EDE

CW00551251

ɔan

↑

THE GREATEST CAPE
Volume One

THE BLACK JOKE

by

David Bramhall

Walnut Tree Books

THE BLACK JOKE

First edition 2012
Second edition 2013

I

Though the mountains be carried into the midst of the sea (Psalm 46)

Far off at the western edge of the world, where the green land meets the grey ocean and the wind never falters, stands Bodrach Nuwl, the Old Man of the Mist, rising sheer and tall above the sea. At his head the great gales thunder, whipping the thin grasses and stunting the trees that lean and cling grimly with their ancient roots.

Only on calm days is it possible to stand at the cliff-top. Often a brave soul making the trek to the summit must fall to his knees for the last two hundred yards and crawl, clinging onto sod and tussock lest the wind whip him away and bowl him back the way he has come. Arriving at the very top and inching his head over the edge, his fingers grip convulsively for a great blue well of air seems to suck him down, down, down a thousand feet or more to the foot of the cliff. Once he has calmed himself and overcome the urge to vomit, he will realise that what lies at the distant foot of the precipice is not the sea but stone, cleft from the cliff-face and tumbled block upon block for half a mile towards the ocean.

From the sea Bodrach Nuwl seems to be a sheer cliff, but his scale is deceptive. He is so gigantic that each ledge and crinkle in his face is a little world in itself. On green, wind-blasted lawns the size of football pitches, whole populations of rabbits and foxes lead their lives perched in the air with no inkling of the outside world. Small crevices become great chasms, lined with trees growing from the rock itself, fed by ferny waterfalls and inhabited by finches and great dragonflies. Habitats here have no connection with the world at large. There are species of insect that exist nowhere else, and unknown pale orchids that thrive in cracks and crannies. Great caves loom open that from the sea are like the holes of sand-martins but in reality could swallow a small village and are inhabited by bats and blind snakes.

And constantly there is the wind, beating the rock, fingering the cracks and crannies, prying free the little stones, worrying the plants and making them dig their roots deep and bloom close and modest.

But this is a calm, sunny day. Imagine, then, the great winter gales, how the wind must suck at the rock and uproot the plants, hurling them up to burst at the cliff-top fifty feet in the air before flinging them wildly inland. Imagine those even greater gales, the twenty-year storms that erupt out of the south-west ocean every couple of decades, flinging waves at the shore fifty feet, eighty feet from trough to crest like solid walls of water, waves so huge they have smaller waves crawling up their faces before they curl and break at the cliff's foot with the force of the apocalypse, or of the creation.

But Bodrach Nuwl is the master of even these elemental forces. For a million years he has stood here, thrusting his chest defiantly into the storms. Every thundering breaker that hit him took its toll. First little stones broke free and were whipped away by the receding waves, then larger blocks began to crack and slide, until from year to year vast slabs, whole crags and hills, fell free and slid to the bottom. But this was all part of The Old Man's grand strategy, a contemptuous sop to the ocean.

For where this débris falls, it lies, half in and half out of the water. And though it break and subside and splinter, it does not go away. Twenty years later another great storm will strike and he will cast more of himself to the sea, and so build up the Stonefields, a half-mile stretch of natural breakwater on so big a scale that no wave, be it a hundred feet high and with the speed of an express train, can reach the foot of Bodrach Nuwl any more.

Bursting in plumes of spray on the outermost bastions of the Stonefields it makes a roar that can be heard twenty miles inland, and rushes on between the slabs of rock through narrowing channels so that the water heaps up on itself and breaks again, adding another roar to the tumult and more spray to the

2

mist that blows all the way up to the cliff-top a thousand feet above. And so it rushes on again, but by now it has travelled a quarter of a mile from its parent the sea, and it begins to lose its resolve so that every twist and turn of the channel, every fallen rock that blocks its path, is a discouragement. Slower and slower it travels, lower and lower it rises, spreading and losing its substance to the nooks and crannies, waylaid by skeins of seaweed a hundred feet long, enticed by rock pools the size of swimming pools with sea-anemones two feet across and crabs that can sever an arm. Long before it approaches the actual foot of the cliff, the toes of The Old Man himself, it has lost its way and its will, and humps sullenly in an oily swell at the bottom of deep chasms seaweed-walled and dark.

And so The Old Man looks out across his kingdom of rock and water towards the kingdom of his old enemy the sea, an enemy long defeated, and sneers as only rock can sneer, and that is a long sneer, and a slow sneer, and a sneer that must give grim satisfaction to those entitled to it.

Behind the cliff the windswept moors fall inland and in a steep cleft, protected by the mass of Bodrach Nuwl, huddles the town. Narrow cobbled streets are hemmed in by tall stone houses. There is no greenery among the little alleyways and squares, but plenty of water in every gutter, rushing headlong down to the quay. At the top of the town stand the larger houses of the merchants and factors, while the meaner cottages of the fishermen cluster round the harbour. Halfway up the town is the Market Place, and above the Market Place is the church, tall and gaunt with an ill-proportioned tower. In the church are ranks of pews, and under one of the pews is a boy, hiding from the Vicar.

II

Let his children be fatherless,
and his wife a widow (Psalm 109)

This was where he belonged, thought Pert. He wriggled further under the pew, into the dust on the flagstones, and drew his feet in so they didn't stick out into the aisle. He felt at home down here. The familiar shadows pressed down on him, all the dark weight of the great empty church covering him and hiding him. Far overhead the saints and angels stared down, but they couldn't see Pert beneath the pew.

Ah, there it was, the sound of the Reverend Tench's feet as he stalked deliberately down the aisle, his narrow head peering from side to side, scanning the gloom. He had called Pert, but Pert didn't want to be found.

"Potts?" he creaked. "Pertinacious Potts? I know you're there. Come along, boy, work to be done!"

Pert shivered. Never any heat here, despite the furnace down in the crypt and the iron gratings in the floor. The worship of God was a chilly business. His groping fingers found something in the dust, a coin fallen from last Sunday's collection plate which he, as altar boy, had to carry in front of his surplice up to the vicar waiting before the altar. He had no idea what happened to the money after that.

The feet stopped at the end of Pert's pew. "Boy? Boy? I know you're there! Come on, you pestilential nuisance, show yourself!"

Pert lay still. Could Tench really know where he was? Did the thumping of his heart give him away, or his panting as he shivered on the floor? Then a hand on his ankle, and a strong pull dragged him backwards through the dust and out into the aisle. He rolled over and looked up.

"I was just …" he stammered, "… I thought I saw …" His face brightened. "I finished in the vestry, sir! I hung up your cassock, and the hymn books are all neatly stacked. And I took the hymn numbers down off the board, and straightened all the hassocks, and then I thought I saw something glinting." He held out the coin. It was a silver sixpence, bread for a week.

"Stupid child," the vicar sneered. His beaky nose resembled a wading bird, a heron perhaps. "I've better things to do than chase around after you. You're nearly sixteen, you're not a baby any more. Stand up, boy!"

He slapped Pert round the head, using the hand with the big signet ring. It hurt.

"Christmas, Potts, Christmas to think about! Services, matins and evensong and midnight mass, Potts. Need you, Potts, need you for the services!"

Pert's heart sank. "Sir, not all, sir? You can't expect me to do them all, sir?"

"Why not? Why ever not, you idle wretch? I have to be here for every one, so why not you?"

"Because you're the vicar," Pert thought, "and you're paid, and you'll sit down to Christmas dinner with the Widow Dolphin and Mrs.Wheable, and you won't do all the services anyway, because you'll go to Sir Humphrey Comfrey in the evening and sit by the fire and have port and chestnuts while poor Mr.Surplice takes evensong and nobody'll come. And I'll be with my mother and we'll eat potato stew same as always, and go to bed cold. That's why."

But he said nothing. Some thoughts you couldn't voice, not if your mother relied on the good will of the neighbours and townsfolk for little bits of sewing and mending.

5

"There's an end to it," creaked the vicar. "No more talk. You be here or I'll know the reason why."

He thrust several envelopes at Pert. "Here, post these on your way home. And no more of your nonsense, creeping and crawling about. Sneaky child you are, like your father and his father before him!"

He turned and flapped back up the darkened aisle towards the vestry, lifting his feet very high.

"You didn't know my father," Pert said under his breath. "And I'm not sneaky. I'm just ... private, that's all." He fled to the great door at the back of the church and let himself out into the night.

Thin snow was falling, whirled into eddies by the wind from the flanks of Bodrach Nuwl. Pert's feet knew every uneven flagstone of the path to the stone arch, and then he was out into the Canonry. He turned downhill towards the Market Place, where the lights of the stalls gleamed on the cobbles and the paraffin lamps hissed as the flakes of snow struck them. Many stall-holders were closing up already, scowling and complaining that business had been slow. Others still stood, stamping their feet and flapping their arms against the cold, hoping for just one or two more customers.

The silver sixpence was still clutched in his hand. What could he buy with it? Brandysnaps? No, he'd get more for the money if he bought toffees, and they'd last longer too. Or ... with a funny feeling in the pit of his stomach ... he might buy a gift for Rosella. He could imagine her surprise as he gave it to her on the door-step, and her eager curiosity as she unwrapped it, and the delight in her eyes as she thanked him ...

He was roused from this pleasant reverie by a bucket of cold, fishy water thrown at his feet. The fish-monger was closing up his stall and didn't care where he swept. He was eager to get off and down to the Drop of Dew to wet his whistle on this raw evening. He had thrown the left-over fish onto the cobbles and a crowd of squabbling gulls were fighting over them.

"Who eats fish at Christmas?" wondered Pert. Fish was for every day. This was a fishing town, and fish was plentiful – though not in their house, of course, with no man to go out in the boats and support them.

With a start he realised that the answer was staring him in the face. The sixpence must be spent, not on himself or on Rosella, but on his family. He thought of his younger sister, so grave and pale and serious. She never complained, she was never in trouble, and no one ever bought her anything. And his mother, always tired and quiet since his father went, scratching a living with her needle in the only way she knew.

Yes, that was it. A gift for each of them. Now, what had the market to offer? Many of the stalls were closed already, but there was still a light shining at Mrs.Toogood's stall, knick-knacks and fripperies, games and toys and ornaments, balls of wool and packets of needles, ribbons and silks and all the little things that Grubb's Emporium was too proud to stock.

Pert spent a long time deciding, picking up first one thing and then another. Rosy-cheeked Mrs.Toogood watched him tiredly. She always tried to keep cheerful but it was the end of a disappointing day, her feet felt like blocks of ice and she was anxious to get home. Still, even a boy's pocket money was worth having with sprats at threepence a pound and firewood like gold dust.

"Is it a present, dear?" she asked. He nodded.

"For your Mum or your sister Fenestra?"

"Both. I've got sixpence ..."

"Well, dear, that won't go very far. Let's see ... how about this for your sister?" She held up a rag doll.

7

"Oh no, she's too old for that! She's thirteen, you know."

"Is she? She always looks younger, poor lamb. What about this?"

It was a little wooden puzzle. You had to twist it this way and that, and little by little the carved pieces would slot into place, and in the end you had a tiny model house with windows and carved flowers up the wall and a little carved cat sitting in the open door. Pert thought Fenestra would like it. She was clever with her fingers, and she could show her friends at school.

"Perfect," he said, and smiled at Mrs.Toogood, who beamed back. "Now, for your Mum ... how is Potentia? Is she managing?" Pert smiled and nodded. He supposed she managed. They ate, they had a roof over their heads, the rent was paid. That was managing, wasn't it? Or should there be more?

"I'll let you in on a secret," said Mrs.Toogood, leaning over the counter and lowering her voice, "people always buy their Mums useful things, like saucepans and forks and darning needles. But what a Mum really wants is something pretty, something that doesn't do anything but is just for them and no one else. I had just the thing here somewhere ..."

She rummaged through her stock, muttering to herself while Pert fidgeted. "Ah!" she said. "I knew it was here!" She held up a small white box. "Look, she can keep buttons in it if she wants ... but really ..."

She opened the box. It was small enough to fit in one hand and made from something natural, with a grain like wood, but not wood for it was too white, almost creamy. Inside the lid and right across the bottom were the smallest little fish you'd ever seen, nosing among seaweed, and shells lying about on the floor, and a crab hiding behind a rock.

"Hold it to your nose," she said. He did, and for a moment there was a brief hint of the sea – not the fishy, weedy, muddy smell

8

down at the quay, but a fresh, clean, salty smell of sun and wind and far away places. "Now listen," she said, and faintly in his ear he heard the swish of the waves and moaning of the great winds that blow across the ocean. It was a wonderful box.

"How much, please?" he asked.

"Just six pence for the two," she said. And she took his money and wrapped the gifts in the prettiest yellow tissue paper, and tied a little length of yellow ribbon round each parcel, and didn't charge him any extra.

"Merry Christmas, thank you!" he said, and ran on. She looked after him for a minute. A polite lad, she thought. Pity about his family.

At the post-office he slapped the hated letters down on the counter. Miss Throstle got as far as "Pertinacious Potts, how dare you …" before he was out of the door. He knew all about the rudeness and lack of consideration shown by the young today, and what else could you expect from that family, and he'd come to a bad end like his father and grandfather before him, you see if he wouldn't. Let her complain about it to her crony Mistress Grubb.

He crossed the street so as not to walk too close to Grubb's Emporium, Fine Fashion, Drapery and Haberdashery. Nobody cared to approach that shop unless they actually had business there.

It was surprising how many people did have business there, though. It was the only haberdashery in town. No other shop-keeper would dare compete with Mistress Grubb.

He thought of the wan little shop-girls who had to work there. His mother had already hinted that Mistress Grubb had her eye on Fenestra. He didn't want his sister to go there and sleep in the garret and run round like a frightened rabbit all day. It was rumoured that Mistress Grubb beat them, and the idea of his frail, wide-eyed sister being beaten was too awful to think about. Rosella would never submit, he thought fondly. She'd shout and kick and run away. She was good at running, and she always wore big boots. You didn't forget a kick on the shin from Rosella Prettyfoot.

He drew his coat around him as he turned into the Bearward. Trudging up the hill the snow hit him in the face, coming straight from Bodrach Nuwl, dark in the twilight over the little town. Up there the wind would be a howling, solid thing carrying the snowflakes horizontal through the darkness, and a man would not be able to keep his footing on the turf. Even down here the gusts whipped round the street-corners and whirled the snow-flakes in the lamplight. Wherever you went in the town, Bodrach Nuwl was always there.

He paused at Rosella's house, and looked at the windows. A comfortable light shone at the edges of the curtains. Rosella was in there somewhere, doing something interesting, always busy and self-contained. In his head he played again the scene where he knocked and presented her with a tissue-wrapped Christmas gift, and she smiled and invited him in, and they stood in the hall quite close together while she unwrapped it and kissed him on the cheek. The packet with the white box was a lump in his pocket. Rosella would love the white box. She'd like him, and smile at him in school.

Pert shook himself. Silly daydreams, he said under his breath, silly, silly. One of his shoes was leaking water so he ran up the narrow hill between the houses and swooped into Pardoner's Alley. As he crashed through the back gate a large seagull on the fence did not so much as flinch. He waved an arm threateningly but it simply hunched its shoulders a little more and gazed at him with a malevolent yellow eye. He went in through the back door and behind him it flapped heavily down onto the dustbin and started to peck and pull at the handle.

"Pert, is that you?" called his mother. She came out of the kitchen wiping her hands. Her hair had come down and she looked tired. She always looked tired since his father went.

"Yes. Sorry I'm late. The old crow made me post his letters for him".

"Dear, you mustn't talk about him like that. He's the Vicar. He's an important man, and you should pay him some respect. Now before you take your coat off, please will you go to the woodshed? The parlour fire's nearly out."

III

*When I remember thee upon my bed, and
meditate on thee in the night watches (Psalm 63)*

They ate at the kitchen table, the warmest place in this narrow house. Supper was the usual, a thin broth with a potato in it, and a hunk of hard bread that hurt your teeth. His sister watched him eat out of the corner of her eye. She loved her big brother. He was strong and quick and not so scared of the big boys at school as she was. He couldn't fight them, but he could taunt them and run away. Her own skinny legs wouldn't carry her fast enough, usually. Just the day before, Darren Durridge and Batty Bunt had cornered her in the playground and tried to lift up her skirt. She had cried and crouched down, but Mr.Merridew came past so they left her alone, with whispered threats to see her again soon. She wondered whether to tell Pert, but knew that he'd probably want to fight them and they'd hurt him. They were big, almost seventeen, and would be leaving school soon and going for the fishing. Perhaps they'd leave her alone then.

After the meal their mother cleared the plates and settled down to some more sewing, and Fenestra went to her room where she would light a candle, wrap herself in the bedclothes and write her secret thoughts in some paper she had stolen from school. She never got into trouble, but she was good at squirrelling away spare paper and pencil ends. One day she would fill out and become a woman, but that day was far in the future. For now, her elbows and knees showed her thin bird-bones and behind the large spectacles her eyes were too big for her face. As Mrs.Toogood said, she looked about ten though she was actually thirteen. She had beautiful skin and a great deal of love to give, but as yet no one to lavish it on except her brother.

Pert went to the attic to see his mouse. He had saved her the crust of his bread. The attic was Pert's kingdom, the place where he slept and could be alone. It was a cold, narrow space under the eaves where the wind lifted the slates in winter and snow would seep in, making little piles on the boards, but as long as he kept his bedding in the middle it usually stayed dry.

His father's old chest was here, a battered thing bound with iron corners and brackets. Pert had annexed it and dragged it up the ladder to the loft, and his mother had never asked after it. In it he kept his books, a few tattered old volumes – *"The Seaman's Vade Mecum"*, *"Ye Dredful Crimes and Justifiyd Execution of ye Blak Pyrate, Benido de Soto by A Sea Captain"*, the back half of a book in Spanish which he couldn't read, but enjoyed looking at the little maps of headlands and harbour installations, and an old Bible which had been in the sea at some time. Many of the pages were stuck together, but in the end papers were notes in pencil by some long-dead sailor: *"Ye 13th June '56 fetched Finis-terro & laid for Ply'th"*, and *"This day three casks ' beef found spoild & ransid"*, and *"Wm.Tabitt ows to me 3 pence for licor"*.

The writing was crabbed and the spelling peculiar so Pert had not been able to decipher many of the entries, even those not spoiled by sea water, but he lived in hope of finding a sentence that read *"Ye tressur is beried 13 paces north by east of ye mark"*, so he could sail off and find ye tressur and return loaded with gold, and buy beautiful dresses for his mother and Fenestra, and stroll into Grubb's Emporium and look Mistress Grubb in the eye and call her "my good woman" as Sir Humphrey Comfrey did, because he had ye tressur safely locked away, and there were a lot of things you could do when you had ye tressur that were impossible without it.

Also in the chest were some of Pert's favourite things: a cow's bone carved with tiny figures by an idle seaman, an empty bottle made of green glass which made the world green and a funny shape if you looked through it, a handkerchief dropped by Rosel-la Prettyfoot at school. He liked to hold the handkerchief to his face and imagine that he could smell her, though in fact it had no scent at all except that of the chest, for he had first put it in there when he was only eleven and Rosella was ten.

Pert always wondered whether Rosella's family, her mother and father and four little sisters, ought to be called "the Prettyfoots" or "the Prettyfeet". Rosella had blonde hair cut short, and a strong fair face, and strong fair limbs that flashed as she ran, and she took no nonsense from anyone. Once in the infants she had kicked the teacher in the shins, and her parents had to be sent for, but she defied even them and teachers had been wary of her since. Pert was wary of her too, although she had never kicked him. In fact, they had never spoken, though they were in the same class.

He broke the bread crust into several pieces and scattered it on the floor near the chimney breast. His mouse lived in a hole in the brickwork. She had got used to Pert and his candle, and would come out every night to see what he had brought her, sitting up like a little old lady and nibbling delicately with the crumbs held between her paws. If he had nothing to give her she would wait until he was asleep and nibble the candle instead. She was a very ordinary mouse, but evidently some male mouse didn't find her ordinary, for once a year and sometimes more she would escort from her hole a little clutch of baby mice as big as your thumbnail.

Pert loved to see the babies scampering around the floor, picking up crumbs and exploring. He didn't even mind when they explored his bed, leaving little black gifts for him. But he did draw the line when they attempted to eat his Bible and Rosella's handkerchief, so he kept the chest firmly shut when he was not there.

Where the babies went to, Pert did not know. Perhaps when they were big enough they set off on an adventure to find their larger family in the house below, rather than stay in this draughty attic. But the mother mouse, Pert's mouse, was always there and Pert felt responsible for her, as he felt responsible for his sister. The mouse's needs were simple, just a place to stay, some warm bedding to nibble and drag back to her nest, and the odd crust. Fenestra's were more complex. He knew she had a hard time at school, but didn't know what to do about it. He had quite a hard time himself. It was part of being a Potts, he supposed. People hated the Potts family because of Grandfather Mascaridus, and that was all there was to it.

IV

The wicked have waited for me to destroy me (Psalm 119)

The following morning Pert and Fenestra were just finishing their porridge when there was a loud knock on the door. Fenestra went to open it, and returned with wide eyes and a frightened expression. Behind her was Urethra Grubb.

"Fetch your mother," she said gruffly, but Mother was already coming down the stairs.

"Mistress Grubb," she began, but the woman cut her off.

"Rent!" she barked. "Christmas tomorrow. Need the rent now."

She stood in the middle of the kitchen and seemed to fill it all by herself. She was almost as broad as she was tall, a squat, toad-like figure. One eye was rheumy and half-closed, the other looked out bright and malevolent over her coarse red cheek, missing nothing. She wore many layers of black shapeless clothing, hung with ribbons and braids, belts and buckles, and stood foursquare on massive legs and large hobnail boots. On her head was a battered hat with a single incongruous flower.

When Pert saw her walking about the town she moved with a strange gait, stomping, head down, her arms not swinging but held straight down and her feet shaking the pavement. She stepped aside for no man, and others would crowd into the gutter to avoid her. She was known to have a finger in every pie, and she stirred those fingers around so that everyone who dealt with her was perpetually off balance, not knowing exactly where they stood, never certain what her motives could be, and what they needed to do to escape her attentions.

She was the kind of woman who walks into a room with her nostrils spread for the smallest odour, the merest speck of dust, who would pick up and read every scrap of paper one left lying around, who thought nothing of peering into dustbins to see what you had thrown away or opening doors in your house to see what lay behind them, who would stop your children in the street and frighten them into telling who you talked to and who visited you and what you said about her. But her worst and strongest weapon was the sheer unrelenting malice she bore the world. She was there, and she would never retreat, never go away, and she let no one forget it.

Pert sat silently watching, and Fenestra scurried to stand behind him. She put her hand on his shoulder, and Pert felt her shaking.

Their mother hesitated, confused. "But ... you usually ... there are five more days, surely?"

"Now, Potentia, if you don't want to spend Christmas in the street. Get it now."

His mother turned and ran up the stairs, returning with a cloth purse. "I may be a few pence short ..." she muttered, and emptied the contents into Mistress Grubb's hand.

The woman counted under her breath. "Six pence short. Bring it tomorrow."

"But it's Christmas ..."

"Tomorrow. Send the boy."

She transferred her attention to Fenestra. "When are you going to send this one to work in the shop?" she barked.

"Please," faltered Fenestra, "I don't want to work in the shop ..."

"Silence! You'll do what you're told. Do something useful, stop cluttering up that school, fooling around with boys ..."

"Please, I never ..."

"Be quiet. How old are you?"

"Please, thirteen."

"Hmph! You look about ten, scrawny little scrap, you are. Need to work, build you up a bit. I'll take you when you're fourteen. Time your family did something useful instead of robbing and sneaking around. No argument!"

She glared at Pert and his mother, and stumped out. The floor shook, and the door slammed behind her.

"I never robbed anything," Fenestra squeaked, and began to cry. Her mother came and put her arms round her.

"What did she mean?" asked Pert.

"Nothing, she meant nothing. It's just the way she talks," his mother said. "I'll find the six pence and you can take it to her after morning service."

V

Horror hath taken hold upon me because of the
wicked that forsake thy law (Psalm 119)

It was generally agreed that Mistress Urethra Grubb, proprietrix of Grubb's Emporium (Fine Fashion, Drapery and Haberdashery) and owner of most of the poorer houses in town, was the worst, most truly awful woman in the world. Short and stout and square and strong, her broad red face lit the street like a beacon as she stood in the shop doorway. Her nostrils were revoltingly broad and her mouth under an undeniable moustache had the wide gape of a frog or toad.

Always truculent and never known to smile, her voice was coarse and vicious as she hectored the little shop-girls and sent them scurrying to fetch bolts of silk, rolls of fine dress material, bobbins of cotton, packets of pins and all the other things necessary to dress the town's womenfolk. She modified her tone but little when addressing the other members of the Town Council or the Poor Relief Fund or the Workhouse Governors, for she was afraid of nobody and would not be gainsaid.

Nor on those obligatory occasions when she was invited by the town's tradesmen and dignitaries to their social gatherings, did she condescend to smile graciously and lower her voice by the slightest degree. Did she not know all their secrets, and were they not just as afraid of her as the little girls who scurried and cried behind her counter?

The tradesmen did not want her in their houses, but such was the power of her overbearing will that they had no choice. Neither did the girls want to work at the Emporium. It was just that once Mistress Grubb had set her mind on you, sensing some innocence to be spoiled or vulnerability to be explored, it became mysteriously difficult to find employment anywhere else.

From the seaweed-fronded harbour to the great grey church on the hill, from the quayside hovels of the fishers to the elegant crescent where the civic dignitaries and the owners of the better shops ruled their households with sarcasm and petty cruelty, you would be hard pressed to find a single person to put in a good word for her save possibly her closest cronies, the Widow Dolphin, sharp-faced Miss Throstle and the Vicar - and who knew what even they thought about her in their deepest hearts?

Her presence made itself felt far beyond the dark confines of the shop she had inherited from her father. Rumour had it that she had poisoned him with a pie made of rotten fish and leaves of purple wightsbane. He had lingered in pain for a week while she had allowed nobody near him, not even the old Vicar, and so intimidated the doctor that he left town and had not been seen since. Why were they interfering, she'd asked them, what did they hope to gain? After the old man's money, was that it? Hoping to catch him in a weak moment and milk him for cash, was that it? Well she was in charge now, and it would be a strange day indeed when some useless quack of a pill-monger or mewling hypocritical fairy-tale preaching priest could put one over on her, oh yes.

As Bodrach Nuwl loomed over the little town, so Urethra Grubb loomed ... not over it but, as it were, through it. Not a gull-stalked street, not a narrow alley, not the broad avenue that led from the Town Hall to the Fish Market, not the cosy flowered lanes at the edges of the town nor the stews and drinking parlours behind the harbour, was free of her. Her malignity crept through the town like a fog, oozing into doorways and round the cracks of the windows, drifting between the curtains, entering every house and home to sour the family supper and dampen the beds, flattening the singing in church and chapel, wilting the lettuces on the market stalls, frightening the dogs and startling the horses, a miasma of wickedness that touched everything and everyone and made life dark and pointless.

Strapping lads failed to live up to their promise and became gamblers and drunkards for no reason. Fair maids in the rosy glow of youth squandered their innocence, contracted diseases, gave painful birth, despaired and took to wandering the streets dragging their grizzling children behind them. Prosperous merchants closed the doors of their fine houses and spent the evenings counting their money, ignoring their wives and children and bothering the servant girl in the garret.

Honest shop-keepers scowled at their customers, abused the delivery boy, short-changed anyone they could, and closed early. The Vicar read his sermons from a book and drank half a bottle of whisky before every service. Schoolmasters found amusing things to do with children who misbehaved or couldn't say their lessons, instilling in them such fear and disgust that many, arriving at half-past eight in the morning, had soiled themselves by ten and spent the rest of the day sitting in their own ordure. It was a rotten town full of rotten people, with Mistress Grubb curled like a maggot at its rotten heart.

VI

*I call to remembrance my song in the night: that ye may
tell it to the generation following (Psalms 48 & 77)*

The following morning it was Christmas. Fenestra and her mother put on their least tired clothes and went to church, Pert having left earlier as he was altar boy and had to put his surplice on and lay the prayer books out and the hymn numbers in the board above the pulpit.

The Vicar gave the same Christmas sermon every year, but Pert never listened anyway. He paid just enough attention to spot the peculiar intonation that would signal the end of the address and the dedication that followed it, because while the congregation mumbled the final hymn he then had to carry the collection plate and hand it to the Vicar at the altar. He rather liked being the only person other than the Vicar who was allowed past the sanctuary rail, though in truth there was nothing of interest there except the boxes of old papers hidden behind the altar cloth.

Pert had spent a number of hours searching through those boxes, hoping to find some books of stories which his sister would enjoy, or old papers about treasure and adventures. There had been a treasure once, in the town, but it had disappeared and no one knew what had happened to it. People didn't talk about it, though a small boy had once walked up to him in the playground and asked him about it.

"Don't you know where the treasure is?" the boy had said.

"No. Why should I?"

The boy looked disappointed. "Oh. I thought you would," he said, and ran off to join his friends. Pert guessed that this might have something to do with the unpopularity of his family, but neither his mother nor his aged Aunt Gittins would tell him anything. Aunt Gittins had raised his father when Grandfather Mascaridus disappeared and Grandma Floribunda died of shame and poverty. Then his father had disappeared too. He thought it was rather a distinction to have two of his forebears disappear mysteriously, and wondered if he would have to disappear too, in his turn. He hoped he would have time to sort something out for his sister first, to save her from the Emporium. He also hoped he would get to kiss Rosella at least once.

Rosella and her family sat in the pews behind the most important people of the town, Sir Humphrey Comfrey and his family, the merchants, Mrs.Wheable and the Widow Dolphin and Mr.Trumbull Underdown the fish merchant and his fat wife who was rather nice and once gave Pert a boiled sweet. Further back were the pews for the poor families, and it was here that his mother and Fenestra had their places.

Pert was glad when the service dragged to a close and the congregation left, rather more quickly than usual for Christmas dinner awaited them at home. The Vicar didn't linger either, but took a draught from the brown bottle he kept in the vestry cupboard, put on his coat and stalked down the aisle on his way to the Widow Dolphin's house at the top of the town.

Pert did his chores, straightening the hymn books and prayer books which would be needed again later, and changing the hymn numbers, and washing the vessels from the Christmas Communion earlier that morning. So long as it was daytime and the Vicar was elsewhere, he rather enjoyed being in the church. It was a gloomy place, but there was a lovely smell of old stone and old wood and damp paper. When you opened the cupboards in the vestry there was an added tang of incense long burned, and ancient cloth from the cassocks that were never used these days after the church choir dwindled and died.

He wondered whether to slip under the altar while he had the chance, and do a little more research in the boxes, but he still had to take the money to Mistress Grubb and then get back to lunch. He locked the great west door of the church with the key that was too large to fit in anyone's pocket, hid it under the usual stone, and ran down the hill.

The door of Grubb's Emporium (Fine Fashion, Drapery and Haberdashery), was open when he pushed it, though the sign said "closed". He walked hesitantly into the dim cave, walled with shelf after shelf of cloth, and lined with polished walnut counters. He wondered what the shop-girls did for Christmas. Did they get the day off so they could go home to their families, or did they have to stay here and have a cheerless Christmas meal in the basement?

"Can I help you?" asked a small voice. From the shadows at the back of the shop emerged a girl, plainly clad and pale. She was older than Pert, and had long straight hair that fell over her face.

"Oh, I didn't know if anyone would be here," he said.

"They aren't. There's only me and Mistress Grubb, and she's gone out."

"Why are you here? Have all the other girls gone home?"

"Yes. But I ain't got one to go to, so I has to stay here."

"That can't be much fun."

She laughed shortly. "Ain't never much fun round 'ere, an' that's a fact!" she said. When her hair fell away from her face Pert could see that she was ... not pretty exactly, but nice. She looked as if she might have known what fun was once, but had forgotten.

"That's sad," he said. "You could come home with me. We're only having potato stew, but I'm sure there'd be enough. You could meet my sister. Mistress Grubb's offered her a job when she's fourteen."

"No!" the girl hissed, and grasped his arm hard. "No! Don't let her come! Keep her away from here! It's dreadful, and the little girls cry themselves to sleep every night, and we're all so scared all the time … you have to stop her!"

Just then heavy footsteps sounded outside the door, which was flung open with a crash. The girl leapt back and shook her hair over her face again.

"What's this? What's this? Having a little social intercourse, are you, my girl, behind my back? We'll see about that!" said Mistress Grubb, advancing heavily into the room.

"No, she was just telling me that you weren't here," said Pert.

"Can't you read? We're closed! Oh, it's you. Well, I am here, so that was a lie, wasn't it? And lies are counted and have to be paid for later, Christmas or no Christmas. Got my money?"

"Yes."

He held out the six pence. Grubb took it and sniffed. "Well, you'd better cut along then, hadn't you?"

Pert wanted to speak to the girl again, to say something kind to her, but could not with Mistress Grubb looking on, so he went to the door and stepped out onto the pavement. It was cold and bright, a weak sun groping its way down into the narrow street and making the cobbles shine.

On the opposite pavement Rosella was marching down the street towards him. Behind were her four little sisters, unremarkable children, keeping up and holding hands nicely and not walking on the cracks. Pert crossed the road and stopped, but she strode past without acknowledging him, her big boots clumping on the pavement. Her legs were too thin for comfort, her skirt a little short for fashion, and her chin too high for casual conversation, but the smallest Prettyfoot smiled at him and turned her head to look over her shoulder. Pert walked on, feeling all right. A smile from even a tiny Prettyfoot was encouragement of a sort. Perhaps if he was patient he could work his way up the family, winning acknowledgement from one after the other until he reached Rosella herself.

Pert's Christmas presents were a great success. He brought them down from the attic before they sat down to lunch. The mouse had nibbled some of the tissue paper on one, but not so much that he couldn't tuck that bit in so it wouldn't notice. Fenestra was delighted with her puzzle. She ran round the table and flung her arms round his neck and gave him a rather wet kiss on the cheek. His mother smiled and said it was the most beautiful box, and he showed her how to smell the briny smell and listen to the sea. She didn't say much, but her eyes went a bit blurry so he knew she was happy. Or something.

She had made them both long knitted mufflers, made from wool she had rescued from all over the place so they were rather mottled. The predominant colour was dark blue, though, so he guessed that the main ingredient was wool from old fishermens' jumpers. The mufflers smelt slightly of tobacco and fish, but that was all right and they would be warm. Fenestra had made him a story, written quite neatly in pencil on assorted pieces of paper and tied together with a bootlace. It was about a beautiful princess who lived in a castle and was very unhappy all the time. He gave her a dry kiss this time, and said he would read it in bed.

The meal was potato stew as Pert had forecast, but there was some fish in it as this was a special occasion, and there was a treacle tart for afters. There was a bit of a delay at the start because Fenestra insisted on saying grace first. It was quite a long grace, and she included thanks for a great many things apart from food – her Christmas presents, the sun, snow, flowers, trees, shoes to keep your feet dry, her mother and her brother, and next door's cat of which she was quite fond. Then they ate.

As the last crust of treacle tart was finished, Fenestra asked her mother "What did she mean, Mother?"

"What did who mean?"

"The old witch, yesterday?" Fenestra said. Pert giggled.

"Hush, Fenestra, really! Don't ever let anyone hear you talking like that!"

"There's no one here, only us."

"Fenestra, darling, you should know by now that there's not much in this town that woman doesn't know about. She hears everything. I don't know how she does it, but she does. You must be careful always, wherever you are, never to say anything that might annoy her if she hears. Not even at home."

Fenestra shrugged. "All right. But Mother, tell me what she was talking about? She said we were robbers! We aren't robbers, are we? If we were robbers, we wouldn't be poor!"

Her mother sighed. "That's true enough, Lord knows. But she didn't mean anything by it. I said yesterday, it's just the way she is."

"But Miss Throstle said something as well," put in Pert. "She's said it before, too. She says I'll come to a bad end, like my father and my grandfather. How did they come to a bad end? I thought Grandfather Mascaridus was lost at sea? I know that's bad enough, but it happens to plenty of fishermen. That wasn't what she meant, was it? And my father – he just went off, didn't he?"

His mother looked at him for a long time. Her face was pale.

"Your father was a good man," she said slowly, "and no one knows what happened to him. He would never ..."

She closed her eyes and breathed heavily. Fenestra left her seat and put her arms round her neck.

"It's all right," Mother said. "I'm all right. It's just that ... it was such a blow when he went, and not knowing, and wondering all this time, and people gossiping, and that bloody woman ..."

"Shh, now you're doing it!" cried Fenestra, and tried to cover her mother's mouth.

"Sorry, darlings. I must pull myself together. Come, Fenestra, sit on my lap ..." she pushed her chair from the table and pulled Fenestra to her, "and I'll tell you what I can. Which isn't much.

"When your father disappeared I swore to myself that I'd do my best to shield you from the rumours and the ugly accusations. This town is riddled with gossip, you'd think they had nothing better to do."

Pert knew this was true. The traders in the Market Square gossiped all day with their customers, the shop keepers in the High Street gossiped with theirs, women gathered together in the street or on front steps to gossip, the fishers gossiped over their nets and the fishwives gossiped in gangs on the quayside. He had noticed how the young women went through a sudden transition – one moment they were fresh-faced, plump laughing girls in the top class at school, the next they stood with the other young wives on the fish dock, arms folded, hard faced and tight mouthed, watching the world suspiciously over their shoulders. Even the school playground was awash with gossip, as though children kept so sternly to their tasks in the classroom had not time to run around and play, but must spend their pent-up energy on a web of scandal, resentment and petty feuding to make up for the life they missed during lessons.

"I thought I could protect you," his mother continued, "but I see now that I was wrong. You were bound to hear about it sooner or later, so you'd better hear it right."

"I was only a baby when your Grandfather Mascaridus died, so of course I knew nothing about it. All I knew was from things people let slip while I was growing up. There was talk of money, a treasure of some sort, which disappeared at the same time. But there was a great storm, some say the worst for a hundred years, and the wind tore the roofs off houses and the waves came right across the quay and stove in the windows of the Harbourmaster's office.

"Your grandfather was out in it. No one knew when he left, or why he went out when the weather was so dangerous. It was nothing but lunacy, but his boat, the *Bight of Benin*, was gone and his second mate was gone as well, and no one ever saw hide nor hair of them since.

"But the rumours started, you see. The treasure disappeared at the same time, so everyone just jumped to the obvious conclusion. The treasure was gone and Mascaridus was gone, so therefore they must have gone together. Your grandmother Floribunda died a year later, of grief, so they say."

She paused. "Fenestra, could you get me a drink of water, please?"

Fenestra slipped off her lap and went to the pitcher, then returned and sat on her mother's lap again. Pert could tell she was beside herself with joy – a knee to sit on, a story to be told and a secret to cherish were all the things his sister held dear in life.

"What sort of man was my grandfather?" he asked.

"Well, I didn't know him as I said, but until that dreadful night, people say, he was a fine and respected man, a leader and an example to younger men. He was one of the Free Fishers, the little group of fishermen who made decisions for all the rest and saw that they all behaved fair and proper. After he went, a sort of rot set in. One of the other Free Fishers took to drink and fell in bad ways, and was killed with a knife when he got into a drunken argument in the tavern, and another started beating his wife so her family beat him back. And now there are no Free Fishers left, and everything's gone to wrack and ruin and Urethra Grubb is the most powerful person in town."

"And my father? You must know more about him?"

"I know he was the bravest, quietest, truest man you could meet," she said, "and I know he loved me. He was a skilled and respected fisherman, friends with everyone. He was even a lay reader at the church, and used to read the lessons quite often. He would never have left us, me with three children and the youngest still in arms – that's you, Fenestra."

The girl smiled and kissed her mother. "We never talk about my sister, do we?" she said.

"No. We never do. Vernilia was my first-born, and the hardest. She was a difficult birth, she kicked and struggled as though she didn't want to be born at all, and as she grew up she never stopped kicking and struggling. She was an awkward, rebellious child, and when she got to the age when young men started taking an interest, she became completely wild.

"With your father gone nine or ten years before, I just couldn't manage her on my own. Your Great-aunt Gittins tried to talk some sense into her – for all she's a gruff old thing, she's got a good heart. She took your father in when he was orphaned, and brought him up to be good and God-fearing. But Vernilia wasn't going to take any more notice of an old woman than she would of me. When she was fifteen she told me she never wanted to see me again, and ran off with a sailor. And never a word since."

She sniffed, and held more tightly to Fenestra. "That's why you're so precious to me, the two of you. You're all I have now."

Pert thought Fenestra might cry, so tried to divert the discussion. "But my father, what happened when he went?"

"It was sudden, and I knew nothing. He said nothing unusual, he did nothing unusual, he spent his days in the way a fisherman does – mending nets, going out to sea, coming back, eating his supper, once in a while a pint of ale in the inn, church on Sundays, just normal things. But one evening he ate his supper, said he was going to the Drop of Dew for a pint, and that was the last anyone saw of him."

"But why do people lump him with his father, and the robbing and everything?"

"I don't know. It's not logical, but malicious people don't require logic. There was no evidence that Mascaridus had anything to do with the treasure, but they still accused him of stealing it. I don't think most of them even knew what the treasure was, or if it really existed at all, but that didn't stop them."

"And when my father went, they did the same thing ..."

"Exactly. His father was a thief, they said, so the son must be a thief as well. Whether they thought your father Obadiah knew what his dad had done with the treasure and went to recover it ... I don't know how their minds work. All I know is that we've had black looks and curses and bad luck ever since, and that you'll probably be tarred with the same brush, though you're as honest a son as I could ever wish. But at least you'll probably be able to find a fisherman who'll take you as a foredeck hand. Some aren't fussy. But Fenestra ... when she's old enough, I don't think anyone will employ her because she's a Potts. So the only thing she can do is go to the Emporium ..."

Now his mother began to cry in earnest, and so did Fenestra. Pert managed to choke back his own feelings. A fine end to Christmas Dinner, he thought, and went to get ready for Even-song.

As he left the house the same enormous seagull was in the yard. It had managed to get the lid off the dustbin, and food scraps and pieces of paper and cloth blew along the bottom of the fence. It glared at him with its mad yellow eye, and did not flinch when he shouted at it. Seagulls were everywhere in this town, great arrogant birds that stalked the streets and intimidated the dogs and terrorised the cats, perching on cradles and prams and alarming the mothers, tipping lids off dustbins and rummaging inside, stealing food from the market stalls and investigating any open window. Their cries were a constant background and their droppings fouled every roof and chimney, corroding the stonework.

Poor Mr.Surplice, the curate, was already in the vestry when Pert arrived, flapping his hands and muttering to himself. Pert always thought of him as "poor Mr.Surplice", and he was indeed a sorry specimen, thin and wan and scant-haired, his weak eyes peering through thick spectacles at a world he seemed not to understand at all. He lodged with a fisher family in the poorer part of town, and was bullied by the Vicar.

"My cassock ... my cassock ... I'm sure it was here ..." he said to Pert in a tone of despair. He was quite good on scripture and the meaning of various holy days, but ordinary things like clothes and food and money were incomprehensible to Mr.Surplice.

"It's in the cupboard where you left it," said Pert, fetching it and holding it out for him to put on. He wondered if dressing curates was part of his job. When he had to help the Vicar with his robes he usually smelled whisky, but Mr.Surplice smelt only of fish and mothballs.

"Thank you, you're a good boy," the curate said, and looked vaguely around. "My surplice ...?"

Pert held it up and dropped it over his head.

"A surplice for a Surplice!" the curate said, "ha ha!" He had made the same joke every Sunday for the last three years.

Pert smiled politely. "That always cracks me up," he said. "Do you know anything about treasure?"

Mr.Surplice stared at him round-eyed. "Treasure? Whatever are you talking about?"

"I keep hearing things about treasure," Pert said, "and I wondered if you could tell me anything about it."

"Well, there was a treasure, I believe ... at least, not so much a treasure, but some plates and cups and things, quite valuable. But they vanished long ago."

"Do you know how I could find out about them?"

"Why do you want to know?" Surplice grinned suddenly, and Pert realised that he was actually quite a young man. "Going on a treasure hunt, is that it? I say, what fun!"

"No, not really. It's just that people seem to think my grandfather had something to do with it."

"Oh. Well, it was an awfully long time ago. Forty or fifty years at least. I wasn't even born, and when I was, it wasn't here. Nor was the Vicar, or ... well, hardly anyone. I suppose there might be some mention of it in the Church Council minutes, if they could be found."

"Church Council minutes? Where would they be?"

"No idea, I'm afraid. And we wouldn't be allowed to look in them anyway. I expect they've been destroyed long ago. There hasn't been a Church Council these ten or fifteen years so far as I know. The Vicar does it all now. We could ask him, I suppose ..."

"No, don't." Pert didn't know why, but it seemed a bad idea.

"Mm. Yes, I expect you're right." He lowered his voice to a hoarse whisper. "Just between you and me, I try not to ask him anything if I can help it."

"He's not very encouraging, is he?" Pert said.

"No, he isn't. I haven't felt encouraged for a long time ..." He thought for a moment. "There's just one thing ... my old tutor at the seminary was a noted scholar, Canon Flitch. His special interest was the history of this diocese. I venture to say that no man knows more about it than he. I could write and ask him. If I present it as merely an academic interest in the history of this church, he won't think to tell anyone about it. Yes, I shall do that! Now, it must be nearly time. Are the hymn numbers up?"

"Yes."

"Good ... er, well done. Do you think you could close up after Evensong? If I don't get home promptly Mrs.Gammage won't wait supper for me, and lunch was ... a bit of a disappointment, if I'm honest. She's a God-fearing woman but I think she may have missed the bit about the milk of human kindness."

Evensong was, as Pert had suspected, a wan affair. There were only a handful of old ladies in the congregation, and when the hymn was announced the only voices Pert could hear were his own and Mr.Surplice's. Pert was embarrassed by singing, and thought he didn't always get the tune quite right, but was pretty good at the words which probably made up for it. Mr.Surplice had rather a nice voice, a bit thin and reedy but tuneful.

The curate stumbled through a very short sermon about the true meaning of Christmas. Pert tried hard to take his duties and religion seriously, but the idea of being born twice was ridiculous however hard you looked at it. It was bad enough being born once. Mr.Surplice fled from the pulpit with a look of confusion and relief on his face. He almost tripped at the bottom where the uneven step was, but Pert was waiting and grabbed his arm.

"I can't remember what comes next!" Surplice hissed.

"Hymn, Offertory and Benediction," whispered Pert.

"Oh, right. Thanks!"

The curate did his duty, doffed his robes and ran for supper. The congregation, their duty done, shuffled out into the windy night. Pert did his own duties with a light heart, skimming hymn books across the tops of the pews, then blew out the candles and felt his way through the dark to the back of the church. Inside the west door he paused and looked back. On the altar a single candle wick still showed a minute cinder which glowed and then winked out. The tall dark pressed down, and Pert thought of the saints and angels up there in the roof, peering down with sightless eyes. It couldn't be much fun being a saint. You spend your life in good works, get put to death in some uncomfortable and undignified fashion, and they reward you by hanging you in the roof and keeping you in the dark.

The Church Council came into his mind. If there were still any papers about the Church Council, perhaps they were in the boxes under the altar? He'd creep in during the week and have a look, he decided, and closed the door behind him.

He trotted through the deserted streets, windows and doors bolted against the cold wind. By the time he got back to Pardoner's Alley his sister was in bed and his mother dozed beside the embers of the fire. She stirred as he locked the door, and got up and gave him some milk and a piece of bread which he took up to the attic with him.

On the way he opened Fenestra's door and peeped in. She was asleep, huddled under the blankets, and on the pillow beside her face, one hand holding them safe, were the muffler and the puzzle. He felt a strange welling of emotion, as though he wanted to cry. Poor Fenestra, he thought, she doesn't ask for much.

He wriggled under his heap of blankets, shivering. The attic was icy-cold, and the thin wind seeped under the slates, moaning. He put his candle into an empty jam jar on the floor so it wouldn't blow out, and carefully broke off part of the bread and put it on the floor boards near him. He drank the milk, and chewed on the rest of the bread. He wondered whether to read one of his books for a while, perhaps the one with the little diagrams in, but it was too cold to get out from under the blankets again.

His mouse appeared, pausing at the mouth of her hole in the chimney bricks, her nose twitching to see what he had brought her. Her little black eyes glowed in the candle light. Satisfied that he had done his duty by her, she ran across the floor and picked up her crust, and sat up not eighteen inches from his face and nibbled at it. It was bigger than she was. He slowly put out his hand and she dropped it and retreated a few inches. He used his fingers to break it into two, and put the pieces down again. She picked one up, ran with it to her hole and disappeared inside. A moment later she came for the second one, and carried that off. At the mouth of the hole she paused, looked at him for a moment, then vanished.

That was all the thanks you got, he thought. He blew out the candle and carefully tucked the edges of the blanket round his face so that only his nose and mouth were showing. He was generating a little warmth now, so he wriggled his toes to push his shoes off and stretched luxuriously. The wind whistled on the roof, the sound rising and falling. He imagined what he would see if the slates weren't in the way, the sweep of sky dusted with stars, the black bulk of Bodrach Nuwl stooping over the town and blotting out half the heavens, and the swooping wind curling round gable end and chimney pot, poking its fingers in every chink and cranny, sucking out what warmth it could find.

It had been a funny day. All this stuff about treasure. It was interesting that Mr.Surplice thought there really had been something, but what evidence was there that anyone in his family had anything to do with it? How could anyone possibly know? They didn't know for certain that the treasure had ever existed. And if it did, where did it come from? Where did they keep it? Had anyone ever actually seen it?

It was probably a load of old tosh. People believed what they wanted to believe, not what was real. They wanted to believe there was a treasure, and they wanted to believe that his family had stolen it, not that there was the tiniest bit of evidence. They wanted to believe it, because it was cosy to have someone to hate, someone to feel superior to. It made you a kind of gang, didn't it? If everyone had someone to hate, then they weren't hating each other, so they could feel they were all on the same side.

His mother had been right, though. It was hard to see what lay in wait for Fenestra. Nobody would give her a job if Grubb said not to, and she had to support herself somehow, at least until he was in a position to do it. The Emporium would be her only option.

It would be all right for him. He might be one of the hated Potts family, but he was already a skilled boatman. He could sail, and sew nets, and catch fish. He already knew some of the good fishing places. Each summer for several years he had gone out during the school holidays with old Walter Glibbery, who was so often drunk he didn't care who he sailed with. He was a good fisherman, or had been once, before he took to drink. He knew the best places, went out in the worst weathers, and could go further into the Stonefields than any of them, hauling crab-pots and looking for eels and lobsters. His boat was small but he took good catches.

Trouble was, no sooner was his catch sold than he was in the alehouse spending it. When it was all gone he'd stagger home and his old wife would hit him with a chair leg. The next day he'd do it all again.

For Pert this had been an advantage. No one else would sail with a fisher who made no money, so Walter was glad to have him, and while the old man sat back with his bottle shouting instructions and advice, Pert had sailed and steered and cast and hauled and made himself a fisherman. When he had finished with school or school had finished with him, he would go out with Walter every day, and take his share of the catch, and save the money. And eventually he would have enough to buy a little open boat, and he'd go into business for himself. He would be all right, let them hate him or not.

Perhaps he could take Fenestra out with him. He thought fondly of sunny days, bobbing on a kindly sea two or three miles from shore, the willing fish in his net, and Fenestra sitting in the stern steering while he worked. Then suddenly Rosella was there too, hauling nets with him, brown and smiling and tossing her blonde locks, and the wind reached its fingers between the slates and ruffled his hair, and he slept.

VII

And in thy book all my members were written (Psalm 139)

In two days' time school would start. Pert decided to take this opportunity to visit the church and look into the boxes under the altar. As he went out into the back yard he found Fenestra. She was sitting on an old box, showing her puzzle to next door's cat and singing a little story to it. The cat yawned and looked bored, but evidently had nothing better to do. Once in a while it would stand up and rub against her knee, and she would stroke it and tickle it under the chin before continuing the story.

She looked up when Pert appeared. "Where are you going?" she asked.

"Up to the church," he replied. "I have something to do there."

"Can I come? The cat's heard this story before. He's just being polite, he doesn't really want to listen."

"No, I'd rather you didn't."

She got up and hung on his arm. "Oh please, please, please?" she pleaded. "If you take me with you I won't get in the way and I'll give you a bit of my supper and I won't tell Mother about your mouse!"

"How do you know about my mouse?"

"I went up into the attic when you weren't there, and it came out and sat there bold as brass. And I knew you must have been feeding it, otherwise it would have run away."

"It's a she. And you mustn't tell."

"Silly, I wouldn't. I was just saying that. It was rather a nice mouse. Can I come anyway? I meant it about the supper."

39

"Oh, all right then," he relented. "And you can keep your supper. But you'll have to be my lookout. I don't particularly want the vicar to know what I'm doing."

She hung on his arm on the way down to the Square and then up the hill towards the church, skipping and talking gaily. Market stall holders scowled at her. They weren't happy, so what right had she? They passed one of the Emporium girls, carrying a shopping basket. Fenestra smiled but the girl scurried past, ignoring her.

"Pert, what've you got to do?" she asked.

"Look for something."

"What something?"

He laughed. "I don't really know till I've found it. Just something."

"That's not a very good answer."

"If I find it, I'll tell you. Now, here's the church gate. I want you to sit here and keep watch up the hill. If the vicar comes, run in and tell me quick."

"All right. Suppose anyone comes who's not the vicar?"

"That's a point. Look, don't stay here, come and wait in the doorway and tell me if anyone looks like coming into the church, anyone at all. And try and look as though you're doing something normal."

"What do you mean, normal?"

"Well, something that girls normally do."

"I'll just read the gravestones. I've never seen anyone else do it, but it's normal for me," she said.

Pert took the key from its usual hiding place and unlocked the door. He slipped inside, pulled the door to behind him so no one could tell from a casual glance that it was open, and crept up the aisle. He listened carefully, then went and checked the vestry to make sure it was empty. He put his ear to the door that led down to the crypt, and the one that opened into the organ loft where all the pipes were. They seldom had an organist these days, just Miss Tizzard on special occasions. She wasn't very good at it, and mostly held a chord with one hand and played the tune with the other. When she felt especially adventurous she would spend several seconds groping for a different chord and hold that.

There was no sound. He had the church to himself.

Under the altar cloth it was dim and dusty, making him sneeze until he got used to it. The boxes lay in a muddle. He remembered roughly which ones he'd looked at and which he hadn't, and decided to start at the other end.

The first box held great leather-bound books filled with records in tiny, crabbed hand writing. "Burials" he read, underlined in red ink. Then a list ...

Zebedee Walduck, 79, fisher, 12th March 1848
Rachel Vacher, 38, wife, 19th April 1848
Simeon Trusting, 46, clerk, 22nd April 1848
Unknown seaman washed ashore, --, ---, 30th May 1848
Mabel Scrutch, 27, woman, 6th June 1848

... and many more. He wondered about poor Mabel Scrutch. What was so lacking in her that she could only be described as "woman"? And the "unknown seaman washed ashore" - who had told his bewildered family? Did they ever know that he'd received a proper Christian burial, miles from home?

He turned to the next book. More burials. And the next. The dates had reached 1883 now, a year before he was born.

The next book was more interesting. The heading, again underlined neatly in red ink, was "Births". The dates began in 1870,
and progressed steadily upwards. In 1884 he found ...

*26th September 1884 to Obadiah Potts, fisher, and ys wife
Potentia Potts, a son Pertinacious.*

In 1887 ...

a daughter Fenestra.

And turning back to 1881 ...

a daughter Vernilia.

And in 1885,

*11th August 1885 to Patroclus Prettyfoot,
haberdasher, and ys wife April Begonia Prettyfoot,
a daughter Rosella Fortunata.*

Pert leaned back against the leg of the altar. This was something
worth knowing. "Rosella Fortunata Prettyfoot" - this was name
indeed, a name to cherish. But wait – her father was a haberdasher? But there was only one haberdashery in town, and that was
Grubb's Emporium. There could be no other.

Here was a mystery. Had Urethra Grubb or her father (or her
murdered father, so people said) taken over Prettyfoot's business? Had they bought him out, or just forced him out somehow? And how was he making a living now? Rosella's house was
a nice one, comfortable and neatly kept. Mister Patroclus Prettyfoot and ys wife April Begonia Prettyfoot were plainly not penni-
less. Perhaps they'd found ye tressur?

No way to find out, he thought. I can hardly ask. Rosella scarcely
knew he existed. And what could he say to Mister Patroclus
Prettyfoot? "You don't know me but I'm in your daughter's class

and I worship her from afar, so can you tell me where you get your money from? Have you got ye tressur hidden in your cellar, and if so can I have some because it was my grandfather that stole it in the first place?"

Pert pulled himself up with a jerk. He was getting as bad as everyone else, weaving fairy tales where none existed.

He heard the door burst open. "Pert? Pert?" his sister called. She sounded shaky. "Oh Pert, quick, they're coming!"

He put his head out from under the altar cloth. "Who's coming?" he called, but instead of answering she ran helter skelter up the aisle towards him. She was crying.

"Who is it?" he whispered fiercely, reaching out and pulling her under the cloth.

"Oh God, help me, Pert!" she sobbed, "it's Darren Durridge and Batty Bunt! They saw me in the churchyard and they came after me. They're going to come in!"

He held her and tried to quiet her tears, fearing that she'd give them away. As he did so there were footsteps at the west end of the church. He put his hand over her mouth.

"Come out, come out, wherever you be?" called a voice, and another voice sniggered. The footsteps moved towards them.

"Come out, skinny little sneak, and take your medicine!" There was a bang which made them both jump.

"Show yerself, Potty girl!" More bangs. They were kicking the pews as they came. Pert risked a peep under the cloth. Darren Durridge and Batty Bunt were making their way up the aisle, looking under every pew.

"We're going to give you Potts, Potty girl! We'll Potts you one way, and we'll Potts you the other way, until you won't know which way up you are, Potty girl!"

Fenestra put her hands over her ears, and Pert held her close. Her eyes were screwed shut.

There were a few moment's silence out in the church. Then the footsteps receded. The bullies had given up, for now.

As they reached the door, one yelled "We'll get you, you skinny little freak! We'll pull your skirts up and smack your skinny bum, see if we don't!"

The door slammed behind them and they could be heard going down the path to the Canonry, whooping and calling. Fenestra whimpered and burrowed into Pert's chest. She was shaking. "Are you supposed to say 'bum' in church?" she whispered.

"I don't think so," he said. "I don't understand why they're picking on you, though. Why not me?"

"You can run faster'n me. I can't get away. I'm easy," she said. Pert thought that was probably about right.

"We need to give them time to go further away and find something else to amuse them," he said. "While you're here, you can help me search."

Her eyes brightened. "What are we looking for?"

"Anything to do with the Church Council".

"What's a Church Council?"

"I'm not quite sure. I just know there used to be one, years ago. I'll carry on with this box, you look in that one."

44

They worked on. Pert found more records of births, and then some volumes of marriages. He didn't want to know whether anyone was married, so he left these to one side. He looked across at Fenestra. She sat cross legged on the floor, a great tome on her lap, reading avidly. She had gone in a few seconds from abject terror to complete happiness. She was a funny girl, his sister.

Right at the bottom of the box there was a bundle of loose papers. The top one was headed ...

Diocesan Audit, Western Area, Year ending
31st December 1850

... and began *"one vestment chest, oak, with lock"*, and *"lectern in shape ' eagle, oak w.iron pediment"*. Pert knew these items. The vestment chest was still in the vestry. "Vest" meant "clothes" in church, not the sort of vest you wore under your shirt, but church robes, cassocks and things. So the vestry was where you put your clothes on, and the vestment chest was where you kept them when you took them off again.

The lectern in shape ' eagle, oak w.iron pediment was behind a curtain in the south west corner of the church, in a heap of broken chairs.

He read on, and towards the end of the second sheet he found an entry that read ...

Silver dish, 18 inches, chased with angels, ancient

This was a surprise. He'd never seen anything like that in the church. The vessels used for communion were crude, pewter things, and when you had to carry them they were heavy.

Further down there was another:

Communion cup, eleven inches high, ancient. Gold.

And another ...

Cross, two feet and 5 inches, with stones
at extremities, gold.

With increasing excitement he rushed through the rest. In all
there were three silver dishes, two silver communion cups, one
gold one, several gold and silver candlesticks, a gold cross and a
number of enigmatic entries he didn't understand but which
used the words "gold" or "silver". There was a treasure after all.

The next three sheets were dated 1852, and all the same entries
were there. They were worded a little differently in some cases,
but it was plain that they were the same valuable items.

The same was true of 1854, 1856 and 1858. But in 1860 they
had all disappeared. Pert felt a little downcast. His joy at finding
that there had been a real treasure here in this church was
spoiled by the realisation that at least half of the stories about
his family were probably true. If there had been a treasure, then
perhaps Grandfather Mascaridus really had stolen it.

"Pert," his sister said, "is this it?" She had pulled out another large
book. "It says 'Ye Parish of St.Severus of Ethiopia'."

Pert crawled over to her and looked over her shoulder.

"Ye Parish of St.Severus of Ethiopia" he read on the cover in gilt
embossed letters, very faded. Inside on the first page was written in fine copperplate *"Proceedings of the Parochial Church
Council, Sunday 23rd Aprille 1849"*. Below that was a list of
members present.

"Are there more like this?" he asked.

"Yes, two more. But the last one's nearly empty. It stops in 1882
and there were only two people present, look."

She held out the third book. The list of members held just two names. One was Tench, and the other was U.Grubb.

"I'm going to take these," he said. "No one'll miss them, and I want to look through them all."

He began to select some of the audit papers and put them between the covers of the books.

"You can't," Fenestra said, "you'll have to walk all through the Market Place and people will see you and wonder where you got them from."

"That's true. Let's see ... I'll hide them in the churchyard, and then I'll slip out after dark and get them. No one will see me then."

"Can I come?"

"Absolutely not. Mother'd kill me if she knew I'd involved you this afternoon. If I take you out of the house after dark, she'll kill me twice."

"I could tell her it was my idea?"

"No, she'd still kill me. She'd kill you a little bit, and me a whole lot."

And so it was. They left the church and locked it behind them, and Pert stuffed the books under one of the tombs whose walls had crumbled in. That would do until night time, then he would slip back and recover them.

It was not easy for Pert to stay awake that night, but he dare not venture downstairs until he was sure his mother was asleep. He read by candlelight for a while, and managed to decipher another entry in the old bible. Once he had puzzled it out it said *"Aug^{ste} ye 9th 57 sight^d Campeachy weyre is log woode"*.

Pert knew what this meant. He had heard sailors, deep sea sailors who had turned to fishing instead, talk of the Bay of Campèche in the Caribbean Gulf and the logwood trade. But what of the year? Did it mean 1857, or 1757, or even 1657?

He turned to the front of the bible and read the front page. There at the foot of the page were the words *"Prynted in Bristol at ye house of Thos.Thomson 1741"*. So that was it. The bible was probably a hundred and sixty years old, and the mariner who had owned it dead for a hundred and forty.

Pert wondered how the man had died. Attacked by pirates, perhaps. Or perhaps he was a pirate himself – Pert had heard that Campeachy was a pirate haunt. Or simply a ship-wreck, which was why the bible was so damaged by the sea. And what kind of man had he been? A drunken, ignorant lout as so many seamen were in times past? But he had kept written records, he evidently wished for some order in his life. And he had been a man of some education, for he would hardly own a bible he wasn't interested in reading.

Tiring of this speculation and feeling his eyelids drooping, Pert pushed off the bedclothes and deliberately kept himself cold. He had saved a small crust for the mouse, and broke it into tiny pieces. He put one tiny piece on the floor quite near his bed, and waited. Before long his little friend appeared, sniffed the air with her whiskers, and scampered out for the crumb.

When she returned to see if there were more, he had put the next crumb actually on his bed. He knew she ventured into his bed sometimes, for he had found her droppings there. But she'd never done so while he was on it. She paused, sniffing, evidently tempted. Then she made a brave dash, leaped onto the bed, snatched up the crumb and fled.

He smiled. This was a splendid new game. Who knew, he might by small stages be able to coax her to take food right from his fingers, or even sit on his hand. But now he judged it was time to make a move. Surely his mother was fast asleep by now. He left the rest of the bread on the floor, pulled his shoes on and crept painstakingly down the stairs. He knew from experience which steps creaked and which did not.

VIII

Thou hast visited me in the night (Psalm 17)

Outside the night was cold and moonlit, a great wind rushing high up and carrying small clouds lit silver from above. The streets were quiet, grey and ghostlike, no colour anywhere. He trotted as silently as he could down to the Market and turned up the hill, keeping to the shadows.

The churchyard held few fears for him, for he was used to it. To find the tomb and withdraw the books was the work of a moment and he turned for home, but as he regained the Market Square he halted. There were footsteps ahead of him. He found a doorway and hid, not wanting to be seen in the streets so late. Peering out he saw a group of men, three – no, four of them – walking up towards him. They were walking quietly, not speaking. They crossed the road in front of him, and as they passed through a patch of moonlight he was able to make out one or two of the faces.

One he recognised as Will Durridge, the father of Darren, one of Fenestra's two persecutors. The one at the back was George Bunt, father of the other bully. He thought that a third was Spotty Bunt, Batty's older brother, a sullen oaf of a man with nothing but scowls and kicks for anyone who crossed his path. The fourth he did not know, but thought that if one had to pick four of the nastiest villains on the quay, one might come up with just such a gang. Roaming the town at this hour they could scarcely be up to anything good.

To his surprise, the group made their way to the door of Grubb's Emporium. The door was evidently open for them, for they did not pause but disappeared inside.

Pert waited for a while, but they did not come out. This was a mystery. Urethra Grubb was a wicked woman but she also ran what was, on the face of it, a respectable business. Were they here to rob her? That would be brave indeed.

An alarming thought struck him. In that building were the young serving girls, including the poor lass he had wanted to befriend. Suppose these men meant them harm?

He tip-toed to the very corner of the Bearward where it left the Market Square and led up the hill to his home, and put his books quietly down behind a dustbin where he would find them again. Then he crept across the road, his heart beating wildly, and approached the door of the Emporium. It stood slightly ajar, and with his heart in his mouth he pushed it gently. It creaked, just a little. He took his hand from it and froze, straining his ears.

"What was that?" he heard someone say. He recognised the harsh tones of Mistress Grubb, and got ready to fly for his life.

"I heard the door upstairs," he heard. "Did one of you good-for-nothings leave the door open?"

There was a mumble which he could not catch.

"Can you not be trusted to do even a simple thing like closing a door? No, Spotty Bunt, it wasn't the wind. I'll give you wind! I'll wind the wind out of you with the tip of my bodkin if you give me any more of your wind! Now go up and close it properly, before I close you for good!"

There were steps inside, and the door was roughly slammed in Pert's face. He breathed out, carefully.

He knew there was an alley running down the side of the Emporium. He used it sometimes to get to the baker's shop in Low Street. It sloped down sharply, barely three feet wide, and because it sloped it started level with Grubb's front door but ended level with her cellar window. Down here he crept, and stood beside the window. Lights burned inside, and he could see clear enough although the glass was dirty. On the table were three or four candles, and round the table sat the four men, and at the head of the table stood Mistress Grubb. Behind her in the shadows was someone else, a tall dark figure.

He found that by putting his head close to the frame of the window at one side, there was a crack through which he could make out what she was saying.

"No," she said, "you'll do no drinking at my expense, you worthless layabouts. What d'you think I told you to come for, a party? This is business, my slimy pustular friends, important business, desperate business, and business that could make us all rich. That's if you can keep your blabbering mouths shut."

One of the men muttered something, and Grubb punched him hard on the side of the head. His head snapped sideways with the force of the blow from her great ham of a hand. He pulled his feet under him and made to get up, but in a flash she was on him, her fists moving twice more, and he was bundled out of his chair and fell to the floor.

"Don't you ever, ever think to get the better of me, Will Durridge or any of you! It'll be a fine day when I don't see you coming, and I've ways to make you rue the moment you thought you'd tangle with me. Now, get that sack of blubber up on his seat and pay attention."

When the man was seated again, she continued. The dark shadow was motionless behind her, and Will Durridge wiped the blood from his face with his sleeve.

"This gentleman ..." she motioned to the figure behind her, "... this gentleman has come to me with a business proposition. He came to me because he knew I could be trusted. He knew I could be trusted to know what goes on, and he knew I could be trusted to make things happen the way I want them to happen, and he knew I could be trusted to find filth like you to help me. And so I have."

She turned slightly, and gestured to an empty seat at the table. "Won't you sit down and make yourself known, Captain?"

The man sat, and his face came into the candlelight. He was old, older than the other men, his face lined and seamed and burned by the sun and the wind and the salt spray, but it was a strong face that spoke cruelty and ruthless determination. He was tall, and dressed like a gentleman in the old fashioned way with fine silks and lace at his throat and cuffs, but he did not seem like a gentleman. He did not seem gentle at all.

His voice was low, but he formed his words clearly. This was a man accustomed to making himself understood, understood and obeyed.

"My name is Trinity Teague," he said, "and I am the Master of the brig you've no doubt seen down at the quay. She's called *The Black Joke*, in honour of a great man I should very much like to have known. Unfortunately he died before I got the chance. His ship was called the "Burla Negra" which is "Black Joke" in Spanish, so I took that name for my own ship, seeing as he had no further use for it."

Pert drew in his breath. He knew who Teague was talking about. It was in one of his books, *"Ye Dredful Crimes and Justifiyd Execution of ye Blak Pyrate, Benido de Soto by A Sea Captain"*. This man was surely a pirate, and called his ship after that commanded by the infamous Benido, or Benito, de Soto. What were pirates doing in the town, and what was a pirate captain doing with Urethra Grubb and four of the biggest ruffians on the waterfront?

"I am here to recover something that belongs to me," the man continued. "It belongs to me because I stole it. It belongs to me because I killed for it, and it belongs to me because I want it. I lost it, to my eternal indignation, and I mean to steal it again, and I'll kill for it again if I have to. You're going to help me, and if you work well I'll be generous. This could set you up for life. Beer, rum, tobacco, food, a soft bed and a willing woman to fill it. Or a berth on my ship, if you prefer, for a life of power and adventure on the high seas, with no one to say you nay. Now, what do you say?"

"What would we have to do?" asked one of the men.

"What you're told," growled Grubb.

"No, no, let him ask!" said Teague. "Let him ask, if he wants to know. Let him ask and I'll tell him, straight. All you have to do, my dear friend," he leant forward and a great curved knife had appeared in his hand from nowhere. He did not seem to have moved, but suddenly the knife was at the man's throat and his other hand was behind the man's head, "all you have to do is follow my bidding without question or hesitation, my friend. Is that clear enough for you?"

The man's eyes were wide but he dare not move his head.

"Grunt once if you agree, my friend, and twice if you'd prefer that I open your veins now."

The man grunted once, showing the whites of his eyes.

"Good," said Teague, and the knife had vanished again and he was lolling at ease in his chair, "it would have been a pity to spill blood all over this clean floor and put the little ladies to the trouble of cleaning it up in the morning. Now, I think we all understand each other?"

He stood up, and bowed to Mistress Grubb. "I shall return to my ship, and the refreshing sleep that rewards a job done properly."

He moved to the door, paused and swept the men with his eyes. "Here is my first instruction to you. Go home. Let no one see you out on the streets. And find out ... *where is Obadiah Potts?*"

So shocked was Pert to hear this that he jerked upright, and hit his head on the top of the window opening. Inside he heard the scrape of chairs thrown back. He took to his heels, down the alley towards Low Street, and as he ran he had the presence of mind to yowl like a cat and then yap like a dog, hoping to allay their suspicion. At the bottom of the alley he ran as hard as he could up Low Street, and from there circled back to the top of the church yard. He slipped over the church yard wall and hid behind some gravestones, breathing hard, and listened.

He heard nothing, no shouts, no following footsteps. He waited. Still no sound.

After half an hour crouched on the ground, the cold seeping into his bones and up through the soles of his shoes, he judged it was safe to emerge. With infinite care, ready at any moment to fly for his life, he slid noiselessly down the road to the corner of the Bearward, recovered his books, and trotted for home.

IX

There go the ships: there is that leviathan,
whom thou hast made to play therein (Psalm 104)

Today was the last day of the holidays.

"I'm going to see Aunt Gittins, do you want to come?" Pert asked Fenestra. She was at the kitchen table with a sheet of paper in front of her.

"No, I have to stay in. I've got a story to write."

"What's it about?"

"It's about this princess who lives in a castle, and is unhappy most of the time."

"Only most of the time?"

"Yes. She's happy when she's playing with her pet mouse."

"What's the mouse's name?"

"Mouse, silly. Mice don't have names. They're mice."

Pert moved towards the door. "All your princesses seem to be unhappy," he said, "aren't there any happy ones?"

"No. It's tough being a princess these days."

Pert decided to go down to the harbour before visiting Aunt Gittins, to see the pirate ship. It was a bright day, still cold but with a hint of spring to come. The seagulls were wheeling high over the town.

He walked along the quay, stopping to say good morning to one or two fishermen he knew. They had their nets spread out on

56

the cobbles, and sat on the mooring bollards, sewing and smoking. Their boats lay moored to iron rings in the harbour wall, rocking gently. They had odd names, like *"Lady Bountifull"* and *"Here we goe"* and *"Second Chance II"*. Pert wondered if the fact that she was the second *"Second Chance"* meant she should really have been called the *"Third Chance"* instead. Old Walter Glibbery's little boat, one of the smallest with no cabin at all and only one sail, was named *"Better Times"*.

On the other side of the harbour hard against the stone breakwater lay a black-hulled sailing ship with tall sides and two masts painted white. She had a high-raked bowsprit with a yard on it. He turned and walked back so he could go along the breakwater and get a better look.

Close to, she had a weather-worn look. Streaks of green algae from her scuppers told of waves shipped in rough waters, and her rigging, tarred in the old-fashioned way, was frayed and knotted. Her sails lay untidily along their yards, grey with salt and sun. A wisp of smoke rose from her little deck house chimney, and three rough-looking men were leaning on the rail amidships, smoking pipes and spitting in the water.

He walked to the stern, and looked at the curved line of windows. That must be the Captain's cabin, he thought, and shuddered as he remembered the dark man and his sudden knife. In faded gilt letters under the windows was her name, *The Black Joke*, and her home port of Philipsburg. Pert didn't know where that was. It sounded German, or Dutch.

He walked back along her side and spoke to the rough men.

"Please, where's Philipsburgh?" he asked politely.

One of the men took his pipe out of his mouth and spat over the rail deliberately. "St.Martin Island," he said. "It's one of the Leeward Islands in the Carrib Sea. Who wants to know?"

Pert had heard of the Leeward Islands, but the man pronounced it in a funny way, "Loo'rd".

"Please, my name is Potts," he answered.

"Oh, is it now?" The man glanced at his companions. "Well, my curious Master Potts, is you a seeker after knowledge?"

Pert didn't know quite what the man meant by this. "Er ... yes, I suppose I am," he said.

"And does your seeking after knowledge extend to ships and the rollin' sea?"

Pert was on safer ground here. "Yes. I can sail a boat."

"So per'aps you'd like to come aboard this 'ere wessel and take a look around, like?"

"Yes, I'd like that very much."

"And so you shall, Master Potts as thirsts for knowledge." The man sauntered towards the stern where a gang-plank joined the ship to the quay. "Come you along this way, Master Potts, and trot you up this 'ere plank, and you shall see what you shall see."

Pert walked up the gang-plank carefully. It had slats of wood nailed roughly across it every foot or so, to stop your feet from slipping, but there was no hand-rail or rope to hang on to. The plank sprung under his feet, but he balanced himself with his arms and made it to the deck.

"There, young Master Potts," said the man, "now you is aboard a proper ship, not some fiddlin' little fisherboat, but a real queen of the seas, what's ranged from the Americees to the Africees, an' seen some rare ol' sights on the way. She seen the black whale fish a-spoutin', and the dolphin a-leapin' in the bow-wave, and the little flyin' fish a-scatterin'. She seen the blackamores a-caperin' on the African beaches, she seen the rivers in the Americees that come down solid mud and turn the sea brown, an' she seen the pretty parrots a-fly between the trees, an' she smelt the green wind that blows off the jungle ... now, you come along back 'ere ..."

And the man took him on a tour of the ship. They looked at the binnacle on the after deck, with the compass in the top of it, and Pert put his hands on the great wooden wheel and turned it a little way, and felt the resistance of the wooden rudder far below and the ropes that turned it. He looked down into the hold, a cavern of a place that smelled of turpentine and tar and other smells he didn't recognise, and he climbed halfway up the rat-lines, the rope ladders in the rigging that led from the rail to the cross-trees of the mast. The man would only let him go up a short way, and then he had to climb down again.

The man seemed kind, but there was something else about him that made Pert feel uneasy. Perhaps it was the way he didn't look at you when he spoke, but always seemed to be peering over your shoulder with his eyes screwed up, or perhaps it was the livid scar down one cheek that pulled down one corner of his left eye in a permanent wink, or perhaps it was the crude wood-en handle of the seaman's knife in his belt, but Pert tried to keep his distance.

The ship's two masts looked about the same height. "This 'ere's a brig," the man explained, "an' a mighty fast one too, an' handy in a tight corner. Them's the courses ..." he pointed out the sails bunched along the crossyards on both masts, "and them's the stays'ls ..." indicating the fore and aft sails hanging in stops between the masts, "and them's the 'eadsails what go down to the bowsprit. And aft ..." he turned towards the back of the ship where a great sail lay furled between two enormous yards, the gaff and the boom, "she's the spanker, what keeps our head to wind and steadies us."

"And where does the Captain live?"

"The Capting? 'E lives in the stateroom, right aft. You can't go there. 'E's not exactly the welcoming kind, if you know what I mean." The man jerked his head, and spat over the side again. "You want to watch out for the Capting," he said, leaning closer and leering unpleasantly. "'E'll spit a plump young chicken like you, Master Potts as wants to know so much, e'll spit 'im and truss 'im and send 'im to the cookhouse if 'e so much as looks at you!" He put his horny hand on Pert's shoulder, and hissed in his ear, "Where's yer Dad, Master Potts? Where's he at?"

Pert wriggled away. "I don't know," he said, "no one does. He vanished, years ago."

He thought it was time to go.

"Thank you for the tour," he said, "you've been very kind," and ran along the deck and down the plank. The men watched him go. One of them called after him "Where's yer Dad, then?" but he walked away quickly towards the town.

When he reached the base of the breakwater he turned and looked back. He hadn't noticed before, but in front of the hold and just behind the foremast (abaft the foremast, he told himself, not behind it, abaft it) was a hunched, sinister shape shrouded in a tarpaulin. There was another in the bows. Could they be guns?

Two of the men were still leaning on the rail. One of them gave a mocking wave. The third man, the one who had talked to him, was walking quickly aft towards the Captain's quarters.

Further down the quay he came upon Walter Glibbery. His little boat was tied up by the wall and rocking gently, and the old man sat in the stern with a net on his knees. A black bottle was by his side. The *Better Times* was like its master, time-worn and decrepit but sound at heart. Her battered planking had been painted and repainted so many times it was hard to tell what colour she was supposed to be. Fish boxes lay between her thwarts, and coils of rope and a crab pot or two. Her old tan-coloured sail lay across the thwarts, wrapped round its single yard. *Better Times* had one mast and one sail, spread upon a single long yard, lugger fashion. She had no boom at the bottom of the sail. A boom spread the sail a bit better when the wind was aft, but it was one more thing to bang your head in a seaway, so most fishers did without.

"Ahoy, young Pert!" he called, "come aboard, come aboard! Come to visit ol' Walter, have ye? That's nice, come you aboard!"

Pert climbed down the slippery iron ladder let into the face of the harbour wall, and stepped on board. There was a strong smell of fish. He sat on a thwart and grinned at Walter. This felt familiar and safe, despite the rocking.

"Hallo, Walter, it's good to see you," he said. "Have you been out yet?"

"No, no, it's a bit too early fer I. Mebbe this afternoon, if the wind serves. Want to come?"

"No, I can't. I'm going to see my Great Aunt Gittins."

"Ah, fine ol' girl she be, I remember she! Great dancer she were, in the day."

The old man wagged his head and smiled, remembering. "I'd've married she, if'n she'd 'ave me, but she wouldn't. Pity. She wouldn't've hit my old 'ead with no chair leg, like my missus do. No, she'd've used the whole chair!"

He doubled up with laughter at his own wit, and took a draught from his bottle.

"I've been on that ship over there, the *Black Joke*," Pert said.

The old man didn't look. He sniffed. "Ah, proper ship, she be.

61

She've seen some sights, I be bound. An' done some deeds, too, I shouldn't wonder."

"Do you think she could be a pirate ship?"

"Ah. Could be, per'aps. Could be. They say there's no pirates any more, but you never know. They thought they'd caught 'em all in the sixteens, but they never. And then they thought they'd put a stop to 'em in the seventeens, an' that was wrong too. An' they thought there were no more of 'em in old Boney's time ..." Pert knew he meant Napolean Bonaparte, "... when the navy were so big an' went scouring the seas for Frenchies and privateers, but up pops that ol' Benido an' led 'em a pretty dance!"

"Is that Benito de Soto?" said Pert. "I've got a book about him."

"'E's in books now, is 'e? Ah, 'e was a bad 'un, old Benido. 'E caught the *Mornin' Star*, 'e did, off the Azorios on 'er way back from the Indies, an' e' did dreadful things, dreadful things as one can't 'ardly speak of. Mind you, it caught up with 'im, 'cos 'e battened the passengers down below an' scuttled the ship, an' they broke out an' plugged the 'oles with the ladies' petticoats, 'an sailed 'er home. An' then they spotted ol' Benido on shore, walkin' down the street bold as brass, an' they cried out an' told everyone 'This 'ere's Benido, that naughty man what robbed us!' An' they took and 'ung 'im, an' good riddance, say I! Ah!"

He took another draught. "An' they thought that was an end to it, but then they was Pirate Hicks, what they hanged on Bedloe Island an' they say ten thousand people came to watch 'im swing. An' they thought that was an end to it, an' up pops Bully Hayes, what was murdered by Dutch Pete, or so they say. Ah, they never goes right away, does pirates. There's always someone what thinks 'e can make a better livin' by robbin' than by honest sailorin'. Ah!"

"Have you heard of Trinity Teague? Is he a pirate?"

The old man sat up, his eyes aghast. "Trinity Teague, you say. Where'd you 'ear that name?"

"I think he might be on that ship."

"Trinity Teague? Lor, love us! Trinity Teague? He disappeared forty years ago, along a' your granddad, and never 'eard of from that day to this! Trinity Teague? What makes you say that?"

"I ... just heard he was back. What sort of man was he?"

"Ah, a black-browed, broodin' sort of fellow, 'e was. Kept to 'imself, didn't talk much. Young, but a great sailor. 'E was your grandaddy's second mate, until the Great Storm ..."

"And they disappeared together?"

"Aye, vanished off the face of the ocean, they did. People talked, but it was just talk. One minute they was 'ere, walkin' round the town, an' the next they was gone. Now, young Pert, when are you goin' to come a-fishin' with ol' Walter, eh? There's mackerel out there with your name writ on 'em!"

"I have to go to school tomorrow," Pert said. "When the Easter holiday comes, I'll go with you."

"Ah, that's what. You see, we'll 'ave them mackerel for supper come Easter. It'll be mackerel this, an' mackerel that, an' mackerel for breakfast an' mackerel for lunch. Them mackerel, they'll be linin' up to jump in the boat by themselves, so they will! An' crabs as big as your 'ead in between."

Pert stood, swaying slightly with the motion of the boat. "I must go," he said.

"Ah, you cut along! You're a good boy, whatever people say. Never I saw a truer course than steered by you. Remember me to your Aunt Gittins, an' tell 'er she should come an' 'ave another

63

dance with ol' Walter for ol' time's sake, he he! We could still cut a caper!"

And he waved his bottle, and giggled, and Pert climbed the ladder and set off for Aunt Gittins' house, full of thought. So Trinity Teague had known his grandfather. That seemed important, but he was not sure how.

Aunt Gittins was Pert's grandmother's sister, and she lived at the edge of the town in a street of stone cottages which would be flowery and bright with window boxes in summer but for now just looked neat and well cared for. If you stood at Aunt Gittins' bedroom window you could see the roofs of the town falling away down the hillside, and the sea sparkling in the sun.

Aunt Gittins was very old, over eighty, and sometimes Pert wondered if she would die and leave the house to his mother. It would be nice to live up here in the sun and watch the sea and not have to pay rent to Urethra Grubb. But Aunt Gittins showed no signs of being ready to die just yet. In fact she was a vigorous and cantankerous old woman who liked her own company and seldom sought anyone else's. She was tall and square-jawed, and wore little wire-rimmed glasses, and seldom smiled. She looked forbidding.

Nevertheless she welcomed Pert nicely enough, and gave him milk and biscuits and made him sit at the kitchen table and tell her the news of his family. He also gave her the message from Walter Glibbery, which made her snort.

"Walter Glibbery?" she exclaimed. "That old soak? Mind you, he's right, he was quite a dancer in our youth, and a charmer. But he was a weak man. A good fisher, they said, but weak and foolish and easily led. How that poor woman has put up with him all these years I'll never know."

"She hits him on the head with a chair leg," said Pert.

"Good thing too. I'd have done the same."

"He says you'd have used the whole chair."

"I probably would, I probably would. Of course, she wasn't much to look at, very plain girl she was. She probably knew he was the best she'd get, so she hung on to him. And she's clung on ever since, and he's been faithful enough to her, so perhaps one shouldn't criticise."

She looked out of the window, her mind elsewhere. Then she gathered her thoughts together.

"Now, your sister Fenestra, you haven't told me about her. Why didn't you bring her with you?"

"I asked her, but she was busy. She's writing a story. She writes lots of stories."

"Have you read them? Are they any good?"

"Yes, I think so. She has very neat hand-writing."

"A funny little thing, your sister. Too much thinking, and not enough laundry and embroidering. But a good girl, not like Vernilia ..."

"Was she as bad as Mother says?"

"Worse. I tried my best to help, but once she got the idea that the boys were interested in her, there was no holding her. Who's going to listen to an old woman like me?"

"I listen."

"So you do, so you do. So did your father, bless his memory. But Vernilia – ah, she was wild and wilful. It was a mercy when she went off with that sailor lad. Not that he had much going on between his ears, I should think. But at least it left a little peace for your poor mother."

"I wanted to ask about my father. Mother was telling us about when he disappeared."

"That was a bad business, and so unexpected. So unlike him. He was a steady boy, a bit of a worrier really, always anxious to do the right thing. You know he lived with me when he was a lad?"

"Yes. After his parents went."

"Mascaridus went first, and then my sister Floribunda. They say she died of a broken heart, but it was more like shame. When they said he'd stolen that money she just couldn't hold her head up any more. Never went out of the house, but just faded and faded until there was nothing left."

She sniffed, and blew her nose. "Your mother looked like going the same way for a bit, but she's made of stronger stuff. Not strong enough to cope with Vernilia, but strong all the same. Obadiah, your father, doted on her. She was a pretty thing, very quiet, but pretty. Fenestra takes after her. She was a Twitchett, you know. A good family, but all gone now. He thought the sun shone from her apron pocket, he did. Why he would ever have left her I just don't know. It must have been something dreadful."

"What sort of thing?"

"Who knows? I know he used to think about his father a lot, even when he was a boy. He came to me when he was but eight years old, an only child, very sad and lost. I never married and never wanted children, but it was my duty to take him in so I did. But I know he always wondered what his father had done and what had happened to him. It might have been something to do with that."

"Might there be any other members of his family who'd know?"

66

"There is no other family, dear. Mascaridus Potts didn't come from here, he was an incomer. A seaman, I think, who hove up here one year and decided to settle. Swept my sister off her feet, bought a boat – a good one, so he must have arrived with money – and set up as a skipper. He changed the name of the boat to the *Bight of Benin* – nasty, heathen name, I thought. I was always told it was bad luck to change a boat's name. Anyway, he soon became respected. People looked up to him. He was a big man, and hard, and he took no nonsense. But he was fair, and well-spoken. People like that in a man."

"I didn't know that. What's the Bight of Benin, what does that mean?"

"It's a place in Africa somewhere, that's all I know. Yes, there was just him. He started the Potts family, and you're left to carry it on. Have you thought what you're going to do when you leave school?"

"Yes. I'll go fishing with Walter, and learn from him."

"You make sure you learn the right things, then. He's got a few wrong things to teach."

"He's taught me a lot already. He says I'm as good a helmsman as he's ever seen. And I'll save money, and then buy a little boat and go on my own account."

She looked at him shrewdly. "That's a good plan. Start small, act prudent and work up. That'll do. And have you a little lady love yet?"

"No," he said, feeling embarrassed. "Well, there is someone ... but she doesn't know I exist, even."

"Ah well, plenty of time for that. Make something of yourself and she'll soon start to take notice, you mark my words. Girls are like that."

Pert kissed his Aunt, and set off home to see if there was any lunch. Sometimes there wasn't, but he'd had biscuits. On the way down past the church he came up with Rosella, marching her little brood behind her. He hurried to catch up, and said "School tomorrow!" but she ignored him and suddenly turned up a side street. Her train obediently wheeled to follow her, but the last two both turned. The tiny one grinned at him, and the other made a face and put out her tongue. That's good, he thought. That's progress, of a sort.

There was no lunch at home, his mother said. Having to pay the rent five days early had upset the family budget, and although she had some sewing to do for the Widow Dolphin and a dress to make for Horatia Fencepiece's little girl, she hadn't been paid yet.

"I had an idea about money," Pert said, pouring himself a cup of water from the pitcher. "Why don't we take a lodger?"

"A lodger? Where would we put them?"

"I thought you might put them in Fenestra's room, and she could come and share the attic with me."

"I'm not sure that's a good idea," his mother said. "Some great hulking noisy fisherman, smoking and dropping his boots on the floor ..."

"I thought about that too. Mr.Surplice is not happy where he is. I don't think he gets enough food, and they aren't nice to him."

"He wouldn't get enough food here, either."

"But you could buy more food with his rent money!"

"Well ... Fenestra, what about her? Kicking her out and sending her to the attic? That doesn't seem very fair."

"You could ask her. She might not mind."

In fact Fenestra didn't mind at all. When Pert put it to her she was ecstatic – sleeping in an attic with a mouse was the most romantic idea she'd ever heard. She would write stories about a little servant girl who lived in an attic and a mouse was her only friend and she'd be unhappy most of the time. Brilliant!

Their mother said she'd think about it. She said it with her hand over her mouth, and Pert thought she was trying not to laugh.

X

For the needy shall not always be forgotten (Psalm 9)

He spent the afternoon puzzling over the Church Council books. It was hard going for an active boy with better things to do, but he thought it was necessary. The Minutes didn't tell you very much, because they didn't report any of the discussions that must have taken place, simply the decisions that resulted from them - *"Resolved that ye sum of 13/6d be payed to ye Curat fr new chasubel"* for instance, or *"Resolved to accept Wm. Walduck, his quotatioun of £3/7s/9d in respect repares to chauncel roof"*.

13/6d seemed rather a lot for a new chasubel, whatever that was, Pert thought. Thirteen shillings and sixpence would have bought quite a few Christmas dinners for poor Mr. Surplice, and Mr. Surplice did not own any chasubels at all so far as Pert knew. He would try and remember to ask him.

At the beginning of the books which started in the year 1743 the Church Council was quite large. At each meeting the members were listed, and it was interesting to see how the membership changed slowly over the years. Many of the names were familiar, and must refer to the ancestors of families still living in the town. In 1761 Jeremiah Scattock evidently died or retired, and his place was taken by Joseph Scattergood. Joseph only lasted three years before he gave up his place to Hosea Scattergood – his son, perhaps.

In 1822 the first woman appeared on the council, Amerelia Scutch, wife – there were still some Scutches in the town, Pert knew, and there was a girl in Fenestra's class called Meriella Scutch. More women appeared as the years went by, until in 1882 came the first appearance of the name Urethra Grubb, spinster. She was a permanent fixture from then on, but the total membership quickly dwindled from year to year. A. Dolphin, widow, dropped out in 1884, and H. Wheable, wife, in 1885. Sir H. Comfrey attended only spasmodically in 1885, and then

70

stopped. Finally in 1887 there was one meeting where the only council members were U.Grubb and S.Tench, Vicar. That was the last one.

Pert closed the last book and sat thinking. What had brought about this rapid decline? Was it that there was less and less business to discuss? Or perhaps they'd simply bowed to U.Grubb's overbearing ways and let her get on with it? Or had she deliberately set out to offend and humiliate until there was nobody prepared to serve except herself and the Vicar, who was obliged?

And if she had done that, why? Why did she want to be on the Church Council at all? She never came to church.

If there were to be any clues, they might lie in the decisions of the meetings where she had held sway. He decided to concentrate his researches on the meetings from 1882 to the end.

Although there were twelve Church Council meetings every year, there was one group of items that recurred only once a year. Each December the Minutes included ...

> *"Resolved to accept ye accounts of ye Parishe Fund"*
> *"Resolved to accept ye accounts of ye Poor Box"*
> *"Resolved to accept ye accounts of ye Funde for*
> *ye Relieve of Destitution"*

Pert did not know what any of these were. Besides, where were ye accounts? They weren't included in the book. Perhaps they were among the Diocesan Audit papers? He searched quickly. Nothing headed "ye accounts". Pert wasn't certain what accounts were but he knew they were something important, and if the Minutes said that the Council had accepted them, they should be somewhere.

This was something else to ask Mr.Surplice.

There was one more thing to look up. He knew his grandfather had disappeared during the Great Storm of 1860. Would there be any mention of that in the Minutes? The treasure disappeared at the same time – surely they'd have discussed that at one of the meetings? He read right through all the meetings in 1860, and went on halfway through 1861 just in case.

There was nothing. The Great Storm was mentioned all right, for the wind had taken the weather cock off the top of the tower, and blown down some of the gravestones and one of the yew trees, but nowhere could he find his grandfather's name, and no mention of the treasure at all. It seemed that the church had owned all those gold cups and plates, had reported them faithfully to the diocese, and never mentioned them to the Church Council at all. Did the Church Council not know about them?

Suppose the treasure had been a secret? Suppose these fine cups and plates were not used in the church services at all, but were hidden away and never taken out? Perhaps they didn't even belong to the parish but had simply been placed there for safe keeping? In that case, who would have known about them? The Vicar, presumably. But that wasn't the Reverend Tench, he wasn't old enough. There must have been another vicar in those days.

He turned to the list of members present at one of the 1860 meetings. There at the bottom was the name *"J.Tench, vicar"*. Surely the Reverend Tench was not that old? - he must have been only a boy in 1860. But wait – the Vicar's name was Silas Tench M.D., so J.Tench must be someone else. His father, perhaps? Did vicarages get passed down from father to son? Pert had no idea.

All this research had made Pert's brain ache and the dim light in the attic was straining his eyes. It was almost supper time, but he still had half an hour and he knew where Mr.Surplice would be at this time - it was Tuesday evening, so the curate would be taking the children for their Catechism in the vestry. Pert had done his some years before, though he had promptly forgotten every word of it. He clattered down the stairs and raced down the street.

In the vestry all was orderly and quiet, which was surprising. Pert remembered these classes being rather rowdy, as Mr.Surplice was not adept at keeping discipline. As he pushed open the door and slipped in, he found that ten little children were sitting still and repeating their sentences after the curate like little angels. Two of them were the two middle Prettyfeet, and then Pert realised why everything was going so well. On the windowsill perched Rosella, her skirt hitched up to her knees and one big boot swinging, watching over the class grimly, daring them to misbehave. She ignored Pert as usual, so he sat on the vestment chest and waited for the class to end.

Before long Mr.Surplice reached a convenient point, rose and praised the children's attentiveness, and dismissed them vaguely. Rosella got down from the windowsill, gathered up her two charges and marched them out of the vestry. One of them looked back at Pert and winked. Pert winked back. He was getting the hang of this.

"Why Pert," said the curate genially, "how nice of you to drop in! Surely you haven't come for a refresher course, have you?"

Pert grinned at him. "No. I came to ask you a couple of questions. What's a chasubel?"

"Ah well, a chasuble, well, it's a sort of frock a priest wears for communion. It's round with a hole in the middle, and you put it over your head and it hangs down all round, but you can still poke your hands out to pick up the communion things. The vicar has a lovely embroidered one."

"Have you got one? Do curates have them?"

"My goodness no, I couldn't afford it. They're expensive, and curates aren't paid very much, you know. And even if I could afford one, the Vicar would just say I was showing off, and stop me wearing it."

Pert frowned. "All right, next question: what's the Parish Fund?"

"Why, that's easy. It's all the money the parish collects, mainly from the plate going round on Sunday but also from bequests – you know, often people leave a sum of money to the church when they die, and rich people sometimes make an annual grant as well. The vicar's stipend is paid from it, and the upkeep on the vicarage, and repairs to the church and so on. And the curate's tiny mite, too!" he laughed sadly.

"So quite a lot of money, then? Is that where the money goes that I collect and give to the Vicar on Sundays?"

"Yes, it is. And quite a lot, I would say. Several hundreds of pounds a year."

"And the Poor Box?"

"That's the money box that sits at the back of the church, and people put their pennies in. It's kept separate from the Parish Fund because it's dedicated to helping poor people. It says so on the box."

"And the Fund for the Relief of Destitution?"

"That's quite different. Ah, we should sit down. I can't explain this very simply."

He pulled up a chair to the table, and planted his elbows. "The Destitution Fund doesn't belong to the church at all. It's money raised by collections and bequests, by a levy on property and generous donations from rich people to help those who have fallen on hard times."

Pert wondered why his mother had never received any of this money. Her times had been hard enough. "So who's in charge of it?" he asked.

"Well, it depends. In some places it's the mayor. In others there's a special committee formed to do it. And in others it might be the Parish Council or the Church Council."

"It's the Church Council here," Pert said. "I saw it in ... some papers I happened on.

The curate didn't seem to notice Pert's slip. "Is it really? That's the first I've heard of it. But there is no Church Council, is there, so who has the money and who gives it out to the needy?"

"No idea," said Pert. "It's a mystery."

"It is indeed. Any more questions?"

"Yes. Where are the accounts kept?"

"What accounts?"

"The accounts for the Parish Fund and the Poor Box and the Destitution."

Mr.Surplice sat and thought for a moment. He was beginning, Pert could tell, to realise that here was something rather serious. "I don't know," he said slowly. "Perhaps the Vicar keeps them."

"Could you ask him?"

"Oh no, I couldn't possibly. He'd be ever so cross if I did. Oh no, no!"

"I've one more question," Pert said as he got up.

"Yes?"

"Would you like to come home with me for supper?"

"Oh, how lovely! Yes, yes, by all means, how very kind!"

Pert could hardly keep up with the curate as he galloped down the Canonry and up the Bearward, his nimble feet skipping on and off the pavement to avoid the rubbish thrown there. It was rather like showing a dog a piece of steak, he thought, or a rancid fish to a seagull. Mr.Surplice's thin legs twinkled as he raced up Pardoner's Alley.

"I brought Mr.Surplice home for supper," said Pert as he ushered the curate into the kitchen. He watched his mother, hoping desperately that there was some supper to offer, but she rose to occasion wonderfully.

"Oh Pert, what a kind thought!" she said. "Mr.Surplice, do come in and have a seat, you're very welcome! It's only simple fare, I'm afraid, but the butcher had some knuckle today and I've made a broth. Pert, go and call your sister."

The meal was a great success. There was enough to go round, although Mr.Surplice ate two great bowls of the broth and nearly half a loaf of bread. He listened with rapt attention while Fenestra recounted the tale of the little servant girl who lived in the attic and had a pet mouse. It was quite long. The servant girl endured indignities that surprised Pert who couldn't think how his sister could imagine such things, but rose above them thanks to the love of the mouse which brought her crusts and nibbled at her bonds when she was tied up, and all was well in the end.

At the end Mr.Surplice thanked her, and praised the story. Fenestra glowed.

"Are you going to come and live with us?" she asked. "Then I can go and sleep with Pert in the attic. We have a mouse too, that's where I got the idea!"

Pert hid his face with embarrassment. He should have seen this coming. He looked sideways at his mother, but once again she seemed to be trying not to laugh. She didn't seem cross at all.

"Oh, Fenestra," she said, "you and your big mouth! Mr.Surplice, we had a conversation here the other day about taking a lodger, and Pert wondered if you might be looking for alternative lodgings."

Mr.Surplice looked from one to another with growing astonishment. "Well, my goodness!" he exclaimed. "Oh my, oh my! I ... well I never! How kind! I ... well, yes, my present lodgings are ... not very convivial, that's true. I don't know what to say."

"Say yes, then, you silly man!" said Fenestra, and sat on his lap. She ruffled the thin hair on the top of his head and dislodged his glasses.

"Fenestra!" gasped her mother, "you wanton, you can't sit on a clergyman! Get off this instant!"

The curate seemed to be in the grip of some powerful emotion. His eyes filled with tears and he gazed around wildly. He gently put Fenestra down on the floor and stood up, wiped his eyes with a rather dirty handkerchief, and said "Dear lady, dear boy, and dear little girl ..."

"Don't forget the mouse," muttered the dear little girl.

"Yes, and ... dear mouse, if it can hear me ... I can't remember the last time anyone treated me with such kindness. I am quite overcome. But yes, if you'll have me, I should be honoured."

"Don't you want to see the room?" asked Pert.

"Frankly, no," he said. "I've seen the people, and that's quite enough. Oh thank you, thank you!" and he shook first Mother's hands and then Pert's and then Fenestra's. "I shall move in tomorrow, if I may!"

"Whee!" said Fenestra, leaping for the stairs. "I'm going to tell the mouse!"

Later, when they had managed to disengage themselves from the curate's gratitude – and he did seem to have an awful lot of it – Pert asked his mother if she was really content with the idea.

"Oh, yes," she said, "though I wasn't quite prepared for Fenestra to blurt it out like that." Fenestra looked not in the least abashed. "I had thought about it, and decided it was a good idea, though a curate ... I thought clergymen would like something a little more comfortable."

"I think he's only a very small clergyman, and not much used to comfort," said Pert. "I'm sure he'll be fine."

XI

They are all together become filthy (Psalm 14)

The next day dawned dismally, a thin rain blowing in from the sea and hardly light at all. Trudging through the wet streets to school, Pert thought the day matched his own mood. As they neared the bottom of the town they were joined by other children walking in ones and twos, shrouded in raincoats or old sacks according to their status. No one ran, and no one smiled. There were few greetings. School was not something to look forward to. Fenestra was silent and withdrawn, walking by his side with her hood over her face.

"Are you going to be all right?" he said. He knew what was worrying her. She was two classes below him, so he couldn't keep an eye on her. "Perhaps if you keep with the other girls at playtime?"

"No, they're no good," she said. "If anything frightens them they just run away squeaking. And they don't like me all that much, except for Esmerelda, because I'm Potts. And Esmerelda's scared of her own shadow."

"I'll come and find you as soon as I get out," he said. His class had their playtime a little later than hers, with only a short overlap.

"It'll be all right," she said. "I'll ask Miss Clutterbrick if I can tidy the bookshelf at playtime. Esmerelda can help. And then we'll do it very slowly so it lasts for the afternoon as well."

"That sounds like a good plan," Pert said.

At the gates Esmerelda was waiting. She was Fenestra's only friend, a tiny waif of a girl with pale ginger hair and knock knees. They greeted each other with timid enthusiasm and disappeared towards their classroom.

Pert's own class, the oldest, were housed at the far end of the building. The room smelled of generations of chalk dust, powdered ink and boy, though these days there were girls in the class as well. One of them was Rosella, but she hadn't arrived yet. She was always the last to arrive because she would march her sisters to school and then escort each one of them to the correct classroom first.

Pert sat next to a boy called Vachel, a dim lad who spoke only in grunts and hated everybody including Pert. He was already in his place, his desk lid up. He had a dead mouse in his desk, and was busy sticking pen nibs in it. Pert greeted him but received no reply.

In the desk in the far rear corner sat Fenestra's tormentors, Darren Durridge and Batty Bunt. They were great hulking lads, far too big for school but far too stupid to leave and too clumsy and sullen to find a berth on a fishing boat, at least with any skipper who valued the happiness of his crew, so there they sat with their boots up on the desk, chewing balls of paper with spit and throwing them at the girls.

Pert felt a tap on his shoulder. In the desk behind him were two brothers, Seth and Solomon White. They were slim and dark and quick, lively lads who got on with everyone.

"See who's come up from Mr.Trump's class?" hissed Seth, pointing towards the far front corner of the class. There sat a new boy, tiny and tousled. His clothes were an astonishing ensemble of other people's cast-offs. His shirt had evidently been a lady's blouse, for it had little purple flowers and horseshoes on it. His jacket was many sizes too large and hung off his shoulder. He had rolled up the sleeves so his grubby wrists and hands could get out, and one lapel was torn completely off. His trousers were also too large and torn in an embarrassing place, while on his right foot he wore a wellington boot and on his left an elderly plimsoll with the toes out.

"Who's that?" asked Pert.

Solomon White put his head beside his brother's. "Billy Moon," he whispered. "His mum's Primrose Moon. She's a ... you know!" He winked, and dipped his head to one side meaningfully.

"She's a what?" Pert asked.

"You know ... she goes with men. Our dad calls her a good-time girl."

"And our mum says time's not all she's good for," put in Seth, "but she charges by the hour!"

The pair collapsed in a fit of sniggers. Pert examined the new boy. He had a snub nose and a great mop of tangled hair through which bright eyes shone. His mouth was wide, and half open in a happy grin as he gazed round the classroom. His face was extremely dirty.

Before Pert could complete his examination, Rosella arrived, her big boots clattering on the floor and her nose in the air. She quick marched to her desk, flung her books inside it, slammed the lid and folded her arms, as if to say "Right! I'm here now, so get on with it!"

She was tall and slender, built for speed. She could have been elegant, but moved too quickly and decisively for that. Her nearly-blonde hair was cropped and always untidy from the speed of her passage through life. Her dark eyes and delicate features spoke of pleasures not yet discovered, and her lips invited soft kisses though probably not from Pertinacious Potts.

He and Rosella Prettyfoot had a secure and consistent relationship and both knew exactly where they stood. Pert had always adored her, and she had always ignored him.

The classroom hubbub died abruptly as Mr.Merridew walked in. He stalked to his desk and surveyed the ranks before him, his hands in his pockets.

"White and White, stop giggling like a couple of girls," he said quietly. "And Potts, face front. Bunt, the cane's hanging behind the door. Do you want to get it for me?"

Bunt shook his head, mute.

"Well you will, if I see you throw one more piece of paper at the unfortunate girl in front of you, though I've no doubt she invited it, the hussy. And before you go out at playtime you'll pick up every scrap of paper from this floor. If I return and find just one, tiny, miniscule trace of paper," his voice sunk even lower, full of menace, "I'll make you crawl on your stomach and lick it clean, so help me. Am I clear?"

Bunt nodded.

"Good. Any boy or girl want to draw themselves to my attention at all, before we start work? Anyone feel the need to flirt with danger or experiment with humiliation? Anyone fancy baring their spotty bottom to the world so I can demonstrate with my cane the futility of their pathetic existence? Yes, that boy? Are you volunteering?"

The boy next to Billy Moon had his hand up. "Sir, please sir, no sir. Sir, please sir, can I move? He smells!"

Merridew looked at him for a long moment. "Smells, does he? How unfortunate. Well, Moon, do you smell?"

Billy Moon, unabashed, grinned at him. "Prob'ly. We ain't got no bath in our 'ouse, mister!"

"Mm. If I were so importunate as to have no bath in my house, I'd keep quiet about it. Yes, you may move. There's an empty place in the second row. And you, Moon, come out here. Fetch the cane from behind the door."

A stir went round the class, a mixture of fear, disgust and glee at the discomfiture of another. It wasn't so bad, seeing someone caned, as long as it wasn't you.

The teacher took the cane and bent the boy over the high teacher's desk. With a gesture of distaste he used the very tips of his fingers to yank down the trousers, and laid two strokes of the cane across the skinny buttocks.

"In future, boy, you will address me as "Sir". I do not answer to "Mister", and I'll cane you every time you forget it. And do not come to my class again smelling like a midden, or I'll have Bunt and Durridge take you outside and throw buckets of water over you. They'll enjoy that, no doubt. It will appeal to what they laughingly regard as a sense of humour."

Billy Moon pulled up his trousers and returned to his seat. He was still grinning, but not quite so widely. The rest of the class relaxed. Now Merridew had got that out of his system they might get through the first half of the morning unscathed. There were few boys who did not know what it was like to bend over that desk for some small crime or other, and few of the boys' bottoms that had not been exposed to public view, from the White brothers' slender buttocks to the great pimply hams of Bunt and Durridge. No girls were punished in this way, but the fear that it might happen one day kept that half of the class subdued all the same. There was always a first time.

Merridew stood and looked out over his class, rocking on the balls of his feet. "Take out your bibles. Potts, you will begin."

Pert started reading aloud. *"He sitteth in the lurking places of the villages: in the secret places doth he murder the innocent: his eyes are privily set against the poor,"* he read. They had got as far as the Psalms.

"He lieth in wait secretly as a lion in his den: he lieth in wait to catch the poor: he doth catch the poor, when he draweth him into his net."

Merridew rocked, and threw a piece of chalk idly from hand to hand. He was a cadaverous man, long of face and misshapen of jaw, his eyes small and his brow insignificant, a mop of lank grey hair obscuring it. He dressed like a magister from one of the great schools, in flannel suit and long black gown, but in his heart he knew that he was not cut from that cloth. He knew himself for a weak man, a man of limited intellect and fibre, a bully who had found his proper niche in life terrorising the youth of this abject little town.

"He croucheth, and humbleth ..." Pert went on, but Merridew interrupted him.

"Next," he said quietly, and Seth White took up the verse: *"humbleth himself, that the poor may fall by his strong ones ..."*

Pert wondered what that meant. Who humbleth himself, and how did the strong ones make the poor fall? He liked the psalms. He specially liked *"They grin like a dog and run about the city."* Dogs did grin, too, and hung their tongues out at one side.

But his favourite was *"The waters are come in unto my soul. I sink in deep mire, where no ground is. I am come into deep waters, and the floods run over me."* That was a proper fisherman's psalm, that was. But they said that the psalms had been written by desert people who lived in sand and rode around on camels and never saw the sea. Perhaps riding around in boring old sand all day made you have a good imagination, he thought.

The turn had reached the back now, but Pert didn't allow himself to relax. Merridew had a habit of suddenly picking someone out of turn, even someone who had read already, and woe betide you if you weren't in the right place. Now Darren Durridge was reading, his head down and his face scarlet.

"How long wilt thou forget me, O Lord?" he read. *"For ever? How long wilt thou hide thy face from me?"* Darren Durridge had got an easy bit, but he hated this embarrassment and someone

would pay for it later. *"How long shall mine enemy be exalted over me?"*

Pert felt cross with the camel-riders. They were always moaning. They were always surrounded by enemies, and the Lord was always forsaking them, and all they could do was complain about the unfairness of it all. Why didn't they get off their backsides and fight for once?

And on the rare occasions when the Lord did come through for them, and sent out his arrows and scattered their enemies and shot out lightnings and discomfited them, they behaved with unseemly glee and did rejoice a bit too much in his opinion, for the enemies soon regrouped and came back strong as ever. You'd think they'd have learned by now.

He gathered his wits together and tried to concentrate, for it was Rosella's turn to read. *"The fool hath said in his heart, there is no God. They are corrupt, they have done abominable works, and there is none that doeth good,"* she read. She read fluently but rather quickly, and did not stumble over the word "abominable" as most of them would have. *"The Lord looked down from heaven upon the children of men, to see if any did understand, and seek God. But they are all gone aside, they are all together become filthy: there is none that doeth good, no, not one."*

She rushed through this in clipped tones that made it clear she had no truck with any camel-riders or their whining. Pert felt pleased that she evidently shared his misgivings about them. Surely you could doeth good and not be filthy without seeking God? The Vicar presumably sought God regularly, but his collar was frequently grimy and he smelled of whisky. Perhaps he sought but did not understand? That would be a nice distinction, wouldn't it? Suppose you were thick like Batty Bunt and you just couldn't understand something – did that make you wicked? It earned you the cane, but did it make you wicked?

"Miss Prettyfoot, you read accurately but you make it sound as though you would as soon read from a laundry list," drawled Merridew. "Perhaps you find this beneath you?"

Rosella looked at him coolly. "Did I make any mistakes, sir?" Pert felt his heart thump in his chest at her bravery.

"You did not, but you read it without sense or understanding," Merridew said. His relaxed pose was gone, and he rose to his full height, his cheeks flushing. "Have you any idea what you just read?"

"Certainly sir. I was reading from Psalm Fourteen. The psalmist is observing that anyone who doesn't believe in God must be wicked, and that he can find no one who seeks to understand the truth. It is an interesting point, sir, to consider whether a non-believer can do anything that is not a sin. If you believe and give a poor person some money, that's a good act. Is it a wicked act to do it without belief? The Vicar touched on it in his sermon two Sundays ago."

Merridew twitched. He never went to church. His mouth moved convulsively. From his position at the front Pert felt sure he heard him mutter under his breath "I'll touch on you, you impudent hussy, see if I don't!" but the teacher covered it up by walking to his desk and sitting down with a swish of his gown. "Moon! Read on!" he barked.

Pert was musing on the wonderful congruity of his thoughts and those of Rosella. He would like to be able to talk to her about this wickedness thing. He found a lot of what went on in the church rather hard to stomach, but he didn't feel wicked. He couldn't remember hurting anyone, or even being rude to them. Did this mean he was a good Christian really, but hadn't realised it yet?

He was disturbed from this train of thought by the sudden silence that gripped the room. Billy Moon had no book in front of him, and sat sideways in his seat, grinning.

86

"Sir, can't read, sir!" he said cheerfully. "Never learned it! I tried sir, but all them little 'ooks and curly fings don' mean squit to me, sir. But I do likes listenin' to the story, sir!"

This can only end badly, thought Pert. Surely there was another caning in this.   The class held its breath. Merridew rose to his feet. Two pieces of defiance in as many minutes could not be borne, his face said, and one must be made to pay for the other.

Just then the bell rang outside the door, and the class breathed a sigh, relief for some, frustration for others. Merridew never let a moment of playtime be wasted, for he was addicted to his pipe and his nerves must be on edge by now. Without a word he wrapped his gown around him and swept out of the door and up the passage towards the staff room. Behind him a gabble of voices broke out, and a surge towards the playground and fifteen minutes of freedom.

Pert had been in the staffroom once, sent by a teacher to fetch something forgotten. He could imagine it now, the ancient leather armchairs stained with ink and food and other unfathomable substances, collapsed on their springs under generations of magisterial buttocks. The air would be fusty and smoke-filled as Merridew and his companions Trump and Bristle stoked up their pipes, bubbling and sucking and filling their corner of the room with fumes. Trump, who taught the class below Merridew's, was a lazy, soft pudding of a man who used the cane just enough to secure adequate discipline but could not be bothered to do much more. The idea of actually teaching his pupils anything was a step too far, in his view. He left that energetic sort of thing to Merridew and Miss Clutterbrick.

Miss Clutterbrick was the only woman teacher, and the only one with any kind of formal training for she had spent two years at the diocesan training college in St.Portius. She excelled at lists, forms, schedules, reports, posters and anything that required several different coloured inks. Her class was orderly, the children mostly complaisant and rather baffled by the exercises they were required to do. They liked the nature table, which held bunches of flowers, shrubs, grasses and dry sticks in jam jars according to season, and odd coloured stones the children found on the beach, some seaweed that was supposed to tell you if it was going to rain, and a fish. The fish was changed once a week. They also enjoyed the daily story which was invariably of a moral and improving nature intended to demonstrate that virtue will always be rewarded in this world and vice will get you nothing but illness and degradation. It never occurred to them that this was entirely at odds with the world they saw around them and in which their parents had to live, which consistently rewarded corruption and ignored virtue. It was a story, after all.

Fenestra was in Miss Clutterbrick's class, and saw through her completely. She knew the stories were absurd, and preferred her own, where cruelly abused princesses were made miserable through no fault of their own. In Fenestra's stories virtue was never rewarded, which made Fenestra herself a rather remarkable little girl for she was always virtuous and harboured no malice for anyone except, possibly, Batty Bunt and Darren Durridge who hunted her unmercifully.

Miss Clutterbrick avoided the staffroom, feeling the eyes of the male staff upon her and fearing that they harboured mad, lustful designs upon her person. This was probably not true, as she was a thick, ungainly person with coarse features and an unfortunate habit of sniffing, but she believed it sincerely all the same and found it a vaguely satisfactory obsession to see her through the long lonely evenings in the two rooms she rented over the butcher's in Low Street.

In fact the conversation in the staffroom tended to revolve not around the feminine charms of Miss Clutterbrick but around the various depraved acts of the children in their charge.

"What the bloody hell do you mean, Trump," demanded Merridew sucking furiously on his pipe, "what do you mean by sending me that stinking illiterate? What do you expect me to do with him?"

Trump chuckled lazily, watching spirals of blue smoke ascend from his own pipe to join the blue cloud layer that hovered near the ceiling. "It's your turn, old boy. I've put up with him for two years, so now someone else has to take him on. He does no harm. He just sits in the corner and grins, and smells. If you don't disturb him, he won't disturb you. And it's generally a good idea not to disturb him, because while he's still the smell doesn't spread so much."

"He does disturb me, though. He disturbs me very much. Do you know he called me 'mister' this morning? He soon learned the error of that particular way though, with a couple of cuts from my cane on his miserable backside. Bristle, why can't you have him? He can't read, so he ought still to be with you!"

Bristle waved slackly. His pipe was refusing to draw, and he had sucked at it so long that the tobacco was now wet with spit and never would burn. He was a long, lean, cadaverous man whose clothes didn't fit. He had a wife he was unpleasant to, and several children whom he alternately ignored and chastised.

He taught the very youngest children to read, and had discovered a simple and efficacious method of doing it. His class learned one letter a day. On the first day of term he taught them the letter A. They practised writing it, they looked through their books and found all the words like 'and', 'apple', 'apostate' and 'antediluvian' that began with A, and repeated those words in chorus. In the afternoon they did it all again. The next morning they were tested, and any child who could not remember either A or 'apostate' received a cut of the cane. Then they moved on to B.

It was a method of beauteous simplicity, and in some cases it worked. But it had not worked with Billy Moon, who seemed to feel little pain and would distract himself and others by asking the meaning of 'apostate' and 'antediluvian'.

"No point," Bristle said, "he's unteachable. Deep, deep stupidity, entrenched and undiluted. Trump's right, it's your turn, Merridew."

Merridew crossed his legs angrily. "And another thing," he said, "that girl Prettyfoot! If I don't wipe the superior smile off her face before this term's out, I'll ... I don't know what I shall do. She thinks she's so clever, does she? Thinks she can get one over on me just because she's read a few books, does she? I'll bend her over my desk and take it out of her hide, you see if I don't!"

Trump giggled. "Oh, whacking girls are we now, Merridew? That's a new departure, isn't it?"

"Sounds good to me," said Bristle morosely. "I never saw why they should be treated any different. My girls at home get the cane, same as the boys."

Trump sat up and took interest. "Do they, my dear Bristle. Do they? And for what heinous crimes do you cane your daughters, pray?"

"Oh, anything," Bristle waved his sodden pipe vaguely. "They don't have to do anything much. I just give 'em a lick once a week to keep 'em in shape."

"Splendid, splendid," groaned Merridew, hauling himself with difficulty from the depths of his chair, "I wish one could do the same in school. It would save no end of trouble. Just line the little bitches and the little bastards up with their trousers down and their skirts up and give them what for down the line and back again, and they wouldn't dare step out of line the rest of the week!"

"I believe Mistress Grubb operates a similar system at her Emporium," said Trump amiably. "But I imagine our dear Headmaster might find it just the tiniest bit draconian. Well, once more to the chalkface. Ours not to wonder why, ours just to do or ... what's the word?"

"Die," said Bristle, and followed him out into the corridor.

At lunchtime instead of marching out of the classroom as usual, Rosella came to Pert's desk, and he put his books away and lowered the lid to find her standing over him.

"You need to keep a closer eye on your sister, Pertinacious Potts," she said. "I found Batty Bunt and Darren Durridge having a go at her at playtime." And she turned on her heel and walked off.

This was a red letter day indeed, when Rosella actually spoke to him, but the news was alarming. Pert hurried to find Fenestra.

"Oh yes," she said, "They grabbed my arms and they said they were going to take me in the bogs and turn me upside down."

"Why are they picking on you?"

"Don't know," she shrugged. "Because I'm here. Because I haven't any friends, only Esmerelda and she ran away. I asked Miss Clutterbrick but she wouldn't let us tidy the books. She said they were tidy already."

"So what happened?"

"Rosella Prettyfoot came, and she wasn't scared at all. She said to let me go or she'd kick them where it hurt most. And Darren Durridge said they ought to take her in the bogs instead and show her something, so she hacked him on the shins and they swore at her and then they went away. I was scared, but she didn't seem to bother."

They went to sit on the playground wall to eat their sandwich. Fenestra prattled, and Pert watched. Rosella would not appear again, he knew: she had a hot lunch in school, which their mother could not afford. Instead he kept an eye open for Bunt and Durridge. Billy Moon wandered out into the playground, and passed by them, grinning. He sat on the wall a few feet away and swung his feet.

"Who's that?" whispered Fenestra. "Why's he got odd shoes?"

"Billy Moon. He's in my class. I think he's poor."

"Poorer than us? Coo!"

Billy Moon sat on his hands and grinned. He grinned at the school building, he looked up the street and grinned towards the church, and then he stretched his head up and looked at the top of Bodrach Nuwl, where cloud was streaming inland.

"Old Man's got 'is 'at on," he grinned to no one in particular. "Rain later."

"How do you know that?" asked Fenestra.

"Always rains when Old Man gets 'is 'at on," said the boy, and came to stand in front of them. Pert caught a whiff of pungent odour, a mixture of dung and wellington boot and stale clothing.

"You're a bit smelly," Fenestra said, holding her nose.

"Fenestra, really!" Pert said, but the boy laughed. When he laughed his eyes crinkled up. "Yeah, I do whiff a bit," he said. "Everyone says. It's on account of not washing."

"Why don't you wash, then?" asked Fenestra. "Haven't you got any lunch? Would you like some of my sandwich?" Without waiting for an answer she tore off half and handed it to him.

"Cor, fanks!" he said, sat on the wall and stuffed it all into his mouth at once.

"Why don't you wash?" she asked again. "Everyone washes!"

"You arsk a lot o' questions, don'cha? I jus' never got in the 'abit, like. No water in our 'ouse. No bathroom, no sink, no nuffin', 'cept a bucket, an' then my mother 'as to carry it all the way from the pump in the Square. So I don' want ter waste it wiv washin', do I?"

Fenestra had no answer to that. After a few minutes of grinning, Billy Moon got up and stood in front of them.

"Wot's yer name?" he asked. "I knows you, you're Pert in my class. But what's yer lady-friend's name?"

"This is my sister, Fenestra."

"Fenestra?" He pronounced it carefully, as though it were something precious. "Fenestra. Cor, that's posh. You're pretty," he said. "I got to run aroun' now. I 'as ter run around a lot, otherwise I can't sit still in class, see?" and off he dashed.

"He's a funny boy," Fenestra said, "I like him. But he does smell. Couldn't we take him home and wash him? There's the tap in the yard, and we've got lots of soap."

"No, silly. You can't start taking strange boys home and washing them. You'll get an odd reputation."

"I've got one of those already. Am I really pretty? No one ever said that before."

XII

In the volume of the book it is written (Psalm 40)

That afternoon during the lovely time between the end of school and supper, Pert got out the Church Council books again. He turned to the pages holding the Minutes of the last few meetings. By this time whoever was writing had stopped bothering to list the accounts by name as they were accepted, and simply put *"Accounts accepted by generall consent"*. Goodness, thought Pert, they didn't even bother to have a vote.

He seemed to have drawn rather a blank so far, so he turned back to the older books. Perhaps he might find something interesting in his grandfather's time. Here the minutes were much more detailed and there had been many more decisions to be made. Most were trivial, like the new chasubel for the curat, but once in a while something major would turn up. It had cost the Council the princely sum of £23/5s/9d to have a new roof put on the vicarage, for instance. The vicarage was not a place Pert was familiar with. He knew where it was, of course, further up the hill towards the top of the town with a circular drive so carriages could pull up, deliver their passengers and go away again, but he had never been inside. He didn't think very many carriages called there these days, for the Reverend Tench was not a sociable man.

He worked backwards through the early books, and finally came across something in the very first one that took his eye. In November 1770 the Church Council had been asked to approve the sum of £2/0s/3d for repairs in *"ye crypte under ye vestrie"*. That was a puzzle. The church had a crypt, certainly. It was a gloomy, sinister place under the nave, though the door opened off the vestry right enough. You went down a flight of narrow stone stairs, and there was a long vaulted space lined with tombs. Some had figures lying on top to show who was buried there, while others were plain.

On the walls were more plaques to the dead, and Pert had a nasty feeling that behind them were the actual bodies.

These days the crypt was a storage place, full of broken chairs, old altar cloths, clumsy wooden furniture and the like. And many piles of hymn books, torn and mutilated, many without covers, dating from a previous age with music written in big white notes. Hymns must have been very slow in those days, Pert thought, even slower than now.

Perhaps it was just the words that were peculiar? Ye crypte certainly opened off the vestry, but it wasn't *under* the vestry. Maybe the long-dead scribe had been careless in choosing his words? There was no crypt under the vestry that he knew of. Another question for Mr.Surplice.

The thought of Mr.Surplice reminded him of the time. The curate was supposed to have moved in today. He hastily tucked the books away and clattered down the stairs to supper.

Supper was the usual, potato stew. There was no meat in it, but in honour of their guest there was a bit more potato, and fresher chunks of bread to dip in it. Mr.Surplice didn't seem to mind the plain fare, and indeed seemed already more relaxed and not so drawn about the face as before. He was a model guest, appreciative of everything put before him, and talked easily with Fenestra and Pert though he seemed to be a little in awe of their mother.

He asked them about their day at school, and Fenestra told him about Billy Moon. Her mother looked rather alarmed to hear the name, and she and the curate exchanged glances. Pert thought he knew why, but said nothing.

Fenestra explained about the smell, and her desire to wash him. "Pert said I couldn't because I'd get a reputation," she said, "but I wouldn't care. Why can't I?"

"I think "reputation" is a very appropriate word," said the curate, "though I can't say I've ever heard anything against the woman, apart from her profession."

"She isn't the first," said Mother, "and she won't be the last. On her own, out on the streets and Billy to feed, what was she supposed to do? I remember her when she was younger. She liked a good time, like many others. I can't condemn her for that. She was always pleasant enough."

"Quite right," replied Mr.Surplice. "And in any case it would be quite wrong to ascribe the sins of the mother to the soul of the child, would it not?"

"He can't read," put in Pert. "And he got the cane today for calling Mr.Merridew 'mister'".

"Mr.Merridew! Hmph!" his mother said, but would add nothing more.

The conversation turned to the bullies, Bunt and Durridge. Fenestra was too proud to be specific. She said they had been horrible to her.

"In my experience," said Mr.Surplice, "which is considerable on this subject, there is no solution except to endure. They quickly tire and move on to some other amusement. And you always have one great satisfaction from it – they never, ever, feel any better for doing it. They bully others because they are bullied themselves, perhaps, or because they are unhappy, or because they know themselves to be of little worth and that they will never prosper in the world. So their bullying profits them nothing, and that is our revenge, if I may be permitted to use such a word."

"Were you bullied?" asked Fenestra.

"Oh, goodness, yes! At school, terribly. I was a weak little thing, and couldn't stand up for myself. But I endured, and they went away. Then there were others, at the missionary college – would-be priests, just imagine! - and they went away too. And look at me now. I am a world authority on tolerance, for I have tolerated the sticks and arrows of outrageous misfortune and the slings and stones of ridiculous vicars. There are many virtues, they say, but tolerance is my favourite, because I'm really, really good at it. And I am a curate, I have a job, and thanks to yourselves I have dear friends and ... a home, if you'll permit me the liberty."

He beamed round the table, and Mother patted his hand and said "Of course you're permitted. Now, as this is a special occasion, I made a treacle tart. Just don't expect it to happen every day, that's all I ask!"

On his way up to bed, Pert was waylaid by Mr.Surplice, who popped out of his room – Fenestra's old room, that is – and whispered urgently.

"I found something out about the accounts!" he said. "There are some in the locked cupboard in the vestry. I sneaked a look when the vicar's back was turned. They run until about five years ago, but there are none since."

"We need to get a look at them, then."

"How? The cupboard's always locked, and I don't know where the key is."

"Well, there must be a way ... we could find the key. Or wait until the vicar's out in the church and then pinch some and run off with them. Or break the door and pretend it was burglars or something!"

The curate looked shocked, but evidently wasn't all that shocked, because he said "I know! The communion service! While the Vicar's giving the sacraments don't you sometimes have to go

97

back in the vestry to top up the wine? You could take some of the books and hide them somewhere and go back later!"

"Perfect!" said Pert. "I'll start planning. Er ... you're sure you're all right about this? You are a curate, after all."

"Those are public documents. They should not be locked away where no one can see them. Oh, I know it'll be bad for me if we're found out, but we're doing nothing wrong."

"Good. Now I've got something else to ask you. What's under the vestry floor?"

"Earth, I should think."

"Only I found some mention of another crypt, under the vestry."

"Never heard of it, I'm afraid. Mind you, anything could be under that carpet. I think it came out of the ark!"

"Probably still has camel-poo on it," said Pert, thinking of the enemies that keep exulting over me. "Good night!"

In the attic Fenestra had taken his bed-space and put her own mattress in it. She had moved his behind the chimney breast, where the spiders were. The mouse was nowhere to be seen either, probably because she had already fed it. He felt a little aggrieved, but watched her sleeping. Her puzzle was still clutched in one hand and she was snoring gently. She *was* quite pretty, really. How odd that he'd never noticed, and Billy Moon did.

XIII

They go to and fro in the evening: they grin like a dog, and run about the city. Behold, they belch out with their mouth (Psalm 59)

The following day after school Pert and the White brothers took Fenestra home and then ran down to the quay to look at the pirate ship.

"There was a fight last night, in the Ring o' Bells, between some of the fishers and some of the pirates!" said Seth. "Only their captain showed up and put a stop to it."

"What was it about?" asked Pert.

"Nothing, really. Just the fishers don't like the way they're hanging about and taking all the best seats, and that."

"And have you seen Spotty Bunt and his mates?" put in Solomon, "parading round the town with scarves round their heads and big knives in their belts, trying to look like pirates themselves? Real silly, they look!"

As it happened they were just passing the Drop o' Dew, and there on a bench outside, sitting in the sun and stretching out their big seaboots, were the same three pirates Pert had met before. As he approached the one with the scar got up to meet him.

"Well, Master Potts as wants to know so much, where be you off to this sunny afternoon? 'Ave you come to see us poor seamen restin' from our labours?" he said, and put his arm round Pert's shoulders. "'Ave you brought your little friends to see our pretty ship, per'aps? You should 'a brought that pretty sister o' yourn, too!"

The other two waved at Pert, and raised their glasses.

why don't you, an' tell us about yer dear departed daddy," urged the man, steering Pert towards the inn.

His arm was heavy, and Pert ducked under it and pulled away. "Thank you," he said politely, "but I don't think I'm old enough, if it's all the same to you. We've just come to look. My friends haven't seen the ship close up."

"Well, feel free, young master, feel free!" the man waved airily. "But you watch out fer the Capting. He's got 'is spit ready!" The man walked back to join his friends. He said something to them in a low voice as he sat down, and they laughed.

Pert ran to catch up Solomon and Seth. Seth looked at him with awe. "I didn't know you were friends with the pirates," he said.

"I'm not really," replied Pert. "I just talked to them once. They seem to know a lot about my family."

"Everyone knows a lot about your family," said Seth.

They made their way along the breakwater until they reached the side of the ship, and Pert explained what all the sails and spars were. He pointed out the captain's cabin with its great windows across the stern, and the name *"Black Joke"* in gold lettering beneath.

He was about to show them the hunched shape under the tarpaulin which he thought might be a gun, when a dark figure loomed in front of them on the breakwater, blocking their path. Pert recognised Captain Teague. He looked smaller in daylight, but still threatening. His face was pale and lined, and his hat threw his eyes in shadow.

"So, Pertinacious Potts, I believe?" the Captain said politely. Pert felt strange. It was odd how everyone seemed to know who he was.

"Please, yes. I'm showing my friends your ship."

"Quite right too. A boy should be interested in ships. He should be interested in travel, and adventures, and stories of treasure, and triumphant returns and all that sort of thing, should he not? That's what boys are for, is it not?"

"Er, yes, I suppose so. Are you having a triumphant return, sir? Is that why you've come back?" Pert felt very daring, and took comfort from the two companions at his back who stood staring in awe at this terrible man.

Teague looked at Pert for a long time. "So you know who I am? That's remarkably perspicacious of you. And no, I am not yet enjoying a triumphant return. A return, certainly, but the triumph will come later, when I have recovered that which is mine."

He turned, and motioned the boys to walk with him. "You might be able to help me with that," he said conversationally. "What can you tell me about your father, honest man that he was?"

"Not much, sir," said Pert. "Only what my mother told me. One day he was there, the next day he was gone. That was all she said."

"Is that all? That's all, is it? I wonder, dear boy, if I should not pay a visit to your mother one of these afternoons. To pay my respects, as it were, and offer my condolences for her loss. I understand it's not just her husband that she lost?"

"No sir. My sister went off too."

"That would be your older sister? Not the little one with the over-active imagination?"

"No, my older sister Vernilia. She went away with a seafaring man."

"As many do, sad to say. It must have been a sad trial for your poor mother. I shall definitely call. But what of you, young Master

Potts?" He put a hand on Pert's shoulder and steered him towards the side of the ship and away from his friends. "What of you? What do you like to get up to, at night, perhaps, when the streets are silent and the naughty men creep in the shadows?"

He leaned down and looked in Pert's eyes. His own were black and deep and without feeling.

"Why, nothing," Pert faltered, "I don't ... I have to stay at home and look after my sister ..."

"And you don't go skulking, at all? Skulking down alleys and outside windows, skulking and listening and poking in business that isn't yours?"

"Sir, no sir."

The Captain straightened up. "Yes, I'm sure you don't, nor ever would," he said. "Skulking's a risky business, and not for upright young men with sisters to protect."

He turned to Seth and Solomon. "So, young masters, would you like to come aboard my vessel?"

They nodded in unison. Pert could see the thoughts flooding through their heads. To board a pirate ship and talk with a pirate captain ... this was the stuff of dreams. What price Mr.Merridew now?

The captain led them up the gang plank and showed them the decks and the masts and the spars.

"What's that?" asked Pert, greatly daring. "What's that under the tarpaulin? Is it a gun?"

"Ah, I can see I shall have to get up early in the morning to put one over on you!" said the Captain. "Poor sailors need to protect

themselves, now, or don't they? Eh? They must protect themselves when wicked privateers roam the sea and harass honest
mariners, or mustn't they?"

He strode to the mound and whipped the tarpaulin off with a
flourish. There sat a heavy cannon, black and pitted, mounted on
a swivel so that it could be turned and point in any direction. It
looked squat and menacing.

"Wow!" said Solomon. "Do you ever use it?"

"Use it, young master? We practise with it once in a while, when
we're far out at sea, so we know what to do when the time comes.
So yes, we use it."

"Wow!" Solomon said again. "Where are the bullets?"

"Balls, young master. This is a cannon, and it shoots cannon balls.
They're by your feet."

They looked down. In a triangular wooden frame rested seven
round cannon balls made of rusty iron. The Captain seized the
end of the gun and pulled it round till it pointed at the town.

"You see the Harbourmaster's office, there, at the end of the
quay?" he said. "I could put a ball right through that window and
land it right on the Harbourmaster's desk, if I chose. Or ...
where's your house, Master Potts? Up there on the hill, is it not?
To the left of the tall chimney and beyond the church tower? I
wonder if I could reach that far? Perhaps not ..."

Pert felt a chill. That had sounded almost like a threat, however
innocently phrased. The Captain began to cover the gun up
again, and got Seth and Solomon to help him. Then while the
boys ran up to the focs'le and looked at the bowsprit and down
at the great anchor slung below the bow, he took Pert and
leaned with him over the ship's rail.

"You must come and visit us whenever you like, young Master Potts," he said conspiratorily. "There's no love lost between the townsfolk and my crew. Splendid fellows though they are in every way, some of my men don't have the knack of making themselves popular. Rough diamonds, they are, in a manner of speaking, and they do rub gentle people against the grain, as it were. You can put in a good word here and there. Diplomacy, cooperation, that's the ticket!

He leaned closer. "And speaking of cooperation, I should very much like to see your father again. I remember him well. A fine, upstanding man and honest as the day. I should like to speak with him and remember old times ..."

You can't be serious, Pert thought. My father was only a little boy when you left the town. You couldn't have known him.

"Sir, we don't know where he is," he said aloud. "He disappeared when I was three years old, and no one's heard of him since."

"Well, if you hear anything, let me know. Perhaps I'll call on your lovely mother one afternoon, and meet the rest of your family. It would be an honour and a privilege. And if you do ever hear anything about your dad ..." he took Pert's hand and pressed something into his palm, "... you won't find me ungrateful. Now, I think your little friends have finished their tour of inspection, so I'll bid you farewell!"

The Captain strode off to the stern, and Pert followed Seth and Solomon down the gang plank. At the root of the breakwater they stopped, and Pert looked in his hand. The boys crowded round to see.

"Gosh!" said Seth. "Is that gold?"

It was a small coin only the size of a farthing but heavy for its size, with faint embossings on the face of it and little ridges round the edge. It glistened when he turned it to catch the sun.

He rubbed it with his thumbnail to take some of the dirt off. It was indeed gold.

He looked around and slipped it into his pocket. He felt guilty, somehow. And he knew Seth and Solomon. They were good lads and pleasant company, but it was not in their nature to be discreet. He knew that by the morning everyone they knew would have heard that Pertinacious Potts was in the pay of the pirates.

They walked back past the Drop o' Dew and the three pirates were still in the same place. One of them appeared to be the worse for drink. As Pert approached he called out "Where's yer daddy, then?" and laughed uproariously.

The spokesman got up and stood in their path. "Don' mind my friend," he said. "So, you see the Capting?"

"Yes, thank you," said Pert. "He showed us round the ship and showed us the cannon."

"Oh, did he now? So yer getting' friendly like, with the Capting? No 'arm in that, no 'arm at all."

He sat down again. "Walter Sabbage is my name, young master," the man said, and held out his hand. Pert shook it.

"Sabbage by name and Sabbage by nature," said the man next to him.

The third man looked bleerily into his empty glass and seemed to be swaying over the table. "Cabbage!" he muttered, "Cabbage by nature!" and he giggled to himself.

It seemed only a casual flick, but Walter Sabbage's hand flashed in the drunk man's face and knocked his head sideways, leaving a streak of blood at the corner of his mouth.

"Why, you ..." he growled, and made to get up, but seeing Sabbage's hand hovering over the handle of the knife at his belt, he shrugged and fell back in his seat, mumbling to himself.

Sabbage poured him another measure of rum from the jug. "There, yer useless drunken sot, get that down you an' stop tryin' to be witty, 'cause you ain't got it in yer!" he said. "Afore you go, young sir, you'll allow me to introduce my friends, formal like. On my left, Matthew Shattock, and on my right is Squance, what believes 'e's a wit, which 'e ain't. 'E don't 'ave no Christian name, on account of 'e ain't no Christian. Also it's yer parents wot gives yer a Christian name, an' 'e never 'ad no parents, did yer, Squancy?"

Squance spat on the cobbles. "Oh very funny, Wally Sabbage, your playful sense o' humour enlivens my days, I don' fink!"

Pert said "Surely everyone has parents, don't they? I mean, you can't be born without parents?"

"Not Squancy. 'E was found as a baby in a lobster pot in Bideford 'arbour, weren't you, Squancy?" Sabbage leaned closer, and whispered loudly "'E also 'as very unpleasant personal 'abits, wot we don't like to mention, young sir."

Squance stuck his finger in one ear, wiggled it about and inspected the result. "Well, they're my 'abits, an' I likes 'em well enough," he muttered.

The boys took their leave. At the corner of the street where it turned away from the quay and went up towards the Market Square slouched Will Durridge, George and Spotty Bunt, and the fourth man Pert didn't know. They looked truculently at the boys who walked in the gutter to avoid them.

Will and Spotty wore tattered old scarves round their heads, and George had an ancient three-cornered hat he had found somewhere. It was dented and crushed, but he had added a bright feather of an unlikely colour no bird ever wore. The fourth man had no hat, but sported sloppy seaboots. All had thick leather belts with knives thrust in them. They looked more like pirates than the real pirates did, but not so dangerous. They were too fat for that, and not drunk enough.

One of the men said something to the others, and they all turned and watched Pert as he went by.

At the Market Square Seth and Solomon said they'd see him in school the next day, and ran home for their suppers. Pert lingered in the market for a while, kicking at the rubbish on the cobbles and looking at the wares on sale. He wondered how much his gold piece would buy. He didn't think he dared show it to any of the stall holders, though, except perhaps Mrs.Toogood and she wouldn't have enough change. He patted his pocket to make sure it was still there. He would keep it in his chest until he knew what to do with it.

He felt a small hand curl into his, and looked down. It was the tiniest of the Prettyfeet, looking up at him with a big smile. She tugged at his hand and he bent down to see what she wanted.

"I know you," she whispered. "You're the one my sister likes!" and she turned and trotted away, slipping between the legs of the shoppers, and was lost to view.

Pert walked home in a turmoil. Pirates, Church Councils, gold pieces, cannon, crypts and now this. His life was a mess, and getting more and more unlikely. Which sister had the little tot been talking about? She had four sisters, some not much bigger than she was. Come on, Pert, he told himself sternly, you're being soppy. You can't take seriously anything a five-year-old tells you.

XIV

*Thou hast covered my head
in the day of battle (Psalm 140)*

At school the next morning Pert felt that his classmates were looking at him a bit strangely. The twins' busy tongues had been wagging about the Captain and the gold piece. It would be all over the town by evening. He watched Rosella carefully but she gave no sign that anything had changed. She behaved, as usual, as though he didn't exist. To be fair, he thought, she behaved exactly the same about everyone else in the class.

At playtime he went as usual to find Fenestra, and she was nowhere to be seen. Esmerelda was sitting with another group of girls.

"Where's Fenestra?" he asked her.

She looked abashed. "I'm not to be friends with her any more."

"Who said?"

"Everyone." She turned her eyes to the other girls. "Them."

"And do you always do what the other girls say?"

She looked abashed, and nodded her head.

"But where is Fenestra? Did she stay inside?"

The girl held out her hand, mutely pointing towards the toilets in the corner of the playground. Pert walked towards them. He saw Solomon and Seth waving at him to join them, but kept walking.

As he neared the toilets he could hear voices, one deep and the other high. He began to run. There was no one in the boys' side, so he ran to the other end where only girls were allowed. Inside the two sides were identical, a little roofless yard walled in with brick, and several cubicles with half doors.

Against the wall was Fenestra, tears streaming down her face. In front of her stood Darren Durridge, and beside her was Batty Bunt. He had her arm up behind her back and was twisting it. No one else was near, and Pert knew this was because everyone knew what was going on and wanted no part of it.

Bunt saw Pert approaching and grinned. He gave Fenestra's arm an extra twist and she shrieked. "Well, look who's here!" he said. "Sneaky little Potts, come to rescue the potty little sneak!"

A blind rage came over Pert and he rushed at Bunt. His onslaught took the bigger boy by surprise. Even as Darren Durridge reached out a beefy arm to grab him, his head connected with Bunt's chin and the bully went down on his back, hitting his head on the brick wall on the way down. He rolled onto a ball, pressing his hands to his head. The wall had hurt him more than Pert had.

Pert grabbed his sister's hand and pulled her with him. He ducked under Durridge's outstretched arm, and shoved Fenestra towards the exit, kicking out at Durridge and catching him on the knee. Durridge swore and reached for him, but Pert was gone.

They took hands and ran for the school building, hearing threats and imprecations behind them. Inside he took Fenestra to her class. The teacher was already there so she should be safe enough. Then he turned towards his own classroom, mingling on the way with the crowd of boys and girls returning from playtime.

"What happened to you?" said Seth as he fell into his seat.

"I had a run-in with Bunt and Durridge," he said. "They were after my sister."

"Cor, rather you than me," Solomon said. "What happened?"

"I knocked Bunt over and banged his head."

"You'll be sorry. They'll get you later," said Seth.

"Thanks for your support!" Pert turned away. He'd always known it would come to this. He'd always known he would be on his own when it did.

Last into the room were Bunt and Durridge. Bunt had a livid bruise on his jaw where Pert's head had struck him, and was still rubbing the back of his head. Durridge was limping.

Durridge stopped in front of him, and leaned over him menacingly. "Dinner time, Potts! We'll be waiting!" he said, and hurried to his seat as Mr.Merridew arrived.

It was maths until lunch. Pert had no idea how he managed to get through the hour, for the little x's and y's in his algebra book danced before his eyes and wouldn't keep still. At the best of times he couldn't really understand why x's and y's were so important, or why they kept changing their value from chapter to chapter. Any sensible letter would decide what it was worth, and stick to it. He knew what he was worth, and that was practically nothing at the moment. He felt sick, and when he wrote with his pencil the writing was shaky like an old man's.

He could feel eyes on the back of his neck, and was certain that somehow the word had got round. No one dared chatter in Merridew's class, for that would certainly earn a bare bum and a thrashing, but somehow they knew, they all knew that Potts was going to get a beating at lunchtime. It was going to be the show of the year, and none of them would miss it for the world. Like Merridew's canings, they knew it wasn't fair and they knew it wasn't right, but so long as it was happening to someone else they'd be there and take a dreadful pleasure from it.

The hour dragged on and on, and Pert felt more and more frightened. What was he going to do? Should he try and run for it? Should he pelt across the playground and out into the town and hide somewhere?

But that would leave his sister alone and unprotected at play and at the end of school.

Should he tell a teacher? That might save him a beating, but he'd be labelled a coward and a sneak for the rest of his life. So long as he lived in this town, he'd be the sniveling little weakling who hid behind the teacher's skirts.

Should he do the sensible thing, and just curl up in a ball and take it and hope it didn't go on too long? That would probably be Mr.Surplice's advice, and it was probably the most practical option. At least Rosella would be at her lunch and wouldn't be there to see his humiliation.

The bell went. Pert put his books away very slowly, while the rest of the class went gleefully past him and flooded out into the playground to get the best view. He left his sandwich in his desk. He wouldn't be needing that. He went towards the door into the playground. The teachers were all either in the staff room, or in the hall with the lunch eaters. He could hear the sound of cutlery and a hum of conversation from the hall.

In the playground the rest of the class stood in a large semicircle. Bunt and Durridge stood in the middle, waiting and smiling. The crowd were silent. He seemed to be seeing everything with the most dreadful clarity. He could see Billy Moon with his grin. He could see the twins, looking serious. He could see one boy chewing his sandwich unconcernedly, waiting for the entertainment to start. He could see a fat girl, a friend of Durridge, smiling and winking at him, nodding encouragement. He saw a disturbance in the crowd as Fenestra pushed her way to the front and stood beside Billy Moon, her face ashen and her eyes enormous.

He knew what he was going to do now. He was going to fight. He would get as many blows in as he could before he went down. Sooner or later – probably sooner – their weight and size and reach would bear him down and once that happened he was finished, but until then he'd do his best to mark them.

He walked slowly to his left, to the side where Bunt stood waiting. Bunt was the fatter and the slower of the two. He tried to get Bunt in between him and Durridge so he only had one to deal with. Bunt smiled, and came towards him.

As he had before, Pert put his head down and charged. His head went into Bunt's stomach, and a howl went up from the crowd. Suddenly there was a tumult of noise, shouts of "Fight! Fight", screams and excited laughter. He punched with both fists, punching at anything he could find. He felt blows on his back and sides, but he kicked out furiously and broke away.

Bunt was still in front of him, looking slightly surprised but otherwise unfazed. Durridge had circled round and was approaching from behind. He went to dodge between them and escape, but at the last minute jinked towards Durridge and lashed out with his fist. A hit! he realised with a spurt of joy. His fist had connected with something soft. He had hit the bully square in the eye.

Joyful suddenly, a feeling of blood-lust in his heart, he turned and tried to follow up his advantage. He took another shot at Durridge's head but as he did so he felt the dead weight of Bunt's mass seize him from behind, pinning his arms to his sides and lifting him off the floor. Then two massive blows from Durridge hit his stomach, driving the wind out of him. He doubled up in pain. He could not breathe, his chest felt like a band of fire, he felt another fist strike his forehead. This was the end.

But suddenly the screaming of the crowd rose to an even higher pitch. Something was happening. Another body was joining the fray, and as Bunt dropped him to the ground to meet the new onslaught he saw slim legs, a yellow dress, and two big boots that hacked viciously at Bunt's shins, one, two, and danced back, and returned again to kick twice more.

Pert got to his feet and lunged into Durridge, hitting and scratching at anything he could reach. Another figure was below him, clinging on and biting the youth's great legs. Billy Moon was small, but he was fast, wriggling and squirming like an eel, an eel that couldn't punch very hard but could grip and squeeze the places that hurt the most, and bite the others. His vicious assault made Durridge forget Pert, but as he covered up and thrashed at the tiny boy he was hit by a fresh wave as Seth and Solomon launched themselves onto the great back. Durridge staggered and went down and Billy Moon swarmed all over him.

Pert turned his attention to Bunt. He was still moving forward, wary of Rosella's feet. She danced in front of him, smiling savagely, her eyes alight with fierce hatred. She had a scratch down one cheek and a bruise on her forehead. She moved away from Pert, drawing Bunt with her, and Pert launched his own attack from the side. He hit Bunt on the side of the jaw with a mighty swing, and felt a tooth crack under his fist. Then he hit again, one, two, left, right, all at the head. Rosella darted in and planted two solid hits on Bunt's legs and the lout swayed, covered his head with his arms, and fell forward at her feet. She didn't hesitate, but kicked him again, this time in the stomach.

Durridge had managed to wriggle free of his attackers. He staggered to his feet and began to push his way through the crowd, which parted reluctantly. His trousers were in tatters, and his shirt was torn completely off, hanging on one shoulder. He had lost his shoes, and began to limp painfully towards the playground gates. He was weeping.

Pert pulled Bunt to his feet and pushed him towards the gate, and he took to his heels, also limping. His clothes were more or less intact but his face was bloody and swollen and his right eye almost closed.

A small body ran from the crowd and threw its arms round him. It was Fenestra, kissing him on both cheeks. Over her head Pert and Rosella looked at each other, breathing hard. There was a look in her eyes of savage exultation which was mirrored, probably, in his own, but the crowd suddenly began to melt away and the tumult died down.

Merridew and another teacher stood before them. Fenestra let go of Pert and ran to catch up her classmates. The five of them, Pert, Rosella, Seth and Solomon and Billy Moon were left. Merridew made a motion with his head, and they trooped obediently back to class.

Inside, the room was silent. In the back row the empty seats of Bunt and Durridge sat accusingly. Pert's warriors stood in line.

"Brawling," said Merridew. He took down the cane from its hook behind the door. "Brawling," he repeated, his voice a little higher, "brawling in the playground like common ruffians! Have you any idea how this reflects on me?" His voice was still rising, the colour inflaming his cheeks. "You know what they will say? That I can't control my classes? That I am a laughing stock and my pupils free to rampage round the school, brawling like common ruffians?"

He paced back and forwards once, evidently trying to control his temper. This was a Merridew they had never seen before. Normally his cruel punishments were inflicted with calm, sardonic enjoyment, but this rage was something new, the loss of control both frightening and at the same time diminishing.

"Who was the ring-leader? Who?" he yelled. "As if I didn't know! It was you, Potts. Wasn't it?" He poked his face in Pert's. His sour breath washed around Pert and he took a step back.

"Don't you move away from me!" the man yelled, grabbing him by the neck. "Nasty, sneaking little thief, rotten criminal fomenting rebellion in my class ..."

He dragged Pert to the desk and thrust him face down. Pert felt his trousers yanked down his legs and a rain of vicious blows, four, five, six ... it went on for a long time, but Pert didn't care. He felt immune. Pain was just pain. Victory and justification were more powerful.

At last the onslaught slackened, and Pert was able to step aside and pull up his trousers. Merridew ordered Billy Moon forward, and started on him. Billy made no sound and didn't wriggle once. His stoic grin was intact when he was finally released. It was as if he knew that he had made a friend at last, and that while the position at the foot of the class was probably his for life, he was nevertheless somebody, a name to be reckoned with and re-spected. Pert thought that for such a small and filthy person, he had a colossal pride. He admired him.

Seth and Solomon were less stoic, but the rage had gone from the man and their punishment was shorter. Merridew stood and rested. The colour had gone from his face, and the fury had been replaced by something colder, something more hateful.

"Now," he said, "Prettyfoot, come here. Bend over!"

There was an intake of breath around the class, and Pert felt his head swim. Rosella did not move.

"Bend over the desk, girl! If you can brawl in public like a com-mon harlot, you can take a common harlot's punishment. Get over that desk!" He pulled at her arm, and she resisted.

"Sir, sir!" said Pert. "You can't! Sir, she's a girl, you can't!"

"Shut up, Potts! I've put up with your insolence, girl ..." he dragged her to the desk and started pushing her head down.

"Sir, stop it! Cane me again instead! I'll take her punishment!" Pert burst out. "Sir, she was just trying to help me, it was me, not her! Cane me!"

Merridew stopped what he was doing. Without a word he pulled Pert to the desk, tore down his trousers and caned him six more times. He did it with malice and accuracy, laying the cane right on top of the weals he'd already made, and Pert started and hissed in agony at each one. Then he was allowed to stand.

"That was for interfering!" said Merridew. "Now, girl, your turn ..."

As he reached for Rosella again, Pert dashed towards him. "No!" he shouted, and shoved the man backwards. "No, don't touch her!" He shoved again and the surprised teacher tripped on the corner of the dais and fell flat on his back. The cane skittered across the floor, and every child in the class rose and laughed.

"Quick, you fool, run for it!" said Rosella, took his hand and dragged him towards the door. "Come on, run!" she said, and hand in hand they fled down the corridor, out of the door and across the playground, screeching with joy and excitement. They skidded at the gate and turned up the hill, running helter-skelter through the Market Square and past the church. Sometimes when they came to a lamp-post they loosed hands and split up, but always their hands came together and Pert ran with a fierce joy and abandon, nothing mattered, only this headlong flight up the town with Rosella, her warm hand tight on his.

They ran and ran, saying nothing, but laughing and whooping, up past the vicarage, up the sandy lane where the little cottages began to peter out, up beyond the town and out onto the moor and the sandy lane turned to springy turf beneath their feet and the cottages gave way to peaty tussocks and heather and clumps of gorse already yellow, and they ran until their breath failed and finally they fell and lay on their backs, laughing up at the sky and kicking their legs with glee.

At last, exhausted by running and laughing, they fell silent. Pert rolled onto his side and looked at Rosella.

"We can't go back," she said.

"We'll have to eventually."

"But not yet."

He grinned at her. "There'll be a hell of a row when we do. Have you ever been right to the top?"

"No. Have you?"

"Yes. You have to crawl, or the wind might pick you up and blow you."

"Will you take me?" He stood up and held out his hand, and she took it, and they started walking. "I don't care what they do," she said. "It was worth it."

XV

The perfection of beauty (Psalm 50)

In later years Pert would look back on that afternoon on the moors with Rosella and think it the most perfect thing in his life, the one event that made sense of everything he had ever done in the past or might do in the future. Whatever befell him, he would always have that afternoon.

They made their way slowly uphill, sometimes walking on soft turf kept short by rabbits and scattered with their fragrant droppings, at other times hopping from tussock to tussock of springy peat. They stopped occasionally and listened to the cries of curlews and an early lark that dropped its sweet pebbles of song from the sky. They passed little brakes of trees, small and stunted by the wind, and once huddled in the lee of one while a rain-shower passed, finding that some creature had already scraped out a little sandy hollow for them. They sat close together while the rain blew, and Rosella pressed her round back to his shoulder, and he smelled her hair.

When they got up she stood very close to him, looking down, and he put his arms round her. "I've never seen you be shy before," he said.

"I've never done this before," she answered quietly, not looking up. He kissed the top of her head, and then her forehead, and coaxed her head up with his hand until he could put his lips to hers. They were very soft. She kept her eyes shut. He felt hot tears pressing at the back of his own eyes, and had to hold her hard to stop them coming. She put her arms round him.

Afterwards they walked on, not minding wet feet or wet clothing, and passed to the high uplands where the wind boomed and snatched at them, for they had reached the very shoulders of Bodrach Nuwl. As they climbed the way got steeper and they went on all fours, crawling like ants on a floor up towards the edge of the cliff. There was no path, and little vegetation, just bare rock, seamed and rutted by the wind.

At the top the wind was like a wild thing, fingering them and trying to get underneath to dislodge them. They lay flat on their stomachs and crawled, inching bit by bit towards the edge. And then they were there.

The first thing they knew was that the wind instead of clawing at their backs was now under their chins, blasting up the face of the cliff. Only with great effort of will could they open their eyes and look down into it. Pert held Rosella tightly by the arms, and she crawled close to him as they peered cautiously down into the abyss.

First they saw acres of grey rock streaming down away from them, and beyond that seabirds, kittiwakes wheeling and settling, guillemots sitting upright with their black backs, and small razorbills flying low and straight, and all too far below to hear their cries. Below them were slopes and stands of stunted trees, and crevices and dark defiles falling steeply down, and then the grey jumble of the Stonefields looking like pebbles strewn in the shallows of a beach but actually vast crags and boulders the size of many houses. And out in front of them was the blue, the hazy mass of solid air moving towards them from the ocean, so tangible you felt you could hold out your arms for balance and walk out on it and never fall.

Later they ran and tumbled down the hill again until they came to a little valley where rivulets and peat-springs came together into a stream trickling over rocks, sheltered briefly from the wind. Ferns and water plants had taken hold, and miniature silver birches and hazel and rowan trees huddled low, and a pair of little grey wagtails flirted on the rocks.

They traced the stream downhill, through bare patches and a deep cleft in the bog, and eventually into a much deeper valley sheltered and warm, the air still and full of insects droning, and taller trees hanging over the water.

Every so often they came to a series of rocky pools where the stream could rest a while before going on its tumbling way. They took off their shoes and waded into one, balancing on stones and laughing until Pert fell in up to his neck. He washed the blood off her face, and then she wet her skirt and used it to cool his poor bruised head and jaw. She was calm and serene, and Pert wished his sister could be here to see how a real princess would be.

Afterwards they sat on a big rock under the trees to dry. Rosella's blonde head was in a patch of sunlight, and a little turquoise demoiselle fly perched on her hair, each segment of its long tail a tiny jewel. She held still, and another came, and another until she had four on her head together. Then she laughed and startled them and they flew off. Pert tucked the memory away to treasure, feeling that if he thought about it too soon or too much, his heart would break partly from happiness and partly from the certainty that they could never be this joyful again.

Back in the Bearward they stopped outside her house. They looked at each other, and he summoned his courage and kissed her again, but there was really no need to kiss. They knew what they knew, it didn't need saying. She turned and went indoors without a backward glance, and he trudged up Pardoner's Alley and home.

XVI

*Lover and friend hast thou put far from me, and
mine acquaintance into darkness (Psalm 88)*

Mother, Fenestra and Mr.Surplice were seated at the kitchen table, the remains of a frugal supper in front of them.

"Oh Pert," said his mother, "just look at your clothes."

He looked down at himself. His shoes were wet through, his trousers were out at both knees and his shirt was torn right down the front.

"And your face," said Fenestra. "Your poor face, does it hurt a lot?"

"No," he said, sitting down. "I'm jolly hungry though."

His mother got up to fetch the bowl of broth and a piece of bread. Pert ate hungrily, while Mr.Surplice looked on with a gleam in his eye.

"Fenestra's told us what happened," Mother said. "I don't know what's going to happen. There's bound to be a heap of trouble from this."

"There, dear lady, what can't be cured must be endured," said the curate. "From what Fenestra tells us it doesn't sound as though there was much choice."

"No, there wasn't really," said Pert, pushing his empty bowl away. "But it would have been much worse without Seth and Solomon and Billy Moon. And Rosella. Especially Rosella."

Mother and the curate exchanged glances. "Where is Rosella now?" she asked.

"Gone home."

"And where did you go? You've both been missing all afternoon."

Pert looked at her, wondering why it mattered where they had been. They could hardly have stayed in school, after knocking a teacher down.

"We went up on the moors," she said, "and up to the top of Bodrach Nuwl."

"And what else?"

"Nothing else. We paddled in a pool, and then we came back. We knew we had to keep out of the way."

Fenestra came and stood beside him and stroked his hair. "Billy said you knocked Mr.Merridew over. Did you really?"

"Yes. He was going to cane Rosella. He'd given us the cane, me and Seth and Solomon and Billy, and then he started on her, so I sort of shoved him and he fell."

"Who else attacked him?" asked Mother.

"I never attacked him!" he said hotly. "It was just me, but I never attacked him. I just pushed him away from Rosella and he sort of tripped. So we ran."

Once again the two adults exchanged a look Pert didn't understand. "Er, can I be clear ... your teacher was going to cane a girl? In front of the whole class?"

"That's what Billy said," put in Fenestra. "And Pert got two lots!"

Mother got up and started tidying the table. "Well, I can see nothing but trouble coming from this," she said tiredly. "I think you two had best go straight to bed, and Pert must stay home from school tomorrow. I can't imagine he'll be welcome there."

They moved towards the stairs, but on the first step Fenestra stopped. "Mother," she said quietly, "you won't let anyone forget, will you, that Pert was just looking after me? Those boys had me in the toilet and they hurt me, and Pert stopped them."

"No," said his mother. "No, we won't forget that. Whatever happens, we won't forget that."

It was strange, not going to school. Fenestra went, reluctantly. Pert walked her to the school gates, and there leaning against the wall was Billy Moon. She brightened up when she saw him waiting.

Billy followed her through the gates. "I'll look after 'er, guv!" he said to Pert. "Don't you worry about a fing!"

Pert wandered up through the Market Square. Some people he passed stared, and pursed their mouths, and turned muttering to each other. But one or two smiled at him, and nodded. As he passed Mrs.Toogood's stall she called out to him.

"Hallo, dearie, I hear you've been in the wars! Here, take this – a man needs a little something to set him up, doesn't he, when he's been standing up for his family?"

She handed him a stick of peanut brittle. He thanked her, and she smiled and beamed at him as he went on his way. His pleasure evaporated at the sight of Urethra Grubb standing massive and threatening in the door of the Emporium. She looked at him hard through her one eye, and Pert felt the force of her malice clear across the road.

He decided to go down to the quay to see if Walter Glibbery had any jobs for him to do. Down at the corner of Market Hill the four would-be pirates were lounging again, and Pert wondered if they might come after him. They simply scowled, though, and made no effort to follow.

He heard a shout behind him, and found that the twins were running down the hill.

"Hold up!" they called, "we're bunking off school today, our Mum said we could, in case he gave us the cane again!"

Pert greeted them with pleasure. "Our Mum's livid!" said Seth gleefully, "you should've seen her! I thought she was going to explode!"

"She said we were just sticking up for you against those bullies, and we shouldn't have got the cane for that, we should've got a medal," said Solomon, "and she's a good mind to go up to that school and wrap that cane round Merridew's head!"

"And when we said about you knocking old Merridew on his backside, cor, our Dad did laugh! It was prime!"

They walked on past the Drop o' Dew. It was a bit early for pirates, probably, for there was no one sitting outside.

"Billy's in school, though," said Pert. "Have you heard anything about Rosella?"

"I don't think Billy worries about anything, much," Seth said. "He just does what he wants to do, regardless. He can't half fight. No, we've heard nothing about Rosella. Coo, didn't she kick, though?"

At the root of the breakwater they ran into Walter Sabbage. He was on his own today, and stood waiting for them, his hands on his hips and his gazed fixed somewhere over Pert's shoulder.

"Well, well, cometh the bold warriers, I 'ear!" he greeted them. "Fightin' and scrappin' an' half-murderin' the masters, an' wipin' the floor wiv giants twice yer size, whatever next?"

The thing about Sabbage, Pert thought, was that you could never tell whether he was serious or whether he was poking fun at you.

"We didn't murder anyone," he said, "I just pushed him and he fell over."

"Must 'ave been an almighty push, then! We 'eard all about it in the alehouse last night. Talk o' the town, you are, Master Potts. 'Alf of 'em wanted to go an' give you a good kickin', an' the other 'alf wanted to elect you Mayor. You cert'nly stirred 'em up, an' no mistake. But listen 'ere ...", he grasped Pert's shirt front and pulled him close, "you listen 'ere, young Master, if'n any o' these louts an' hobbledehoys gives you any grief, tell 'em to take it up with Walter Sabbage. I'll tickle their ribs with my little rib-tickler, see if I don't!"

He gave a cackle and let Pert go. "An' don' ferget the Capting, lad, 'e's powerful taken with you, is the Capting, an' 'e wouldn't like for anything to 'appen to yer!"

"Don't worry, Mr.Sabbage," called Seth, "we're keeping an eye on him now! He'll be safe with us!"

Pert felt heartened, but uneasy all the same. Protection from pirates was liable to be a dubious comfort – there would be a price to pay at some point. He just wished he knew what it was.

Solomon too was in a realistic mood. "They'll get us back", he said. "Never mind Merridew, there's still Bunt and Durridge. They aren't happy with us."

His brother snorted. "What are they going to do? We beat 'em once, we can beat 'em again!"

"Don't be daft. They won't come at us all together. They'll follow us, and pick us off one by one."

"Look here," said Pert, "what Solomon says is right, but we mustn't get too worked up about it. For a start, we can all run faster than they can, so as long as we avoid dark alleys and dead ends and always have an escape route in mind, we can get away from them, easy."

"True!" said Seth.

"Also, they won't try anything when there are people about, so don't go out at night, and stay in the busy streets all the time."

"Also true," said Seth, "gets my vote every time!"

"And it should be easy for you, because there are two of you. Just don't ever split up and go round on your own."

"On our own?" mused Solomon, looking at his brother. "We never go anywhere on our own. Tell the truth, it never occurred to us."

"Yeah, we even get the cane in tandem!" laughed his brother. "We've got to go now, our Mum said she wanted some chores done, and the mood she's in ... will you be all right?"

"Yes, thanks. I'm going to have a chat with Walter Glibbery. I can see him in his boat over there!"

The boys shot off, but Pert did not do as he said and seek out the old fisherman. Instead he followed the twins, more slowly, back up the town, thinking he would wait outside Rosella's house and see if she was all right. As he turned up the Bearward the two oldest Prettyfoot girls were coming down, holding hands. They did not smile or even look at him, but as they passed him one of them hissed "Follow us! Don't let anyone see!" so he stopped as though he'd forgotten something, then sauntered back the way he had come.

At the corner he couldn't see where they had gone, until an arm appeared from behind one of the market stalls and beckoned furiously. He ran, and the two girls grabbed him and dragged him behind the canvas of the stall.

"Rosella's locked in her room!" the taller one said. "They've taken

126

her boots away, and locked her in, and she's crying!"

"Can't you rescue her?" said the other. "We don't know what's going to happen to her, and we're scared!"

Pert was stunned. Rosella never cried. He could not even imagine her crying. Rosella was strong. She was always in control.

"Have they ... done anything? Like, have they punished her?"

"No, just the locking up. But there's something going on, we know it. No one took us to school, and Mistress Grubb came to the house this morning, and she and father talked for a long time in father's study. They were shouting about something."

Pert felt numb. This shouldn't have happened. This wasn't fair. What was he to do? He needed to ask someone ... his mother? Mr.Surplice? Aunt Gittins, that was it! She was old, she must be wise, she knew the town and its habits ... yes, that was it – Aunt Gittins! He would go straight away.

"Look, I've got to get some advice about this," he told the girls. "You go home and watch and wait, and if anything happens, you need to get a message to me somehow. You could tell my sister at school, or give her a note or something. And if you get the chance to speak to Rosella, tell her I know and I'll think of something. Now run along – I don't think you ought to be seen speaking to me."

The little girls wasted no time, but were off. Pert looked round. No one had seen. He was about to set off for Aunt Gittins' house but thought it would be a good idea to follow the girls up the Bearward and make sure they had got home safely. He saw them turning into their gate, but stopped. No sooner had they gone in than Mr.Prettyfoot came out, and marched briskly up the hill towards Pardoner's Alley. Pert couldn't imagine that the Prettyfeet knew anyone in Pardoner's Alley, for only poor people lived there.

Goodness! He must be going to their house! What was going on? Was he going to give them news about Rosella or what? Pert ran up the hill, turned into the Alley, then skidded into their yard and crashed through the door.

Mother sat at the table, looking pale and tearful. Mr.Surplice stood at the foot of the stairs, his eyes wide. Over the table stooped Mr.Prettyfoot, his fists clenched.

Mr.Prettyfoot was, like his daughter, tall and fair. Pert thought he must once have been a good looking man, but his features had ... slipped, somehow. His eyes looked as though they had seen some things they didn't like, and his mouth was slack and wet-lipped as though driven to pronounce words that had disagreed with them. His cheeks were flushed, and as Pert entered he thumped his fist on the table.

"Never!" he said harshly. "Never again! You see to it, madam, or I will!"

He realised that Pert had come in, and turned to face him.

"You," he ground out, "you spawn of Satan! You vile, filthy little grub! How dare you put your dirty hands on my daughter? Fifteen years we nurtured her and protected her from scum like you, and you take her up the hill and ... I'd kill you with my own hands, but that would be too quick! I'll ruin you, I'll make your life a misery!"

He paused for breath. His face had steadily got redder and redder, and his cheeks by now were almost purple.

"Sir, I don't know what you're talking about," Pert began, but got no further.

"And don't you ever imagine," the man went on, "that you'll get within a stone's throw of my daughter again. I've taken steps! I'm sending her somewhere you'll never get to her! She'll learn the error of her wickedness, and she'll be safe from you!"

He rushed to the door and shoved Pert aside. At the door he turned, and delivered his parting shot. "And you, madam, I blame you for this! You would do well to consider who owns this house, this den of filth where you bring your children up to connive with criminals and seduce innocents! Like grandfather, like father, like son – never a truer word!"

With that he was gone. Pert stood and looked at his mother.

"Oh Pert," she said sadly, "you didn't?"

"I don't think I did," he said. "What?"

His mother put her head in her hands and did not answer. Mr.Surplice stepped forward and put his arm round her.

"Pert, Mr.Prettyfoot says you took his daughter up on the moors and ... did something with her you ought not to have done. He says you ruined her."

"I did not!" Pert said hotly. "I told you what we did. We went up on the moors and we paddled in a pool, and then we came back. She was a bit dirty, but she wasn't ruined."

"Nothing else?" asked the curate.

"No! We were happy, and now you're turning it into something else, something dirty. It's foul, you have no right! You have no right!"

Mother raised her head. Her eyes were wet. "Pert, if you say that's what happened, that's what happened. You're my good boy. Come, come and give me a hug, you're my good boy, oh dear, oh dear ...."

Later, when they had all recovered themselves a little and the curate had kindly made them all a cup of tea, they sat round the table and discussed the matter more rationally.

"I hope the tea is all right," Mr.Surplice said, "I had to make it twice, because I forgot to put any tea in the pot first time."

"It's perfect, thank you, Mr.Surplice," his mother smiled, and patted his hand.

"Oh, that's a relief," he said. "Making tea is one of the many accomplishments that have eluded me so far. Dear lady, I wish you would call me by my name, my first name I mean. If I am to live under your roof, it seems more appropriate. My name is Septimus, Septimus Surplice."

"Dear Mr. ... dear Septimus, it will be my pleasure."

"And you too, my boy. We are friends, are we not?"

"We are," said Pert, but could not gain any satisfaction from this exchange, for weightier matters bore down his spirits.

"Of course, we know who's at the root of this, I think," said Mother. "Urethra Grubb."

"She visited the Prettyfeet this morning, Mother. One of Rosella's sisters told me. They were shouting in his study."

"Oh yes, that'll be it, then. She always manages to turn things dark and twisted. She's an evil, manipulative woman and she likes nothing better than to drag everyone else down to her level."

"Dear lady, in my profession I feel obliged to give everyone the benefit of the doubt, as Our Lord would have done, and offer forgiveness for even the blackest sinner. But in this case I fear you are not too far from the truth. I have only had the doubtful pleasure of speaking to the lady once or twice, but I formed the impression of great malice, a deadly hatred for anything good and bright. Not that my impressions are likely to be any help in finding a solution."

"I can't think of any solution at all," said Pert. "Poor Rosella's locked up in disgrace, and all she did was step in to help me when those bullies were beating me. And my name's mud, and everyone'll think I did something wicked to her and I can't go back to school because of Merridew, can I? I'd better start fishing with Mr.Glibbery as soon as the weather opens up. There's one good thing, though ... Billy Moon's decided he has to look after Fenestra when I'm not there."

"Oh my goodness!" said Mother. "He's the last person ..."

"Now, now," interrupted Septimus, "you said yourself you never had anything against the mother. But he's very small ..."

"Oh, don't let that worry you," said Pert. "He's small but he's vicious. I think he'll manage very well."

Later he went down to the school to meet Fenestra. She was waiting with Billy at the gate. She looked happy, and Billy was grinning as usual. Billy walked up the hill with them, explaining that he had nothing better to do, and since he couldn't read he never did homework anyway

"Oh Pert," Fenestra said excitedly, "I've had such an interesting day! All the other girls were being much nicer to me than usual, and Esmerelda wanted to be my friend again but I'm not sure I'm going to let her because ..." she thought for a moment, "well, perhaps I will. It's not her fault she's little and scared. I'm a bit scared myself, sometimes."

"Don't you be scared of nuffink, Ferny," said Billy. "I'll sort you out, no trouble!"

Ferny, thought Pert? Ferny? Where did that come from? Fenestra didn't seem to turn a hair.

"And anyway," she went on, "the Headmaster came to my class and took me outside, and I had to tell him everything that happened yesterday, about those boys in the toilets and everything, and then he just said "Thank you Fenestra" and sent me back."

She skipped a couple of paces. "And Mr.Merridew ... well, perhaps Billy ought to say, because he saw it."

"Yeah, I saw it all right," Billy said. "'E come in with this big bandage round 'is 'ead, and a face like thunder. I fought 'e were goin' ter start whackin' us again, only you and Rosella an' the twins were away, so I fought blimey, Bill, it's all down ter you today, you're goin' ter get what for ...."

"But you didn't, Billy, did you?" said Fenestra.

"No, 'cos the 'Eadmaster come in an' another teacher come an' sit wiv us while Merridew 'ad to go outside, an' when 'e come back 'e was all white in the face, an' e' din't say 'ardly anyfink the rest of the day an' 'e din't cane no one. I fink 'e got it in the neck, did Mister Merridew!"

"And all the children are saying that you and Rosella and Batty Bunt and Darren Durridge aren't ever coming back to school again, is that right, Pert?" asked Fenestra.

"I don't know. It wouldn't surprise me. I shall go fishing instead, I suppose. But just because Bunt and Durridge aren't at school doesn't mean they're not going to be around the town. We need to be careful."

"So who'll take me to school and everything, if you're out fishing?"

"I will, Ferny!" said Billy, grinning even wider. "I'll come an' meet you in the mornin's and walk you 'ome after. Don't you worry, they won' ever get near us, I'm too quick for 'em!"

"Oh. All right then," Fenestra said, looking pleased.

When they got home Fenestra went in and got some bread and dripping and a cup of tea for Billy. He refused to go into the house because of the smell, he said, and he'd much prefer to sit on the dustbin instead. Mother looked a bit relieved.

Then before Pert had to have his own supper, he and Billy ran down to the quay so Billy could look at the pirate ship. But Billy didn't go straight down the road to the bottom. He knew a better way, he said, and dived down a little alley at the foot of the Market Square with Pert at his heels.

Pert had lived all his life in the town, but plainly there were things and places he had never discovered. Billy led him up little stone staircases between the buildings, and ducked under archways. At one point they inched along a six-inch stone ledge above the river, their heads so close to the open windows of the buildings backing onto the river that they could hear the conversations within. Eventually they came out in a wider alley that ran, so far as Pert could judge, parallel to the quay but behind the houses and inns that faced the sea.

Billy had just pointed to a little passage that would lead them onto the quay itself when Pert heard a familiar voice.

"Oh yes," it said, full of scorn, "oh yes, William Smy, you're a fine one to talk! 'Oo was it said 'e'd served with ol' Benido, but 'e never? 'Oo was it said 'e knew where them trinkets was that Bully Hayes left on Trocadero, but 'e never? 'Oo was it said Dutch Pete would never 'ave the nerve, an' 'e did, so there?"

It was unmistakably Walter Sabbage. Pert stopped. The voice came from a window, slightly open, above his head. At his frantic signal Billy Moon crept back to join him.

"All I said," replied another voice, deeper and hoarser than Sabbage's, "all I said was if someone do know where the stuff is, an' someone won't tell, what's wrong with throwin' a tarpaulin over someone and stowin' 'im away neat an' tidy in a ship we know of, an' stickin' pointy things in 'im until 'e tells us where it is? Eh? What's wrong with that?"

There was a murmur of agreement. This was evidently quite a large meeting.

"Where is this place?" Pert whispered to Billy.

"Back room of the Drop o' Dew," he answered.

"What's wrong with that," Sabbage said, "is it ain't what the Capting wants, an' since we elected 'im Capting, we has to re-spect 'is ways. Or don't we?"

Again there was a murmur of agreement. Plainly powerful argu-ments were being deployed on both sides.

"Well whatever you say, it weren't Dutch Pete what done the deed, it were the Capting, so squits ter you, Sabbage! I would 'a thought you'd a' knowed that!"

A laugh ran round the table, and calls of "One in the eye fer you, mate!" and "You tell 'im, go on!" and "Where's that slavey? This jug's empty!"

But now Sabbage's voice fell. Pert could picture him leaning forward over the table, cajoling and persuading. Only occasional words could he hear, words that sounded awfully like "treasure" and "hidden" ...

"It's the pirates, but I can't hear what they're talking about!" he moaned to Billy.

"No problem, guv!" Billy grinned, and wriggled away down the passage.

Pert waited. The conversation went on, voices rising and falling. Pert heard "them townies" and "slit their gizzards" and laughter. There were occasional oaths and disagreements, but it sounded as though Sabbage was winning them round slowly.

Suddenly one of the voices said "'Ere, what's that smell?" and then there was pandemonium, rough voices shouting, chairs crashing over, a short scream and a cry of "I'm bit! I'm bit!" and another shout of "'old 'im, 'old 'im, cor, e's a slippery li'l devil ..."

Pert knew exactly what had happened. Billy had wormed his way into the room, probably under the table where the pirates were plotting, and then been discovered and captured. It was up to him to do something.

He ran down the passage and came out, as he expected, on the quay right beside the Drop o' Dew. He dashed inside, through the dim bar room, and made for the back of the building, where there was an open door and lights and noise.

In the back room were a dozen pirates at least. Walter Sabbage was the least disreputable of them and looked positively angelic beside the squalor and lust of those faces. There were scars, and eye-patches, and extravagant moustaches with beads threaded in, and three cornered hats and pistols in belts, and in the middle of the table lay Billy, every limb pinioned to the wood, and at least three knives at his throat. He was still grinning, but it was the sort of grin you wear when you are very scared and can't think how to escape.

"Oh, let him go, let him go!" cried Pert. "He's my friend! He wasn't doing any harm, he was looking for me and thought I was in here with you!"

Sabbage's face broke into a smile. The rest of the faces did not.

"Why, Master Potts as ever is!" he said. "What a welcome surprise! Gents, this is the very young 'ero I was speakin' of, as

135

vanquishes bullies five times as big, and floors the very teachers and makes off with bootiful young maids! If ever a young master deserved a seat at this table, this is 'im!"

The faces began to relax. They especially liked the bit about the bootiful young maids.

"Oh, please, I didn't ..." he stuttered, "it wasn't like that, exactly. She made off with me, really. Please, will you let my friend go, he meant no harm."

He drew himself up and tried to sound as honest as he could. "I will vouch for him."

"Vouch? Oh well, in that case ..." said one voice, and another "If it's proper vouchin' 'e's doin', why that's a diff'rent kettle o' fish" and another called out "let 'im in, 'e's practically one of us ..."

Billy was released, and the pair pressed to take a seat at the table. A glass was placed in front of each of them, and liquid poured from a jug. Billy knocked his back immediately, but Pert sniffed and then sipped it, and found that it burned the back of his throat and made him cough. The man next to him slapped him on the back and said "Go on, you'll soon get used to it!" He had one ordinary hand, and the other was a hook with a ribbon tied round it. He smelled strongly, rather like Billy but with less wellington boot.

But the conversation didn't return to its original subject. Billy and Pert had evidently spoiled the mood, and there was no more mention of tarpaulins or treasure. Instead, they fell to recalling old shipmates they had sailed with, and the dreadful fates they had met. It did seem as though every sailor who had ever sailed the sea, met with an unusual and picturesque end. It made Pert wonder if there were any sailors who made it home and died in their beds.

Billy downed a second glass of liquor and sat happily grinning and listening. Pert was still on his first one, not liking the taste but getting used to the burning sensation as it went down. He felt happy, pleased to be accepted into the company of these brave and experienced old salts. His face kept breaking out into a silly smile, and he wondered if he had caught something from Billy.

Several of the old shipmates seem to have fallen foul of someone called Davy Jones, which puzzled him.

"This Davy Jones," he asked the man next to him, the one with the hook, "he seems to be a bit of a nuisance. Why hasn't someone sorted him out? Who is he, anyway?"

There was a sudden silence. The very old man at the end of the table put his glass down on the table with a bang.

"Who's Davy Jones?" he said scornfully. "Who's Davy Jones, 'e asks!" He leaned forward and fixed Pert with a rheumy eye. "What ignorant little squit is this, as don't know Davy Jones?"

"Careful now, Secret ..." warned Walter Sabbage, but the old man ignored him.

Pert squirmed in his seat. All eyes were upon him and he didn't know what to say. "Please," he faltered, "please, I never heard of Davy Jones. Please, he doesn't live here, or I'd know him."

"No," the old man said slowly, "e' don't live round 'ere, that's right enough. Davy Jones lives in the sea, that's where."

Round the table there was a movement, a sigh, a relaxation, for these rough men knew when a story was coming. There was a murmur of "Go on, Samivell, tell 'im." Stories were a real and living pleasure to them, stories were what kept them alive round the focs'le lantern on dark nights at sea, stories were what drew them together.

137

"Right at the bottom of the sea, right away out in the deepest bits off the Azorios, down among the wrecks an' the bones an' the fishes, 'e lives. And 'e comes up to the surface when the weather's bad, and 'e bobs about on the waves and 'e sees a ship comin', and 'e swims across and 'e talks to the tars on the deck, and 'e calls to 'em!"

There was an appreciative murmur from the men, leaning forward and listening intently. This was the kind of story they liked, this was a story that touched them where they lived.

The old man drew on his pipe, and continued: "An' Davy Jones, 'e knows which o' them sailors will live an' which will die, and them as'll die, 'e calls to, puttin' 'is hooky hands out o' the sea and beckonin', beckonin', and when they get close 'e lays hold an' ... loves 'em, like ..."

"Loves 'em?" asked a voice.

"Aye, loves 'em. He'll love you all right, will Davy Jones, if'n 'e gets his hooky hands on you! He'll put 'is clammy fingers on your privates, an' he'll put his cold lips on your'n, an' he'll wrap his slimy arms around you, and you'll gasp for breath and yer chest'll heave and he'll pull yer down with the foam in yer throat an' he'll hold you fast and down you'll go, down to the fishes and the mud, where no one'll remember who you was or what you did. Cold you'll be, an' wet you'll be, and yer eyes'll stare and yer mouth'll gape, an' down you'll go, an' down an' down ..."

Old man Secret broke off with a cackle that turned into a choking and he pulled at his glass and the spell was broken. Men began to shift in their seats and look around for more drink, and one began to sing in a tuneless voice ...

> "Davy Jones is King o' the Sea,
> An' grief's his tax, and death's his fee;
> When seamen on the oceans roam,
> King Davy he will call 'em home ..."

And the rest of the men joined in with the chorus, very quietly and tapping their pots on the table ...

> *"... be you young or be you old,*
> *The ocean mud is wet an' cold;*
> *When food an' drink an' love is past,*
> *King Davy he will love you last,*
> *King Davy he will love you last ..."*

Pert was starting to feel a bit strange. His head was nodding and he was finding it hard to keep his eyes open. Sabbage noticed, and brought proceedings to an end.

"Now then," he said, "we don' want to get the lad in more trouble than 'e's already in, do us? Roust 'im out and escort 'im into the cold air, that'll set 'im right!"

He was right. As soon as Pert felt the fresh sea air outside he felt better, and he and Billy walked up the hill. "You know," said Billy, "there might be somefink in this washing lark after all. I mean, they smelled me in there, that's 'ow I got caught. Imagine, wiv all their own pong ...!"

It looked as though Fenestra might get her way after all.

In the Market Square there was a strange atmosphere. The stalls were still crowded with shoppers at this late hour, but no one seemed to be buying anything very much. Instead, they stood around in groups muttering to each other, their eyes roving round. Pert felt some hostile glances as he threaded his way up the hill.

As he was about to turn up the Bearward, he felt a tug at his sleeve, and a little hand slipped into his. The tiny Prettyfoot looked up at him, smiled nervously and disappeared. In his hand she had left something small. He closed his fingers round it and continued innocently up the Bearward. Not until he was safely back in his own yard did he look to see what it was.

It was a note, tightly screwed up and written in red ink on a piece of school notepaper.

> Dere Mister PHS
>
> Roseld is still loked in her room but she has stoped criing so much and nuffen els have hapen.
>
> hop you are kwite well
>
> A frend (a gurl?)
>
> PS but not a gurlfrend ha ha
>
> PS PS you no wot I mean
>
> PS PS PS its April Prettyfoot reely

Pert smiled sadly. This was news, not good news exactly, but it might have been worse. If only he could speak to Rosella, reassure her, comfort her in some way. If only he could get closer to the house.

He left the yard again, and walked further up Pardoner's Alley. He knew that at the top it turned into a muddy track that wound uphill past some abandoned farm buildings, and then onto the moor. It was turning chilly, and he pulled his coat around his ears.

Past the farm buildings he left the track and began to make his way to the left hand side, over coarse grass and boggy patches where he had to leap from tussock to tussock. Below him was the straggle of roofs that was his own Alley, and beyond that the broader swathe that was the Bearward which went up past Rosella's house and then curved back on itself and down into a muddle of smaller houses. He stopped and spent some time trying to work out which was the Prettyfoots', and eventually narrowed it down to one grey roof. It was directly below him, across a paddock of thin grass and a tumbledown stone wall. He picked his way across the paddock, and an ancient horse ambled across to see what he was up to. He patted its nose and it snorted gently at him and sauntered away.

Peering cautiously over the wall and being careful not to dislodge any more stones, he found himself looking down a steep bank and at the bottom, a trim lawn with some fruit trees. This must be Rosella's back garden. Beyond the lawn was a flower bed, and beyond that the rear wall of the house. He counted eight windows, three downstairs and five up. He had no idea which was Rosella's. He guessed that her room was probably at the back, but which one?

He stood for a long time, willing something to happen that would help, but there was no sign of life. The house might have been deserted, though he knew it was not. The rain was heavier now, and his shoulders were soaked. His hair was soaked too, and water ran down his neck and into his shirt. He was doing no good here. He should go home.

As he squelched back down the hill, he ticked off on his fingers the things he had to deal with.

One, he was out of school, in disgrace and jobless.

Two, Rosella had seemed within reach and was now snatched away again. Worse still, she was in trouble and unhappy and he could do nothing to help her.

Three, he knew there was something sinister in the town, to do with the church and the Church Council, but he didn't know what it was.

Four, he knew there was something mysterious about his father but he didn't know what.

Five, there were evil forces in the town, mainly in the shape of Sabbage and his friends, and they seemed to want something from him but he had no idea what it might be.

Six, there was a vague mystery about treasure and he had, at least, found out that it existed once upon a time, but there was no clue what had happened to it.

Seven, the two bullies, and presumably their families, had a score to settle. They had not shown themselves yet, but they might any day.

And eighth and last, everyone seemed to think it was all his fault. Well, not everyone, but quite a lot of people. He hadn't done anything to Rosella that he shouldn't have, and he was certainly not in league with the pirates as some suggested.

All in all, he thought this was a pretty dismal tally. He wondered what he had done to bring all this trial and disaster on his head. Was there some act he had committed, some seemingly trivial wrong decision, that had set matters in train and enmeshed him? He could think of nothing. The only things he had done were to try and protect his sister, and to admire Rosella. They didn't seem like dreadful sins, exactly.

As this approach had produced a fairly damning list of problems, he decided to try and redress the balance by listing all the things he had in his favour.

One, he didn't have to go to school any more. Admittedly this meant he couldn't see Rosella every day, but as she was locked in her bedroom he wouldn't have been able to anyway.

Two, he had a sort of career available to him, in the shape of Walter Glibbery and his fishing boat, the *Better Times*.

Three, Fenestra's problems seemed to have evaporated for the time being, and for some odd reason he trusted Billy Moon to care for her.

And four, financially they were a little better off because of Mr.Surplice's rent money, and Mother seemed to be happy having him around.

Well, he said to himself, they say "count your blessings", but it's not very encouraging when you do and find out that for every blessing you can count, there are two curses. Still, it was a clarifying exercise, trying to sort things out like this. Perhaps if he did the same with his options. What options did he have? What actions could he take that might help?

First, he knew how to get hold of the Church Council accounts, which might solve one mystery, and there was a communion service on Sunday morning.

Second, he must, must, must get to see Rosella. Perhaps the little Prettyfeet could help? He resolved to write them a note.

Thirdly he could make a start on his new career. He would go out with Walter Glibbery tomorrow.

And fourthly he needed to find out more about the pirates' quest. As he was already regarded as half a pirate himself, it wouldn't hurt to continue talking to them.

That evening he wrote a note to the Prettyfeet. It said ...

Dear April Prettyfoot

I need to know which is the window to

Rosella's room. Can you draw me a picture?

Signed

Your servant

P Potts

Pert went to bed early that night, on purpose to catch Fenestra while she was still awake. He found her sitting up in bed. On her hand sat the mouse, eating a piece of treacle tart.

"That was my mouse," he said, "and you've tamed her. You're very annoying."

"I know," she said, smiling at him sweetly. "Pretty, though."

Pert rolled his eyes.

"Look," he said, "I need you to give this to April Prettyfoot at school tomorrow. Don't let anyone see. It's a secret."

"Can I read it?"

"I suppose you'd better. You'll only look when I'm not there."

She opened it, read it, and grinned. "Wow," she said, "how exciting!" and she slipped it under her pillow.

"I don't even know which one is April," he said.

"She's the one that's oldest after Rosella. But May Prettyfoot is in my class, shall I give it to her? She's the next one."

"Yes, I suppose so. Only you have to make her see that it's a deadly secret," he said.

"It's all right. I will," she said sleepily. "Goodnight."

"Goodnight."

"I was speaking to the mouse."

He rolled his eyes again and went to sweep the spiders out of his bed. He was just climbing between the blankets when there was

144

a patter of feet on the floorboards and Fenestra jumped on top of him and kissed him.

"I'm sorry," she said, "I love you really. It's just that I feel all peculiar at the moment and I don't know why. Mother says it's because I'm growing up. Bit scary, really."

She hugged him once more and she was gone.

XVII

*The fowl of the air, and the fish of the sea, and whatsoever
passeth through the paths of the seas (Psalm 8)*

Seen from a mile out to sea, as it would to a weary seaman
approaching land at the end of a stormy voyage, the town looked
peaceful and benign. Pert thought how misleading that was.
Distance lent an enchantment it didn't deserve.

Walter Glibbery sat in the stern of the fishing boat *Better Times*,
one arm draped over the tiller, while overhead the single sail
slatted back and forwards as the boat rocked. Pert was baiting
up, threading small pieces of fish on the hooks that hung one
after the other from the long mackerel lines. Every so often he
dipped his hands over the side to wash off the slime and scales.
The water was cold, the sea still in the grip of winter. On land the
first signs of Spring had come, but out here although the air was
bright and the little waves sparkled in the sun, it was the coming
equinox with its gales that waited over the horizon.

Pert felt happy, doing something he was used to, something he
knew he was good at. He smiled at the waves and the light wind
lifting his hair, and looked shorewards. To his left rose Bodrach
Nuwl, impossibly high, sunlit and serene with no cloud at its
head. The sun on the sheer cliff face made the rock look almost
white, and the lower slopes gleamed emerald green and fresh.

To the right the cliffs swept down to sea level, and there was the
entrance to the winding creek that led up to the quay, with the
town sprawling up the flanks of the hill. This was a wet land,
watered by the west winds that rose over Bodrach Nuwl and
turned to rain or snow, soaking the heather and peat, gathering
into tiny rivulets that joined together and carved out little channels for themselves, joining again and getting bigger, cutting
their way down to the rock and tumbling towards the town,
growing all the time.

Soon they became the brawling river under the trees that Pert and Rosella had waded in, then down through the town sometimes in stone-walled defile and sometimes in arched tunnels with houses over the top, until it flowed through the little harbour and out towards the sea.

Leaving the harbour it lost its momentum, meeting the salt tide coming the other way, and the two streams tussled in and out, first the fresh water gaining ground, but twice a day giving way to the sea as it carried the little fishing boats and larger vessels up to the quay. Its constant wrestling had over the years caused it to twist and turn, and where it met the tide it was forced to pause and drop the cargo of silt and gravel it had carried down from the hills, so that a broad plain of mud and sand had built up on either side. Here reeds and coarse grasses found a foothold, and water fowl nested.

Pert finished the baiting, and began to put the lines over the side, carefully so they didn't tangle. As he did so, the old man hauled in on the sheet. The old patched sail filled with wind and *Better Times* dipped her venerable head as though to say "Here we go again, old man!" and began to forge ahead. A gurgle of running water formed under the forefoot, and the boat heeled slightly with the wind. Little waves slapped against the bow, and once or twice a cloud of silver droplets came over the rail and wet Pert's back. He shivered with joy and watched the lines trailing astern.

Drunk or sober, Walter always knew where the fish were to be found, and Pert could tell that already the lines were twitching as mackerel drove in for the bait and found themselves hooked. "This is the life!" called Walter, and raised his bottle. "Nothin' better'n this, my boy!"

Pert grinned back at him. Before long the old man would have finished the bottle and would nod over the tiller. Pert didn't mind. He knew the *Better Times*, he knew the fish, and he knew the winding channel that would take them home. He could do this single handed if need be, and would be happy doing it as the old man was happy to let him. If he was really lucky, the old man would sleep right through the landing, and Pert would take the baskets up to Trumbull Underdown's shed and collect the money. Then he would run to give some of it to Walter's wife before handing the old man his share for ale or rum.

By mid morning the baskets were full of handsome blue and silver fish, sliding and twitching, and Walter was still awake.

"Aye, a grand mornin's work, young Pert," he said. "Let's go an' 'ave a little look in Stonefields afore we goes 'ome. We'll be needin' to think about crab pots soon. Big 'uns, an' all!"

Only a lunatic or a landlubber would ever think of approaching the edge of the Stonefields when any sea at all was running, but today it was bright and calm and the onshore wind was light. Walter Glibbery knew these crags and rocky outposts as well as any man, and Pert was calm and confident as they made their way in. He was anxious to learn. He had been here several times before, but there were miles of twisting channel to know. A boat could get lost in here, and never be found, for the tumbled slabs of rock rose forty and fifty feet in the air in places, way above a fishing boat's mast so it would not be spotted from land or sea.

Although the sea was calm there was a deep underlying scend under the wavelets, remnant of some long-forgotten storm far out on the other side of the ocean, and as the rocky walls rose around the *Better Times* the waves died and only an oily swell was left, heaving and sucking at the seaweed fronds and making the boat pitch uncomfortably. The wind went out of the belly of the sail, but there was still a breath higher up and Walter slacked off the sheet so the sail could find it.

In times of storm and tumult this deep defile would be a maelstrom, a hell of huge white waves breaking and crashing and drawing back, only to meet more breakers coming in so that the two would meet and send plumes of spray a hundred feet into the air. The noise would be heard miles inland, and no boat could live on the water and no man could live on the rock.

But today was peace, and sombre shadow. Onwards they drifted and the swell grew less. White and grey limpets covered the rocks in their thousands, and at the margin goose barnacles nodded on their flexible stalks, and little yellow crabs crawled among the bladder-wrack. Above them Bodrach Nuwl filled the sky. Now that they were close to him, he seemed to lean over them, teetering and about to fall. Halfway up his sunlit flanks the seabirds wheeled and cried, but down here they were in deep shadow.

On their left an opening appeared and Pert found himself looking across a lake of dark placid water. Walter pushed at the tiller and *Better Times* wallowed round, sail slatting gently, and drifted into the entrance. They were in what would be a rock pool anywhere else, but here was a vast cistern of still water, dark and clear. Pert leaned over the side and saw patches of sand, and fish darting from one weed to another. He thought of the box he had given his mother, with the little fish in it. On rocks clung huge dark red sea-anemones, their little tentacles waving as they sifted food from the water, and once he thought he saw the quick movement as a moray eel, startled by their shadow, drew back his head.

The *Better Times* cast a black shadow on the sandy bed, and Pert watched it undulate with the shape of the bottom. A crab saw them pass, and stopped and raised its claws threateningly. It was the size of a dinner plate.

"We'll put some crab pots here," said Walter, "after the big storms have passed through."

"They'd better be jolly big ones," said Pert.

Walter put the helm down and the boat turned slowly round. There was little wind left, and Pert got out the oars, settled them on their pins and began to row gently. They passed out through the entrance to the pool and turned left again towards the cliff.

"We'll go a little further in, since it's quiet," said Walter. "I saw a boat in here once."

"What, another fisher? Surely we aren't the only people who come here?"

"No, no, I means a wreck. All smashed and stove in, she were. An' old. Real old," Walter replied. He reached into his pocket and began to stuff his pipe with tobacco from a greasy pouch.

"Where was this?" asked Pert.

"Well, if I'm honest ..." Walter struck a match and sucked at his pipe, "... if I'm honest I'm not too sure if it happened or not." He sucked again, and blew smoke out. Pert rested on his oars and *Better Times* slid on under her own momentum.

"See, I'd had a bottle or two, like. As you do when the weather's quiet an' the fish aren't keen an' yer wife's been 'ittin' you with the chair leg ..." He smiled fondly at the memory. "Ah, she's a grand ol' girl, so she is. Anyways, I were jus' sculling in all peaceful like, and singin' to meself, an' I jus' kept goin' in and in, and there she was."

"On the bottom?"

"No, sort of 'alf an' 'alf, as it were. 'Er bows was up on a little beach, on the stones, an' er stern was down under water. Not a lick o' paint left, all grey and silvery timbers, an' a few shred o' sail. Just sittin' there peaceful under the cliff, like she bin there an 'undred years."

"Where was this?" Pert's mind was working frantically. Could this be the remains of the *Bight of Benin*, Grandfather Mascaridus's old ship?

"Right in close, I thinks. I looks up, like, when I sees 'er, and realises that I've come in too far under the cliff. She's loomin' over me, like as if to fall on me 'ead, and there was little stones droppin' down every so often. Dangerous in there, bits of cliff fallin' on yer 'ead. Whole lot could come down any minute. So I backs water and gets out o' there as quick as I could. I don't know nobody as goes that close in to the Ol' Man, 'e don't like getting' 'is toes trod on."

"So probably no one knows about this wreck."

"Ah, prob'ly. Like as not she's lyin' there still, less'n she's been squashed."

"And nobody knows about her. Can you tell me how to get there?"

"Jus' don't turn", the old man said. "I seen 'er, right up the end, tucked nice and tight between two big rocks. Years agone, it were." He was getting vague, the drink fuddling his old wits. Pert used the oars to turn *Better Times* around and began sculling towards the sea.

"Go on," he urged. "Don't turn, is that all there is to it? Are you sure?"

"I thought I seen 'er, anyhow, but I might've dreamed it, being in licker, like. But it might be there. You goes on past the crab pots, and when you sees a big red rock what sticks up, the main channel turns to the left but there's a little one what go straight. Well, don't turn, take the narrow way and don't turn, just keep goin' straight till it gets all high and dark, and there she'll be. There she might be ... perhaps ... it were a long time ago ..." The old man sucked on his pipe, and his eyes closed.

Pert rowed on through the looming rocks until the boat began to lift to the swell, and the top of the sail filled with wind. He shipped the oars and took the tiller from Walter. The wind came from seaward and they were travelling to seaward against it, so he made a fine game and a challenge of tickling her along, sheeting in when the puffs swung favourably and the boat could get some drive, and letting the sail flap so she could drift under her own momentum in between. In this slow way he reached the end of the rocks, put the helm up so the sail could fill properly, and enjoyed a sparkling beat to windward until the mouth of the creek opened up.

Then he put the helm up with one hand, grabbed the whole sheet in a bundle with the other, gybed the sail across with a bang and ran up the creek with the wind behind him. He felt happy, and proud that he could do this so well and without help, and pretended that he was the skipper of his own craft returning from a voyage of adventure. He wished that Rosella could see him, and was waiting anxiously for him on the quay.

Gliding up to the quay he threw a mooring line to one of the fisher boys who were always hanging around in the harbour. The boy slipped it through a ring and tossed the end back to Pert so he could make it fast. That way when you wanted to slip out of harbour again you didn't need any help from the shore.

The same boy seemed happy to help, so between them they hauled the baskets of fish up to the quay. The boy ran to bring a little two-wheeled cart and together they hauled the catch to Trumbull Underdown's shed. Pert haggled with the foreman, who he knew would try to pay him less than the fish were worth. He thought that had he been older he might have got a few pence more, but on the whole he was content that he had been only slightly cheated. He gave the boy a threepenny bit, earning a grin and a cry of "Thanks, guv!" and hurried to Mrs.Glibbery's little cottage in the street behind the sea front.

"Walter's sleeping in the boat, missus," he said when she opened the door. "Here's the money from Trumbull's. I kept a bit back for Walter. And I brought some mackerel for your supper, fresh caught." The old woman looked at him suspiciously, then realised who he was.

"Eh, you're growed, young Pert," she said. "Look at you, you're all sunburned and growin'! You not at school any longer?"

"No, I pushed the teacher over and I had to leave," he said.

"Ah, I 'eard something about that. That's my boy, I said to meself, that's the boy to stand up fer 'imself! An' that girl, that pretty Rosella, she was in it too?"

"Yes. I was trying to protect her."

"Well, what I 'ear she needs some protectin'. That Grubb'll get 'er soon, so you wants to get 'er out o' there, you do, mark my words! Nobody get fat and flourish in Grubb's 'ouse. I remember when Grubb were younger. She were always objectionable, like. She spoke coarse, an' she looked coarse, an' she acted coarse, always lookin' fer a fight to pick or someone weaker ter pick on. And her dad, that were a rum business an' no mistake. One day he were 'ale and 'earty, big gruff man 'e were, but people respected 'im. An' the next day he were an invalid an' took to his bed, an' she stood guard over 'im an' no one ever saw 'im alive again. She din't even let Vicar read 'is Last Rites! Now, I got to go an' polish my chair leg fer when Wallie gets 'ome. 'E expects a proper welcome, does Wally!"

Fenestra was waiting when he got home, full of secret self-importance.

"Here!" she said, pushing a piece of paper at him. "May drew it. She showed it to April at playtime and they agreed it was right."

It was a piece of paper torn from the front of a schoolbook. On it was a childish drawing of a house, complete with a curly stalk of smoke coming out of the chimney, and a dog with only three legs standing in the flower bed. But the windows were well and accurately placed, and in one very small one upstairs there was drawn a sad face.

"Now, listen," said Fenestra. "May says that Rosella shouted at her father, and threatened to jump out of the window, so he got a hammer and nailed the window shut. But she's allowed to go to the bathroom, and the window of that opens. But it's too small to climb through."

"I don't think I'd got as far as getting her to climb out," he said. "That would make things worse. And where would we put her? I was just going to talk to her."

"Well anyway, she can't get out. But her bedroom's the one next to the bathroom, and has a door to it. And listen, May says everything's really strange in their house. Their mother just locks herself in the dining room and won't come out most of the time. And Urethra Grubb keeps coming in. I think that's what makes Mrs.Prettyfoot hide, probably. I would, if it was me.

"And Mr.Prettyfoot just stays in his study and when he comes out he talks funny. And no one is looking after them, and April's having to do it and she can only make jam sandwiches.

"And April found the key and tried to let Rosella out, and her father heard and smacked her over his knee and she daren't try again, and he's hidden the key anyway. Now, did I leave anything out?"

"I think that's enough to be going on with. Crumbs, what a mystery. All this over one afternoon bunking off school? It doesn't seem right. There has to be something else. And what's it got to do with the Grubb?"

He sat and puzzled over it, but no ideas came. This was yet another item to add to the eight imponderables he already had on his list.

Pert waited until the house was asleep, dressed and crept downstairs. Outside it was a gusty night lit by a fitful moon, which would allow him to see where he was going at least. He trotted quietly up the Alley and round to the paddock. The horse was still awake, and came to greet him. He wished he had brought an apple or a bit of bread for it. It seemed a nice horse.

He found a place where the stone wall had almost completely collapsed, and slithered down the bank, stinging his wrists with nettles and getting caught up on brambles. Goodness knew what his mother would say about the state of his clothes in the morning.

He followed the sides of the lawn, keeping in the shadows as much as possible. Reaching the wall of the house, he stopped and listened for a long while.

The house seemed silent and dark. He went to the flower bed and picked up a handful of earth and pebbles, and threw them at the window next to the bathroom, his heart in his mouth. What if he'd misunderstood the drawing, or if the little girl's knowledge of architecture was wrong?

Nothing happened for quite a long time, and then there was movement at the window. A pale face peered out. Then it disappeared, and the little bathroom window was raised a few inches.

"Pert? Is that you?" came a whisper, so quiet he almost missed it.

He stepped out from the wall and looked up.

"Rosella?"

"Oh Pert, they took my boots!"

"Who did?"

"Father and that woman, Grubb. She's in the house half the time now, and she shouts and shouts, and when she goes, Father shouts at Mother. I don't understand what we did so wrong?"

"Nor do I. Do you think we could get you out of there?"

"I don't see how. Unless I just smashed the window with a chair and jumped."

"Don't do that! You'll hurt yourself, and there'll be glass and everything."

"All right ... Pert, I think there's someone moving about downstairs. You'd better go!"

"All right. I'll try to come again."

"Pert, I'm glad you came."

The window was closed, and Pert fled across the lawn and up the bank and didn't stop running and scrambling until he felt the horse's hot breath on his cheek.

"Hallo, horse," he said, patting its long nose, "I wish I'd got something for you. I hope you're having a happier time than I am."

XVIII

Thou hast made us to drink the wine of astonishment (Psalm 60)

Sunday morning was Communion, and Pert had planned how he would get into the vestry cupboard while the Vicar was busy with the sacraments. He intended to be particularly efficient so as not to arouse any suspicion, but his plan foundered at the first hurdle, for the Vicar was there before him, sitting at the vestry table.

"Potts!" he said, "been waiting for you. Stand there."

His face was flushed, and Pert smelt spirits. It was ten o'clock in the morning and the Vicar had started already.

The Vicar planted his elbows on the table and fixed Pert with a beaky glare. "Where is it?" he said sharply.

"Sir, where's what?"

"Where's the money you stole?"

Pert was floored. Now they were accusing him of theft. He'd already been convicted of assault and battery, of defiance and rebellion, and of unspecified crimes against the virtue of Rosella. Now it was theft.

"I've stolen nothing," he said truculently. If he resisted, if he was stubborn, was there much they could do?

"Liar!" screeched the Vicar, and rose to his feet. "Liar, and thief! Thief and liar!" He advanced round the table, his knees very high and his hands outstretched. Pert braced himself for flight.

"Where is it? Where is it, you unspeakable little blackguard?" the man yelled in his face, and gripped his lapels. "Where is the sixpence you stole from the collection?"

Pert breathed a sigh of relief. Was that all? Was that all it was about? Sixpence found on the floor, which he had kept and spent on presents?

"Sir, I found that money. I didn't steal it. And I've spent it."

The Vicar's narrow face flushed with anger and his little eyes grew round. He shook Pert by the lapels. He was strong, too strong for Pert to break away. What should he do? Rosella would have kicked with her big boots, kicked at his shins, that would have done the trick but Pert was wearing ordinary shoes, the shoes he used for church, with soft soles so they didn't click when he walked about during the service.

"Sir, let me go! I'm not a thief. I found that money, and I believed it was all right to keep it. If you want, I'll pay it back. I can give it to you tomorrow." He did his best not to sound scared, though he was. Not of the Vicar's violence, but of the label "thief", of the word that the Vicar would put round the town. But, he thought, whether he paid the money or not, that wouldn't stop Tench and his crony Urethra Grubb from noising it abroad that he had stolen – and stolen from the church, at that. What worse crime could there be?

The Vicar let go of him. He thrust his great nose in Pert's face, and barked "Pay it back? I guarantee you will pay, my sneaky light-fingered friend. Oh yes, you'll pay all right, with this to add to your other sins!"

He calmed at this, and sat down again. "You will bring me six-pence tomorrow. Bring it to my house. And you are fired from your post as altar boy. You will serve at this morning's commun-ion, and then you will never darken the doors of this building again. This is the house of God, and black spirits like yours have no place it its observances!"

Pert watched him, and felt an icy calm spread over him. Be rational, now, Pert, think calmly and work it out. Do you mind not being an altar boy any more? No, not in the least.

Will you still be able to accomplish what you set out to do, and purloin the parish accounts? Yes, you will. You'll do it now.

Will you pay back the six pence as you promised? No, not in a thousand years. Let the Vicar whistle for the money. It wasn't his, and there was nothing he could do about it that he wasn't already going to do anyway.

Pert felt a surge almost of joy. He was free, somehow, as though a shackle had been released from him. Here's to a life of crime, he thought, and beggar the consequences!

"Very well," he said, trying hard not to smile. "Shall I get the wine and wafers out now? Could I have the key to the cupboard?"

The service followed its usual course. The usual prayers were intoned, the usual hymn was sung though this time Pert didn't feel it was incumbent on him to take part in it. As usual the Vicar made his mystic passes over the pewter cup and the pewter plate, and the usual worshippers rose from their pews and shuffled forward to take communion.

Sir Humphrey Comfrey was always first, followed by Mrs.Wheable and the Widow Dolphin, then other town dignitaries, the fish merchant and his wife, the headmaster, then down the pecking order, Miss Throstle, then the harbourmaster, then the more ordinary people, shop keepers and stall holders and fishermen and their wives.

"This is my blood ... shed for you ... drink it in remembrance of me ..." and sip, and wipe the rim with the cloth, and turn it a little so that the next person drinks from a different place though there are only so many different places, thought Pert, so you've got to share someone else's spit anyway, just not someone of your own social class.

159

Then the wafers, thin, poor little things from a packet printed "Makepiece & Thorogood, communion wafers, economy grade", and "this is my body ... in remembrance of me ..." and the worshippers struggle to their feet and file back to make room for those behind.

Pert had deliberately given the chalice half-measure, so he could be absolutely sure he would have to go and refill it. There were two chalices, in fact, both coarse pewter things, so that there would be no break in proceedings. He had only half filled them both.

When the Vicar handed him the first empty chalice, Pert walked swiftly to the vestry, went to the cupboard which the Vicar had, perforce, to leave unlocked. On the top shelf were the bottles of communion wine and spare packets of wafers. He slopped some of the thin red stuff into the chalice, hurriedly put the bottle back and looked at the lower shelves.

Mr.Surplice had not been mistaken. There they were, a number of notebooks with stiff covers of marbled cardboard and red cloth backs, partly hidden under a mess of old robes, boxes of candles and prayer books. He pulled them out and put them in the bottom of the other cupboard that held the old choir robes. This one was never locked. Pert had never seen a key for it. He put an old cassock over them and closed the door.

In the main cupboard he rearranged the candles and the old robes so the gap would not be noticeable, and returned to the sanctuary with the chalice.

At the altar rail a new row of parishioners knelt while the Vicar moved up and down. He put the chalice back on the altar, and took the wafer plate. "This is my body ..." he intoned, placing a wafer on the tongue of each supplicant. Pert picked up the almost empty chalice and took it back to the vestry.

Here a wicked thought struck him. He stood transfixed by the enormity of it, then acted. His final duty as altar boy would be one to remember. He went back to the special cupboard. Right at the back of the highest shelf was the Vicar's special bottle, the whisky. It was half full. Pert emptied it into the chalice, replaced it, and took the chalice back to the altar.

He waited just long enough for the Vicar to take the chalice and begin to administer it to the fishermen and their wives who knelt before him, and to see the look of surprise on their faces as they sipped. The first ones crossed themselves and rose to go back to their pews, grinning. That was a communion and a half, that was!

Pert slipped back to the vestry, threw off his robes, and grabbed the accounts books. He pulled open the door from the vestry into the churchyard, ran down the side of the church beneath the yew trees, along the path to the lych gate and out into the Canonry. Leaping and bounding at the mischievous freedom in his heart, he fled down the hill and turned for home.

For the rest of the morning Pert was half expecting that the Vicar might call to vent his anger on Mother, but nothing happened. After all, he mused, how could the Vicar admit that he regularly drank a half bottle of whisky before officiating at holy orders? And the chances that he had missed the accounts books were slim – no one had taken any notice of them for ten or fifteen years, to judge from the dust. Just in case, he took them up to the attic and hid them behind a loose brick in the back of the chimney breast. He must remember to get them out before the mouse found them and fancied a snack, though.

IXX

The mouth of the righteous speaketh wisdom and in the hidden part thou shalt make me to know wisdom (Psalms 37 & 51)

After lunch Mother complained about him and Fenestra cluttering the place up, and suggested they go out for a walk, the day being fine. They went slowly down the Bearward, Pert looking out of the corner of his eye at Rosella's house which still seemed dead and silent. As they reached the bottom of the street they heard a shrill whistle behind them, and running feet, and they were joined by a grinning Billy Moon.

"Well, fancy meetin' you 'ere," he said, hardly puffing at all.

"It's quite amazing, Billy Moon, how often you seem to be in this neighbourhood," said Fenestra airily. Pert could tell that she was not put out at all.

"Oh, yeah, it is, innit?" laughed Billy. "It jus' so 'appens I often 'as a bit o' business round 'ere, like!"

Fenestra said nothing, but walked on holding Pert's arm in her best ladylike manner.

"How's school?" asked Pert.

"Borin'," was the reply. "No fights, no wackin's, nobody knockin' no teachers on their arses, nuffink interestin' at all, jus' borin'!"

"Billy Moon, school's supposed to be boring," reproved Fenestra, "and you're not supposed to say arse."

"You jus' said it!"

"No I didn't!"

"Yes you did, you said arse!"

"I was just saying what you said ..."

"Children, children, would you behave?" laughed Pert. "Can't we have a more grown up conversation?"

"But we aren't grown up, are we? We're children," said Fenestra. "Who's that standing in the middle of the road?"

Pert looked. It was Batty Bunt, and just as they had spotted him his brother Spotty appeared round the corner, followed by Darren Durridge.

"Uh oh," said Billy Moon, "lout alert!"

"Let's go back," said Fenestra.

They turned. From the alley beside the Emporium sauntered Will Durridge and George Bunt, and further up the hill were two more burly figures strolling down towards them.

"Bert Millidge an' Fisty Marrow," said Billy. "This isn't good. We better make ourselves scarce. Run!"

They took to their heels and immediately a shout went up. "Get 'em!" yelled George Bunt, and there were whoops and jeers from the rest. Batty Bunt and Darren Durridge were running heavily up the hill towards them, and the rest of the men spread out across the street in front and behind. They were cornered.

But the men hadn't reckoned with Billy Moon. "This way!" he called, and darted downhill to a small opening between two houses. He waited, and Pert and Fenestra reached the opening just before the hands closed on them. They tore down an alley so narrow Pert wondered if the bullies would be able to follow them at all, but knew from the noise of thundering feet and the heavy breathing that they were not far behind.

Billy turned up another alley just as narrow, and immediately stopped. He handed Fenestra up into an opening in the wall, bounded through behind her, and pulled Pert in behind him. "Go on, Ferny, go up!" he said, and they followed her up a flight of steps and out into another alley. Pert glanced right and left, and saw burly figures at both ends, but Billy led them straight across, into a yard piled with timber and building supplies. He ripped open a shabby door and pushed them into a building, then led them across the floor to an open gate and out into the street beyond.

Pert couldn't even recognise the street but thought it might be one of the little rows that led down to the harbour. Still Billy ran. Fenestra was flagging now, her skirt awry and her blue cloak flapping. Pert was out of breath. He knew he could carry on longer before they had to turn and make a stand, but he was worried about his sister.

But Billy was master of the situation. He led them through another door, into someone's garden, up the side of their house and into yet another street, then across and into a shabby cottage.

"Mum!" he yelled, "look after 'em! I'm goin' to draw 'em off, the great lummocks!" and he was gone, the door slamming behind him.

Pert leant against the door and looked around him, chest heaving. Fenestra had collapsed on the floor, kneeling on all fours and fighting for breath.

"Come in, come in, my dears," said a fat, kindly voice, and a plump, rosy woman waddled into the room. "Come, sit you down," she said, sweeping a pile of old clothes from a sagging sofa, "sit you down an' get your breaths, an' I'll make a nice cup of tea!"

They did as they were bid. Fenestra leaned against her brother and gradually their breath returned.

"Now, here we are, drink up and let's see who we've got! You must be Billy's little friends, Pertinacious and Fenestra? He's told me. Phew! Just let me get the weight off my feet ..."

She turned and backed into an enormous easy chair, and sat with her feet off the floor.

"We won't worry about Billy, the lamb, because this quite often happens to him. He's quick, though, and he wriggles and sneaks in and out and he knows every nook and cranny of this place, so they never can catch him, bless 'im!"

"You're Billy's mum," said Pert. "Sorry, that's a bit obvious, isn't it!"

"Yes, I'm his mum, bless him, for all the good it's done 'im. My name's Primrose Moon, and your mother will have told you about me, I dare say. She probably doesn't approve of me, not one little bit!"

"Actually," said Fenestra, "she says you're pleasant and she doesn't see what else a body is to do ... I think that's what she said."

"Did she now?" said Primrose, her eyebrows raised. "Did she now, did she say that? Well, bless her for a wise and forebearin' woman. I think I'd like to meet your mother. There's not many in this town would be so generous."

"I don't understand really," said Fenestra. Pert wished she would keep quiet, but when Fenestra asked questions in that innocent tone of voice, and gazed at you with that wide-eyed look, there were few people who could have resisted. "Why do people disapprove of you? Is it because you're fat?"

Primrose gave a great shout of laughter, and her chins wobbled, as did several other parts. "Why, you little madame! I thinks you knows exactly why, so don't you play the innocent with me!"

165

Fenestra looked only slightly abashed. Her innocent look was fireproof.

"People say I'm a naughty woman, my dear, because I got a child and no husband, and I has gentlemen visitors occasionally. Well, most nights, really. And I like a drink and I like a dance and I like a laugh, and what's wrong with that?"

"And would you mind if we washed Billy, because he does smell rather a lot?"

Another shout of laughter. "Cor, you are a caution and no mistake! If you can get him to wash you'll be a better woman than I am, my love. Billy does what Billy wants, and I've never managed to get the hang of him at all. When he's home I feeds him, if I've got anything in the house, but otherwise he's his own boy, is Billy!"

At that the door opened and his own boy came in, not breathing hard at all. He slid down the door and sat at ease on the floor, grinning.

"That was easy!" he said. "I led 'em right out to the edge of town, right up near Throssell's farm, an' then I doubled back. It'll take 'em an hour to get back, rate they go, great fat slow things they are, and they'm knackered already, an' arguin' whose fault it was. Batty Bunt already got a clout round the 'ead from 'is dad, and I reckon they'll all be fightin' before long!"

"That's my good boy," said Primrose fondly. "I likes your friends, Billy, especially this one. Right little charmer, she is. Mind you," looking at Pert, "you're going to be a handsome lad before long, and all the girls will set their caps at you!"

"They'll be wasting their time, then," said Fenestra, "because he's spoken for!"

Pert felt himself blushing. "Oh yes, I heard. Poor lass," said Primrose. "Trouble is, once Grubb gets involved, anything can happen and it's always nasty."

"I don't understand how Grubb's involved as it is," said Pert. "What's it got to do with her, me and Rosella?"

"Well, my guess is that she's got something on the girl's father. That's the way she usually works. She finds out something, or gets 'em involved with something shameful, and then she's got them in her power, like. See, people like me and your mum, we're not in so much danger from her, because we ain't got any secrets. I'm a naughty woman, true enough, but everyone knows it and there's no secret to be covered up. And your mother's an honest woman, I judge, and the same applies.

"Mistress Grubb knows secrets, see. She knows lots of secrets, does Mistress Grubb. How she finds out, nobody knows, but find out she do. She knew when I took Alice Trivett's dinner-money from her pocket at school. She knew when Gadarene Tyler pulled little Victoria Sponge into the bushes and made her do things, not that she minded much. She knew it was Amos Rossage what burned the dockyard paint shop down, though she never said nothing.

"She's always found out which careless youth fathered which poor little bastard. She knows who cheats, or steals, or beats the servants, or blacks his wife's eyes and breaks her teeth in a drunken rage. She knew when Thomas Millidge hid his own father's will so he could keep the lot – she probably done the same herself. For years, Ovary Makepeace used his advancing years and the promise of a legacy to rule his grown children in misery, and they at each other's throats all the while, and she knew about that. It was probably her idea."

She took a sip off her tea, and sat forward to fix them with her eyes.

167

"She knows who can't resist one more drink, which is half the men in this town. She knows who takes their comfort with Primrose once in a while, which is the other half. She knows who lusts after the neighbour's daughters – like Reverend Tench lusts after your Rosella, young sir ..." Pert felt his eyebrows go up and Fenestra sat up very straight and put her fingers down her throat as though she was being sick, "and she knows who's scared to stand up for what they know to be right, which is the whole damn lot of 'em. Oh, she knows, all right. She knows ..."

There was a silence. Then Primrose gathered herself together.

"Now then, I think it's probably safe for you to take these babes home to their mum, Billy. And I've got an appointment down at the Drop o' Dew, so I'll take my leave. And by the way, young lady, I ain't fat. I'm comfortably upholstered. Men like that, some of them. You skinny little waif, you wouldn't understand it, but you will one day."

Fenestra had the grace to look just a little embarrassed. She grinned sheepishly, and Billy took them to the door.

That evening Pert went up to bed early, and while Fenestra sat on one side of the chimney breast and told the mouse a rather long story about a princess who was being chased by some bad men and had to be rescued by a handsome prince, he sat on his mattress on the other side with a candle and opened the parish accounts. As he'd expected, they were difficult to decipher, but after a while he began to get the hang of it.

On each page there were two columns, one labelled *"Income"* and one labelled *"Expend're"*. Down the left hand side were various headings, like *"Fabric"* and *"Emoluments"* and *"Misc. Disbursements"*, and against each heading there were entries of money in one or other column or sometimes both.

	Income	Expendre
Fabric		
ye chauncel window	-	£1/6s/9d
V.Throstle, carpenter		
for repares to ye pews	-	17s/2d
	Expendre	£2/3s/11d

	Income	Expendre
Emoluments		
J.Tench, viccar	-	£4/11s/0d
P.Scutterbuck, curat	-	£2/4s/3d
S.Tench, altar boy	-	12s/6d
Mistress Tizzard, organ	-	£1/0s/7d
Ezekiah Mould, sexton	-	£1/15s/8d
	Expendre	£10/4s/0d

Pert stopped reading. S.Tench had been the altar boy, and had been paid 12s.6d. for it? Pert had never been paid a penny. He couldn't really remember why he had become an altar boy. The suggestion had come from the Vicar who had spoken to his mother, and it had never occurred to him to refuse, that was all. He read on ...

Misc. disbursements

Mrs. Throstle, ye flowrs	-		6s/4d
R. Meakins, chandler, for candels	-		11s/10d
R. Meakins, chandler, for coals	-		£1/1s/7d
ye Destitute	-		£5/0s/0d

Expendre £6/19s/9d

ye Collections

Sunday 7th Aprille	£1/9s/4d	-
Sunday 14th Aprille	£2/1s/1d	-
Sunday 21st Aprille	£1/12s/9d	-
Sunday 28th Aprille	£2/7s/11d	-

Income £7/11s/1d

ye Bequests & ye Foundationnes

Comfrey	£5/0s/0d	-
Osakiah Wheable, gent.	£15/10s/0d	-
Rossage	£1/0s/0d	-
Millidge	£2/10s/6d	-
a seaman	2s/5d	-

Income £24/2s/11d

At the bottom of the page the expenditure for the month had been subtracted from the income, and the Parish Fund was richer by £12/6s/4d, a handsome sum, he thought. At the foot of the page was the signature of the people who had drawn up the accounts, Tortice & Wetlow, solicitors. But what of ye Poor Box and ye Funde for ye Relieve of Destitution? He found these on a separate sheet. They were very simple ...

ye Poore Boxe   13s/8d   13s/8d

ye Funde for ye Relieve of Destitution
    Town levy on ye houses   £11/13s/3d   -
    from ye Parish Fund   £5/0s/0d   -
    ye needy   -   £16.13s,3d,

                                            _____

                                            £0.0s.0d.

So the money people dropped in the Poor Box at the back of the church was just given to poor people straight away. Pert wondered who did the giving, and how they decided who needed it. But at least it was a simple system. The Funde for ye Relieve of Destitution was more complicated. Mr.Surplice had been right about the levy or tax on the houses of the town. Money was collected from every householder, the Parish Funde added a little to it, and the money was distributed to ye needy, though how and by who was not clear.

Pert checked the date at the top of the sheet. These were the Parish Accounts for the meeting in May 1879. What about the accounts a little nearer the present? 1880 was little different, nor was 1881 or 1882.

But 1883 was written in a different hand, and looking down the page Pert found one or two new entries, for instance ...

to Reserve Account £10/0s/0d

... and ...

Diocesan Levy £8/10s/0d.

Right at the foot of the page were the words ...

Reconciliation £6/2s/11d.

... and conveniently this was the exact figure that was left after all the Income and Expenditure were added and taken off. Pert looked at the next month, and the one after that. Similar entries, and the Reconciliation at the bottom again wiped out any remaining balance. Perhaps this was just a word that meant "what's left"?

Then Pert's eye fell on the signature. It was no longer "Tortice & Wetlow, solicitors". It now read "Patroclus Prettyfoot".

Pert took out the Parish Minutes and hunted through until he found 1882. Ah, here it was – the first appearance of the name U.Grubb as a council member. So the year after she took office, the solicitors were no longer keeping the accounts and Patroclus Prettyfoot was. Pert felt this was important. It was a clue. He had no idea what it meant, but it was definitely a clue to something.

XX

He that worketh deceit shall not dwell within
my house for their deceit is falsehood (Psalms 102 & 119)

The next morning he slipped out of the house as early as he could, and walked down to Low Street. The names Tortice and Wetlow sounded familiar to him. He was sure he had seen them somewhere.

Keeping a weather eye out for any Bunts or Durridges, though he thought it was probably much too early for them to be out of their beds, he wandered up one side of Low Street and down the other. This was a street of tall narrow buildings that leaned over and shut out the light. It was here that some of the business people of the town had their offices, the marine factors and chandlers and other desk-bound mariners who made a living off the sea without ever leaving their chairs.

He found it without difficulty. He must have walked past it a hundred times, and remembered it without thinking. Near the top of the street where it turned left to pass above the church, at the top of a flight of worn stone steps, a tarnished brass plaque beside a door announced *"Tortice & Wetlow, Solicitors, Convey-ances and Commissioners of Oaths"*. The door didn't look as though many people had used it for a long time, but it gave at his touch.

He found himself in a long, low passageway, dim and redolent of old paper and older cooking. On his left was an open doorway, and inside the doorway at a vast desk sat a tiny man. The desk was covered with piles of papers, and the floor was too, and the chairs, and the bookshelves and the fireplace and the occasional table that stood in the window looking over the street.

"Yes, young man, can I help you?" said the tiny man. He was almost dwarfed by the desk and its cargo of papers, and had a pair of glasses sitting on top of his head.

"Er, could I speak to Mr.Tortice or Mr.Wetlow, please?"

"I'm Wetlow. Tortice hasn't been here these ten or fifteen years, and I've never got round to taking his name off the door. Always so much to do, you know ... I can't seem to find ... can you see my glasses?"

"On top of your head."

"Oh! Of course, how silly of me! Can't find anything these days!" The man smiled. His face was weak, and his eyes rheumy from too much staring at fine print.

"I'm surprised you can ever find anything in here," Pert said, "I've never seen so many papers!"

"Yes, it is a bit daunting, isn't it?" Mr.Wetlow stood and gazed round in consternation. He was hardly any taller standing up than he was sitting down. "I used to have a system, you know. I could put my hands on the right papers in a trice. But it all seems to have got ... on top of me a bit. Now, how can I help? A will, is it, or a conveyance? Or do you want to swear an oath? I'm good at those!"

"No, thank you. My mother doesn't like me swearing. I was look-ing for some information."

Wetlow sat down. "I'd invite you to sit, only I'm not sure what there is to sit on," he said vaguely. "Information? What about?"

"The parish church accounts."

Wetlow suddenly look wary. "What about them? They're nothing to do with us. Or with me, rather. I know nothing about them."

"But you used to, didn't you? You and Mr.Tortice used to sign them every month?"

"Oh, but that was years ago. Before Tortice ... um, went, you know."

Pert lifted a pile of papers from a chair, set them carefully on the floor, and sat down.

"I've been looking at the accounts from after you and Mr.Tortice stopped," he said. "There are one or two things I don't understand. What's "reconciliation"?"

"It means an agreement between two parties who are in dispute, but I can't think what it has to do with the parish accounts. There hasn't been a dispute, has there?"

"No, I don't think so."

"Then there can be no reconciliation. Was that all?"

"Not quite. There seems to be something called "Reserve account", and another one called "Diocesan Levy". Do you know anything about them?"

"Nothing. There were never any such things in my day. What are they?"

"They just appear in the accounts, and money goes into them."

"Hmm. Makes no sense to me, but you really ought to ask the vicar."

"He's not very pleased with me at the moment. I put whisky in the communion wine."

The man's face brightened. "I say! Did you really?"

"Yes. And it was his whisky."

"Well, perhaps you should speak to whoever does the accounts now?"

"There aren't any. There haven't been for ages. There's no church council either, just the Vicar and Mistress Grubb."

The man paled. He stood up. "In that case, there's nothing more I can do for you. Thank you so much for calling. Can you find your own way out?"

"But you haven't told me anything yet."

"And I'm not going to. Young man, if Mistress Grubb is involved with this, then I am not. Now, I don't know your name ..."

"Sorry, it's ..."

"No!" Wetlow held up a hand to stop him. "I don't know your name and I don't want to know it. This conversation never took place. You were never here. Do I make myself clear?"

Pert did not move, but stared at Wetlow for a long time. "You're scared," he said slowly. "It's Grubb, isn't it? You're scared of her."

"Me? No, of course not. A man of the law has no reason to fear anyone. Now, please leave."

"No. You'll have to throw me out. And I'm bigger than you."

"Get out! I'll call ... er ... I'll call ..."

"Who you going to call? Listen, I'm Pertinacious Potts. I knocked the teacher over!"

Wetlow gasped. "Please," he said, glancing round as though someone might be watching, "I can't help. I dare not. Not after what happened to Tortice. Please leave me alone."

"What did happen to him?"

"His trousers ... she ..."

176

"What about his trousers?"

The man sat up straight and seemed to make an effort to pull himself together. He took a deep breath and said "She came to see him one night. I heard her shouting at him. I couldn't hear what she was saying, but he kept saying 'No, I won't', and then she slammed out. And the next night he was found in the church-yard with no trousers. He was all tied up, and covered in mud and ... other stuff, awful stuff, and the ladies from the choir found him when they arrived for choir practice, and people started to say he was some kind of mad man and was doing ... peculiar things ... and the next thing I knew he'd gone. He packed his bags and left, and I've been on my own ever since."

"And you don't know what it was she wanted of him?"

"No idea. Please, I can't tell you any more."

"How did she get on the Church Council?"

"Get on the Church Council? How do you expect me to know? We just did the accounts, we didn't have anything to do with it."

"But you must have heard things. Was she elected?"

Wetlow slumped in his chair. "You don't give up, do you?"

"No."

"You have to promise this won't go any further? You must prom-ise me, or I'm saying nothing."

"I promise."

"Well, I can only say what I heard. I never went to any of the meetings or anything, it was only talk. No one elected her or appointed her. I think she just turned up one day, and no one had the courage to tell her she shouldn't be there. She was one of the leading businesswomen in the town, you understand, she had a finger in many pies, she had a hold over too many people, so they simply let her sit there. And gradually she took over. She'd hector them, just shout down any ideas she didn't like. She could make them vote for motions she proposed by plain force of character and persistence."

"And they let her? Even people like Sir Humphrey?"

"I think they realised that if they didn't agree with her, she'd just go on and on in that dreadful hoarse voice of hers. That huge wet mouth flapping and those big red cheeks staring round daring anyone to contradict her, until she got her way. And if anyone opposed her, she'd accost them in the street, buttonhole them in that unpleasant way she has, and polite society people can't stand that. She'd always choose a time when they were late for an appointment, or they were with friends whose good opinion they valued, or at some other time when they would be most embarrassed, and she'd hold them by the arm and talk, talk, talk at them until eventually they just caved in from sheer exhaustion and revulsion. It was only the Church Council, after all. It was worth it to get rid of her."

"I can imagine."

"And did they get any thanks for it? No, she remembered every tiny slight, every raised eyebrow, every heavy sigh, every glance at the clock or at the door. She'd note every resistance, however feeble, and one way or another, sooner or later, they'd pay. Oh, she was a terrible woman. Still is. Now, that's really all I can say. Please, go now, I don't want to end up ... I have no desire to be exposed before the ladies of the choir, thank you. Please, young man ..."

"But there isn't a choir any more."

"Maybe not. But there are trousers, and I'd rather hang on to mine. Good day to you!"

When Pert reached the bottom of Low Street he ran into the twins.

"I say," said Seth excitedly, "what's this we hear about you and your sister being chased all over the town by Bunt and his cronies? How did you get away?"

"Oh, it was easy," he said airily. "We slipped down an alley and hid out at Billy Moon's mother's house. Then when they'd gone, we went home."

"You went to Primrose Moon's? Wow! What was she like?"

"Rather nice, actually. She says she wants to meet my mother."

Solomon laughed. "I think your mother might have a thing or two to say about that!" he said. "Anyway, there's something going on this morning. There are people standing around in the street, looking daggers and muttering. Something's upset them."

"And Bunt's dad and Durridge's dad are going round asking questions," said Seth. "They pushed Amos Rossidge up against a wall and said they'd bash him if he didn't tell them where your dad is!"

"How would Amos Rossidge know anything about my dad? He doesn't know what day it is, half the time."

"I don't think it's him, particularly, they're asking anyone who might be scared of them, and leaving the ones who aren't. My dad walked past them earlier and they didn't bother him." The twins' father was a small man but a well known pugilist in the town, and their mother had a famous right hook.

"We thought we'd go down to the quay and see if anything's going on down there. Want to come?"

Pert thought he would. If nothing else he could have a chat with Walter Glibbery.

The twins were right, it seemed. The quay was more crowded than normal, and there was less work going on. Boats were unmanned, and nets were draped unmended over the cobbles. Knots of fishers stood around, scowling. Members of Bunt's gang were moving from one to the other, but Pert noticed that the fishers were not being very welcoming. He thought that if the ruffians were seeking information among the fishermen, they'd find it in short supply.

Because of the fishermen Pert and the twins thought it safe to walk along the quay. If Bunt or Durridge approached them, they'd face up and the bullies wouldn't dare do anything. So it proved, but Pert felt uneasy all the same, for not all the bluff fishermen's faces looked friendly. There were some smiles, from those he knew well, but others were suspicious.

This is to do with the pirates, he thought. They're getting fed up with the pirates, and they think I'm in league with them because I was talking to them. That means they probably think I'm in league with Bunt and Durridge as well, which is ridiculous because I'm not. And I'm not in league with the pirates either. The pirates want something from me, so they're being friendly. I bet that could change in an instant if they thought I wasn't going to cooperate. Perhaps I should try harder to find out something about the treasure, and then I could tell them and they'd go away and it would all be over.

He realised that Solomon had been saying something to him. The boy was pointing towards the Drop o' Dew. Out of the alehouse door issued a file of pirates, Sabbage at the front. They were singing and laughing and pushing each other. The fat land-lord stood at the door and watched them go, looking relieved.

As the pirates swaggered along the quay, a knot of fishermen drifted across and blocked their way. Then another group began to move as well. Pert and the boys stood transfixed. Something was happening. There was going to be a confrontation. He looked around for Bunt and the gang, and they too were aware that something was up. They had gathered together, and stood uncertainly between the two opposing sides. Clearly they didn't know which side they were on.

There were perhaps a dozen pirates. Pert recognised Matthew Shattock and Squance, with the very old pirate Samivell Secret in the middle, and the looming bulk of Will Smy at the back. They walked towards the fishermen calmly, their hands on the knives at their belts.

The fishermen spread out to block their path, but Sabbage kept walking towards them, a grin on his face.

"Now then, my hearties, what be you a-wantin'?" he called. "You surely can't be a-wantin' to interfere with your fellow mariners what's goin' about their lawful business, can you?" He stopped in front of the fishers. Pert's heart was in his mouth. This was going to be bad.

But Sabbage was speaking again, speaking with power and authority that got him heard on a busy quarterdeck in battle. He was calling names.

"Tom Suffling," he called, "Andrew Skedge! Show yerselves! Tobias Smnith, and Jed Scurrell and John Scutter, step you forward!"

Up the steps at the root of the breakwater came more pirates. They had evidently been resting and waiting there for just this eventuality. They were behind the fishermen, and they were armed with pistols and blunderbusses.

"There now," said Sabbage jovially, "was there still something you gentlemen wanted to discuss, or can us God-fearin' seamen go back to our ship fer our wittles, what Cooky 'as been a-slavin' over this livelong mornin'?"

He waved towards the ship, and all eyes turned towards it. In the bow stood Trinity Teague, behind the gun he had uncovered.

It was pointing straight at the fishermen, and its black mouth gaped threateningly. In the midships stood another figure, an old pirate with a wooden leg and a stocking cap. He stooped over the second gun, even larger, and in his hand was a smoking match.

"Need I say more?" said Sabbage sweetly. The fishermen dropped their heads and shuffled back. The pirates grinned and grimaced as they walked through the blockade, the armed men falling in behind. Once they had gone aboard, Pert noticed that two or three of them remained perched in the bows, keeping lookout. These pirates knew a lot more about military tactics than the innocent fishers. He also looked round and found that Bunt and his gang had vanished quietly away.

"There's no Diocesan Levy in this diocese," said Septimus later that night.

They were in his room. He sat in the chair, and Pert and Fenestra perched on the bed. Fenestra stared round, fascinated that it looked so different with someone else's clothes and books strewn around.

"This used to be my room, and now it feels all strange," she said. "I'm amazed."

"I'm sorry to have dispossessed you, my dear," he said.

"Oh, that's all right. I like it in the attic. Pert's there, and my mouse, and you can get really cosy under the blankets when the wind blows. It's romantic."

"You were saying about the Diocesan Levy?" Pert interrupted.

"Oh yes. Well, there are some dioceses that do it, but I've been in this diocese all my life. I was born not far from St.Portius's over on the other side, and I trained at the cathedral seminary, and my first curacy was in the poor part of town before I came here. The cathedral is a small one, but it is very richly endowed, and the bishop is a saintly man of frugal habits, so they have no need to levy the parishes. No, trust me, there is no levy."

"And the other things? The Reserve Account and the Reconciliation?"

"There could certainly be a Reserve Account, a bank or savings account where money could be put for safe keeping, but if there is, there ought to be another accounting of it, and there isn't. And Reconciliation, well, I have heard the word used in financial affairs, it's true. I think it means when you take two lots of accounts and fiddle around until they match. But there's only one set here ..."

"You know what this means, don't you?" said Pert. "This is cheating. He was relying on the fact that nobody would know what he was talking about, to pull the wool over their eyes."

"I fear you are right, my dear boy. This is fraud of a simple and rather blatant kind. I wonder where the money went to?"

"I reckon Grubb's behind it," Pert said. Fenestra stopped gazing round and looked at him wide-eyed. "She tried to get Tortice and Wetlow, well Tortice really, to do something similar, and he wouldn't, so she got rid of him, in a nasty way. And then she pushed her way onto the Church Council and wangled it so Prettyfoot could do the accounts, and he did it. They probably shared the money between them."

"Why didn't Sir Humphrey stop them?" asked Fenestra.

"I think by then he was getting fed up with being on the Church Council. Grubb was bullying everyone and getting things her own way, so he lost interest and dropped out. So did all the others, one by one. Mrs.Wheable, and the Widow Dolphin and those others. It was easier to just sit at home and let her get on with things than it was to fight with her. I expect if they'd fought her, she'd have done something nasty to them, and they knew it."

"And that's why they have a nice house, the Prettyfeet," Fenestra said. "It's all the church money."

"I found something else, too. Once they'd all gone and there was only Grubb and the Vicar running things, the payments from the Destitute Fund and the Poor Box kept coming in, but nothing went out. They kept it all. And then the accounts stop altogether."

"Oh, my goodness!" exclaimed Septimus. "That is really wicked! So all the householders in town are paying their tax and it all goes in Mistress Grubb's pocket?"

"And the Vicar's, and he sits in that big vicarage drinking it in whisky and lusting after Rosella," said Fenestra. "Whatever that means ..." she added unconvincingly.

Pert grinned at her. "I think you know exactly what it means," he said.

She jumped up and said indignantly "No I don't! Well, perhaps I've got just a tiny idea. Eugh, I've just thought – do you think he lusts after me as well? I'm pretty too! How disgusting!"

Pert ignored her. "The thing is," he said, "what can we do about it? Who could we tell, and would they take any notice?"

Septimus thought. "I suppose the proper person would be Captain Mattheson Fludd," he said, "he's the magistrate. But I'm not sure ..."

"He's a crony of Grubb's," said Fenestra. "April Scutch in my class, her mum's the cook there, and she says Grubb's always up there, and she comes in the kitchen and complains if the food's not to her liking, and it isn't even her house."

Pert knew of Captain Fludd. He had a very large house at the top of the town, and several servants, and a carriage with two horses. He was a big, florid man with a red face, and a reputation as a drinker. His wife was a small, pale woman who rarely spoke, and his many children were also small and pale. They had a tutor, and didn't go to school, so whether they spoke or not, Pert didn't know.

"So," he counted off on his fingers, "we can't tell the magistrate, we can't tell the Vicar because he's in it, we can't tell the Mayor because there isn't one, we can't tell the Free Fishers because there aren't any of them either. And if we tell the town, half of them won't believe us because they're scared to, and the other half will believe us but be too scared to do anything about it. What about the bishop?"

"The bishop. Yes, there's the bishop," said Septimus. "But as I said, he's a good and unworldly man. He wouldn't know what to do, faced with such wickedness. Oh, he has the power. He could dismiss the Vicar on the spot. But he's never had to do anything like it, and the first thing he'd do would be to take advice from some of the other senior clergy, and the thing would leak out and get back to Grubb before anything could happen. She'd cover her tracks, and her revenge ...", he shuddered. "I'm pretty scared of the Vicar, to tell the truth, so what she'd do would be ten times worse."

"She'd probably put it about that you've been lusting after me," said Fenestra smugly.

"Fenestra, you are truly impossible! I think I liked you better before you started growing up," said Pert. "Isn't it about time you were in bed? Come on, we'll both go. We can talk about this till the cows come home, but we're not going to think of a solution tonight."

"All right," she said. "I've just thought of a story anyway."

"I bet there's going to be some lusting in it, then," Pert said as he shut the door behind them. He hoped she didn't really know what it meant, because he wasn't sure himself. But he didn't like the sound of it.

XXI

I am a stranger in the earth (Psalm 119)

Septimus Surplice was not a courageous or active man. Not for him the posture of bold defiance, or the two-handed swing of the cudgel when wicked heads needed breaking. But he had his principles, he knew right from wrong, and like most meek men he had one or two tricks up his sleeve. As he had promised Pert some days before, he had written a letter to the head of his old seminary in St.Portius, and finally a reply had arrived. Before breakfast he took Pert into his room and read him the letter.

My Dear Surplice, it began ...

How very satisfactory to hear from you, and to know that you are happily placed in a worthwhile curacy. As you know, most of your classmates are rectors or vicars by now, and Gammon Major is a deacon, but temporal advancement is not for everybody and service to the Church can not be measured by mere rank.

The treasure you inquire about, could only be one thing. As you know, this diocese is a wealthy one, but its wealth is entirely in endowments and land rather than money or precious things. There has only ever been one treasure that I know of, and that was the fabled Hoard of Saint Erwald, lost these many centuries ago.

The Hoard was kept at the Monastery of St. Erwald. In times past these coasts were often infested by Moorish pirates, who came ashore and plundered the coastal settlements for gold, women and slaves, carrying them off to heathen parts. Bolder and bolder they grew until, meeting little resistance, they assembled a large fleet and landed in the north of the diocese. They marched inland, looting and burning as they went, and soon invested the Monastery of St. Erwald.

Before they were overwhelmed and put to the sword, the monks divided the Hoard and sent it away to all four corners of the diocese for safe keeping. After that the records reveal little. The pirates tired of the rain and cold and went home. The treasure remained hidden in different places. We know that some of it was lost when the Great Keep at Castle Fortitude burned down in suspicious circumstances. Much of it must have been purloined and sold or melted down by greedy clerics, or even by greedy bishops if they could find any of it, for we have not always been blessed with such a saintly leader as we are now.

So I would guess that the rumours you mention refer to some small part of that Hoard, sent into your remote fastness for safety and there forgotten. It is just as well that they are only rumours, for if there were any substance to them, it would be a long and tedious and divisive business to establish ownership.

That is all I can tell you. You may not have heard that I am to retire soon. My Lord the Bishop has granted me a pleasant house in the cathedral close, the Widow Makepiece has kindly agreed to keep house for me, and I plan to spend my days completing my twelve-volume History of the Diocese from 1520 to 1650, growing roses, and practising the art of pipe smoking, a pleasure I have only recently discovered, *for as long as the Good Lord shall spare me before He gathers me to his eternal garden where I understand mature horse dung is available at knock-down prices.*

Until then I remain,

Affectionately your proud Friend and Mentor,

Aloysius Flitch, Canon in Ordinary

"There!" the curate beamed, "my dear old tutor remembers me and sends me the most kind regards. How gratifying that is! And he has been able to shed a little light on the alleged treasure. We may not know where it went to, but we now have an idea where it may have come from. And it never belonged to the town or the church, but was simply sent here for safe keeping."

"That's good to know," said Pert, "but it really doesn't move us forward at all. I'm sorry to say ..." he added, looking anxiously at the curate in case he was disappointing him.

"No, no, that's quite correct," said Septimus. "I understand your reservations entirely. It was just a case of leaving no stone unturned, you know. If the information was to be had, it was only right that we should seek it."

"Speaking of seeking, and stones unturned, there is one stone we haven't tried to turn yet, and that's the floor of the vestry," Pert said.

"But I understand that you are no longer a *bona fide* servant of the church. I hope you aren't suggesting that I should dig up the vestry floor while the Vicar's back is turned? I don't think I'd be very good at that."

"No, not at all. I may have been sacked, but I still know how to get into the church, don't I? Today's Tuesday, so the Vicar will be celebrating spoken Evensong this evening. And he's usually fairly drunk by the end of the service, so with a bit of luck he'll lurch off home to sleep it off. That'll be my chance!"

He spent the afternoon with his mind whirling with plans for the evening's escapade. Should he take a shovel? Might he need rope? Was he indeed getting his hopes up for nothing? – there had only been that one little indication that anything at all lay under the vestry floor, the phrase *"ye crypte under ye vestrie"*. It might just have been careless writing, and he might be reading more into it that he should.

Because he was so preoccupied, the dreadful news was all the more shocking when it came. Fenestra burst into the house with Billy in tow, and thrust a crumpled note into his hand.

Roseld hav been sent away

a new gurl as come to look after
us she is nice but can you get
Roseld bak plees

April Prettyfoot (miss)

Pert felt his face grow pale, and he sat down hard at the foot of the stairs. What had they done with Rosella? Where had they taken her? Indeed, who was "they"? Was it her father? Or ... dreadful thought but all the more likely, was Urethra Grubb involved?

"Oh Pert," his sister said almost in tears, "what's going on? She only ran away with you for an afternoon, it's not as if she killed anyone! I think I'm going to cry, sorry. Sorry, Billy, thank you for bringing me home, but I have to go now ..." and she ran upstairs.

"I know how she feels," said Pert. Billy said nothing. It was incredible, but he managed to grin and look sad at the same time.

"Guv, I'll go an' sneak around an' see if I can find out anyfink," he said. "There's places I can creep an' conversashuns I can 'ear, an' people speak unguarded when they don' think Billy's anywhere near. You leave it ter me!" and he disappeared out of the back door.

Pert sat for a moment, feeling desperate, but he knew Billy was right. Billy was far better placed to get information than he was. It was odd how you trusted Billy. He was the most unlikely person, dirty, ignorant, smelly and completely disreputable, but somehow you knew you could leave things to him and they'd get done.

Meanwhile, he had his own job to do. Later would be a time to act on Rosella, once Billy had learned what there was to learn. Now, it was time to go to church.

He hid in the churchyard until he judged the service was nearly over, and then ran round to the vestry door, keeping low behind the yew trees. He heard voices at the west end as the congregation left – only a few people at this time, he knew. Soon the vestry door opened and the Vicar came out.

Pert watched from his hiding place as the Vicar stooped and locked the door behind him, then walked round the end of the church towards the Vicarage. He walked slowly, his long limbs like the stilts of a wading bird, lifting his feet high. His sharp nose moved from side to side as though seeking prey between the tombstones. Seeking whom he might devour, thought Pert, remembering the scriptures in school.

When the Vicar was safely out of sight Pert walked to the west door and found the great key in its hiding place under a flag-stone. He opened the church, slipped inside and locked the door behind him so he could not be disturbed. The tall darkness waited for him, the saints and angels gazing down, wondering what this sinner was doing here. The silence and the damp hymnbook smell were familiar yet strange, no longer belonging to him, nor he to them.

In the vestry the cassocks and surplices hung on their hooks as always. He dragged the big table from the centre of the room, and then with difficulty turned it on its side. Beneath it lay a large rug of something coarse and prickly, coconut matting, he thought. It had lain there as long as he could remember, and when he grasped it by one end and started rolling it along the floor it left thick dust on the floor in a herring-bone pattern.

There in the middle of the floor, scarcely distinguishable from the stone flags under the dust, was a square shape of a different texture. He swept the dust aside with his hand, and found planks of wood, knotted and dry and old. It was a trap door.

The wood was a tight fit against the stone, and had clearly been so for many years. Pert looked in the cassock cupboard for a tool of some sort, and found the broken end of a candle-snuffer. The conical snuffer had come off, leaving only the flat end of metal to which it had been soldered. He used this to scrape around the edges of the trap door, and then tried inserting it in the gap he had created, but when he levered upwards it bent.

He needed something more substantial. Taking a stub of altar candle from the shelf and a box of matches, he opened the door to the crypt stairs and let himself down between the stone walls.

In the crypt he ignored the flickering shadows, stubbornly not thinking about what else might lie down here in the darkness, and rummaged in the piles of broken furniture until he found the massive iron leaf of an old door-hinge. The end looked thin enough to fit in the crack.

It proved to be the right size, and the iron strong enough to be a lever. Several minutes of desperate, sweaty work round the edges of the trap, and he found which was the right side to lift. With a creak the door surrendered and lifted an inch or two. A little gust of cold air came up, bringing a smell of damp stone and earth and darkness long confined. He propped the door up with a hymnbook, and levered again, gaining another two inches. Another hymnbook, and he was getting somewhere at last. With a crash the door came up and fell back on itself, and there at his feet was a stone stairway leading down into the shadows.

He waited a while to be sure the noise hadn't alarmed anyone, lit the candle again and began to go down the stairs. He felt very frightened, but thought of Rosella. She must be even more scared than he was. He thought of Billy, too. Billy was never scared. Billy would just grin and get on with it, and so must he.

His feet reached earth at the bottom, after a dozen or so high steps, and he felt rather than saw a wider space around him. He stood at one side of a room, and in the flickering candle light he could see a flat, beaten earth floor, some wooden shelves, and a wall on the other side of great worked stones. These must be the very foundation stones of the church, and that was the outside wall of the nave. There was very little litter. The room had clearly not been used, like the crypt, for general storage. One or two items lay forgotten on the shelves, and he went to examine them. A roll of cloth, that fell apart with a musty smell as he lifted it. Some pieces of paper with writing so faded it was indecipherable. And a little bundle wrapped in what felt like soft leather. It had an oily texture, so perhaps it had been greased once upon a time to make it last. He laid it on the floor and unwrapped it. Something small winked at him in the folds of leather. It was a spoon, a pretty little spoon no longer than his hand, made of yellow metal with chasing on the handle and elegant curlicues of the same metal extending onto the back of the bowl. Was this gold? It felt heavy for something so small, heavy and old and somehow warm, as though it wanted to be found and taken into the light, away from this eternal darkness. It was not a creature of the cold shadows, but yearned for the sun. He slipped it into his pocket.

At the far end of the room was a doorway. A single step led into another room, completely bare, again with stone walls and an earthen floor. For the first time he looked up at the ceiling, and saw curved stone vaulting, carefully shaped to support the weight of the earth and stone flags and pews above it. The air was cool and damp but not musty, and he thought that there must be some outlet that let the outside atmosphere in.

There was yet another doorway ahead of him. He judged that he must by now be halfway down the nave of the church, but right at the northern edge of the nave against the foundations of the north wall. On his left must lie the main crypt, behind stone and earth and then more stone. He walked to the new doorway and looked in, holding the candle high.

This was not a third room, but a passageway, a tunnel with stone sides and roof. It sloped sharply downward and away to the right. It must pass under or through the church foundations, under the yew trees and down towards the Market Square. He walked cautiously on, and presently found tangled roots that had eased their way down between the stones, looking for moisture. When they had failed to find it, they had died and hung there. They were probably the roots of the yew trees, he thought.

His candle was guttering now, so there must be a tiny breeze coming up the tunnel towards him, but it had burned very low and was starting to hurt his fingers. Time to go back, and come again another day, better prepared. Also, he had left the vestry quite long enough with the table and carpet pushed aside. He needed to cover his tracks.

Back in the vestry he closed the door quietly, then put the candle and the matches back on the shelf and hid the tool he had found. Then he rolled the carpet back over the door, and manhandled the table. This took a long time as he had to lift one corner of the table at a time, move it a little way, then do the other side, so as not to ruck up the carpet.

He was just looking round one more time to check that he had left everything tidy and normal, when he heard the scrape of a footfall on the path outside the vestry door. Someone was coming. He ran to the door into the church, but there was no time to make his escape that way – the west door of the church was big and heavy and the latch always clanked. It could not be unlocked and opened and then closed again without making a noise.

He scampered to the cassock cupboard and climbed inside, then sank down in the corner and pulled the cassocks over and round him with a wildly beating heart. He felt scared, not so much of the Vicar – he thought he could probably manage the Vicar provided he was alone – but of being found out so that he would not be able to come here again and pursue this mystery. A tunnel, a tunnel from the church, secret rooms and a tunnel. This was a puzzle that needed exploration. And in his pocket was the gold spoon, so if he was caught he'd be stealing again.

"Why do we have to come here?" grumbled the Vicar's voice, and the key rattled in the lock. "If you want to talk, why can't we do it at the Vicarage?"

"Because of ears," was the gruff reply. Pert stiffened. It was the voice of Mistress Grubb. "I don't trust your servants. You don't have them scared enough, you weak fool. I'm not running the risk that one of them might have a sneaky ear glued to your keyhole. And there's something here we need to find."

Heavy feet stamped at the door and shuffled into the room. The door closed behind them.

"Very well, Mistress, what is so important that it must be said now and must be said in such privacy?" grumbled the Vicar.

"You can stop the sarcasm," Grubb replied. "Don't you sarcasm me, you weasel! I'll have your hide if you sarcasm me! I'll beat your scrawny body, and I'll expose your filthy soul, and I'll have you dragged through the streets for a thief and a drunkard and a lecher! I know your secrets, right enough, don't I, vicar? How's that for sarcasm?"

The Vicar said nothing.

"Now. With that blackguard Teague sitting in the harbour and his men swarming all over the place, we need to do a bit of house-keeping. I can control him for the moment, because he thinks I'm helping him get his hands on the man Potts, if he still lives which I doubt, and the treasure, if such a thing exists which I also doubt. But it won't last. There'll be trouble sooner or later, and I have to make sure it goes my way and not his."

"Madam, I see your point, but what has this to do with a humble clergyman?"

"Humble clergyman my eye! Dirty old lecher with his brains in a bottle, more like! What this has to do with you, is that I need to be sure there's no record of our financial dealings. Prettyfoot's taken care of, but I'm not taking any chances. What records are there still?"

"I don't know. I never look at them. There are some boxes under the altar, but I don't know what's in them."

"Get them out. Get them out and destroy them, do you under-stand? I'll send two of my girls up here in one hour's time, and they can carry the stuff out into the churchyard and you'll have

197

a bonfire, is that clear? And keep your hands off my girls while you're at it! You can give 'em a kick if they slack, but that's all, d'you hear?"

"Madam, I ..."

"Shut up! Now what else is there?"

"I think there used to be some books in the cupboard behind you."

"Books? What sort of books?"

"I don't know, thin books, handwritten. Old. I need a drink."

"You can wait. Get these books out!"

There was the sound of the key in the lock, and the squeak as the cupboard opened. Pert tensed. This could be very awkward.

There was a scuffling sound. "Madam, I can't ... they don't seem to be here."

Suddenly there was a crashing sound, and a gasping, and the Vicar cried out in pain.

"You bloody idiot!" shouted Grubb. It sounded as though she had him by the throat. "You pathetic, addle-brained, perverted old Bible-thumper! Have you nothing in your worm-riddled head but whisky and looking up young girls' skirts? What have you done with them? You'll find them, you'll lay your hands on 'em or I'll lay my hands on you! I'll throttle you till you're dead, and then I'll wake you up and throttle you some more! Then I'll tear bits off and stuff them down your throat, so help me!"

The Vicar was whimpering and kicking, but evidently couldn't escape. "Madam ... please!" he whispered, his voice strangled in his throat, "I don't ... what's so important about them?"

"They're probably the accounts, you idiot! If anyone got hold of them, they might be able to figure out where all the church funds have gone, and the Town Levy. If they've got any brains, that is, which isn't likely round here."

"I didn't realise it was written down anywhere," said the Vicar sheepishly.

"That fool Prettyfoot was so proud of himself, with his weasel words and his subterfuges. I told him to just stop keeping accounts, I told him as soon as I found out what he was doing, but he thought he was so clever ... well, he soon found out just how clever he was, didn't he, sitting up in that nice house with his nice family. Oh, I squeezed him dry, I did! I squeezed on his neck until his eyes popped! I throttled him until he was offering me anything I wanted. And I took it, too – money, his business, his house is mine now, the deeds all tucked safely away in my drawer ..."

She chuckled. It was a horrible sound to hear, full of ancient malice.

"And now I got his daughter! Stroppy little madam, but I'll break her, you see if I don't. I'll whip her legs and make her howl! I'll give her stripes and make her sing!" and she broke into song herself, a terrible sound, grating and foul and frightening ...

> "Smile, my pretty, laugh and flirt," she sang,
> "Beguile the men with all your art;
> I'll drag you back into the dirt,
> and make your pretty bottom smart!"

"... and then ..." she continued in a dreadful whisper, "then, when I've finished with her, I'll send her up to you. You could do with a new scullery maid, couldn't you? The old one's just about used up by now, I should think. I'll send her up to the Vicarage."

"You will?" The Vicar's voice sounded thick and hot, somehow.

"Yes, I said, didn't I? No one cares what happens to the miserable little slut, and her father's in no position to complain. Take my advice – give her a damn good whipping first, and she'll be no trouble. It works for my girls at the shop. But remember this, my friend ..."

Her voice sunk even lower. "You only get her if you find those accounts for me. You find those accounts, Tench, or I'll Tench your gullet and I'll Tench your liver and I'll Tench your lights out, and you'll get no little pretty to wash your dishes and play your games with!"

"Madam, I'll ... do my best ..." but Grubb was gone with a stamp of her big boots and a slam of the door. Pert could hear her heavy tread all the way to the west door.

He listened while the Vicar, from the sound of it, made another desperate search for the missing accounts books. Pert grinned, knowing they were safely hidden in his chimney breast. It didn't sound as though Tench were going to get his hands on Rosella in a hurry, which was a relief.

Then the cupboard door was locked, and the the vestry door banged, and the Vicar was gone too. But he would be back in an hour, to sort out the boxes under the altar, so Pert must be quick. He emerged from the cassock cupboard, slipped out of the vestry and down the length of the church, and locked the great door behind him. Then he sauntered casually back to the Canonry. For all his desperation for Rosella, he felt strangely satisfied. All his fear of the Vicar had vanished. How could you take anyone seriously when you'd heard him being throttled against the wall, whimpering while a woman told him how she was going to tear bits of him off and feed them to him?

Night had fallen while he was under the ground, and the lights in the Market Square were going out as the stall holders packed up for the day. He kept a weather eye open for bullies or pirates, but it was Billy he found at the bottom of the Bearward.

"What ho, guv!" said the boy cheerfully. "I found 'er, I knows where she is, all right. Grubb's got this boy, see. Everyone thinks it's just the shop girls, but she's got this little lad as well, weedy little streak o' wind, 'e is, wouldn't say boo to a goose an mortal scared o' Grubb! But I talks to 'im sometimes, see? I climbs up on the fence when 'e's out in the yard doin' the dustbins an' that, an' I talks to 'im over the wall!"

"What did he tell you?"

"She's in the cellar, locked up. An' she's been kickin' up a terrible rumpus, shoutin' and yellin' an' bangin' the door, an' all the other girls is runnin' roun' scared out of their wits in case Grubb might take it out on them. Grubb went in there to give 'er what for, and Rosella attacked 'er with a chair an' smashed it over 'er back, so now she's locked the door and says she'll see what 'unger an' thirst'll do."

Pert laughed. "That sounds like Rosella, all right," he said. "I wonder if there's any way we could get to her? Either get her out, or at least bring her some food and water?"

"Prob'ly is, guv. I'll nip back an' recco ... rec ... you know, that word ... 'ave a look round!" And Billy was gone.

He returned after supper, and was invited in and sat, legs swinging, at the kitchen table and ate a bowl of Mother's broth. Mother looked a bit askance at the smell whenever she got near him, but seemed to accept him. He had earned her trust by looking after Fenestra so faithfully, turning up every morning early, waiting in the street and grinning as she appeared.

"I tell him my stories," Fenestra had explained. "I tell him the first bit on the way to school, and then a bit more at playtime and a bit at lunchtime and a bit more in the afternoon, and then I try and spin it out so we get to the end on the way home. And Mother, could I take two sandwiches, so I can give one to him and still have one myself?"

"It's incredibly patient of him," said Mother, "to listen to your stories every day all the way through."

"He likes it. He thinks my stories are good. He says he wants me to write one that has him in it."

"That seems only fair," agreed Mother. "I'll make two sandwiches tomorrow."

Billy finished his broth and wiped his mouth on his sleeve. "Nice, mum, thanking you," he said. "I found out, guv, what we was talkin' about. We can't do the one, but we can do the other."

"What's he talking about?" asked Fenestra. Pert wondered whether they ought to have this conversation in private, but decided it was too serious not to share.

"Grubb's got Rosella locked up in her cellar," he said. Mother gasped and put her hand to her mouth, and Fenestra paled.

"Why?" she said.

"Don't know. Because she can. Her father let it happen. And Rosella's been shouting and carrying on, so they've locked her up and they're starving her."

"I bin down there," put in Billy. "I sneaked all aroun', an' I can't see no way we can get 'er out, not unless we 'ad someone on the inside, so ter speak. But I foun' something else."

"Go on," said Pert.

"There's this grating thing, see, in the pavement down the alley on the far side. Tiny little alley it is, no one don't 'ardly use it. An' the gratin' leads into 'er cellar where she is. It sort of curves, it don't go straight in. I fink they used ter tip coal down it."

"Could we lift the grating and get her out that way?"

"No, I tried. It's stuck fast. Two or three big men might do it, but not any of us. But we could speak to 'er through it, an' we could put food an' drink down it, and she could climb up an' snag it an' pull it down. It would have to be thin food an' drink, though, mum, 'cos the 'oles in the gratin' isn't very wide."

"Slices of bread?" asked Mother.

"Yes'm, they'd go."

But drink's a problem. Let me think ..."

"Balloons!" said Fenestra. "We could use balloons! Fill them half full with water so they're floppy, and push them through the grating. Then she could just pinch the corner out and drink it!"

"Brilliant! Have we got any?" said Pert.

"I think we have, but not many," said Mother. She searched in the kitchen drawers, and found five balloons left over from Christmas. They experimented, and found that it worked much better if you blew the balloon up first, and then let it down again and poured water in. Only one balloon burst, so they filled four and knotted the necks. Mother sliced bread thinly, spread it with butter and wrapped each slice in kitchen paper.

"Right!" said Billy. "I'll do the first lot. I'll do it now. But four little mouthfuls of water and a few slices of bread aren't goin' ter last very long. We'll 'ave to do it again tomorrow night."

"Mrs.Toogood will have balloons, I'm sure. I'll buy some in the morning," Pert said. "And I'm coming with you now. I can't not speak to Rosella."

Fenestra rolled her eyes at her mother, but Mother said "Of course you must. Just take care you're not caught, either of you. And you're both to come back here so I know you're safe. What will you use for money tomorrow? We're getting very short this week, and I've Septimus's suppers to think of."

"I've got something," said Pert. "Leave it to me."

It was exciting, slipping down Bearward as quietly as they could, carrying their little cargo of contraband, and it was exciting that they were going to speak to Rosella, too. They flitted from shadow to shadow, Pert following Billy's lead, then sprinted across the Square and into the narrow alley mouth.

"'Ere it is," whispered Billy. "This is the gratin' wot I said."

It was indeed an insignificant thing, set into the cobbles and slightly overgrown with moss and weeds round the edges. It clearly hadn't been lifted for many years, but Pert wondered what a lever and fulcrum might do. He'd been pretty successful with the trap door in the church.

He put his head down to the grating and whispered "Rosella?", and listened.

"Rosella?" he said a little louder. Billy crouched above him, looking up and down the alley.

There was a little sound, and then a tiny voice. "Pert? Where are you?"

"Rosella, I'm up here in the alley!"

"Your voice is coming from a hole in the ceiling, but I can't see anything!"

She sounded hoarse, and weak, and not happy at all.

"We can't get you out yet, but we've got some food and drink for you," he whispered. "I'm posting it through a grating. You need to get up to the hole and feel around in it."

"There's a chair, I can stand on that. I broke the other one, hitting Grubb, so she locked me in and left me!"

Pert began posting the little parcels between the slats of the gratings, and heard them fall with a soft "plop!". There was a scrabbling sound, and a flash of white fingers at the bottom of the hole.

"Got one!" she whispered. "Oh, Pert, you're a genius, thank you so much!"

"There's four balloons and five bits of bread. We'll be back with more tomorrow night."

"Pert, Pert? Listen, I need my boots. I have to have my boots! I can put up with anything if I have my boots, but without them I feel so defenceless!"

"I don't know how I'll get them past the grating," he said, "but I'll try and find a way. I've got to get them out of your house first."

"Thank you, Pert. Who's that with you?"

"Billy Moon."

"Coo, who'd have thought? Thank you Billy!"

"'S'all right, miss! We got ter scarper now, 'case someone comes. No point pushin' our luck, like."

Reluctantly Pert tore himself away, and they crept up to the top of the alley and out into the street. Billy led the way past the front of the Emporium and then paused at the top of the next alley, the one with the window where Pert had listened and first seen Trinity Teague.

"Jus' a quick look," hissed Billy. "You stay 'ere an' give a little whistle, quiet-like, if anyone's comin'."

He was back in a moment. "Come on," he said, sounding serious. They ran over the road and up the Bearward. When they reached Pert's gate, Billy stopped.

"'Ere's a turn-up an' no mistake!" he said. "There's pirates in there!"

"What, in Grubb's cellar?"

"Yeah, in that room where the window onto the alley is, an' you can see in. There's those two from the Drop o' Dew, Shattock and Smy, sat there at the table bold as brass! They's got pistols on the table, an' their knives out, an' they're sittin' there in Grubb's basement smokin' their pipes."

Pert thought. This was, indeed, a turn of events. Were the pirates there to guard Rosella and make sure she didn't escape? Or were they there because Teague didn't trust Grubb and wanted to keep an eye on her? It was a mystery. Poor Rosella, things just kept getting worse and worse for her, and he was further and further from saving her.

"We'd better get in the house," he said, "Mother will be worrying."

Billy left shortly after, taking a great hunk of bread and butter with him. Pert drank some milk and went up to bed. An alarming idea had just come to him, and he needed to think it through. If they couldn't rescue Rosella from the cellar of the Emporium, perhaps they could rescue her from somewhere else. If Grubb got the accounts books back, she'd promised to send Rosella to Vicar Tench.

It would be a lot easier to rescue someone from a vicarage, with ordinary doors and windows and servants coming and going, than it would be from a cellar guarded by pirates. But that meant in the first place giving the accounts back, and more importantly delivering Rosella into the hands of a cruel, deeply unpleasant man who might have sinister plans for her. Any rescue would have to be quick, and it would have to be successful.

XXII

A very present help in trouble (Psalm 46)

Pert had thought of the gold coin Teague had given him. If he could sell it or change it into ordinary money, he'd be able to buy the balloons, but he didn't know how to go about it. He decided to ask Mr.Surplice.

"Oh no," said the curate, turning it over in his fingers. "No, I don't think you should do anything with this, not right now. If you took it to the bank or to a solicitor and asked them to change it, there'd be questions. What is it, where did you get it and so on? The alternative would be to find a jeweller or goldsmith to buy it from you, and I can't think that there is such a person in the town. And if there were, the same would apply – awkward questions!"

"And if it got out, people might guess it was pirate money and they'd be even more certain that I was in league with them," said Pert despondently.

"What do you need the money for?"

"Balloons."

"Oh, I say, balloons? Are we having a party?"

"No. It's ... look, it's difficult to explain. I just need balloons, that's all. It's really important." Pert had not yet told Septimus about what he had heard in the vestry, and what he had found underneath it. He meant to, and he meant to tell him about Rosella too, but it was going to be a long story and he wanted to pick his time to tell it. And there was always the risk that the curate would be all grown-up about it, and advise him to stop what he was doing. And he had no intention of stopping at all.

"Well," said Septimus. "I'll tell you what. I have a few coppers put by. Why don't I buy the balloons? Only if there is a party, I trust you will invite me to it!"

"I promise," said Pert. "When there's a party, you'll be the first to know!"

He took the curate's coppers gratefully and ran down to Mrs. Toogood. Sure enough, she had two packets of balloons tucked away.

"They're only one packet of blue and one of yellow, though," she said. "I sold all the red ones."

He assured her that blue and yellow were his favourites of all colours, and ran back in time to walk down to the school with Fenestra and Billy. At the school gates they came upon a little crocodile of Prettyfeet, all holding hands. Leading them was a girl in grey, plain clothes. From the back she looked a little familiar, and when they came level it was the shop girl he had spoken to at the Emporium.

"Hallo," he said, "what are you doing here?"

"I'm not supposed to talk to anyone," she said nervously. Seen in daylight, she was less pale than he thought, and had a pleasant, rather plump face. This time she had tied her hair back so her face wasn't hidden.

"Who says?"

"Her. Mistress Grubb."

"Oh. That is a problem, because I really want to talk to you."

The girl looked up and down the street in panic. Her little charges had vanished into the playground with Fenestra and Billy.

"I don't ... oh, all right, I'll take a chance. Look, walk behind me, just casual like, as though we're not together but just walking the same way."

"We are, aren't we?" Pert said, falling in behind her.

"Yes, but you never know who might be watching," she said over her shoulder.

In fact they said nothing until they turned up the Bearward, and then she evidently felt a little safer.

"You're the boy who came into the shop Christmas morning, aren't you? And you're Rosella's friend?"

"Yes. Do you know anything about Rosella? What are you doing with her sisters? Do you know where her boots are?"

She laughed over her shoulder at him. She had a nice laugh. "That's a lot of questions," she said. "Mistress Grubb sent me up to look after the little girls, because their mother keeps locking herself in the dining room and there's no one to look after them now Rosella's at the Emporium. And I'm supposed to tell Mistress Grubb what's going on, but I ain't."

"Aren't you scared of her?"

"Of course I am. Everyone's scared of her, an' I ain't no different. Only there's nothing much to tell. The little girls are no trouble, really, and Mrs.P's locked in the dining room an' cries a lot, and Mr.P justs sits in 'is study and doesn't do much. 'E looks at me a bit funny, mind. I put a chair under me doorknob last night, in case 'e decided to come in, but 'e never."

"What about Rosella?"

"Ah, she's causing a stink, an' then some! Screaming an' shoutin' an' bashin' about, an' smashin' a chair over Grubb's 'ead, it were really somethin', that were! I wish I were brave like that!"

"But she's been locked up for it, hasn't she?"

"Yes. Silly of 'er really. If she jus' did what she were told, an' got on with it like the rest of us, it wouldn't be so bad. Servin' in the shop's all right, you don't get hit when there are people lookin'. An' if you keeps yer nose clean, you just get the odd kick when she feels like it, and a reg'lar whippin' once a week, which she says as keeps you "pliant", whatever that is."

"Whipping? Does she use a real whip?"

"Yes. One o' them little ones they use on 'orses," she said. "It 'urts, that does, especially when she does it on yer bare skin. I could show you some bruises, I could. 'Cept I'm not goin' to," she added.

"So you're better off here, then?"

"Coo, yes, I should think! Long as Mr.P keeps 'is 'ands to 'imself, I'm well suited!"

"What about the boots?"

"Don't know. I'll look around, see what I can find out. I got to go in now. Mr.P might be watchin', an' I got to start lunch. It's rolled pork, an' that takes ages."

Pert stopped and let her get ahead. She paused at the Prettyfoot gate, and looked back.

"What's yer name again?" she whispered.

"Pert. What's yours?"

"Floris."

"Isn't that a boy's name?"

"No, it's mine. It might have been a boy's name once, but I got it now. See you!" and she ran up the garden path.

Pert went in and knocked at Mr.Surplice's door.

"Septimus?" he said, "can I come in? I've got stuff to tell you!"

The curate opened the door, and ushered Pert inside.

"Your mother's told me about Rosella," Septimus said. "How awful! That poor, poor girl!"

"Yes, it is awful. But we're feeding her through a grating. That's what the balloons were for. And I've got a plan for getting her out, but it's not finished yet. I've got to think about it a lot, and talk to Billy about it. We'll be needing him."

"Yes, a very useful young man, that. Smelly, but useful. What else did you have to tell me?"

Pert launched into his account of the expedition to the vestry and what he had found beneath it. Septimus was awe-struck by the spoon.

"This is beautiful!" he said. "It looks very old, and I'm almost sure it's gold. It's not tarnished, you see, and that's why people first started to value gold so highly – its beauty never dims. This could easily be part of a hoard."

"So it's a sort of proof that the hoard was in the room under the vestry, then?"

"Well, not proof exactly, but it seems to point that way, yes."

"And after I found it, I found something else - there's a tunnel! It goes under the nave, and out at the north west corner, and under the churchyard and across the Canonry I should think. I couldn't go far because my candle ran out."

"Oh my goodness! This just gets more and more extraordinary!"

"It does, doesn't it? So I need to go back with some more candles, and explore it properly. If the treasure was down there, maybe someone took it out down the tunnel. Or perhaps it's still down there somewhere."

"Well, I'm not sure that's a good idea ..."

"You're not going to go all grown up on me, are you?"

"Suppose the tunnel caves in? Suppose there are hidden traps, or pitfalls, or wild animals? Bears live in caves. Or bats. Or snakes. Or ... anything could happen. You might get lost. It's dangerous!"

"Oh, pooh! There have never been any bears round here. Bats are tiny, and the only snakes are adders and grass snakes. Grass snakes are harmless, and adders are really little. And the other things ... well, I think you've been reading too many stories. I suppose Fenestra hasn't taken to writing about a princess who lives in a cave, has she?"

Septimus laughed. "No, but I expect she will when she hears about this!"

"And there's more. When I was in the vestry, Tench and Grubb turned up!"

The curate paled. "They caught you?"

"No, I had time to clear up and hide in the cupboard. And I could hear them talking, and it was awful! She as good as admitted that we were right about the money – she and Prettyfoot and Tench have been robbing everyone blind for years. And she said that if Tench gave her the account books to destroy, he could have Rosella. They didn't say what for, but it didn't sound good."

"Oh my goodness, this is too much! That there should be so much wickedness in this town, and the church in the thick of it! I really should leave here, go to St.Portius and talk to the bishop."

"No, no, no, that's the last thing! Look, I have a plan. Well, half a plan, anyway. I can't rescue Rosella from Grubb's, because it's too difficult and there are two pirates guarding it. But I probably could get her out of a house, like the vicarage. I haven't worked out the details, yet, but it has to be possible. But I need you to think of something for me ..."

"Anything, dear boy."

"Can you work out how I can get the account books back again so Tench can find them and give them to Grubb, but do it in such a way that we can still prove what's been going on if we need to?"

"Give them to Grubb ...?"

"That's the price she wants for Rosella, don't you see? If she gets them, she hands Rosella over to him, and that gives us a chance to rescue her!"

"Oh my goodness. It all sounds very dangerous to me. The Vicar ... he's a terrible man ..."

"Not all that terrible. Grubb hoisted him up the wall and practically throttled him. He was so frightened he almost wet himself. He's not as scary as all that!"

"Oh. Well, in that case ... I'll see what I can ..."

They were interrupted by a commotion downstairs. They ran down to find a wide-eyed Floris in the doorway.

"Please, let me in!" she said. "Quick! 'E went out, so I come over, but I don't know where 'e's gone or 'ow long 'e'll be!"

"Yes, come in, quick!" said Pert. "Mother, this is Floris. She's looking after the little Prettyfeet, and she was never here."

"Wasn't she?" said Mother, looking confused. "Oh, I see! No, I never saw her!"

"And Floris, this is Mr.Surplice, the curate. Only we call him Septimus."

Septimus stood at the foot of the stairs, with a strange look on his face, as though he had just been struck by lightning, or a pain in the stomach.

"Oh," breathed Floris, "ain't 'e sweet!" Then she recovered her composure and curtsied. "I got the boots, Master Pert! I found 'em in the boot room, where else? An' ..." she fiddled with something under her skirt, revealing a length of plump but shapely calf, "'ere they are!" With a thud, Rosella's boots fell on the floor.

"I tied a string to 'em, and slung it round me waist under me skirts!" she said proudly. "They did 'alf swing about, though. Me ankles are black an' blue now!"

"Won't you get found out?"

"No, I foun' some ol' gardener's boots in the shed, an' swapped 'em over. Boots is boots, to most people. They won't notice unless they looks close."

She stared once more at Septimus, a look of longing on her face. "I got to go! Quick, I got to go!" She vanished out of the door, and the gate swung behind her with a bang.

"Well!" said Mother. "What a surprising young lady!"

"Oh my goodness," said Septimus quietly.

In the afternoon Pert walked down to meet Billy and Fenestra. He and Billy had to plan the evening's expedition to take food for Rosella, and he rather hoped to be able to speak to Floris again and see if he could learn a little more about life at the Emporium. It might be useful.

At the gate his sister was already waiting, with Billy grinning in attendance. Floris was there too, and she glanced round nervously before sidling up to him.

"'Ere," she whispered, "that Mr.Surplice, 'e's lovely! ... 'e ain't ... er ... spoken for, is 'e? There ain't no Mrs.Curate?"

"Er, no ... feel free!"

Floris looked relieved, and moved away as the Prettyfeet came out of the playground. Pert found Fenestra looking at him with an expression of glee.

"Crumbs!" she breathed, "was she saying what I think she was saying? Crumbs!"

She took his arm, and they began to walk up the hill, Billy on the other side. "Of course, that does mean he'll have to stop lusting after me," she said quietly. "I'll just have to make do with Billy. But Billy," she turned and said sternly, "there'll be no lusting until you've had a proper bath! I mean it!"

"Oo-er," said Billy, grinning.

Septimus was waiting for them when they got in.

"I think we may be able to get the accounts books back," he said furtively. "Can you go and get them?"

Safely ensconced in his room, with Billy and Fenestra perched on the bed, Septimus took the books and flicked through them.

215

"If I take these and hide them under some other rubbish in the cassock cupboard, with a bit of luck Tench will find them and think they were there all the time," he said. "I can't believe he ever took much notice of them before, so we should get away with it."

"And how do we manage about keeping some of the evidence?"

"Well, we ought to keep one book to show how the accounts used to be kept, before Prettyfoot came on the scene. Tench and Mistress Grubb won't be certain when the accounts started, so if we hang on to the very earliest book they won't be any the wiser."

He searched through the books and set aside the oldest one, from 1879.

"Now, as to the later ones, we daren't keep any of them back. But I thought we might just remove a page or two. This one, for instance ..."

He pulled out the very last book. "If we carefully cut out one or two pages here, perhaps they'll think they just fell out."

"They probably won't even look, they'll just put them on the fire," said Pert. "But I've got a better idea. Let's pull the book to bits, as though it just got battered about in the cupboard and fell apart, and then a few pages missing won't seem odd at all."

And this is what they did. They broke the back of the binding by bending it back and forwards, and then craftily sawed through some of the binding threads with a blunt knife so there would be no neat cut edge. The pages came loose in pairs, so it was easy to remove a couple of sheets. Then they stuffed the whole thing back together again, and it looked exactly like a notebook that had seen some rough use.

"Perfect!" said the curate. "Now, you take the evidence, Pert, and keep it safe and hidden, and I'll smuggle the rest into the vestry and hide it in the cupboard."

Suddenly he looked very serious. "But Pert," he said, "you do realise what you're doing, don't you? You do realise that by giving these back you could be putting Rosella in even greater danger than she is now?"

"Golly, how can she be in any greater danger than she is now?" puzzled Fenestra. "She's shut up in a cellar with nothing to eat and drink with two pirates outside the door!"

"Oh, I think there could be even worse things," said Septimus. "That man Tench ..."

"Don't let's think about it," pleaded Pert. "If I let myself think about it I get all paralysed and can't plan properly! And that's what I have to do now, I have to make a plan that really will work, to get her out of the vicarage pretty much the moment she arrives."

"And once you've done that, what then? Where are you going to hide her? Grubb won't just give up, you know."

"I've thought of that. I'm going to hide her under the vestry. We can put food and drink and bedding and candles down there, and she should be safe enough for a couple of days. But you'll have to help, Septimus, because every time we go in there we have to shift the table and the carpet."

"What are you talking about?" demanded Fenestra. "What's under the vestry? You never told me that?"

"I found a room there, a sort of cave. I thought Rosella could hide there."

"Gosh, hiding in a cave! How romantic!"

"Yes, but cold and lonely, I think," said Septimus. "Not all that much better than where she is now."

"Better than Tench," said Pert. "But what we need to know is where that tunnel goes. I mean, we might be able to get in and out from the other end and never have to go through the vestry at all."

"Indeed, that would be very convenient," agreed the curate. "I have the little people for their catechism tomorrow afternoon. I'm not looking forward to it, I must say. Having Rosella there made it a lot easier. You and I could go early, I could let you down into the trap door and cover up after you, and then let you out when the class is over."

"That sounds like a good plan," said Fenestra. "And I've got an idea, too. I'll come and take Rosella's place. I probably won't be as good as Rosella because of the boots, but I'm sure I could be quite scary if I put my mind to it."

"Oh! What a kind ... oh yes, that would be splendid!"

"But you're not to do any lusting!" she said sternly. "I'm off limits. There's only one person you can lust after now, and that's Floris!"

Septimus blushed deeply and look flustered. "Oh my goodness ... I never ... she is a most ... well, she seems very, er ..."

Fenestra rolled her eyes. "Oh crumbs!" she said. "Do I have to spell it out? Look, you'd better not let her get away, because this might be your only chance. You're not exactly God's gift, you know. I suppose curates are allowed to get married?

"To be sure ... er, yes, certainly ... but I never thought ..."

"Just get on with it," she said, and led Pert out of the room.

Outside he cornered her at the foot of the attic stairs. "Look, Fenestra, do you actually know what you're talking about here?"

"Of course I do. It's a woman thing, you wouldn't understand."

"You're not a woman, though, you're a little girl. And do you really know what lusting is?"

She looked down. "Erm, well ... look, this is strictly between ourselves, right? I'm not quite sure of all the details. They do say things like 'Let's give three lusty cheers,' don't they, so it must be something jolly. But it's just such a lovely word, and when I use it people get all flustered, so perhaps it means something else as well. I expect I'll find out when I'm a bit more grown up!"

Pert let her go. "All right, then. And perhaps when you do find out, you'll tell me!"

She smiled, and patted his cheek. "I will. But I expect Rosella will tell you first!"

The evening expedition to feed Rosella went smoothly, at least to begin with. Pert and Billy delivered a dozen slices of bread and butter and some thin pieces of cheese through the grating, and eight or nine balloons, though one split as they pushed it through. They caught a glimpse of Rosella's white fingers as she reached up and gathered them together.

"Are you all right?" Pert whispered, and thought he heard a quiet "Yes!" before Billy grabbed his shoulder hard. There were footsteps at the head of the alley.

"Quick, run!" breathed Billy, and they took to their heels. There was a shout behind them, and the sound of heavy feet. At the bottom of the alley Pert risked a glance back, and thought it was only one man, a big man who was lumbering and gasping for breath.

"Billy, wait up!" he called. "He's never going to catch us!"

Billy came back. He looked up the alley and grinned. "You're right, guv," he said, "that's only ol' Fisty, 'e couldn't catch a cold, 'e couldn't. But we better keep an eye out in case the rest of 'em's around."

They turned right at the foot of the alley and walked quickly down a steep, narrow street towards the sea. Ahead of them in the distance there was noise, people calling out, and shouting.

"There's somethin' goin' on!" said Billy, and they ran down towards the sound. As they got nearer to the harbour they could hear more clearly. There were many running feet, and more shouting, and over the housetops they could see a red glow in the sky. Something was burning.

Billy led them right and then left into another alley, down some steps and then out into a broader street. At the end of the street was the quay. People ran past, hurrying along the quay, and then someone turned into the street and ran up towards them. He was running hard, and panting, his elbows pumping with the effort. Round the corner came three more men, chasing him, shouting and cat-calling. Pert and Billy shrank into a doorway and watched, wide-eyed.

Half way up the street the man disappeared into a patch of shadow and did not come out. Perhaps he too had slipped into a doorway to hide, but his pursuers were not to be fooled. They ran into the shadows behind him, there was a scuffle and a cry, and then they appeared again, walking back down the hill and breathing hard. As they passed Pert's doorway he recognised Squance, the pirate.

When the coast was clear the boys ran cautiously towards the hunted man. He lay in a doorway, propped up against the door, his hands loose at his sides and his chin on his chest. He did not move, even when Pert, his hands shaking, gave him a shove on the shoulder. There was a dark patch on the doorstep which grew as they watched.

"I think he's dead," Pert whispered, his mouth dry.

"D'you know 'im?" asked Billy.

"I think I've seen him around. He's just one of the fisher boys."

"It's started then. Knew it would."

They walked nervously to the bottom of the street and looked along the quay. All was quiet now, with no one in sight. At the far end, near *Better Times*'s mooring spot, a shed was blazing, and while they watched one wall fell inwards with a crash and a cloud of sparks rose into the air and drifted inland over the rooftops.

Pert looked towards the sea, where *Black Joke* was moored. There was no movement, but he could make out three or four figures on deck, watching the shore, and the great gun amidships had been trained round and now pointed at the town.

"We better get 'ome," said Billy. "Your mum'll want ter know you're safe, and I'd better see if mine is all right, an' all."

Pert left Billy at Primrose's door, and insisted that he could get home safely by himself. The town seemed unnaturally quiet now, the streets deserted. He walked slowly and quietly, keeping in the shadows and darting across patches of moonlight. The stalls in the Market Place were boarded up and silent. He crossed to the foot of the Bearward, and paused, looking across at the Emporium. Rosella, poor Rosella, what must she be thinking? Buried in that miserable cellar with nothing but a few slices of bread and sips of water, not knowing what was to happen to her. He felt tears welling up, and swallowed angrily.

Just as he moved off again towards home, he glanced up at the top floor of the Emporium. He wasn't sure, but he thought he could make out a bulky figure in one window, standing back in the shadows, motionless. He shuddered, and ran for home.

Urethra Grubb stood looking out over the roofs of the town. Slates gleamed in the moonlight, and the streets below were in deep shadow. The shouting and running had died down and stopped a good hour ago, but still she stood, watching.

There was that Potts boy, nasty sneaking little worm that he was. What was he doing out so late, sneaking around? She would have to deal with him soon, before he became a nuisance. But first there was the matter of the accounts to clear up. If Tench couldn't find them, she'd make him pay. She wondered whether it might be best to do something permanent, or just ruin him and get rid of him. He was a wreck, just the remains of something that had once been able to function as a human being but was now a mass of malice and perversion. He wouldn't be useful in future. No, perhaps it should be permanent.

On the other hand, if he came up with the goods and found the accounts, all well and good. He should have his little pretty to play with, just for a while. Not for long, though. Just long enough to break the little harridan's will, reduce her and make her pliant. Then Mistress Grubb had other plans for her.

She looked out again, smiling grimly. So it had started, the fighting and the violence. She had known it would, had even planned it. She wasn't certain just how it was going to work out, but of one thing she was sure – there would be a way to turn it to her own profit. There always was.

Primrose Moon had been right. Urethra Grubb did know everything that went on in this town. She made it her job to know, and if nothing was going on, she often took steps to make sure something did, putting temptation in this man's way, or cajoling another man's wife into some petty betrayal, for people's wickedness and selfishness and weakness were what gave her power.

But for all the secrets Urethra Grubb kept, there was one she cherished above all. It was the one dark secret that only great men know, the one law that rules every other law, the one tenet that masters every religion, the one proposition that guides and controls every manifesto.

She knew it, and she lived by it, and she spread it and propagated it like the plague-carrier who moves calmly from place to place leaving death and suffering behind. She knew it so strongly that it burned within her and threatened to consume her. She knew it so deeply that she was driven to share it, like the missionary who knows a contagious western disease is justified by the conversion of innocent savages before they die, like the mussulman with his curved sword who knows cut throats and disemboweled children are Allah's will, like the zealot who knows that a thousand emaciated bodies in a shallow grave will cleanse and liberate the land that covers them.

She knew that nothing matters. Whatever little lust or whim you have, whatever sleight of hand, whatever greed or envy, whatever urge to cruelty or perversion, there is no reason why you should not indulge it.

What is to stop you? Punishment? That doesn't matter - when it is over, you can do the same again. Only next time you will be more clever, more thorough, more ruthless so that you will not be caught and punished again. The disapproval of your fellows? What does it matter what they think? Next time you will do it to them, each and every one of them, and teach them not to judge you. Death? What does that matter? It has to come at sometime, and until it does you may as well do whatever you want. Suffering? What matters this, so long as it is someone else's suffering and not your own?

Nothing matters, and so you are free. You are free to steal and lie, to violate and burn, to cheat and swindle, to do whatever you want to do. Urethra Grubb knew herself to be truly free, and like a true apostle she wanted everyone else to be free as well. Of course they would also be free to be kind, to be considerate, to help those less fortunate than themselves, to make others happy. But where would be the fun in that? Those who wish to make others happy do so for one reason and one reason only - to gain approval, to make people like them.

Urethra Grubb knew that was a snare and a delusion. *"Oderint dum metuant"* was her motto - "let them hate, so long as they also fear". There was nothing to gain from being liked.

XXIII

And in the hidden part thou shalt make me to know wisdom (Psalm 51)
I may tell all my bones: they look and stare upon me (Psalm 22)

Next day, to take his mind off what he had to do that evening and reasonably certain that Rosella was safe where she was for now, Pert spent a pleasant enough morning with Walter Glibbery in *Better Times*, following a shoal of pilchard that had come too far inshore and attracted the attention of gulls and gannets, larger fish and fishermen alike. The waves were grey and wrinkled, heaving slowly, and a warm wind blew from the west. Walter said he didn't like the smell of it, and worse was to follow. Dull clouds extended to the horizon, and the town from a distance looked wan and desolate.

The quayside had been a sullen place. No one was talking. There had been two dead bodies in the streets the night before, and a building burned to the ground, and the fishermen who had taken part in the fight were feeling defeated, ashamed at their own intemperance, and fearful of what might follow. Few thought that the pirates would be happy to let the matter rest. What the pirates themselves were thinking, no one could tell. The *Black Joke* was still and deserted, though it was certain that there would be unseen eyes trained on the harbour. The pirates knew very well how to organise a battle. The previous night they had been heavily outnumbered, but by an instant and deadly response with superior weapons had carried the night with ease.

Pert and Walter were pleased to leave the harbour behind, and concentrate on casting and hauling their fine-meshed net, bringing in a leaping haul of silver fish to fill their baskets.

"There'll be worse to come," said Walter, "no question about it, young Pert. They fishers are backed into a corner. They can't jus' give up, but they don' know what to do for the best. Pirates are pinned down in one place, but they've knives and cutlasses and guns an' they knows 'ow to use 'em. An' they big cannon, they

225

can lob a ball right into the Drop o' Dew if'n they please. That's a powerful argument, that is!"

"It would help if we knew who was on which side," said Pert. "I know the fishers hate the pirates, but what about all the rest of the town? And what about Mistress Grubb? Where does she stand? A lot of people in the town will just do what she says, but she isn't saying anything. I think she's in league with Captain Teague!"

Walter reached under a thwart and drew out his black bottle. The baskets were full enough, and he put the helm up and turned for home, paying out the mainsheet. "Nay, she don't be in league with anyone, that woman. She be a league of 'er own! Whatever she does, it'll be to 'er profit and others' loss."

"But I saw her talking to Captain Teague days ago."

"No matter. When time's ripe she'll turn agin 'im, or back 'im up, or jus' keep out of it altogether, whatever suits 'er own purpose. You'll see."

Pert didn't answer. Walter probably had the right of it, but if there were a rift it was not certain who would prove the stronger. Grubb had the malice and cunning on her side, but Teague had weapons, and men prepared to use them. If only someone knew where the treasure was, Teague could take it and welcome, and the town would be safe again.

He helped Walter complete his business at the quay, and walked home. He loved the way when you have been to sea, the smells of the land wrap you round the further inland you go. Smells of cooking food, of dung in the gutter, of flowers and plants, and the buzzing of insects all seem warm and vivid when you've been on the ocean which has almost no smell of its own, not out in the middle anyway. Harbours and seaweed and rotting fish smell, but the ocean itself is sterile.

Not all the stalls in the market were open. Pert walked up between them, looking around. Only a few people were shopping. One woman walked by with her basket, and spat on the floor as she passed. She obviously blamed Pert for what had happened last night. How could he tell her it was nothing to do with him, that bearing the name of Potts didn't automatically make him a criminal and accessory to murder?

"Take no notice, Master Pert," called Mrs.Toogood. "She's two sons in the boats with not a lick o' sense between 'em, and that ain't your fault."

Pert saw Batty Bunt at the far end of the stalls, standing half hidden behind an awning and watching him. He walked toward the bully, feeling savage. Perhaps the one thing that might make him feel better today was to feel the bone crunch when he punched someone on the nose, but the fat boy melted away before he could come up with him. He stopped and looked round, but could see no more of them. He felt disappointed rather than relieved as he turned for home again.

At home he collected together the things he thought he'd need for the tunnel – a small shovel from the woodshed, all the string he could find in case he needed to leave a trail to follow back, and some paper and a pencil in case he wanted to draw a plan. He would steal candles and matches from the vestry. No one would notice. In the kitchen Fenestra and Septimus were waiting. Fenestra looked excited. Septimus looked nervous. He had the accounts books tucked inside his jacket.

They walked up to the church together, and after looking round to make sure they were unobserved, let themselves in. In the vestry Septimus tucked the accounts books away under a pile of debris in the cassock cupboard while Pert found candles and matches. Then the three of them moved the table and rolled back the carpet. Pert recovered his lever from its hiding place, and prised up the trap door.

Fenestra quailed when she saw the steps down into the ground. "Spooky," she breathed, and looked at him wide-eyed. He grinned, and stepped in. "Close it up tight," he said to Septimus. "I won't knock when I want to come up. I'll just wait until you open."

With that he stepped down into the room and busied himself with the matches. Above his head he heard the soft thump as the hatch shut him in, and the shuffling sound as they put the room to rights ready for the catechism class.

It was cool in the dark, and no more scary than it had been before. He spent some time looking round first one room, then the other, to be sure he had missed nothing last time. The rooms were dry, and the air not unfresh. With light and food and warm blankets one could hide down here for days quite comfortably.

The tunnel felt narrower now he knew he couldn't run back so easily or so soon. The heavy stones of the walls and the curved arch of stones above his head seemed to press in, and he moved in a feeble circle of light. He found himself turning round, to see the dark close in behind him as he passed.

"Shape up, Pert," he muttered to himself, "you just walked there. You know there's nothing behind you!" All the same he felt better when he redistributed his string and his papers and candles to free his hands, slung the shovel round his neck with a piece of the string, and walked forward with a candle in one hand and in the other the last thing he had picked up in the kitchen, a long pointed kitchen knife. No sense in being unprepared, he thought. A weapon was comforting.

The tunnel went down gently, and turned to the right. He judged that by now he must be under the Canonry. He wondered if he would come out in one of the houses that faced the church, some of the oldest in town. But the tunnel leveled off and kept going fairly straight.

Why would anyone have built such a tunnel in the first place, he wondered? He knew it was traditional for smugglers to make tunnels to move their contraband, and there had certainly been plenty of smuggling here in the past, but why would they need a tunnel? This town was right out on the edge of nowhere. There can have been few revenue agents to worry about. Besides, cargoes could have been landed in all sorts of places, especially across the marshes that bordered the creek, and no one would be any the wiser. It made no sense.

By now he thought he had probably reached the edge of the town, and to confirm his guess came to a flight of stairs that curved up and to his right. They were worn and crumbled and had obviously seen a good deal of traffic at some time in the past. He stopped, lit a second candle from the stub of the first, and began climbing.

The stairs went on and on, always turning to the right, and his legs felt on fire by the time he came to a small archway that opened into a much larger space. He held the candle up and looked around. The ceiling was high, and partly natural rock as though this were a cave, and partly dressed stone blocks. The floor was also uneven stone and mostly natural. He sat down to rest, and tried to sort out the geography in his head.

There had been no side passages or junctions, of that he was sure, so he could not get lost. A cool, steady draught was in his face, so there was fresh air somewhere ahead. The stairs had curved always to his right, and he suspected he had been climb-ing a large spiral staircase in the rock, gaining a lot of height but not covering much ground. Behind the houses opposite the church the hill rose steeply, and then became a cliff, an outlier of Bodrach Nuwl though it faced south across the town rather than west like its parent. He must be somewhere inside that cliff. If there were more stairs he would eventually come out at the top, somewhere behind the precipice of the Old Man himself.

Perhaps this was simply an easy way to reach the cliff? Perhaps people in the past had visited the cliff more often than now, to gather seabirds eggs or the like? But in that case, why start from the church?

He crossed the cave to where the tunnel appeared to continue. If it went up, he was right. If it went on, he didn't know where he would end up – perhaps behind the great face of Bodrach Nuwl itself. That was an awesome thought.

The doorway led, not into more tunnel, but into another, smaller chamber. Once again the floor was of stone, though it sloped away from him this time, and the walls of natural rock with only a few dressed stones in the flaws. On the far side the tunnel continued, but narrower and lower, with a rough floor and walls of natural rock. He bent and went on, and had traveled only a few paces before he came to a place where the walls and ceiling receded and he could stand up straight again.

And where, lying against the bottom of the wall on his right hand side, he found a figure. It lay with its back to him, one arm over its head and the other straight out as though pointing further up the tunnel.

His heart in his mouth, he inched closer holding the candle high and the knife in his hand. He could hear the blood pounding in his ears, and he felt sick with fright. The figure was a man, and had been dressed in a long dark robe which had rotted and fallen away like cobwebs. There were shoes on the feet, but the legs that wore them were bones, yellow in the candlelight. This poor man had been here for a very long time.

Holding his breath, he moved the candle slowly up towards the head. A fringe of hair still clung to the skin, but most of the skin had shrunk away from the skull, and the skull was smashed and shattered at the back. Someone had beaten this man's head with a hammer or a rock until he died.

Pert staggered back and sat breathless against the opposite wall. Was this his father? Was this what happened to his poor father, an honest fisherman, a loving husband and father? Had he come to this place for some obscure purpose, lured to it perhaps, to meet this grisly end? And who had done it? Who hated his father enough, or feared him enough, to beat and beat his head until he died and lay there alone all these many years? Who had then crept back to the town with his guilt, and carried it around with him, and talked to people and gone about his business, and said nothing until he too died and took the secret with him?

Pert sat in the darkness, cradling his pitiful candle, and fought back tears. Why did he have to find this? He was only a boy. He should be in school, not here in this dreadful darkness with the skeleton of his long-lost father. He should be sailing on the bright sea with Walter, or running in the sun with Seth and Solomon, or walking with his sister to school, or watching the turquoise flies on Rosella's hair in the trees, her feet in the water and her hand on his arm ...

He shook himself. This was not good enough. Perhaps it wasn't his father anyway. Have another look, Pert, he told himself. Make sure. There must be some clue.

There was. Round the bony neck was a ring, a circlet of decayed fabric that had once been white, and fallen in among the jumbled rib bones a little cross on a dull chain. This was not his father Obadiah, honest fisherman. This was a priest, with a dog collar round his neck. This might have been a curate like Septimus, or a vicar like Silas Tench, but it wasn't his father.

With a lighter heart he gathered up his belongings and walked on. He still had a few minutes before he should turn back and be ready for Septimus and his sister to lift the trap door. And what a tale he would have to tell them! Maybe there would be another shock ahead, perhaps more bodies. Perhaps there had been a battle royal in this dark place. He thought that now he had recovered from the first shock, any future ones would be mild by comparison. But he held his sharp knife in front of him just in case.

The tunnel wound onwards a little further. It seemed as though the men who had made it were following the line of least resistance, for it went up and down, and right and left, for no apparent reason. One thing became increasingly clear, however. The darkness in front of him was just a tiny shade of grey lighter. He was nearing the end.

Lighter and lighter it grew, until he was able to blow out his candle. He felt a wind now, salty and electric, a sea breeze. And it was cold. He was high up.

Finally he rounded a corner and there in front of him was the ocean, the grey ocean and a vault of air at his feet. The wind snatched at him, and whisked a paper out of his pocket and whirled it away in an instant. He put his hands on the rock and leaned forward. He was on a ledge, high up on the face not of Bodrach Nuwl himself but of his outlying left flank, the cliffs and broken precipices that gradually grew lower until they reached the narrow valley with the town at its foot. From his feet the ground sloped away sharply, then eased to a shallow meadow with storm-blown gorse and bushes. Sea birds were here, crying and landing and stalking about on the hillside, and there were rabbit droppings at his feet.

To his right there was a narrow path of the kind that animals make for themselves, stony and treacherous. To his left there was only rock and air. In his face was the wind, and beyond that the sea. Far below, like toys in a fairy's bath, two fishing boats beat their way to the creek mouth before they could haul the wind aft and glide up to the town. He smiled. He probably knew the men in those boats, and they him, and here he was in another world they know nothing of.

He knew it was time to make his return. It would take twenty-five minutes at least, though it would be downhill this time, and

Septimus and Fenestra would be ready for him, eager to hear what he had found. Just as he was about to enter the tunnel again, he caught a movement in the corner of his eye, and turned. It was a small movement, and a very long way off, but he had seen something move that was not a rabbit or a seagull.

He froze, and looked and waited. He didn't search around with his eyes, but unfocused and gazed at the hillside above him, relying on another movement to alert him. Ah! there it was. He kept close to the rock and watched.

Further towards the sea and far, far above him, looking like an ant, or even smaller than an ant, moved a figure. It was on an area of sloping ground, green and partly wooded with small stunted trees, with sheer cliff above and sheer cliff below. One false step and one would roll head over heels down the grassy slope and out into the void, floating and falling until one hit the rocks below where the sea sucked and broke.

The figure moved slowly, pausing from time to time, stooping. Pert thought it might have been gathering seabirds' eggs, or picking plants. At other times it faced the sea and made extravagant gestures, waving its arms and wagging its head as though declaiming poetry or preaching a sermon. He watched for a long time, but could see no reason for its behaviour, and no hint as to where it came from or where it was going. It strolled, bent, picked, straightened, walked on, paused, made a speech or sung a song, then strolled on again.

He had to go. Someone was living up here in this wilderness, on this wild hillside, someone nobody knew about. He had to go now, but he knew he would not be able to rest until he had come back up the stairs and found out who this hermit was and why he was here.

Back down the tunnel, then, he thought. Past the cleric in his lonely bed, farewell, your reverence, sleep tight! It was all right if you didn't think about it too hard. He knew that once he had passed the spot, he would spend the rest of the journey in fear of the thing behind him, the bony fingers that would clamp around his throat, the bony legs that would wrap round his waist bearing him to the floor, the bony teeth whispering dead obscenities in his ears ...

He was right, too, but a boy can run and has nimble feet that can probably outpace a priest who's been stiff and cold these tens of years. In any event, Pert reached the stairs to the trap door breathless but un-skeletoned, and praise be! the trap door was open. He ran up the stairs and collapsed at his sister's astonished feet, laughing and gasping with relief.

On the way home Pert described his adventure, and told them of the crypt, and showed them the gold spoon, and described the tunnel and the stairs. When he got to the skeleton Fenestra looked frightened and had to hold his hand. And he spoke of the tiny figure he had seen in the distance, stooping and picking and declaiming to the void.

"Who was he? Does he live up there?" she asked.

"I think he must do. I suppose he's a hermit, and lives in a cave and eats berries and stuff."

"Gosh," said Fenestra dreamily, "that's really romantic! Living in a cave. Gosh!"

She was even more excited when he got to the skeleton. "A skellington?" she squeaked, "a real live skellington?"

"Not live, but real enough," said Pert, "and it's skeleton, not skellington."

"I know. But skellington sounds nicer, an' it's what Billy says. I'd like to see a skellington."

Pert laughed. "I bet you wouldn't! I didn't, not at first."

"How do you know it was a priest?" asked the curate.

"Dog collar and a cross. And a cassock I think. Something long, anyway."

"Well, there aren't many people it could have been. There's the Vicar, and he's not dead. And there's me, and I'm not dead yet or I'd have noticed. And the last curate, I met him. He warned me not to come here, but I did anyway. And he wasn't at all dead. So who else?"

"What about J.Tench, the last Vicar? What happened to him?"

"I heard he retired and went to live in a Home for Ancient Clergymen at St.Portius."

"No, he didn't," said Fenestra. "He's in the churchyard. I found him when I was reading the gravestones. He's got an angel on top, and he says "Jedediah Tench 1833 – 1887, Hide me under the shadow of thy wings, I am forgotten as a dead man out of mind.""

"Hm. Psalms seventeen and thirty-one. Wouldn't have been my choice, but still."

"We could look in the Register of Deaths, but they were under the altar so I expect the Vicar's burned them by now," said Pert.

"I wish the skellington had been the Vicar," Fenestra said. "Foul man!"

"Now, now, young lady," said Septimus. "Have you forgotten about forgiveness?"

Fenestra thought for a moment. "But he wants to be nasty to Rosella. How can you forgive someone for stuff they haven't done yet?" she asked. "I know we're supposed to forgive people who've done wrong in the past, but what about things they're planning to do in future? Can you forgive them provided they stop, or do you have to forgive them and then they think it's all right to do it anyway?"

"I don't know. It's an interesting theological point. I don't remember covering it at the seminary."

"Billy doesn't believe in forgiveness. He says he believes in giving them a smack in the mouth!"

"It's a point of view," said Septimus. "A lot of the things they taught us in the seminary seem a bit pointless after talking to you."

When they got home they found Mother sitting in the kitchen with Floris and a strange boy. He had fair hair brushed damply back, and a pug nose, and wore a grey suit which Pert recognised as one he had grown out of two years ago.

"Oh crumbs!" said Fenestra, her hand over her mouth.

"Who's this?" asked Pert.

Mother and Floris were smiling.

"It's me, guv! Billy Moon!" the boy said, and grinned.

"Doesn't he scrub up well?" said Fenestra proudly, and took his hand.

"Goodness gracious, what a transformation!" exclaimed Septimus, but he was looking at Floris, not at Billy.

"I'm amazed," said Pert. "You look almost like a normal person. And no smell!"

Fenestra swelled with pride. "And he can nearly read, too!" she said, "I've been teaching him at playtimes, so he can read my stories instead of me telling them."

"I know P fer Princess already!" Billy said. "I'm good at P. I'm learnin' M next, fer Mouse. An' I know F ..." He glanced at Fenestra shyly, and she blushed.

XXIV

They also that dwell in the uttermost parts (Psalm 65)

With the town in turmoil, pirates ready to rampage at any minute, a gang of bullies out on the streets, Rosella in captivity and mysteries piling up around them it might be thought that Pert and his family would be feeling fearful and cautious, but in some odd way the opposite was the case.

Pert felt in himself a mood of quiet elation and excitement. Something important was going to happen soon, he thought. His plans to rescue Rosella were almost formed, and he was waiting for the news that she had been moved to the Vicarage, for surely the Vicar would find the accounts books soon and run with them to Mistress Grubb, and the deal would be struck. Billy had appointed himself chief spy, and when he was not walking Fenestra back and forward to school he had absented himself from classes and spent his time in the back alleys and passages around the Emporium, peering through windows, climbing on fences and having urgent whispered conversations with the pale little urchin in the back yard.

"She not bin moved yet," he announced. He was sitting in the kitchen, swinging his short legs and munching on a crust of bread and butter. Pert's old suit was looking a bit the worse for wear already, and Pert's old shoes which Mother had given him were scuffed at the toes, but his hair was bright and he no longer smelled.

"That boy says Grubb's not bin near these two days, she's all taken up with other fings. An' the Vicar's not bin round, either."

"Do we know how she is?" asked Mother. "I've got some food ready, and balloons, for this evening."

"I'll see ter that later, mum," he said. "I called down 'er coal-hole this mornin', and she says she's all right but she's mortal bored.

238

An' she was askin' after 'er boots again."

The kitchen door opened and Floris appeared. "Is it all right?" she asked. "Mr.P's out an' I thought it was safe to pop over. I don' think Grubb's got time ter be watchin' me, what with everythin'."

"How are the girls?" asked Mother.

"At school. They're doin' all right, really. That April's a good girl, very sensible. She's a big 'elp. An' Mrs.P jus' sits in 'er room an' mopes, an' Mr.P sits in 'is room an' sulks, and the rest of us, we jus' gets on with it." Her eyes wandered to the stairs that led up to the curate's room. "Er ... is 'e ...?"

"He's up at the church, dear, but he'll be back any minute."

"Oh. All right, I reckon I got ten minutes more 'afore Mr.P gets back." Her voice dropped. "I fink e's drinkin'," she confided, "'e reeks of it when I goes in there, an' e' mumbles. All I want is to ask 'im for shopping' money, an' 'e just chucks a few coins at me and mumbles to 'imself."

"Poor man," said Mother.

"Poor man, my eye!" said Pert indignantly. "He all but sold Rosella to Grubb! He's nothing but a slave trader!"

"Well, dear, he's suffering for it now, I don't doubt. And I'm sure you'll be able to get her out soon."

The latch rattled and Septimus fell into the room. "They're gone!" he gasped. "The account books, he must have found them!"

Billy slipped off his chair. "Right!" he said, "time fer me to keep me ears peeled an' me eye to the ground!" and he disappeared at a run.

"Don't worry, Pert," said the curate, looking at Floris. She looked

239

back with hunger in her eyes. "It'll take hours for him to pluck up the courage to see Grubb, and then I don't suppose she'll just hand Rosella over immediately. She'll want to make him sweat a bit first."

Floris rose. "I need ter get back," she said. "See you later!"

Septimus rose to the challenge. "I'll walk you to the gate," he said, and followed her out. Pert and his mother looked at each other and smiled.

"She's just what he needs, the poor lamb," said Mother. "She told me she wants to cut his hair and organise his wardrobe. She'll mother him, and he'll love it."

"And Fenestra seems very ... happy," he replied.

"Yes. He's a boy, isn't he, that Billy? I like him. I'm not worried about Fenestra at all, though she's my little girl and so young still."

"So it's just you and me, then, isn't it? You and me who know what we want and can't have it?"

"Yes, dear, I'm afraid it is."

Pert walked down to the town, and found it almost deserted. A few fishing boats were out at sea, but otherwise it seemed people were keeping behind closed doors. Only two or three stalls were open in the market.

At the top of the Market Square stood three of the pirates. They were lounging on the churchyard wall, smoking and talking quietly, their eyes on the street. They had pistols and cutlasses in their belts. Further down, past the Emporium, were two more, leaning against a wall.

"Well, then, young Master Potts, where be you a-goin' of?" called one of them. It was the dark-eyed Matthew Shattock. He was fingering his knife as though he wanted to use it on someone. Pert went to walk past without speaking, but the man stood in front of him so he had to stop.

"I'm just going down to the quay to do some jobs on the boat," he said, which wasn't true but sounded reasonable.

"Oh, what jobs are they, what can't wait till tomorrow?"

"I'm ... the mainsheet needs splicing again, it's unravelling where it goes through the sheave, so I thought I'd cut it and long-splice the ends together," he said.

This evidently sounded sufficiently seamanlike to satisfy the man.

"Well, off you go and splice, then, young master. But don't you get no clever ideas, 'cos we're watchin' all what goes on. We control this town now, Capting says, an' 'e's sittin' on the barky with 'is guns loaded wi' grapeshot what'll cut down a crowd o' men an' blow their legs ter bits, and they're pointed right down the quay. You see any of them naughty fisher-boys, you tell 'em. Capting's in charge now!"

"And what does Mistress Grubb think about that?" Pert asked, greatly daring.

The man drew breath to answer but was interrupted by the coarse voice behind him. "What Mistress Grubb thinks is what Mistress Grubb knows," it said scornfully. From the mouth of the alley stepped the woman herself, short and squat and menacing.

Pert felt his heart turn over as she approached and stood at the pirate's shoulder. Her head was level with his breast bone but she looked completely unconcerned about the knife in his hand and the pistol in his belt.

"You, Pertinacious Potts, it's time you and I had a little chat," she said. "I'm sure this gentleman won't mind if I steal you away for a minute, seeing as I have my sharp knife up between his legs?"

The pirate gulped and tried to stand on his toes. "And he wont be needing this, will he?" she said sweetly, taking the pistol from his belt and pointing it at the other pirate. She took Pert by the shoulder and pushed him towards the alley. Her grip was power-ful, paralysing him. At the entrance to the alley she turned, tipped the pistol up so that the ball fell out and rolled into the gutter, and threw the gun on the pavement.

She hustled him down the alley, her great boots pounding on the cobbles, and pushed him into a doorway. The door opened and he found himself in the back yard of the Emporium.

"Now," she said, facing him, her back to the door so there was no escape, "our little chat. It goes like this. Your friend Teague wants his treasure. He doesn't know where it is. I don't know where it is, though I think I know where it's been but isn't there now. But you ..." she paused, and her one good eye narrowed, "you know where it is, or you know where your father is and he knows it. At any rate, I think you have a handle on the thing, and I mean to get that handle from you."

"I don't ..." he began, but she slapped him in the mouth with her gloved hand. He felt his lip split against his teeth, and tasted salt blood on his tongue.

"You listen, you sneaking, idle, thieving little turd!" she hissed. "I've got your girl, and if you don't do what I tell you, I'll take it out of her precious prissy hide! And then I'll give her to someone who'll do worse, and enjoy the doing of it!"

"You ..." he began, but she slapped him again.

"And when I've finished with her, we'll see how you feel when it's your sister down in my cellar, or your mother so bathed in sweetness and light! And if that don't work, when they're ruined and spoiled, I'll start on you. I'll flay your skin off your back, boy, and I'll extract your pretty white teeth one by one with a poker, and I'll puncture your eyes with a toasting fork, and ..." she raised her head even closer to his face, and he stared fascinated at the moustache on her upper lip and the blooming hairs in her broad nostrils, "... I'll rip off your manhood and eat it!"

She stepped back. "And then I'll toss your useless carcase into the street and tell everyone I caught you doing something so rotten that they'll hunt you down and string you up and spit on what's left before the seagulls get it!"

"You've got a pretty way with words, Mistress," he said, "but I don't know what you're talking about. And as for your threats, well, you'll have to catch me first!" He burst into motion. Keep moving, keep moving, he gasped to himself, she's bigger and heavier than you but she's slower, keep moving! He ducked under her arms and dashed to the other end of the yard, turned and threw over a dustbin in front of her feet, dodged one way and then the other as she reached for him with her great mouth gaping wide and her great yellow teeth gleaming for his throat, then leaped up onto a dustbin and vaulted over the fence.

He had no idea what lay the other side of the fence, but were it a fifty foot drop it could hardly be worse than Grubb. What lay on the other side of the fence was, it turned out, Billy Moon. Pert struck him and they both fell sprawling in the dirt.

"Quick, scarper!" said Billy, pulling him to his feet, and they ran hell for leather for the alley and then downhill. Billy led him the usual dance, up this entry and down this yard, through one garden and out of another, until he judged it was safe. They stopped in a side street. Bent over and gasping for breath.

"Whew ... that was ... grand, guv! You told 'er!"

"I was so scared, Billy! I don't care who knows it. I nearly wet myself. In fact," he looked down, "I think I might have!"

Billy laughed. "No you ain't! Bleedin' 'ero, you are, standin' up to 'er! There ain't no one stood up against 'er these fifteen years, I should fink. You're a bleedin' 'ero, an' I'm proud to know yer. Bloody 'eavy you are, though, when you falls on a bloke!"

Both laughing and supporting each other they began to walk towards home.

"What we've got to think about," Pert said, "is what she'll do next. If she wants to come after me, she's either got to use the pirates, or Bunt and his men. I don't think there's much love between her and the pirates, and there'll be even less now. She put a knife to Matthew Shattock's trousers, you know!"

Billy's eyes gleamed. "Cor!"

"And if she uses Bunt and Durridge and Fisty Marrow, I reckon I can keep out of their way all right."

"But she might come at it another way, like."

"Yes. There's Rosella, and there's my sister and my mother."

"Oh! Wait up! I knew there was somefink I never told yer! I meant to say, Vicar came callin' this mornin'. 'E come to the front door of that Emporimum all puffed up and excited, wiv a pack o' books under 'is arm."

"Did she take them?"

"Yes, she took 'em in, but then they stood on the doorstep arguin' for a bit. He was wavin' 'is arms, an' she was shakin' 'er 'ead, and in the end 'e turns an' stumps off lookin' none too pleased."

"I think I can guess what that was about. He thought she'd give him Rosella right there and then, to take home with him, and she wouldn't. But I expect she will later on. We'd better get ready!"

"Where's Septimus?" called Pert as they burst into the kitchen. "Septimus?"

"I'm here, dear boy," said Surplice clattering down the stairs. "Why, whatever's amiss? Why the row?"

"We need to plan!" said Pert. "And I need you to do something important, this afternoon after school!"

They sat down, and Pert outlined his plan. "As soon as Billy and Fenestra get back from school, I want you to go to the church with us and let us into the tunnel. You can pretend you're in there preparing sermons or something, if anyone sees you."

"They won't, probably. Only the Vicar, and he stays away mostly. But why do you have to go there again?"

"I need to check once more. If the treasure's hidden anywhere, it'll be in those tunnels. I need to be sure."

"But Fenestra? Surely you won't take her?"

"Not if I can help it, but I need Billy. It'll be safer if Billy's with me. And another thing – can you remember what Fenestra said was written on J.Tench's gravestone?"

"Why, yes, I think so. Let me see ..."

"Could you write it down for me?"

"I will. Do you want me to do it now?"

"Yes, please. Just that, nothing else, on a piece of paper. I'm going to try and send the pirates on a wild goose chase to divert their attention."

With Septimus's paper in his pocket, Pert ran down the street again, and turned up towards the church. The picket of pirates lounged on the wall, though the guard had changed. He went to them, and as he approached they rose expectantly.

"Please," he said, "I have a message for your captain."

"What's that?" one of the men said suspiciously. It was Will Smy, the big, truculent ruffian.

"It's this," said Pert, showing the paper. "I want you to take this to Captain Teague, and tell him this might be where the treasure is. Not for certain, say, but possibly. It sounds like a hiding place – see, "Jedediah Tench 1833 – 1887, Hide me under the shadow of thy wings, I am forgotten as a dead man out of mind." It says 'hide' and 'under thy wings', and there's an angel on top."

The man looked baffled. "Look, just go and tell him. He'll work it out. And ..." a thought had struck him, "... and tell him I got it from Mistress Grubb!"

Smy took the paper, nodded to his two companions, and began to walk quickly down the Market Square towards the quay. Pert turned for home again.

So, that was one thing done. If the treasure was indeed hidden under the shadow of thy wings, then Teague would find it and he and his men would sail away. Then all they'd got to worry about was Grubb and the Vicar.

On the other hand, if the grave was just a grave and nothing more, then Teague would have wasted time and effort digging it, and there was just a chance he might blame Grubb for it.

One thing was certain, though. Whatever was in that grave it wasn't Jedediah Tench, because he was lying still and bony and forgotten as a dead man under the cliff, and Pert was going to see him that afternoon.

Later, Billy went to keep an eye on the Vicarage and on Jedediah Tench 1833 – 1887 while Pert collected Fenestra from school. They walked up the hill behind Floris and her crocodile.

"How are you getting on in school without Billy, now he's bunking off to help me?" he asked Fenestra.

"Oh, no problem at all," she said airily. "There is this one boy, Feckless Rossage, what started getting a bit picky in the playground, but Billy spoke to him after school, and said that if he came near me again he'd wait for him at the gate and smack 'im in the mouth. And he went quiet after that, and now 'e keeps away from me. An' I'm getting a bit friendly, like, with April and Amy. They're quite nice, they are."

"You're sounding more and more like Billy every day."

"What's wrong with that? I like Billy. He's my best thing. I think I might start lusting after him, now he's washed. Are girls allowed to lust, or is it only boys?"

"I don't know," said Pert hopelessly, "I really don't."

In front of them Floris and her brood had slowed, looking as though they were hoping Pert would catch up. Floris looked over her shoulder and rolled her eyes, meaning "follow me, I need to speak to you". They turned up the Bearward and at the gate of the Prettyfoot house she urged the little girls inside before pulling Pert and Fenestra round the side of the house.

"Listen," she said urgently. "This morning I went shopping, not that there's many shops to shop in, and 'avin' to run the gauntlet of all them pirates on ev'ry corner. But I nipped up to the Vicarage. There's a girl works there as used to be at the Emporium, so I knows 'er. She's called Vera, weedy little thing she is, very scared. And no wonder - I reckon she gets an 'ard time of it up there."

247

She glanced round to see that no one was watching, and continued "Anyway, I sneaks up ter the back door, an' there she is washin' dishes, an' we 'ad a little conversation. She's been told to prepare a room for a new girl, an' make sure the lock works an' the big cane is hangin' in the kitchen. But she 'ates the Vicar, an' I think she's desperate enough to help us. Fer instance, would it be useful to 'ave a little plan of the rooms, like, so we know what's where?"

"Very useful, oh thank you Floris! Do you think she might unlock the door and let us in when we go to get Rosella?"

"She might. I'll try an' get away an' speak to 'er again. I don't think anyone but the Vicar's spoken to 'er in months, she was so pleased ter see me! Would tomorrow mornin' do?"

"Yes. And one more thing. Could you put Rosella's boots in your shopping basket, and give them to Vera? I think Rosella might be able to look after herself if she's got her boots on."

Floris laughed. "Cor, yes! One good kick on those skinny bones'll slow that Vicar down, all right! Damp 'is ardour, that will!"

XXV

But mine enemies are lively, and they are strong:
and they that hate me wrongfully are
multiplied (Psalm 38)

Round about him were dark waters
and thick clouds (Psalm 18)

As Pert had suspected, it was impossible to deter Fenestra from accompanying them to the church. It was not so much the adventure she was interested in, but that wherever Billy went, she wanted to go too. The wind was getting up. As they walked with Septimus up the twilit Canonry, gusts rattled the fences and swooped round the corners, tugging at their clothes and making little whirlpools of litter. Clouds were racing overhead, and the top of Bodrach Nuwl was hidden in them.

"Going to be a storm," said Pert, "Walter said there would. It's the Twenty Year Storm, probably, the bad one. I hope all the fishers are home. My Grandfather Mascaridus Potts disappeared during the Twenty Year Storm, and the treasure, though that was forty years ago. There's been another since then, and now here it is again."

"Where do you suppose the treasure is?" asked Fenestra.

"I don't know. If it's not in the angel grave with J.Tench 1833 – 1887, I have no idea where it is. I thought it might be under the vestry, and I still think it might have been once, but it isn't now. And then I thought it might be in the tunnel or in one of the caves, but it isn't. Our father might know something about it, if we knew where he was, but we don't."

"You talk as though you think he's alive still. Do you?"

"I have a feeling, that's all. It's to do with the person I saw, out on the cliffs when I went through the tunnel before. I don't know what."

"Will we see the person again now?"

"No, we can't go that far in the dark. We're just going to check and see if there's any treasure I missed last time."

"In the dark?"

"It's dark down there anyways," put in Billy, "so it don' make no odds."

As they reached the top of the Canonry and were just about to turn in through the lych gate, Septimus stopped. "Quick!" he whispered. "Someone's coming, a lot of them! We should hide!"

Pert led them over a low place in the wall further up, and over into the churchyard. They crouched behind two gravestones leaning close together. In the twilight they could see the light of a lantern swinging, and harsh footsteps marching, the scrape of a heavily-shod foot on the cobbles, and muttered voices. Fenestra moved closer to Billy.

"Who d'you think it is?" she whispered.

"Pirates," Pert said shortly. "I think they've come to dig up J.Tench, the dead man out of his mind."

The men, six or eight of them, walked in through the lych gate and began searching around, reading the graves. Pert tensed himself to run, but there was a low shout and the shadowy figures converged on one spot. They had found the grave.

There was some muttered conversation, and then the clink of shovels. They were digging.

The men's lantern cast a pool of light and faces swam in and out of it as they moved. Pert could make out Sabbage, who seemed to stand back in charge of proceedings. Shattock was by his side, but he couldn't put names to the other dark figures that stooped and stood up, stooped and stood up again as they worked. There was the odd muttered oath, and once or twice a man would straighten up and drink from a bottle, then stoop again.

"I think we've seen enough. We can't get into the church now, in case they see us. That door always make a noise," Pert whispered.

"What about the tunnel?"

"We'll have to do it another day."

"Are they going to find the treasure?" Fenestra said.

"Don't care. I hope they do, really, and then they'll go away and leave us alone."

"But it wouldn't be fair!"

"Why not? The treasure was no good to us when it was here, and it won't make any difference if it's gone. It's not ours, anyway. Come on."

They moved at a crouch, placing their feet carefully, back to the wall and clambered quietly over, then walked on tip-toe down the Canonry, past the lych gate and into the Bearward. Once there they could straighten up and walk normally. Billy said he was going to check on the Vicarage while they were there, and slipped noiselessly into the darkness.

Getting home was awkward, finding Mother waiting anxiously and wanting to know where they'd been and what they'd been doing, and not being able to tell her. Fortunately there was a distraction in the shape of Floris. "I've locked Mr.P in 'is study," she said gleefully, "'e was drunk as a pig an' snorin', and Mistress Grubb an't been near us these four or five days or more so I reckon she be busy elsewhere, so I've took over the 'ouse! No more creepin' about fer me!"

They congratulated her, but she only had eyes for Septimus, who sat beside her.

"What about the girls?" asked Mother.

"Ah, they're smashin'!" Floris said. "They've 'ad their supper an' gone to bed like good 'uns, an' I found the spare keys an' let Mrs.P out, an' she an' me 'ad a nice little chat an' I gave 'er some supper an' she's gone up to sit with the girls while they sleep. An' Mister's out fer the count, and 'e can't get out of the study, so that's 'im done! Floris is in charge now!" She giggled, and Septimus edged his chair a little closer.

With a sharp rap on the door Billy fell into the room. "Guv, guv!" he gasped, "they done it! They moved Rosella! The Vicar's got 'er now!"

Everyone leaped to their feet in alarm. Floris grabbed Septimus's arm and clung there, and he did not shake her off. Mother had her hands over her mouth, and Fenestra ran to Billy and took his hand.

"When? Is she all right?" Pert said. "Have they hurt her?"

"Not yet, guv," said Billy, sinking into a chair. He drew a long breath and began to tell his story. "I'm comin' past the Vicarage an' I thought I'd jus' pop roun' the back, like, an' see what's what. An' I'm sittin' on their fence at the back, an' that girl comes out, the skinny one."

252

"Vera," said Floris.

"Yeah, that Vera. So I calls out, quiet like, and speaks to 'er. An' she says was I to do with you, Miss Floris, an' if I was, could I tell yer that the boots is on the right feet, an' the person attached to them feet is locked up in the scullery and 'as practically demolish-ised the door already wiv kickin', and is in a right ol' temper."

There was a sigh of relief round the room. "That sounds like the old Rosella," said Pert.

"Vera said they brought 'er up strugglin' an' scratchin' this afternoon, Grubb an' two of the Bunts an' Fisty Marrow, an' quite a job they 'ad of it. They'd wrapped 'er in an old rug to keep 'er still, but she was wrigglin' an' kickin', an' once she got 'er 'ead out of the rug an' bit Fisty in the arm, an' didn't 'e yell!"

Billy paused for breath, and Mother put a glass of milk in front of him.

"Cor, thanks, mum!" He drank deeply and went on. "So Vera lets 'em in the back door, and Vicar comes and says they're to take 'er up to 'is study, but when they took the rug off she stood an' give 'im such a mouthful of abuse an' swearin' that he come over all discombobulated, an' changes 'is mind. So now she's in the scullery shoutin' an' carryin' on an' Vicar's upstairs wiv 'is 'ead in a bottle. Vera says she ain't never 'eard such language as that girl knows!"

"And she's got her boots back?" said Pert.

"Yeah. Good little girl, that Vera. She 'ates the Vicar with a passion, she do. She says one day she's goin' to wait till 'e's drunk and creep up and slit 'is throat wiv a kitchen knife, an' sit an' watch 'im bleed!"

"That's how I feel about Grubb," said Floris quietly. "I could do that."

Septimus had his arms round her waist. "Goodness, that would never do," he told her. "A curate's wife couldn't ... oh!"

Floris pulled away and looked at him. "Did I 'ear that right?" she said, eyes bright.

"Oh my goodness! It just ... popped out! I opened my mouth and there it was, bold as brass!" Septimus said, his face scarlet with embarrassment.

Floris was mistress of the occasion. She gathered the quaking curate up and pushed him towards the stairs. "If you'll all excuse us," she said over her shoulder, "I think we need to go up to 'is room and sort a few things out."

"Cor," said Billy, "didn't see that coming!"

"I did," said Fenestra, looking smug.

Floris left ten minutes later, stepping lightly down the stairs, saying that she didn't ought to leave the little darlings alone too long even if their mother was with them, and she ought to check that Mr.P was all right and hadn't thrown up on the Persian carpet.

Pert and Fenestra ran to Septimus' room and looked in. He lay on the bed, staring at the ceiling. His face was still deeply flushed, and he was muttering, over and over, "I do ... I do ... I do ... I do ..."

When he noticed them at the door he broke off. "Oh, there you are! I ... er ... I appear to be engaged. To be married, you know. I feel very strange. I think I'd like to be alone, now, thank you. I do ... I do ..."

Fenestra closed the door quietly. "Weird," she muttered, and went up to bed.

Pert returned to the kitchen. Mother was pottering around, clearing up. He sat next to Billy.

"Septimus says he's going to be married."

"Good," said Mother. "Just what he needs, a girl who knows her own mind."

"Bit sudden, though," said Billy.

"Oh, I think that when it happens, you just know," said Mother, and looked at Pert for a moment. "And when you do, you might as well get on with it."

XXVI

For innumerable evils have compassed me about (Psalm 40)

The morning dawned, if that is the right word, dark and wild and rain-lashed. The wind thundered overhead and wrenched at the roof slates. The few trees in the town flogged back and forth wildly, and rain squalls terrorised the cobbled streets.

No one thought about school. Billy turned up early, and he and Fenestra sat in the kitchen with Mother, waiting to see what Septimus looked like the morning after. Pert walked down to the town.

The Market Square was a wreck. Every single stall had been smashed, overturned and battered to matchwood, the débris scattered far and wide from the church to the Emporium and beyond. People stood around numbly, looking at the destruction.

"Pirates did it," said a voice in Pert's ear, and he turned to find Seth and Solomon behind him. "They went digging for something in the churchyard, and they didn't find it so they smashed everything up in a temper!"

"Where are they now?" said Pert, "do you know?"

"Back on their ship, swearing an' carrying on. Our dad says we all need to get together and sort them out."

"And when our dad says sort 'em out, you can bet there's going to be some sorting!" put in Solomon. "And our mum. Wicked right hook, she has."

But the pirates have guns, Pert thought, a wicked right hook might not be enough. "Can you help me tonight?" he asked out loud. "I have to rescue Rosella. She's locked up in the Vicarage and I need a diversion while I break in and get her."

"Cor, yes, that'll be a lark!" said the boys. Pert explained his plan, and the boys agreed to meet in the churchyard after dark. The diversion might not be necessary, Pert thought as he walked down the Market Square, but it wouldn't do any harm and it would be good to have two spare bodies on hand in case something unforeseen happened.

"Satisfied, now, are you?" said a man as he passed. The group he had been talking to all turned and stared at Pert.

"Satisfied? You pleased what your friends did, are you?" said the man again.

"They're not my friends," Pert replied. "This is nothing to do with me."

"Yes it is," another man said, stepping towards him. "Getting all pally with them ruffians, an' then they go an' do this. You should be ashamed."

Pert turned to walk away, but the group fanned out in front of him. "We ought ter scrag 'im," one said.

"There'll be no scragging," said the twins' father, crossing the road towards them. He was a small man, but tight and powerful with big muscles in his arms. "If you want to scrag anyone, Dick Trundle, scrag them pirates, not kids. You start scragging kids an' you'll have me to reckon with. Now then!"

The group muttered and shuffled out of the way. "You best keep off the streets, young Potts," said his rescuer. "Things are turning ugly, and they're going to turn uglier before the day's out. You take care!"

"Thank you Mr.White. I will. Seth and Solomon are up at the top of the Square, if you're looking for them."

The man grunted and turned away. Pert walked quickly on,

thinking that in a way he was indeed responsible. It was he who had told the pirates to look in the grave, and he'd had a good idea they'd find nothing. He should have guessed that they'd be angry and look for revenge. He had done it partly to create a delay and divert their attention from himself, and partly in the faint hope that the treasure might be there after all, and they'd take it and sail away. Perhaps it hadn't been such a good idea after all. "Too clever by half, Pertinacious Potts!" he said to himself.

The quay was deserted again, and dark catspaws of wind rushed across the surface of the water. Fishing boats rocked and sucked at their moorings. He could see *Better Times* surging and tugging at her painter, but there was no sign of Walter. This was not fishing weather. This was sitting indoors with your feet in the hearth weather.

Across the marshes beyond the breakwater the reeds were heaving in the wind and there were white horses all the way up the creek where the outgoing tide fought against the onshore gale. It would be unpleasant sailing, the wind in your face trying to get behind the sail all the time, and the short seas kicking up spray over the bows. It wouldn't be dangerous. If the wind did catch you aback you could always drift into the marsh and sit there safe enough. It was when you reached the mouth of the creek that things would get seriously worrying, for the waves would be building up before the storm and would break in your face as they hit the shallows of the creek.

And further out, and especially round in front of Bodrach Nuwl where you took the full force of the westerly blast, there the waves would be big, the size of a house, and down in the trough you'd lose the wind and would flounder and be unable to keep the boat's head into the seas, and as the crest came up under you the full force of the wind would hit you and make the boat heel and then go careering down the back of the wave into the next trough. Pert had never been out in such a storm, but he knew well what it would be like. It would be very frightening indeed.

The Drop o' Dew was closed, with heavy wooden shutters across the windows, and all the doors on the water front were barred and bolted against the storm and against the pirates. At the far end the ashes of the burned out shed were stirring in the wind, and little clouds of cinders rose into the air and were whipped away inland over the house roofs. It was good that it was so quiet, Pert thought, for people to just stay in and bolt their doors was the best thing. Let what would happen, happen, and then come out and take up your normal life again. He wished he could take up his normal life. He wished he could go to the church and set out the hymnbooks. He wished he could think of the Reverend Tench as merely an unpleasant bully to be avoided, rather than as a lunatic rock-murderer, a patricide with foul designs on a schoolgirl.

He wished he could be back in school, keeping his head down, avoiding the notice of the teacher in class and the bullies outside. He wished he could see Rosella march into the classroom, stamping with her boots and slamming her books into her desk, and looking round with that defiant air. He wished he could spend the playtimes sitting with his sister while she prattled about princesses and castles.

He wished he could rock in the *Better Times* with Walter, watching the glint of the sun on the water and the flash of wet roofs in the town, hauling nets while Walter got slowly drunk at the tiller.

Instead he was here, on this wet deserted quayside, buffeted by the wind and not knowing what the day had in store. The townspeople suspected him of dirty dealing and Rosella was imprisoned and in terrible danger. But he had to square his shoulders, and do what he had come for. If the townsfolk thought he was in league with the pirates, then should any of them be watching, he was going to prove them right. He had to speak with the Captain, find out what he intended, and try to persuade him not to take his wrath out on innocent townspeople. Teague thought Pert was important, for some reason. Pert knew this was a mistake. He knew nothing and wasn't important at all, but if there was any use to be made of that mistake, he should make it.

In the bows of the *Black Joke* two or three pirates sat watching as he walked down the breakwater, watching his feet in case the weight of the wind blew him towards the edge. The ship tugged and fretted at its mooring warps, rocking slightly and creaking. As he approached, more men appeared from the companionway, from behind the gun and under the focs'le. Quite a welcoming committee, Pert said to himself.

"Good morning!" he called, trying to sound confident. There was no reply. Walter Sabbage strolled nonchalantly down the gang plank and waited for him. The pirate was heavily armed, with cutlass and two pistols stuck in his belt.

"Now, young master," he said quietly, "now, young shipmate, this is an unexpected pleasure. Didn't look to see you come a-callin' today, not at all. Not after that bum steer you give us last night. You're either brave, which I doubt, or very stupid, which I suspects."

"I didn't give you a bum steer," Pert said. "I said I didn't know if it was a good steer or a bad one."

"Well, it were a very bad one, my cock, an' we'm not too 'appy with you. Come aboard, then, since you're 'ere."

The pirate followed him up the plank. Pert felt a little faint. At the top he stopped and said "I've come to see the Captain, please."

"And so you shall, and so you shall, young cock, don't you fret. The Capting'll be werry pleased to see you, no doubt. But first we thought we'd like to invite you to our cabin, to sit an' 'ave a drink an' a chat, like."

"I don't drink," he said.

"You did the other night, with your little grinnin' friend. So you can now. Come this way, young master!"

Sabbage led the way, Pert followed and the rest of the men closed in behind him. They climbed down the steep companion ladder, and went forward into a narrow coach compartment with a long table down the middle and benches either side.

"Sit you down there, cocky, 'an we'll all 'ave a little drinky," said Sabbage pushing him down onto the bench. The rest of the men sat down with them.

"Not you, Tom Suffling an' Andy Skedge," said Sabbage sharply, "you gets back an' keeps yer 'eads poked out in case them townies try anything!"

A bottle was produced and passed around, and glasses. Pert shook his head and the bottle passed him by.

"Now, young master," said Sabbage, "you sure you won't drink with us? I gives a toast, gentlemen! To young master, an' to our good selves, and them as went before!"

There was a chorus of agreement, and clinking glasses. They're just playing with me, Pert thought. I wish I could speak to Teague.

"To them as went before," said Samivell Secret, the oldest pirate, "aye, I'll drink to that! To Bloody Bill Surtees, what they 'anged at Deptford, an' Captain Thompson as 'id is treasure on Cocos Island an' no one ever find it since, for all they digged an' digged. An' to Benido, that lovely Benido, the darlin' of 'em all!"

"Ah, Benido, the darlin'!" they drank.

"Did you know, young master, that your grandaddy sailed with Benido?" asked Secret.

"What? My grandad ... my grandfather? He was a fisherman, he wasn't a pirate!" Pert gasped.

261

"Oh, 'e may 'ave <u>become</u> a fisherman," said the old man, "but e' was a pirate afore that, when 'e was a nipper. Ship's boy, 'e was, on the original *Black Joke* – 'cos this ain't the first to bear that name, you know. Benido, he were powerful fond o' that boy by all accounts, an' when they took the *Morning Star* 'e sent 'im aboard to search through the cabins an' see what 'e could find, and 'e found a few trinkets too, I can tell you!"

"Ah, that were a takin', that one. They took that ship, an' took 'er proper," said Matthew Shattock, who sat next to Pert. "They rousted out them passengers, an' they rousted out their ladies, and they rousted 'em all over the barky, they did!"

"But it did 'em no good, mind," continued Secret. "'Cos when they got back to the Portugees the *Black Joke* she piled up on some rocks, an' they all 'ad to sink or swim, an' poor Benido was caught an' they strung 'im up! But 'e didn't mind, not 'im. Laughin' an' jokin', 'e was, right to the end! *Adios todos*, 'e sung as they dropped 'im. *Bye-bye all!*"

"I can't believe that my Grandfather Mascaridus was a pirate, though," said Pert. "He was a respected man, he was one of the Free Fishers, the leaders."

"Ah, well the Capting's a respected man. We all respecks 'im something awful, don't we lads?" said Sabbage. "Here you are, a toast to our respected Capting!"

And they drank to show their respects. "But 'e's still a pirate," said Secret, "an' proud to be one. The Brethren o' the Seas, 'e calls it." He drank deeply. "Ah, the Brethren o' the Seas! 'Ere's to the Brethren o' the Seas!"

They all drank again.

"Bully Hayes," mused Will Smy, "'e were the last of the pirates, they reckoned, but they was wrong."

"Ah, 'e were a lad! But 'e weren't the worst, an' e' won't be the last. An' our Capting took care of' im in the end!"

"It weren't the Capting, it were Dutch Pete!" said Sabbage.

"The Capting!"

"Dutch Pete!"

Pert thought there was going to be another fight. "Why do pirates have all these nicknames?" he asked.

"Only the captains," replied a sallow, ill-favoured man at the end of the table. "It's mostly just the captains." His voice was more cultured than the rest, as though he had been an educated man once. "It's easier to remember a nickname than it is an ordinary name. Like, for instance, my name's Tobias Smnith. The "m" is silent. Who's going to remember that in fifty years' time? Whereas "Butcher Smnith", that would get you remembered, wouldn't it? Or wouldn't it?"

"Butcher Smnith?" scoffed Smy. "The only thing you could butcher is yer toenails!"

"Isn't it a bit odd," asked Pert, "that you all have names beginning with "s"? Isn't that rather a coincidence?"

"No, lad, no coincident about it," laughed Sabbage. "S stands for seaman, which we all are, except for Squance who'll always be a damned lubber however long 'e sails. And S stands for secrets, wot we've got a lot of. And S stands for strong, which we 'as to be for 'aulin on ropes an' such, and S stands for savage, which we sometimes is in defence of our rights, like. And S stands for sorry, which we'll all be if we don't find what we're lookin' for and which you'll be if you don't 'elp us find it, young sir."

"And S stands for sister," added Matthew Shattock. He put his arm round Pert's shoulder and looked him hard in the face. "Wot you've got one of, and a right pretty little thing she is too, an' you need to take great care of 'er in case some 'arm might befall, on account of you ain't told us what we want to know!"

"Oh yes," said Squance with a leer, "very neat, very trim. Is she ticklish at all, your sister? I wouldn't mind ticklin' 'er with my ticklin' stick. I'd make 'er squeal, you see if I wouldn't!"

"You wait in line, Squancy," said Shattock. "I thought of it first, so I gets first tickle!"

"I can't tell you what I don't know," said Pert, standing up. "And you leave my sister out of it!"

"Or what?" said Shattock. "Or what, my fine cockeroo? You'll push us over like you did the teacher? Well, I ain't no teacher, an' you'll find I don't go down so easy."

He gave Pert a shove with both hands, and Pert stumbled with his back to the table. Suddenly there was a knife at his throat.

"I'll slit you from side to side," the pirate growled, his noisome breath in Pert's face, "an' I'll slit yer sister from top to bottom, an' I'll toss the both of you over the side for the crabs an' the hagfish! Now, where's it at? Where's yer dad, and where's what 'e took?"

"Enough!" The authority of the voice made Shattock freeze and blanch. He let go of Pert and the knife disappeared. Trinity Teague stood calmly before them, his feet apart and his hands in the pockets of his frock coat.

"This boy is our ... associate," he said quietly, "and he will not be harmed or threatened unless I say so. Is that clear, Shattock? Squance?"

The men shifted their feet and looked at the deck. "Yessir!" they both muttered.

"Make it so, then, and be sure to keep it so. Mr.Sabbage, I hold you responsible for the conduct of these men. No harm is to come to the boy, or there will be a slitting, I promise you. There'll be a slitting up and a slitting down and a slitting sideways and a crabbing and the hagfish, and it'll be you that's on the pointy end of it, just mark my words! Come, boy. A few words in my cabin, if you please!"

In the cabin the Captain flung himself into a chair and crossed his legs. Pert stood in front of him. "Captain, thank you …" he began, but Teague held up his hand.

"Don't thank me yet, Master Potts, because we haven't got to the end of this yet, and who knows what may come?"

He stood, and turned to look out of the broad windows at the stern, the view of the harbour and the wind-ruffled water and the fishing boats tossing.

"I asked you to work with me to make sure there was no bad feeling between my men and the town, and you failed. There is so much bad feeling that two nights ago my men left two dead bodies in the streets, and a mob of louts and ruffians marched up the breakwater demanding blood. I had to unveil my little toy on the deck, and then they ran away sharp enough!"

He laughed bitterly. "And now I've had to waste time and effort digging up an empty grave, thanks to you and your Mistress Grubb. Though why the grave should have neither gold nor a corpse in it is a mystery I don't care to bother with."

"Sir, that's not my fault," Pert said, sounding braver than he felt. "You think I'm in league with Mistress Grubb, and I hate her and she hates me - she said she was going to knock my teeth out with a poker, and cut … well, she was very threatening. And half the town think I'm little better than a pirate myself, and that I'm in league with you, so they hate me as well."

"Little better than a pirate? What does that mean? What can be better than a pirate?" He looked Pert full in the face, as though he had been insulted. "There is no higher calling than to go on the grand account. We roam the seas in freedom and power, and we scorn those that try to stop us. There is nothing better than a pirate, boy, and *you* won't get the better of a pirate, so don't think you will!"

Pert said nothing,

"You know what I want. I want your father, and I want the treasure that is mine by right. If I don't get them very soon, it'll be difficult to hold my men in check, and I shan't bother to try. And they'll know where to lay the blame, and they'll know who it is that's defying us, and they'll know where to find him. And ..." he held Pert with his black eyes, and Pert felt his insides turn to water with fear and loathing, "and they'll know where your sister is, and they'll know where your mother is, and that other little hussy you're so fond of. Oh yes, I know what Mistress Grubb's done with her, and Mistress Grubb will do what I say or I'll blast her blasted Emporium to smithereens. The big sixteen will reach that far, and further. I just have to snap my fingers ..."

Pert swallowed and thought he might be sick. Teague straightened up and laughed. He had evidently decided to lighten the mood.

"Well, there we are! Cards on the table, boy! There's no need for any unpleasantness, and my men can go on to the next port and take their pleasure there instead. Just get me what I want. That's all you have to do. This is my proposal."

He leaned forward over the desk. "This is what's going to happen. It is now ten o'clock in the morning. You have until noon. You will go to the town and tell them that unless I have either Obadiah Potts or the treasure in my hands by noon, I will open

266

fire on them."

He sat back. "You tell Mistress Grubb that. She thinks she can outsmart me, but it's pretty difficult to outsmart a long sixteen that's loaded with grape and pointing at your bedroom window. Tell her that. Twelve o'clock, or it starts. You can go now."

Pert ran from the room. At the gang plank the crew loitered threateningly, but made no move to stop him as he left the ship and ran along the breakwater to the town.

Pert had no intention of delivering the message. There was no point. Neither he nor the town could deliver the treasure, and he had no father. What he had to do now, he reasoned, was to keep his head down, stay out of sight and let whatever was going to happen between the pirates and the town, happen without him. He had something far more important to think about. Nothing must interfere with the rescue of Rosella.

He ran home by a circuitous route, avoiding the main streets and reaching Pardoner's Alley from the edge of the town rather than from the Bearward. There he sought out Septimus.

"Listen," he said. "I need you to listen and be clear. There's going to be trouble soon, bad trouble."

"How do you ..."

"I just do. Your job is to look after my mother, and Fenestra, and Floris and the little girls over the road. When Billy comes he'll help you. Seth and Solomon are coming with me later to get Rosella, so it's all down to you and Billy here. Can you do that?"

"Of course, my boy. What do you take me for?"

"I'm sorry. It's just that you seem a bit distracted."

"Oh. Well, yes, I am a little. But it'll be all right. Leave it to me!"

"Right. Where are Fenestra and Billy, anyway?"

"They're upstairs. Fenestra's giving Billy a reading lesson."

"Good. Now, I'm going to see if I can find Seth and Solomon, or their dad."

He walked quickly down to the town, and found everything quiet, just a few stall holders clearing up and searching through the wreckage for anything to salvage. Whirlpools of wood splinters and paper traveled across the cobbles, and the wind was moaning between the houses. There was no sign of the twins or their parents, so he walked to their house which was in the small streets below Low Street, between it and the quay, near Primrose Moon's.

He decided to call on Primrose and make sure she stayed indoors. She welcomed him warmly, and promised to stay safe.

"The alehouses are mostly shut anyway, an' there don't seem to be much call fer Primrose at the moment. Good thing, probably."

"Yes. Now you'll stay indoors, and stay downstairs?"

"Yes. I don't like it upstairs in this wind, anyway. I can hear the slates being lifted by the wind. It feels eery. Why?"

"I'm afraid of the pirates' guns. There might be shooting."

"Can they shoot straight in this wind?"

"I don't think it matters whether they shoot straight or not."

He went further down the street and found the Whites' house. Seth and Solomon were there, but not their parents.

"They're going round trying to get something organised," Seth said. "My dad thinks if they get enough sensible people they can take the pirates on. Safety in numbers, my dad says."

"When they get back, can you tell them I think the pirates are going to start shooting soon? People will be safer indoors and down low. And I'll see you both in the churchyard the moment it's dark."

His last call was the Vicarage. He could not present himself at the door, of course, but he wanted to spy out the lie of the land for himself. The wind buffeted him and shrieked round the chimney pots as he walked up the hill. He cut through the churchyard where the yew trees were swaying and rustling, and over the wall at the top. He knew he could work his way round behind the Vicarage from there.

He clambered through bushes and up a bank, and came out into a little fenced footpath that skirted the back of the Vicarage. The house had a large garden, but it was mostly on the up hill side. Here nearer the church there was only a back yard, and then the kitchen and domestic rooms.

He climbed up on the fence and looked over. From the plan Vera had given Floris he knew what each window was, and could identify the window of the scullery where Rosella was, unless she'd been moved. It was small and high up, difficult to reach from outside. The glass was very dirty, and he could see nothing moving inside. Beside it was a larger window which gave on to part of the kitchen, and here there was a figure moving about. This must be either the Vicar, or Vera, or one of the other servants. He was not sure how many people there were in the house – that would have been useful to know. But he thought that as this was the kitchen, it was unlikely to be the Vicar himself.

The flimsy fence was moving under him, shaking at each gust of wind. It creaked, but he did not worry too much about noise. The rushing of the wind in the trees was loud enough to cover any small sound he made. From his vantage on the fence, high over the rest of the town, he was able to look back towards the sea.

The creek was covered in white foam now, blowing inland, and little blobs of foam were whipping off the tops of the waves and flying over the marsh. At the mouth of the creek there was a turmoil of white water. To his right Bodrach Nuwl frowned over the tumult, thrusting his great bulk chest first into the gale. At the edges of the Stonefields the breakers were so high he could make out individual waves even from here, two or three miles away. There was a constant tumult of white water over the rocks and in the various channels between them. This was a Twenty Year Storm, and no mistake.

The fence shook under him, and he looked down in panic. Below him, looking up, was a thin, pale faced girl in stained servant's dress, her hair whipping in the wind.

"Get down, you fool!" she hissed. "Get down before he sees you! Have you come for her?"

He looked around. The kitchen door was closed, and there were no signs of movement elsewhere. It should be safe. He slipped off the fence and landed in the yard in front of her.

Close to she was small, a thin figure with hard grey eyes and a tight mouth.

"Are you Vera?" he said. She nodded.

"Is Rosella all right?"

She nodded again. "She's still in the scullery, locked up. I ain't got the key. He keeps it in 'is pocket, or I'd 'a let 'er out already. She got her boots, though. I managed that."

She pronounced the word "he" with particular venom, Pert noticed.

"Has he hurt her or anything?"

"No, not yet. He went in there once but she started shouting and carryin' on, so 'e backed out. But I know 'im, the snake. 'E'll just wait, and wait, until she's exhausted or asleep or something, an' e'll get 'er then. 'E's been workin' up to this fer days. 'E lost interest in me, 'asn't 'it me or anything for days. 'E's savin' it up, the foul toad."

"Who else is in the house?"

"Jus' me an' 'im, an' cook what is eighty an' deaf as a post, an' the boot boy what's a bit simple. It's me as does most of the work, and puts up with 'is little ways."

"I don't understand how he hopes to overpower Rosella if she fights?"

"Oh, 'e's strong." She shuddered. "Once 'e gets a good grip, you can't get out! I should know. When you goin' to come?"

"After dark. We'll make a diversion, and while he's taken up with that we'll try and break the door. You'll let us in?"

"Oh yes, I'll let you in all right. I'd never 'ave dared try an' let 'er out meself, but I've got enough nerve to 'elp you do it. And enough hate. Once you've got 'er away, I've got a little plan meself. I'll serve 'im fer all 'e's done to me, you see if I don't, the snake!"

Pert climbed the fence and got away, feeling that Vera would be as good as her word. As he reached the churchyard he heard a dull thudding noise and looked around wildly. Was the church tower blowing down on him? Then there was another bang nearer at hand. He looked at the church clock. It stood at twelve o'clock. Trinity Teague had been as good as his word. He was going to bombard the town until they gave him the treasure.

Down the street people were coming out of their doors, looking round in puzzlement. He wanted to shout at them, tell them to go inside and keep safe, but dared not. If they knew that he had known about it before, they would think he had something to do with it.

There was another dull thud, and close behind it another. Then a great crash shook one of the houses below the Emporium, and a hole appeared in its roof, slates and bits of wood sliding down into the street. Another crash sounded nearer the harbour. Teague was using both his guns now, and the bigger one, the long sixteen, was aiming at the Emporium. Pert felt a surge of elation at the thought that Grubb might finally get what was coming to her, but then realised that all the little shop girls were in there as well. For all he knew, they were locked in, unable to escape. But they would probably be in the basement, which would be the safest place.

More people were flooding into the street now, shouting and confused, and then a small group appeared at the bottom of the hill, walking purposefully up and keeping close together. It was Mr.White and Mrs.White and some of the older fishermen. They were coming to get organised. Not far behind them, Seth and Solomon flitted from doorway to doorway. Clearly they had been told to stay at home, and clearly they had no intention of missing the fun.

Suddenly Pert felt his arms seized from behind. "Here's one of 'em!" called a voice, and more arms wrapped him around. He kicked and struggled, and caught a glimpse of one of those holding him. It was Spotty Bunt. He jerked his head back, hoping to get his captor on the nose, but the man was too cunning for that. People were turning towards them now, wondering what was happening.

"Here's one! We got one!" Spotty shouted again. "Here's one of them murdering pirates!" The crowd began to move slowly towards them. Pert wriggled and got one arm free, pulling at the great hand that had him by the throat, but the man was too strong. He felt the breath going out of him and wondered if he were going to faint.

"What'll we do with 'im?" asked a voice. It was Darren Durridge.

"Pull 'is trousers off an' kick 'im in the nuts!" This was Batty Bunt.

"Take 'im to Grubb," said another voice, older. "She wants this one!"

But his captors weren't to have it all their own way. Someone leaped onto Batty Bunt's back, and there was the sound of a fist crunching. "Dad, Dad!" someone was shouting. Seth and Solomon were leaping and punching, and their father was hurrying up the hill behind them, with his wife not far behind. Will Durridge went to meet him, burly, a cudgel in his hand. Mr.White hunched up, tucking his chin into his shoulder, and his hands whipped round, one, two, with all the strength of that stocky frame behind each one, a fist to Durridge's midriff, the other fist to his head as he bent over in pain. Mr.White left him and moved in on Batty Bunt. One punch was enough for Batty. He went down and stayed down, twitching. Behind him the twins' mother had arrived. She spread her feet, swung her body and delivered a mighty roundhouse punch to the head of Will Durridge. He went down, poleaxed.

The fight was over. Will Durridge and Batty Bunt lay where they fell, and the rest fled. "Now, you two," said Mr.White, "I thought I told you to stay 'ome! Why can't you do as yer told? An' you, young man," he addressed himself to Pert, "I think you know more about all this than meets the eye, but I judge you to be a straight young feller so I'll give you the benefit of the doubt. All of you, this is no place for boys. You can get off, but stick together and stay off the streets. There's going to be trouble. Find some safe place to watch from! Go on!"

"Let's go up to the churchyard," said Pert. "We can see from there, and it's easy to hide."

273

"Why don't you rescue Rosella now?" said Seth. "Why wait?"

"Because it's not dark ..." He thought for a moment. "Yes, that's it! We wanted a diversion, and here's a diversion been laid on for us, courtesy of Captain Teague! Right, gather round ..."

They sat on one of the tombs for a council of war. The twins would create a second diversion at the front of the house, while Pert went in at the back.

"The only problems are, will Vera be ready if we arrive now? She's expecting us later. And, how do we break open the scullery door? I've never bashed through a door before!"

"Well, a door's only held shut at one point, isn't? Doesn't matter how strong the door is, you've just got to bash in where the lock is. And the lock goes into the door frame, so that's the thing to attack!"

"Seth, you're a genius."

Seth tried to look modest, but failed.

XXVII

Deliver me out of great waters, from the
hand of strange children (Psalm 144)

Pert's plans were laid in one direction, but in another they weren't going well at all. Sweet and timid Fenestra certainly was, but her skinny frame hid a steely determination and she was damned if she was going to stay home and be looked after when there was excitement and romantic adventure to be had.

"The tunnel!" she exclaimed. "Let's go through the tunnel, and do what we set out to do last night. Pert's busy, so we'll help."

"My dear little girl," said Septimus reasonably, "I think that's a job for ... well, for men, not a young lady of tender years."

"Tender years my foot! Rosella's got tender years too, and look at the danger she's in. Girls can be in danger too, and still be brave. And I've got Billy. He's brave enough for both of us!"

"I'll look after her," Billy said. "It's only dark an' that. An' the skellington, but 'e can't do nothing to us."

"But there's gunfire, and men in the streets! I couldn't possibly," began Septimus, but Fenestra would have none of it.

"Dear Septimus," she said reasonably and sweetly, holding his hands and gazing up at him with her eyes as large as she could make them, "I appreciate your kind concern, but I'm going. There won't be any gunfire or men in the vestry, will there? It'll be even safer than here. And I know where the key to the church is hidden, and I know how to get into the vestry, and I'll put a chair behind the door so no one can come in and interrupt, and I'll go on my own if you won't help us!"

She was irresistible, of course, as most determined young girls are. In any event Septimus had no experience in his life that could

275

possibly show him how to hold out against such blandishments, and as Billy knew no fear himself he was not very sensible of danger to others, even to his adored Fenestra. In any case, it was just a tunnel. A candle is a reliable antidote to darkness, and underground there would be no cannon or pirates to worry about.

Billy led them not down the Bearward but by paths and alleys Fenestra and Septimus had never seen before, out of Pardoner's Alley and down between houses and gardens and yards, along narrow ginnels and down crumbling steps and out into the Canonry, across the road and into the churchyard. In the vestry they rolled away the carpet and raised the trap door.

Septimus had brought papers and books with him. "While you're gone," he explained, "I'm going to sit here and be a diversionary tactic. If the Vicar comes I can always tell him I can't work anywhere else because of the noise, and I'm guarding the church in case of intruders. And I think I might actually try and write my own sermon for once. I usually get them from a book, but it would be interesting to talk about something else ... perhaps the dilemma of forgiveness?"

Down the steps Fenestra was very quiet, and held Billy's hand tightly. They carried a candle each, and looked round with wonder at the buried rooms. Then they took to the tunnel, remembering Pert's description. It was less sinister with two candles instead of one. They forged on in silence, no sound but the pad of their feet on bare earth and the rasping of their breath.

When they reached the spiral stairs they felt a little more cheerful and less awed. Stairs were more normal than a tunnel, somehow, even though they climbed in a little circle of light with the darkness pressing in behind. They crossed the two cave-rooms Pert had described, and Billy stopped.

"Now, we'm coming to the nasty bit, Pert said. We'm nearly at the skellington."

Fenestra squeaked and covered her eyes.

"D'you want to wait here, an' I'll go an' look?" Billy asked.

"No way," she said fervently. "I'm not waiting here in the dark. Besides, I want to see the skellington."

"Not scared?"

"Of course I am. But I've got you, haven't I?"

So it was settled. They went slowly on until the dark shape by the wall was in sight. "Oo-er," Billy said. Fenestra's eyes were enormous in the shadows. She kept very close. "Would you put your arm round me?" she said. "Thank you. I feel braver now."

Billy stooped over the skeleton, while she stood very close and looked over his shoulder. As Pert had said, this was an old priest from a bygone age they neither knew nor cared about. They looked closely at the remnants of cloth.

"Yes," she said, "definitely a cassock like the Vicar wears. Look, it has bone buttons down the front." They saw too the collar, once a stiff white circle of heavily starched linen, now mildewed and eaten but still recognisable.

Billy reached down among the jumbled ribs and picked up the cross. The chain was round the skeleton's neck, and would not come free unless he either broke the neck apart or lifted up the skull. As he didn't wish to alarm Fenestra by doing either, he poked the tip of his pocket knife into one of the links and levered at it until the chain broke. He pulled the cross free, and there was a tinkle as more bones tumbled to the floor. Fenestra made a small noise and buried her face in his shoulder.

Holding it close to the candle, they turned the cross over and over. It was a simple thing, cast in some dull, heavy metal, with a small stone inset at the end of each arm. The stones shone with little lustre and did not look especially valuable. On the back of the cross were the engraved initials, "J.T." That was good enough.

"J.T., Jedediah Tench!" she exclaimed. "He's not under the angel at all, he's down here! This is the Vicar's father, the old Vicar." Billy tucked the cross into his pocket and they went on.

The daylight, when they reached it, was stunning. The wind blew strongly, warm and moist. Above were the continuous grey clouds, darker on the horizon. Below them the sullen sea was cold and unfriendly.

They began to look for the hermit, but there was no little figure moving where Pert had described the day before.

"There's one thing for it," Billy said. "We can make our way down this path and then up the cleft with the trees in it, and then us'll be on that green bit at the foot of the cliff. That's where Pert saw the 'ermit. I wonder what 'e thought was so important about an 'ermit?"

"I have no idea. I have a feeling, though."

"I can't see 'ow an 'ermit could possibly have got there either from above or below. There's no paths or nothin'."

"Isn't that the point of being a hermit?" she said. "I mean, you wouldn't be a hermit if you lived in the middle of town."

"But 'e must 'ave come out o' the tunnel," Billy said.

"Oooh! I get it! So he must have got into it from the vestry, and he must know about the skellington! I knew he must be important in some way!"

"Yes, that's the fing! Either be someone important, or know somethin' important. Either way, we wants to talk to 'im!"

The path across the hillside was not so bad provided you watched your feet and didn't look to your left where the grass sloped away so steeply, and then stopped at the vertical drop. The wind snatched at their clothing, and they felt safer feeling their way along with one hand leaning on the grass beside them. The little path meandered up and down. Fenestra wondered what had made it. It looked like the sort of path sheep might make, but there were no sheep here. Perhaps it was rabbits. Their little droppings were everywhere.

Bird bones and bird skeletons and bird beaks were everywhere too, and there were holes in the grass all over the place. She knew that some seabirds like to nest in old rabbit burrows, and make them their own. She also knew that other seabirds – the great gulls, for instance, with their cruel beaks and mad eyes – would wait by a hole until a smaller bird emerged to be skewered and torn to pieces.

They reached the little ravine that cleft the cliffside and sheltered a tangle of small trees and bushes. Here the going was much more difficult because there was no path but at least if you fell, you wouldn't fall very far. Billy took the lead and proved adept at wriggling his way up and finding the easiest route. They were sheltered from the wind though the tops of the trees were tossing wildly, and began to feel hot and sweaty from their exertions and dirty from scrabbling in the earth and the bushes.

At the top they were able to stand and look up. They were at the bottom of the steep meadow where Pert had seen the hermit. Here there were more rabbit-paths, this time a criss-crossing labyrinth of narrow tracks so that whichever way you wanted to go, there was a convenient path to follow. There were more burrows, and more rabbits, and more bird remains. Above them the cliff shot sheer to the sky, and at the foot of the meadow another cliff fell to the rocks although they could not see it.

They set off on a diagonal track so that as they crossed the meadow they were also climbing to its top. They noticed that one

279

or two of the tracks they crossed were wider than others, and turned on to one of them, thinking it might have been made by larger feet than a rabbit's. As they rounded the curve of the hill more bushes came in sight. Running downwards in front of them was another ravine, but deeper this time, with larger trees and the sound of rushing water flowing down. Billy stopped and sniffed the air.

"Can you smell something?" she asked.

Billy sniffed again. "Wood smoke!" he said quietly, "someone's got a fire up here".

On they went, more slowly this time, and presently the source of the smoke could be seen. It rose from among the trees in the ravine, a blue haze that was ripped away by the wind as soon as it got high enough.

"Quite cosy," muttered Billy. "You can have a fire and no one will see the smoke 'cos the wind takes it away so quick. 'Ere, let me go first 'cos I'm sneakier!"

He wound away quickly along the path, and disappeared down into the ravine. Fenestra followed more slowly.

She found Billy standing transfixed at the foot of the slope. In front of him was a little clearing surrounded by bushes and mature trees. A dark cleft in the rock suggested a cave of some size, and in the bushes away to their left there was a stream flowing. In the middle of the clearing was a small fire with something roasting on a branch for a spit, and between the fire and the cave stood a man.

He stood calmly, showing neither hostility to, nor fear of, these intruders. He was thin and brown, clad in rags and tatters of what must once have been ordinary clothes. His feet were bare, and his hair and beard grey and matted. Behind the hair there were eyes of an astonishing blue. It was impossible to judge the face because of the beard, but he didn't look fierce at all.

For a moment no one spoke, just stared. Then the hermit drew a deep breath and said "The Lord preserveth the strangers!"

He spoke in a kind of chant, almost as though he might at any moment burst into song.

He spoke again, "Thou hast visited me in the night; thou has tried me, and shalt find nothing."

"It's still daytime, though," said Fenestra, "and we're not looking for anything. We just came to see who you were, and if you were all right."

"Both young men, and maidens; old men, and children," he said. He reached out a hand and pointed to her uncertainly. "Maidens," he said, as though to reassure himself.

"Yes, I'm a maiden," Fenestra said. "My name's Fenestra. What's yours?"

"How excellent is thy name in all the earth!" the man cried, and held his arms up. Then he hunkered down by the fire and began tearing with his teeth at the roasted rabbit on the spit. After a few mouthfuls he stopped, and offered the rabbit to Fenestra. She smiled and shook her head.

"Man did eat angels' food: he sent them meat ..." the man said. "Are you an angel?"

She shook her head again, and moved closer to him. "Don't you have a name?" she said again.

Pert had said that he thought the hermit had been singing or making speeches. Fenestra realised that he might instead have been preaching, or reading a lesson. Their father had been a lay reader, and read the lessons in church. She bit the inside of her cheek, to distract herself. She didn't want to think this thought just yet, it was too soon.

She was now sitting in the grass near the fire and beside the man. He reached out a gentle hand and touched her hair. Billy had moved closer, ready to intervene if needed, but the man seemed to have no malice in him. He was peaceful.

"Pretty," the hermit said, "out of Zion, the perfection of beauty."

She smiled at him again. "Come on, you can tell us. I'm Fenestra, and that's Billy. What's your name?"

"We will remember the name," he said, stroking her hair again. "I will make thy name to be remembered."

"Your name's Daddy, isn't it?" she whispered. "You're my Daddy."

There was a long, long silence. Fenestra sat and smiled while the hermit touched her hair. Billy sat with his mouth open, not understanding what was going on but grinning all the same and ready for action at a moment's notice.

Fenestra held her breath. How had she guessed? She felt sure she was right, she felt it inside her, but how did she know who this was? She tried to keep her thoughts in check, not daring to let herself believe.

"Fenestra ..." Billy began, but the hermit was speaking. "O ... O ..." Fenestra nodded, willing him on. "O ... O ... O ..." He shuddered and dropped his head. "Can't. Can't!" he wailed. "Thou holdest mine eyes waking! I am so troubled that I cannot speak!"

"You can, you can," Fenestra cried. She got to her feet and held both his hands. "Say it for me. I'm Fenestra. And you're O ..."

"Obadiah!" he said with a great sigh, and beamed round at them. "Obadiah, Fenestra, Billy, Obadiah!"

282

He got up and wandered round the clearing, saying "Obadiah!" to himself. He stopped and looked at them in wonderment. "You know, I had forgotten ... it's been so long ... I never told, you know. I never told."

He paused and looked round uncertainly. "A boy. Another boy. P ... something ... and Ver ... oh, what ... Vernilia? Is there Vernilia?"

"No, not Vernilia, we lost her. But Pert's at home, waiting," she said.

"And ... oh dear ..."

"Potentia? Your wife? Our mother?"

Obadiah nodded eagerly.

"She's waiting for you at home. We can take you home, and you can see her!"

"And now, Lord, what wait I for? No, I ... not yet ... I never ... I never told ..."

"What didn't you tell?"

"Oh, no, I never told!" Obadiah cried, and held his head and rocked back and forwards. "He hath smitten my life down to the ground, but I never told!"

"Ssh, ssh!" Fenestra comforted him, "you're my Daddy, it's all right, I'll take you home, ssh!"

Slowly under her tenderness he calmed, and looked around more clear-eyed than they had seen him.

"I never told anyone, you know," he said reasonably. "I ran, and I hid, and I kept my counsel. It was comfortable here ...", he looked around him.

"But that's over now," she said. "You can come home now."

"Can I? Is that why you came?"

"Yes. We came to take you home. Come!" She held out her hand, and he took it, and followed her quietly as she led the way back up to the meadow. Billy fell in close behind.

"Hold up my goings in thy paths, that my footsteps slip not," said Obadiah.

Across the meadow and slantwise down they went, buffeted by the wind, the girl leading and the man following, and scrambled down through the crevice and the bushes, and then made their way across the first slope, but as they came in sight of the tunnel mouth the man changed.

"No! No, I can't! I saw, but I never! I never told!" he cried, and pulled back wildly. She tried to hang on to him and they struggled. Billy threw himself forward and grabbed her by the waist, fearful that she would be thrown down. He planted his feet in a rabbit burrow and set himself strongly and held on to her. At last she let go and relaxed in his grip, her face tearful and flaming.

"Daddy, it's nothing," she wept, "there's nothing there, just dark, and we have candles!"

The man calmed now he was no longer being dragged towards the cave, and squatted down. He seemed to make a great effort, and then turned to Billy behind him and said "I saw, you know. I was ... it was a shock, I couldn't believe what I saw and my mind went ... I don't know, somewhere else."

"Will it help if you tells us what you saw?"

"I don't know. I'm not sure I can."

284

"Shall we tell you?" asked Fenestra.

"Yes."

"You saw ... a murder. You saw someone strike down the Vicar, and kill him!"

"Yes! No! No, not someone! It was God! The Lord struck him down! I saw The Lord, and the Devil behind Him!"

"God struck him down with a rock?"

"Yes! The Lord at thy right hand shall strike through kings in the day of his wrath!"

"Why were you here?"

"I had found the way under the floor, and thought my Daddy might have come out this way with the cups and plates and things, so I came to find out. And the Vicar he must have followed me to see where I went, and I didn't want him to see me, he was such an angry old man, so I hid. I didn't want him to know what I was doing. But he came after me, he was calling 'Obadiah, Obadiah, I know you're there! You're not to tell anyone about this, you hear? This is a secret, you're not to tell! Obadiah? Come out, I know you're hiding! And then ...'"

He hid his face in his hands. Fenestra stroked his hair and put her arm round his shoulders, calming him. "Go on, and then ..."

He sat up and breathed hard, and continued in a strange, high-pitched voice, "... and then HE came, with his robes and the rock of His wrath, and therefore he was the wrath of the Lord, and behind him the Devil all in black with a flaming torch, and I knew it was written that the Lord shall swallow them up in his wrath, and the fire shall devour them ..."

He buried his face again, and spoke through his fingers, "and I

285

hid, for His fierce wrath goeth over me; His terrors have cut me off, and I <u>was</u> cut off, and I couldn't go back for the wrath was waiting ..."

"Tell me. Tell us what God looked like."

"He looked ... He wore His robes of glory ... He was in His wrath, He rushed out of the darkness, and He struck the priest. He struck and He struck, and He cried "You old idiot, what use are you? Do you plan to live for ever? Vengeance is mine, saith the Lord!" And He struck and He struck until there was no life left, and He had taken unto Him His vengeance. And the Devil held the flames and watched, and the blood, the blood! ..."

"Was it the young priest who killed the old one?"

"Yes. Yes, it was. He was the Servant of the Lord. It was the Lord's work, so I ran and hid in the bushes and I never told!"

"It was only men, Father. They were just men, wicked men, caught up in their evil jealousy and ambition. Just men. It was Silas Tench, and he killed his old father for living too long!"

"It wasn't the Lord?"

"No, just men."

"And women," said Billy in an undertone, "That ol' devil sounds a bit familiar!"

Obadiah said "I can't go in there if he's there."

"Then I'll go and get rid of 'im," said Billy. "I can do that, you know."

They settled her father in the grass with his feet to the sea and the clean wind in his face to blow away the cobwebs of his confusion. Fenestra stayed to mind him, and Billy went into the tunnel alone.

286

He walked until he came to the skeleton, and then he did the hardest thing he had ever done, though he would never admit it. It was harder than Merridew's cane, harder than the bullies, harder even than it would have been if it had been him facing up to Grubb instead of Pert. He gathered up the rattling bones into a bundle in his coat, and wrapped them as securely as he could so he couldn't see the skull grinning at him, and carried them back to the end of the cave. There he pitched the lot over the edge of the cliff. He listened for them rattling against the rocks, but the wind was too strong. The old man Tench was gone, and was forgotten as a dead man out of mind.

The rest of their journey was not difficult. Obadiah walked calmly with Billy and Fenestra in front, and showed no sign when they passed the scene of the murder. Fenestra wondered if they would ever manage to work out just what had happened, and why Silas had bashed his own father's brains in. It was clear that Obadiah's own mind was too addled to make sense of it, and might always be. The enormity of what he'd seen, and the shock that a man of God, a young man of the church whose authority he trusted, could do such an incomprehensible deed, had unhinged him and brought him low.

When they reached the bottom of the spiral stairs, Fenestra said she felt weary, and Obadiah picked her up without a word and carried her. She wrapped her legs around his waist and her arms round his neck without a qualm. As Billy walked behind she looked over her father's shoulder and mouthed "Phew! He does half pong!"

The trap door was closed, so they rapped gently on it and waited while Septimus cleared up his sermon and moved the table. Obadiah set down Fenestra, and they climbed up into the dim daylight of the vestry.

"You've been gone a long time," said Septimus, "I was beginning to worry that I'd have to write a second sermon."

"That would never do," laughed Fenestra, "you don't know the first one's any good yet. Septimus, allow me to present my father, Obadiah Potts!"

There now arose the question of what to do with her father, who was of far too much interest to both Grubb and the pirates for comfort.

"Aunt Gittins!" she said. "She's perfect! She's out on the edge of town, she's old so no one will suspect, and Father will know her and trust her. We'll take him to Aunt Gittins."

This was not accomplished without a great deal of care. Billy made Fenestra and her father hide under the supervision of the curate, while he reconnoitered at every step and street corner to be sure there were no pirates or emissaries of Mistress Grubb wandering about. From the town below they could still hear the thud of the guns, and the occasional crash as a ball struck home, but it did not seem that even the long sixteen could reach up here. The journey out of the churchyard and up the Canonry, then down through the back lanes to Aunt Gittins cottage, was nerve-wracking but successful.

"Oh my Lord!" said Aunt Gittins when she saw them. "I'm an old woman, are you trying to give me a heart attack? Quick, come along in before someone sees! Obadiah, is it really you? Come and give your old aunt a hug! However did you manage to get yourself in such a state?"

"He's been living in a cave, and eating rabbits!" said Fenestra.

Her aunt looked at her over her glasses. "Hmph!" she said. "This isn't one of your fanciful stories, you know! And who's this boy, and what's he grinning about?"

"This is Billy. He's mine. He always grins," said Fenestra.

Billy held out his hand. "'Ow do, missus!" he said, and Fenestra thought there was the trace of a smile on Aunt Gittins' face.

"Now, let's get organised!" she said. "He needs a good bath, so young man Billy, do you go into the kitchen and put the kettle on the hob, if you please. And make sure there's water in it before you do!"

Billy moved towards the kitchen. "I am 'ouse-trained, you know," he said quietly, "more or less."

"And these clothes have to go, and be burned in the back garden. They're disgusting. One of the neighbours will have something he can wear, if I tell them I'm making a scarecrow for the runner beans. And I'll call Elsie Tonkin over. She used to be a hairdresser in her younger days, but she got so fed up asking people if they'd had their holidays yet that when she stopped hairdressing she vowed never to say another word in her life. Nor has she, either, but she doesn't mind getting her scissors out once in a while, just for the practice. She'll tidy him up and keep her mouth shut. Just don't mention holidays!"

She began to help Obadiah out of his clothes.

"And you, young lady, you don't need to be here gawping at gentlemen at their toilet! This nice young curate must take you home and put you to bed. But I'll keep that young fellow of yours for an hour or so if you don't mind. He looks as though he could be useful."

Fenestra did mind, rather a lot, but she didn't argue. She knew when she was likely to be beaten, and she'd done her romantic heroine deed for the day.

"Cheer up!" said Septimus as they threaded their way through Billy's back doubles towards Pardoner's Alley. "He's back now, among normal people. I'm sure just talking normally and wearing normal clothes and doing ordinary things around the house will slowly bring his mind and his memory back. And he has your Great-aunt. She strikes me as a very capable person."

"I'm sure you're right," she said. "I'm just wondering how we're going to break it to Mother!"

"Why don't you leave that with me? If you tell her tonight she'll be rushing out across the town to see him, and that's a bad idea. No woman ought to be abroad alone at night with those pirates around. I'll tell her in the morning, and then I'll go with her to your Aunt's house."

"Excellent," she said. "That's a relief, to be honest. I wasn't sure what to do about it."

Mother was pacing the floor in a lather when they got in.

"Oh my goodness!" she cried, "I've been so worried, what with the banging and crashing, and I looked round and you weren't there. Wherever have you been? And where's Pert?"

Fenestra said "Pert's gone to get Rosella, I think. And we've ..."

"We've been up to your Aunt Gittins', to make sure she was all right," lied Septimus.

"And is she?"

"Yes, she's fine. And we've left Billy there with her for a while."

Fenestra took her milk up to bed with her. She felt exhausted and could think of nothing but sleep, but she pushed open Septimus's door on the way.

"You told a lie, you naughty man!" she said. "It was brilliant, I couldn't think what to say!"

"It was only half a lie," he said shamefacedly. "We did go there, and she is all right. I imagine I might be forgiven."

"I'll certainly forgive you," she said. "You're a lovely man." She put her arms round his neck and kissed his cheek. "There!" She gave him a second kiss. "But this doesn't mean you can do any lusting, you hear? You've got Floris to think of now!" and she slid off his lap and bustled out, leaving Septimus pleased but a bit confused.

She was really a most remarkable child, he thought. But odd, decidedly odd. How was it that you never knew where you were with women, yet you always felt they had you exactly where they wanted you to be?

XXVIII

Surely thou wilt slay the wicked, O God: depart from
me therefore, ye bloody men (Psalm 139)

The wind was like a solid thing, pressing them down as Pert and
the twins crept up through the churchyard towards the Vicarage.
Behind them they could still hear the steady thud as the guns
fired, and sometimes a crash as the ball landed. Presumably the
quieter impacts were when the ball hit a tree, or landed in the
street. Or hit a person, thought Pert, with a shudder. Teague
certainly meant what he said, though. He wasn't about to stop.
This was pay up or have your house bombed sooner or later.
Each gun seemed to be firing every minute or so. That was 60
cannon balls an hour, two guns made it 120 an hour. Pert wondered how many cannon balls the pirates had. Surely not all that
many? But then, the ship didn't have to carry any cargo, which
left plenty of room for ammunition.

Pert swarmed over the Vicarage back fence, which was rocking
wildly in the wind and surely couldn't last much longer before it
fell and blew away. He ran to the back door and knocked very
quietly.

Vera opened it. "It's not dark yet!" she hissed.

"Change of plan," Pert said. She shrugged, and let him in.

"There's the scullery," she pointed. "She's awake. We was just
talkin' through the door."

"Rosella?" he whispered.

There was a movement inside. "That you, Pert?"

"Yes. I've come to get you out. You all right?"

"I will be. Thank you for coming."

292

"Get away from the door, then. When the diversion starts, I'll try and bash it in."

They waited. "Vicar's upstairs in 'is study," said Vera. "But be careful, 'e 'ears everything."

There was a long pause, and then it started. There was a great crash as something hit the front door of the house, and then the sound of breaking glass. Seth and Solomon were attacking the front with rocks and stones. They were hooting too, like a tribe of lunatic monkeys, and giving shrill whistles, and meanwhile pelting the windows with stones. They heard the sound of footsteps rushing down the stairs, and the Vicar swearing.

Pert looked at Vera. "I never heard him swear before," he said.

She smiled grimly. "I bet there's lots of things you never 'eard 'im do before, but 'e does 'em!"

They heard the front door open, and an angry shout. The whoops redoubled, and more stones were thrown.

"Now!" said Pert. He took a run at the door and hit it with his shoulder near the lock. It shook and there was a splintering noise, but it held. He tried it again, but still it held. Then Vera came staggering in with a great log of wood from the yard. It was as tall as she was, and much fatter. She dropped it on the floor, but they picked it up between them and ran and hit the door with it. There was a crash and the door flew open. The door was intact, but the latch had torn right through the frame as Seth had predicted.

"Quick!" said Pert, and Rosella appeared, pale and very dirty, but intact and smiling. He took her hand and ran to the back door.

"Vera," he said, "you come too! I know a place where you can both hide!"

"I'll follow you," she said, "there's something I have to do first."

They could hear more footsteps from the front of the house now, and the sound of monkey whoops fading into the distance. They ran for the fence. As they reached it, part of the fence finally gave up the unequal struggle and let go its hold on the ground. It sailed up in the air and drove inland, revolving as it went. There were two solid thuds from the harbour, and two loud crashes from the town.

In the churchyard they paused and waited for Vera, but she did not come. The wind whipped round their ears. They could see straight into the Vicarage back yard now the fence was gone, and there seemed to be a light in the kitchen. Then there was a whoosh and flames blossomed from the open door. The window blew out with a crash, and flames came out of there too.

"She set the house alight!" said Pert. "That was her plan! She's going to burn the old bugger!"

"But where is she?"

The flames went down a little, and then bloomed once more, but this time from a window on the first floor. The fire was spreading with horrifying speed. There was still no sign of Vera.

"Perhaps she'll go out through the front, it's not burning there yet," said Pert, so heedless of the danger they ran to the Canonry and into the Vicarage drive. The fire may not have reached the front, but you could see it. It was as if the whole back of the house was ablaze, lighting up anything in front of it. As they watched, a figure moved rapidly across first one upstairs window, then another. The wind had found the broken window panes and was reaching in to the fire, feeding it and spreading it.

Then the front door opened, and the figure was silhouetted against the flames. It was not Vera, but tall, spindly, its arms outstretched, its hands like claws. It was burning. It stalked forward, lifting its feet, and down the front steps to the drive and they heard its feet crunch on the gravel as it began to run, taking great prancing steps, bounding high in the air as though preparing to take off, and as it passed there was a roaring noise from its burning clothing, for the wind was whipping at the flames, wrapping them round the limbs and clothing them in fire. With his head held back and his beaky nose raised to the sky, the Vicar bounded past them, his mouth wide in a silent scream, and trailed black smoke and cinders behind him as he fled down the street.

The inside of the house was an inferno now, and with a creak and a crash the interior floors gave way and came crashing down, releasing a cloud of sparks. Flaming wood and fabric rose into the sky, driven by the howling gale, and landed on the house next door. One patch of fire stuck on the roof, and burned, and soon they could see that this house was also burning, and that the roof was alight. Slates toppled down, and the rafters were coated in flame. Another house across the road was also alight, and each cast its cargo of flaming material into the gale to be carried up the road. These were the richest houses in the town, built of fine timber and costly curtains and carpets, and they burned merrily as the wind stalked over them and spread fiery contagion.

Pert and Rosella took to their heels and began to run down the hill towards the Market. Behind them the lowering clouds reflected the inferno back, so that the town was lit by a hellish backdrop to go with the carnage beneath. In the Market Square the Emporium had been hit, more than once. There was a huge hole in its roof, and the turret and bay window at the corner overlooking the street, where Pert had seen Urethra Grubb watching him, now leaned drunkenly and about to fall.

A crowd stood in the Market Square, and in front of them, her voluminous layers of black whipping in the wind, stood the squat, massive figure of Urethra Grubb herself, waving her arms and shouting at them. The children stopped.

"Why don't you move, you pathetic flock of pox-ridden verminous sheep?" the woman was saying. "Must I do everything myself, you flaccid, useless appendages? Go! Go and kill those murdering spawn of Satan!" Her voice was hoarse with fury. She rushed in the crowd and began hitting and kicking at them. "Go, why don't you go?" she yelled.

Suddenly from the Bearward burst the dishevelled figure of Patroclus Prettyfoot. He had broken out of the study where Floris had locked him, and he was incoherent with rage and drink. Waving a bottle in one hand, he weaved across the road towards Urethra Grubb, shouting imprecations.

"Fat, revolting harridan," he yelled, "last time you come t' ... t'my house 'n' bully me ... had enough! Enough, y'hear?" He flung the bottle at Grubb, but missed. It fell without breaking, and liquid glugged from it.

"See what you made ... hic! ... made me do, you fat cow?" he screamed. "I'll kill ..." he staggered forward, "... kill you, taking my daughter ... where is she? What did you do?"

He stopped and planted his feet, swaying wildly. "Don' you lay ... hic! ... finger on my daughter! 'f anyone hits 'er, it'll be me, ungrateful little slut! I'll take 'er hide off, see if I ... hic! ... you give 'er back, Grubb, you ..."

"You shut your mouth, or I'll shut it for you!" Grubb shouted and darted towards him with murderous intent, her face black with rage and her great fists clenched, but there was a hissing sound louder even than the wind, and a cannon ball made a direct hit on the horse trough at the edge of the Square. The trough split in two and spilled its water in a cascade down the gutter, and the ball bounced high into the air and took Patroclus Prettyfoot's head off his body. The ball flopped onto the cobbles, bounced twice and then began to roll with gathering speed down the hill. People leaped out if its way, and it hit the railings outside the bank and went plink-plink-plink-plink on each one and then disappeared down the hill. The head rolled more slowly and did not go plink but made a wet splatter as it looked first at the pavement and then at the sky with an expression of mild surprise.

The other gun fired a moment later and a ball struck a house further down the road, leaving a hole in the roof. The door of the house sprung open and people spilled out into the street, screaming, their thin cries whipped away by the wind.

Grubb turned to look at the trough, and then at the lifeless body of Prettyfoot, and her eye fell on Pert and Rosella standing transfixed with horror. A great shudder ran through the woman, and she pointed.

"There!" she roared, her voice hoarse with emotion, "there! There they are! They did this! Murdering, thieving, sneaking little spy! Whoring little slut! Fetch them here! Go, go, get them, I'll rip them limb from limb!"

A portion of the crowd moved uncertainly towards them, and Pert poised for flight. Grubb began to lumber up the hill towards them, her solid limbs pumping and her feet heavy on the cobbles. Some of the crowd followed her, and some stood still. At the back of the crowd a more coherent group began to move, a group with some leadership. Mr.White was there, and Mrs.White, and the older fishers, grim-faced and silent. It was not clear to Pert whether they were on Grubb's side or his. He began to back up, dragging Rosella with him.

Then the rear of the crowd turned to look down the hill. Around the corner from the quay came a phalanx of men, trotting in tight formation, cutlasses aloft and pistols in their belts. It was the pirate crew, resolute and armed, and they kept close and drove up the hill through the crowd, shoving some aside, cutting with their swords at those who didn't move fast enough. At their head was Walter Sabbage, grinning savagely.

"Grubb! Grubb!" he shouted, "we'm comin' fer you, Grubby! Capting wants you, Grubby! There's a noosy and a swingy and an 'appy little droppy waitin' fer you, Grubby!"

A sigh rose from the crowd, which was swelling rapidly as people poured out of the side streets. The pirates reached the front and drove towards Urethra Grubb. She stopped, torn between flight and the capture of Pert and Rosella.

It was Rosella who broke the deadlock. She let go of Pert's hand and darted forward. With a scream she launched herself at Grubb and hacked one, two with her big boots on the thick shins. Grubb staggered back with a howl of rage, and then launched herself forward. Rosella turned and sprinted, her legs flying and boots clattering, with Grubb behind her. She ran for the top of the Square, and Grubb pounded behind her. A great knife had appeared in her hand.

Pert stepped forward and threw himself at Grubb, but her momentum was too great and her onward rush brushed him aside so that he fell heavily to the pavement. With a shout the pirates broke rank and ran after Grubb, whooping with the thrill of the chase. And behind them the Whites and the fishers finally galvanised the people of the town and the whole crowd ran up after the pirates, up past the church, up past the burning buildings, up and up with the wings of the gale pushing them onwards.

Pert rolled over, winded. Seth and Solomon were there, and helped him up.

"Rosella," Pert said helplessly. "I must ..."

"You can't. Don't worry, they'll never catch her. The pirates'll catch Grubb before she gets Rosella. And the townies'll catch the pirates. They've found a bit of backbone at last, and our dad's there."

"No, Rosella," Pert moaned, "I must find Rosella ... wait!"

He turned and sniffed the air, and looked around. "Something's changed. The wind's changed!"

Behind them the flames roared, the fire was spreading still further up the row of houses, and the clouds threw back the lurid light. The whole upper town was either alight or illuminated. But out to sea, something had changed. Pert began to walk down the hill, an idea forming in his mind. The twins trotted beside him.

Pert knew what every fisherman knows, that whatever direction the wind is blowing, when it reaches the shore it tends to turn so that it crosses the shoreline at right angles. All day long the great west wind had turned to blow slightly from the south as it crossed the shore, thundering up the creek and over the harbour. But so great was this gale, the great Twenty Year Storm, so high had risen the wind, that it no longer cared to notice the puny creek and the flat marshes. It was the West Wind, it had decided, and it would blow from the west as it should. The wind now blew across the creek, not up it.

"If I can cast off the mooring lines of the *Black Joke*, this wind will take her out of the harbour. She'll drift across the wind and down the creek – she won't have any sails on but her hull is high, it'll act like a sail and drive her downwind and crosswind until she strands in the marshes somewhere. Then she can't fire any more. I can stop her, Seth!"

"Come on, then!" said Seth, and made to run down the hill.

"No!" Pert stopped him. "This'll only take one. I can cast off a few lines by myself. I can creep along the breakwater and ... no, I have a better idea, I'll get the *Better Times* and row across to her and do it that way. They're less likely to see me, I expect they'll be busy with the guns, and watching the fire, and wondering how their landing party is getting on with capturing Grubb."

"But ..."

"I want you to stay. I want you to follow the crowd and see if Rosella's doubled back. That's what she'll do. And you can find her and get her somewhere safe. Take her home with you. And if you can't find her, then make sure Fenestra's safe. Please, Seth! Please Solomon!"

"You sure, Pert? We can creep and sneak like anything, almost as good as Billy Moon. You sure we wouldn't be better with you?"

"No, I'm certain. This is seaman's business, and I'm the seaman here. Look for Rosella. She's quick. She'll slip away from Grubb, easy, and get down and hide, and then come back. Find her for me!"

"Righto!" they said, and the boys slipped away, running lightly up the hill. Pert hurried towards the harbour.

XXIX

Deep calleth unto deep at the noise of thy waterspouts:
all thy waves and thy billows are gone over me (Psalm 42)

The harbour was a strange and unfamiliar place, the quay deserted and nets flapping in the wind or blowing in heaps across the
cobbles to rest against the foot of the buildings. The surface of
the water was dark and ruffled by gusts, little waves rearing
their heads only to be mashed flat by the weight of the wind.
Boats tossed and ground together against the wall among a
heaving welter of broken timber and débris.

On the far side the *Black Joke* was still in the shelter of the
breakwater, looking black and hunched. Figures moved on her
deck, but only a few. Then there was a puff of smoke quickly
whipped away by the wind, followed a second later by the dull
sound of the explosion. Another ball was hurling over Pert's
head into the packed houses behind.

He kept low, crouching behind an upturned dinghy, and waited
until the figures were bent over the cannon to reload, then
darted quickly along the quay and hid again. The second cannon
fired, and this time he heard the ball hiss as it passed over. He
watched the figures and only moved when he thought they were
busy.

His progress along the quay was slow, and he had plenty of
opportunities to look around and listen. Further up the town he
could hear shouts and screams, and the crash of falling timber
or falling walls and slate. The sky was scarlet from the fires,
which now spread in a wide arc at the top of town, the lowering
clouds lit with a baleful glare. He wondered whether he should
be worried about his family. No, their house was upwind of the
fire, they were safe. But could the fires spread as far round as
Aunt Gittins'? No point thinking about it, he decided. Anyway,
they had legs, and they had Septimus to guide them, and sooner

or later Billy would be there. He had absolute faith in Billy's ability to get anywhere or do anything needed.

But the other houses in the town, the fishermen's cottages behind the harbour, and Walter and his wife, families and children cowering in the buildings that were lower down and in far more danger, and the ample roofs of the Prettyfoots' house, where Floris and the girls were hiding in the cellar. A cellar should be safe, surely, except from fire? But the fires were moving in the opposite direction, driven by the gale. Then he remembered the shop girls in the Emporium. That was a prime target for the guns, and he wished he could be sure that they were safe in the basement. It was a sorry predicament to be in, caught between Grubb's vicious wrath and the impartial thunderbolts from the ship.

No doubt about it, he thought, this was the right thing to do. He glanced at the ship and the figures toiling there, and made his next dash up the quay. He was at the Drop o' Dew now, boarded and silent with a hole high in the front wall where a poorly pitched cannon ball had struck. He could see the *Better Times* now, straining at her painter and rocking wildly.

He ducked down as the long sixteen fired again. That was the moment when he might be seen, when they were watching the town to see where the ball fell. He heard the ball passing overhead, and then a different sound as it struck, not the ordinary crash of smashed stone and roof, but a loud bang! and a flash. This was bad, he thought. Teague has found some explosive shells and has decided to escalate his attack. He imagined the bursts in the narrow streets, and the stone chips and fragments that would kill and maim anyone out in the open.

He made the edge of the quay in a last rush and flung himself over the edge and down the ladder. *Better Times*' painter was tied to the bottom rungs, and he cast off, tucked the painter round one rung and held the end in his hand as he pulled the boat towards him. She came, bobbing and pitching, and he scrambled over her bows and fell into the well, still holding the end of the rope. He waited a while before risking a peep over the gunwhale. The men on the ship had not seen him, but were bent once more over their guns. There were two more reports, and one dull crash and one sharp explosion from the town. They only had shells for the big gun, the smaller one in the bow was still firing solid ball.

This was the most dangerous time, rowing the boat across the clear water of the harbour. This was the moment they might spot him. He got out the oars and pushed off, letting the painter slip and run out of the ladder. *Better Times* slid backwards and began to turn across the wind. With one eye on the ship he pulled hard on his right oar to complete her turn, then bent to both oars and took three or four good strokes to windward. *Better Times* was a good boat, old but easily driven. Even against the wind she slipped forward into clear water.

He looked at the ship, and as the next burst came he lay back with the oars shipped. With a bit of luck if they saw the boat they would assume it was just a stray, broken free of its moorings and adrift. He hoped they would not be paying enough attention to wonder how she was managing to drift against the wind.

He could feel by instinct that her head was beginning to pay off as the wind bore on her starboard bow, so he glanced out to see the coast was clear and took several more strokes, then lay flat again. Each time the guns fired, he hid and rested. Once he thought the gun crews were busy, he rowed. It was back breaking work, pulling a heavy fishing boat against this wind, and he feared that every time he rested he was losing whatever ground he had just gained, but gradually, very slowly, he was making progress. He tried to remember what the tide was doing. It might just be getting into the ebb, which would be a help as the current moved seawards against the wind.

He was level with the stern of the ship now. Its black windows looked at him, but the Captain was busy on deck, he hoped. The round tower at the end of the breakwater was right above him, and he turned the boat and ran parallel with the breakwater, straight towards the stern of the ship. He was in plain sight of the men on deck. He could imagine the pistol balls whipping round him if they saw him, though they would not be able to get one of the big guns to bear.

The stern of the ship rose tall above his head. From the other side of the harbour she had seemed serene, untouched by the storm, but here he could see how she was tugging at her mooring lines, rocking slightly, her bilges sucking at the water and her big rudder, six inches thick of solid oak, slatting slowly from side to side. Above there was a constant roar of wind in the yards, a shriek as the air tore at the rigging and the loud pistol-shots of halliards frapping on the masts.

Now he had a problem. He was at her stern but he needed to cast her off at the bows first, for that way her high bow would take the wind and fall away from the breakwater while her stern was still held fast, and she would swing by the stern so her guns would be facing the marshes instead of the town.

He stood up in the bow and tied *Better Times*' painter to the rudder stock of the *Black Joke* with a slip knot that would come undone when he pulled on the end. Then he felt under the thwart where Walter kept his big fish knife with the eight inch blade honed every day on one of the thwarts to keep its wicked edge. Tucking it into his belt, he took off his jacket and shoes, and slipped over the side.

The cold water took his breath away and made him gasp. When he had recovered a little he pulled himself away from *Better Times* and into the narrow space where the curve of *Black Joke*'s bilge entered the water and left a tunnel between the ship's timbers and the stones of the breakwater. He pulled himself along, breathing hard, his fingers on the slimy stones.

It was a frightening thing to do with the ship heaving above him and the water black under his feet, and he feared being crushed at any minute although he knew the shape of the ship's hull would allow no such thing. In reality, he kept saying to himself, this was the safest place to be, out of sight and secure, however cold.

When he had pulled and slithered himself along the ship's length he came out into the wider space where the bows rose above him. He had never noticed before that the ship had a figurehead under the bowsprit, a figure of a lady with bare breasts very round and wavy hair, although the sea and shoddy seamanship had left her without a lick of paint and her breasts were seamed by the grain of the wood from which she was carved. He saluted her, and as the ship rocked she seemed for a moment to dip towards him, acknowledging. Perhaps she knew he meant to send her back to her proper element, the sea.

He was close to the pirates at the bow gun now. They were just a few feet above him, and he could hear a word or two, a grunt as they lifted a ball into the muzzle, a command to stand clear and the loud bang as the gun was fired. Then hurried movement as they started the process again.

This was his chance, while they were busy. He swarmed up the slightly sloping stones of the breakwater, fingers and toes finding plenty of wide gaps to lodge between the stones. At the top without putting his head over the edge he was able to reach up and touch the taut mooring line, two inches thick. He pulled out the fish knife and began to saw at the rope. One thread snapped apart, then two more. Walter had honed the knife well, for it went through the strands easily and then when only a few were left the weight of the wind and the ship did the rest. There was a faint twang, and the rope parted.

Pert slithered quickly back to the water and began to make his way to the stern, shivering. As he went he was aware that the tunnel was getting wider and he was now moving in the light.

The *Black Joke* was swinging by her stern.

As he hauled himself over the side of *Better Times* there were shouts from the deck of the ship. They had looked up from their work and realised the ship had moved, their guns no longer bearing on the town. There were loud footfalls and a barked order. He reached over his head, then had to stand on a thwart, balancing wildly as the boat pitched. His knife would just reach the taut mooring warp. He sawed once, twice, three times and the rope parted under the strain. Immediately the ship fell away from the breakwater. He pulled at the rope end that released him from the ship's rudder, and ran back to take the helm of *Better Times*.

The *Black Joke* drifted rapidly out towards the centre of the harbour, still swinging round under her own momentum. In a moment her bows would come right round and she would point to the harbour mouth. Pert knew what the crew would do. There was only one thing they could do, to bring the ship under control. If she were to be prevented from crashing across the harbour and fetching up against the opposite side, held into the welter of fishing boats and floating junk by the press of the wind, they had to hoist a sail and give her some forward movement in order for the rudder to bite.

He also could not allow himself to drift down and strand against the quay. The *Better Times* needed to be under control too. He grabbed the halliard and hauled the single sail up halfway, then threw the end of the halliard round the bunt of the sail so that only the top four or five feet could fill with wind. Full sail would just capsize her, the wind was so strong. *Better Times* staggered as the wind snapped the sail open, then gathered herself and surged forward. He settled himself at the tiller.

Better Times was small and gathered speed immediately, a white bone in her teeth. The ship was large and ponderous, and responded only slowly as the men aboard her inched their way along the main yard and cast loose the furled canvas. Once the ship gathered way she would be much faster, but for now Pert found himself creaming rapidly along her high side, overtaking her. As he burst out into clear water ahead of her there were more shouts. He had been spotted. There were several dull popping sounds, and he was dimly aware of little splashes in the water some feet away. They had fired their pistols, and it would now take them at least a minute to reload. By that time he would be far ahead, but that meant he could not now turn and make his way back to the harbour. He had to continue this headlong flight towards the creek.

The wind came swooping across the marshes from his right, and *Better Times* heeled and settled down to her work. He braced his feet in the floor of the boat and concentrated on the tiller, straining and quivering against his arms as she tried to round up into the wind. This was a broad reach, the point of sailing any boat likes best, and she tore down the first stretch of the creek like a thoroughbred, dashing the little waves aside in clouds of spray. He glanced behind, and saw that the ship was doing the same. There was nothing else he, nor they, could do. They were going to sea whether they liked it or not.

Even with one sail set the ship was gaining slowly, but the creek turned to the right and the next reach was closer to the wind. With her fore-and-aft sail and tall spar *Better Times* could lie closer to the wind than the square-rigged ship, and Pert took full advantage, clawing up to windward while the ship wallowed more slowly, having difficulty keeping the sail full of wind. He adjusted the halliard and tidied the bundle of captive sail at the foot, wrapping the reefing lines round and knotting them so the sail wouldn't escape and fill with more wind than he could handle.

At the next bend the wind came free, howling from over his right shoulder. He slacked off the mainsheet, letting the sail out, and *Better Times* was tearing down the final reach. At the bottom was the open sea, and he could see large waves waiting for him. Already the bows were pitching up and down as the waves rolled up the creek and met him head on, but the wind pressed him on. Behind him there was a bang, and a whistle and a tall plume of water rose from the creek several feet to his left. Spray fell into the boat, but he felt elated. They had fired the bow gun at him, and missed. They would not have another chance before they hit the waves and their aim was spoiled.

Then he was among the smother of breakers at the river mouth, and for many minutes he was aware of nothing but the need to keep the sail drawing and driving, smashing the bows into the breakers as they rushed at him, flinging spray and lumps of solid water aside, soaking him again. The wind pushed him on, and he concentrated on keeping the boat straight. If once he let her yaw to one side or the other, she would lose the wind and falter, a breaker would strike from the side, and she'd be over.

Eventually – he neither knew nor cared how long it had been – the breakers gave way to the big, serious rollers of the open sea. Huge and steep they bore down on him, but *Better Times* shook her head in the troughs and rose bravely to the face of each wave, paused at the top, and rushed down the other side to do the same again. He risked a glance behind. The *Black Joke* had gained, for this was more her element than his, the waves bothered her less, and he could see figures in the rigging. Teague was putting out more sail. He could no longer fire his gun with any hope of accuracy in this sea, but his ire was up and he meant to hunt Pert down and crush him.

Pert began to think, for the first time since he had jumped down into *Better Times*. He had been operating on instinct and excitement, making decisions without thought. He had simply done each obvious thing as it presented itself. Now he must consider what to do next.

At the moment they were sailing straight out to sea, with nothing ahead but a thousand miles of storm-tossed ocean. At this rate there was no doubt that *Black Joke*, by far the faster vessel, would overhaul him in an hour or so. What would Pert do, if he were Teague? He might start using the forward gun again, firing indiscriminately in the hope that a lucky shot might find its target. Or he might wait until he was close enough and try picking Pert off with pistol or musket fire. But probably he would rely on the weight and speed of his ship, slowly overhauling *Better Times* until she was crushed under the forefoot and cast aside in splinters and Pert would drown.

What could Pert do to avoid this? His boat was handy and could turn far quicker. He could put the helm up at the last minute and gybe round into the wind, stopping his boat while *Black Joke* rushed past and would then take fifteen minutes to complete her own turn. But gybing was a risky manoeuvre at the best of times, presenting his stern to the wind and letting the wind get the wrong side of the sail and send it crashing across. In this sea it was suicidal, and as the ship passed they would shoot down at him with their muskets and pistols. Could he then turn the other way, coming closer to the wind and slantways across the seas? *Black Joke* could do that as well as he, but it would keep him closer to the shore and out of the deep ocean. Where would he come if he did that? What lay up to windward?

The answer was obvious, and horrifying. Only two miles to windward was Bodrach Nuwl and the Stonefields. He imagined the Stonefields as they would be now, a seething maelstrom of fury, the great breakers roaring up the narrow gullies and the spray flying a hundred feet into the air. There was no surviving the Stonefields in any storm, leave alone a Twenty Year Storm like this.

Suppose he were able to work his way up to windward past Bodrach Nuwl? What lay there? Pert had little idea. He knew from seeing when fishing that the cliffs fell rapidly and then petered out to sandy dunes and little hills inland, but he knew nothing of the shore. Was it sandy or rocky? In either case the breakers would make landing impossible.

He cowered down in the sternsheets, watching the great grey seas rolling under his bows and feeling the lunatic tugging of the mainsheet in his hand. He wished he had something to eat or drink. His face was wet with spray, his mouth foul with salt. He wished he had some dry clothes to put on. He thought of the kitchen fire, and hot milk, and his mother, and his sister talking quietly to the mouse. He thought of Rosella at her desk, her eyes proud and private. He thought of Billy, so sharp and quick and happy. Then he thought of the shop-girls cowering in their basement, and the little Prettyfeet shivering in theirs and wondering when a shell would burst over their heads and set fire to them, and his good Aunt Gittins in her warm cottage up the hill, and Septimus, the ludicrous Septimus who had only just found someone to love and to love him back. He thought of Walter, relaxing at the tiller with his bottle and his old wife waiting with her chair leg and her love for the silly old fool.

His choice came down to this. He almost certainly couldn't survive himself, but he could make sure Teague didn't either. The man was so full of lust and anger, he would hunt Pert until he was certain Pert was dead. So ... Pert would lead him where no ship could survive, where there would be no making port and firing on innocents, no guns and no Brethren of the Seas, just wreck and ruin. He would lead the *Black Joke* into the Stonefields, and let the sea and the Old Man wreak justice.

He put the helm down and hardened in the sheet, and *Better Times* turned through the wind on the crest of one wave, then slid quietly down its back and rose diagonally up the next, the wind in her face. To sail directly to the Stonefields would be a reach with the wind on the beam, but the waves would be on the beam as well which the boat could not stand. Instead he must beat up to windward, taking the waves on his port bow, keeping control and relying on leeway to carry him along the coast instead of out to sea. All boats make leeway, sailing forward but also slipping sideways at the same time. He would sail slightly out to sea, but in reality would slip along the coast until he reached the Stonefields.

Behind him *Black Joke* matched his course, rising more easily to the seas than he, but probably making more leeway. He dare not relax his attention, for to head too far into the wind would take the drive out of the sail and rob him of the power to steer, leaving him to wallow helplessly in the troughs. He drove onward, every nerve and sinew bent on his own destruction.

It seemed to take no time at all before under his lee he could see white water and clouds of spray, and dimly make out the dull roar as the ocean met the intractable land. He hardened in his sheet and pointed more into the wind, slowing his forward progress, and looked round to see where *Black Joke* was. He hadn't looked at her for a long time, so it was a shock to see how close she was. Her great bows rose only yards away, one moment pointing up to the sky so that he could see the copper under her hull, the next crashing into the trough in a welter of foam. She had three sails drawing now, and in the bow stood a tall black figure.

Pert kept the *Better Times* hesitating a little longer, her sail drawing but her progress almost stalled, so that the *Black Joke* would get close before he changed course. He wanted to do it suddenly so that the pirates would react automatically and without considering the consequences.

He could almost look into Teague's black eyes, he was close enough to see the half open mouth and the savage grin, and the strong hand grasping the forestay, and the eager foot poised on the rail. Teague meant to run him down, and watch as the *Better Times* was smashed under his feet. Pert put the helm up and loosed his sheet. *Better Times* swung obediently, taking the wind from astern, and her bows rose on a white roll of foam as she gathered speed and raced downwind.

When you sail downwind, the wind seems to lose a little of its force and things are quieter, but Pert was approaching a welter of spray and roaring water, and the sound rose to a deafening pitch as the rollers reared up and rushed him towards the rocks. Behind him *Black Joke* reared and plunged, and made another roar of her own from the great bow wave she pushed before her. Pert thought he had never sailed so fast in his life, born landward by the great press of wind and the breakers.

Higher and higher the waves rose, feeling the ground beneath their feet and rearing up to plunge upon it as though they thought they could consume it by the sheer weight. Once Pert looked back and found that while he was in a trough, *Black Joke* was careering down the face of the wave behind him, speeding down towards him as though it could spear right through him and down to the bottom. He thought he could see the lunatic light in Teague's eyes as he turned and shouted to the men at the helm, waving one arm. The roller passed under them, and Pert was on a crest while the *Black Joke* heaved up behind him.

The crest was starting to break, and *Better Times* was picked up and rushed shorewards at a breathtaking speed. She was not going to slide down the face of this wave, for this wave was going to curl and hurl her with it. The water beneath her turned white and green and insubstantial as though she might no longer float, and Pert thought that he was on top of the world, looking down at the rocks and the trough behind him where *Black Joke* still followed, and the white water far below in front. He could see rocks he recognised, but not as he remembered them. No longer did they tower over the entrance to the big gully where Walter had brought him. Instead, Pert on his wave towered over them, and they were consumed in water that rolled over them and poured off their tops still blue and solid.

Then the wave began to break. It was a slow thing, and Pert had time to observe. First *Better Times* sunk suddenly as the bubbles beneath her no longer held her weight, then she tilted sharply forward, her bow pointing down the almost vertical slope, and began to rush quickly down. Pert could do nothing but let go of the tiller and hold on as tight as he could. The boat was tilting further and further, practically standing on her bows, and then the crest hit her from behind as it tumbled down the face, and she was sunk into a welter of foam and water and noise, rushed down and down until she must surely crash into the ocean floor, and turned this way and that, and almost over but miraculously staying right side up and then pushed forward between pillars of rock that flashed past, a wall of white water pushing her inland and inland but losing its force gradually so that she steadied.

Pert was able to look back. Crouching in the stern sheets he clung to the gunwhale and watched. Behind them the next wave towered, rising higher and higher, impossibly tall. Pinioned on its front face was the *Black Joke*, looking like a toy, so steeply raised that Pert was looking down on her deck from above. He saw the black figure in the bow, still grimly clinging, and another figure lose its grip and fall down the decks, and the great gun amidships come off its mounting and tumble into the focs'le and then the wave fell on it all at once, and the ship hit the rock on the left hand side and flew apart.

One moment the *Black Joke* was there, suspended in the air but whole, the next there was nothing, just a cloud of black timbers, half a mast in the foam here, a yard and sail there, splinters flying up and scattering over the rocks, an explosion of wood and canvas and iron and copper that rose in the air and then fell. And then ... nothing.

Better Times rocked, and her forward rush was slowing, but she was upright and little damaged, and Pert crouched in the stern stunned and wide eyed, unable to comprehend what he had seen. A ship, a fine, powerful, wicked black ship with men and guns and masts and ten thousand miles of ocean under her keel, and in a moment, gone. There was nothing. He fell into the bottom of the boat and wept, and then leaned over the side and was sick.

While he lay, *Better Times* ran on. The wind was robbed of its force by the high rocks on either side and by its need to rise up the face of Bodrach Nuwl, but it was still there and the small area of sail still forced her onwards. And the great breakers were spent, but still they surged up the gully and carried her with them. Once or twice she grated on the rocks, but righted herself and ran on.

Quieter and quieter it grew, and less and less the motion, and still she ran more and more gently. Pert sat up and took notice. The seaweed walls slid past. He saw the entrance to the rock pool, and then it was gone. Then the tall red rock Walter had described. Here the main channel turned leftwards, but Pert put his hand to the tiller and guided the boat to the right, into a narrower defile. Don't turn, Walter had said, don't turn. He would not turn.

Overhead the wind still howled, but it seemed a long way off now. Down here was peace, and gloom, and sucking water in the weed. The boat rocked quietly, and slid onwards. Darker and darker it grew, and deeper and deeper the defile, and she slowed and slowed, and then slid to a stop. There was a little grating noise under the bow, and *Better Times* had beached herself.

Pert stood. The cliff face rose sheer in his face, and he had to lean back to follow it upwards. To the right there was a gentler slope, and green, where rocks and earth formed a buttress up the face of the cliff, but here was just vertical rock, silent. They had beached on a little ledge of stones and pebbles. He stepped out and waded ashore, and pulled the boat up to make it more secure.

On his left, only yards away, was a grey hull, the timbers silvery with wear and exposure to sun and wind. It lay canted away from him, low in the water and on the stones, clearly stove in beneath the waterline. There was no mast or rigging, though a litter of old spars lay on its deck. It might have been here for ten years, or a hundred. Here was the boat Walter had seen, and thought he might have imagined.

He looked up to the top of the cliff. The sky was a little lighter there, but lit with a rosy glow. The fires in the town were still burning. In the confusion and fury of the waters he had forgotten the town. There the houses were still flaming and people were wandering in the streets wondering what to do and where to go. But the shooting had stopped, that was something.

Pert found it hard to think about the town, and the people he loved who were in it. Somehow his mind had moved away from them, and for the moment they didn't seem real, but just a story he had heard long ago. He wondered if there were any way back from here. He had never heard of anyone climbing up from the bottom of Bodrach Nuwl. It was impossible to scale a thousand feet of vertical rock. He would have to wait until the storm abated, and then try to sail home. *Better Times* was only a little damaged, she would float.

XXX

Thou hast thrust sore at me that I might fall (Psalm 118)

Rosella ran and ran, with Grubb's harsh panting behind her. She didn't feel as good as she usually did when she ran. She liked running, the feeling of her long limbs working, carrying her swiftly away from what she feared, or towards what she wanted. But she had been days with little food or drink, and she had been dragged and manhandled and frightened, and she no longer felt that familiar live spring in her heels.

She ran up the cobbled Canonry with the woman behind her. Surely she should have shaken her off by now? She was an old woman, big and heavy. She was strong, but how could she run like this? She could hear the laboured breathing, and the heavy clump of the feet. She would get to the top of the lane, and then dart off to one side or other, leap from tussock to tussock, and lose her bulky pursuer, and then she could double back to Pert.

Pert, she thought, why isn't Pert here? She wished Pert were running with her. He had tried to save her, she was sure, but something had gone wrong. She was on her own now, but she still had her good legs and her good thick boots. God, she had caught that woman such a crack! One, two, right on the shins where it hurt the most! She had enjoyed that. But it hadn't stopped the old hag.

A vision of the Vicar came to her mind, leaping and bounding down the drive with his flaming cassock trailing behind. Presumably he was dead now. She hoped so. She had always hated him, the thin beaky face that judged her, and the mean little eyes that watched her when he thought no one was looking, following her, measuring her up and down. She hoped he was dead, and that it had hurt dying.

Run, run, she thought. There were others behind her. Who were they? Who were they after? They must be after her. They were

Grubb's confederates, either the bully gang or the pirates. She knew pirates had been in the basement of the Emporium, though they hadn't bothered her. She had heard their coarse laughter through the door, though, and knew they were talking about her.

Nearly at the top of the lane now, the cobbles left behind and sandy grass under her feet, less easy to run fast on. Her pursuers were still there, the odd shout, and the panting, and the sense of malice following her as she ran. There, now the lane had ended, and she was on springy turf. Now was the time to look for the chance to turn and take to the rough moorland. She looked to one side and then the other. Not yet, not yet, put on a sprint, make a little distance. Legs not responding, can't give that little extra. Keep going, this is a pace that can be maintained a long time, it's just that little extra that's missing.

Pert, she thought, why isn't Pert here? He'd know what to do. That day on the hill after the fight, paddling in the stream, holding his hand. She had relived that perfect day over and over in her dismal cellar. He'd been so nice. Why wasn't he here? He would be if he could, she thought. She knew he wouldn't let her down. She risked a glance over her shoulder. Damn! The woman still plodded behind, heavy and resolute, but the people behind had fanned out. Still behind her, but out on both sides, there were large figures running, one holding a pistol and one a curved sword, a cutlass. It was the pirates. The pirates were after her.

How could seamen run so well? Perhaps she was slowing. Perhaps it wasn't them speeding up, it was her not keeping the pace. Pirates spent the time drinking and scaring people, not running. But here they were, heavy shoes pumping, iron-hard muscle and sinew urging them on. After her, urging them on after her. Behind them in turn were more people, all running. Who were they? More pirates? Or other people from the town?

Who were they chasing? Surely everyone in the world wasn't

317

chasing her? She was just a girl, for goodness' sake, she wasn't anyone important. She hadn't even done anything wrong, except play truant from school for one afternoon. Run, keep running. That's what you do best, Rosella. Run!

She was running on rock some of the time, and the wind in her face was pushing her back. This wasn't going well. Should she turn, go like a rabbit from hummock to hummock, slip between them and back down? She might make it to the stream and follow it down through the trees, they might not know about that. She looked around again. No, they'd fanned out even more, and the outriders had even caught up a bit. The foremost pirates were almost level with her now, but well out to the sides. They would cover any sideways dart she made, or shoot at her with their pistols. A particularly strong blast of wind caught her and knocked her sideways and she almost lost her footing. The gale was fierce here, and behind she could feel rather than see the angry red flames lighting the clouds. Careful, careful, the wind's hitting first from one side and then the other. If you fall over you'll be done for. Grubb's still there, groaning and swearing softly to herself, but she's there.

When she came up here with Pert they'd had to get down and crawl, and the wind was far stronger now than it had been then. But crawling wasn't an option. Pump, legs, keep pumping. At least the wind will be slowing them as well. It plastered her thin dress against her body, wrapping it round her legs and making running harder. She hitched the skirt up and held it with one hand up above her thighs. There was a sort of roaring, flapping sound behind her, and she knew that Grubb had the same problem. Her voluminous clothing, always black, in many different layers, must be holding her up. She looked over her shoulder. Grubb had done the same thing. She had hiked her skirts up and held them with both hands. Her great thick legs were pumping, and she swore in a steady stream of hatred and her horrible piggy eye blazed after Rosella.

Another blast hit her, and she stumbled, and put out both hands to save herself, and then found that she could run forward on all fours just as fast. Her running must have been slowed so much by the wind that she could now gallop just as well. She hadn't realised. She scuttled like a crab, she thought, but forward and not sideways. Thank God for her boots, she couldn't have made half this distance in the flimsy shoes her father made her wear. It was all rock under her hands and feet now, no grass left. She must be nearing the top.

An enormous gust of wind swooped down and got underneath her and for one sickening moment she thought it would pick her up and throw her back down the hill, right into the arms of her pursuers. She might go over the head of Grubb and the pirates, but the people behind them were still coming. She flattened herself, then scuttled on, her dress flogging wildly in the blast. It was torn near the hem, she hadn't noticed when, and the tear was lengthening up the seam at every step she took.

The rocks began to level off, and she realised with a sick feeling that she was nearly at the end. There was nowhere else to go. She crouched near to the rock, and scuttled on all fours, thinking of nothing but avoiding those grasping hands. There were whoops and shouts now, from the pirates. They knew their quarry was finished. There was a yell of surprise, and one of them was rolling over and over back down the hill, knocked over by the wind. Grubb seemed unaffected, too squat and heavy for the wind to get a grip. She was coming slowly now, her arms outstretched, a dreadful grin on her face.

Rosella stopped, crouching. Her dress thundered and flapped around her. Grubb came forward still. Rosella looked from side to side, but there were men creeping forward, men with knives and cutlasses, keeping low but making a semicircle round her and Grubb.

"Grubby, Grubby," one of the men sang, his voice barely audible above the wind. "We've come fer you, Grubby! Come on, Grubby!"

The woman turned and looked at them. "You scum-sucking cowards!" she spat. "Yellow, spineless vermin! All of you, for one woman and a girl? Isn't there one of you with the courage to take on an old woman? Come on, not one?"

"No need, Grubby," grinned another man, crawling forward. "We're not goin' ter make lovey dovey with you!"

"Though we might makes an exception fer the girly," said another.

Rosella didn't move. Grubb backed towards her. The men crept forward. Then suddenly Grubb sprang. She whirled, and before Rosella could move the big hands had her, had her by the arm and the throat, and she found herself lifted into the air, clasped to that iron-hard bosom.

"Is this what you fancy, then?" the woman called, her voice hoarse and foul. "Little bit of fresh meat? See," she pulled at Rosella's clothing, lifting her skirt, "see, fresh and springy. Is this what you fancy? Come on, you can have her! I'll give her to you!"

"Naw, Grubby," said the leading pirate, "that won't swim, 'cos when we've stuck you and chucked you over the edge, we're 'avin' the filly anyway!"

"This is easier. Come, take her! I'll give her to you! You can do what you like with her, I don't care! Take her back to the ship with you! I wanted her for myself, but you can have her!"

Behind the pirates another circle of men had appeared, also crawling up the hill against the wind, but the pirates didn't seem to notice, so intent were they on their prey. They were still moving closer, close enough to poke out with their cutlasses and feint stabs at Grubb and Rosella. Then the leader rose to his feet, intent on making the final rush, and the others rose with him, silhouetted against the flaming sky.

Grubb's grip shifted slightly in response, and Rosella took her chance. She bit down on the hand that held her, bit as hard as she could, bit with her good young teeth and tasted blood in her mouth. The woman yelled and convulsed, and Rosella fell at her feet.

"Why, you vicious little whore ..." the woman groaned and brought out her knife. Rosella pushed herself to her feet and rushed. One last kick, she thought, and hacked one, two, and the woman screamed and seized her by the collar and Rosella continued her rush and kicked and kicked again and pushed and suddenly there was no more ground and the wind rushed in her ears and she was falling.

XXXI

They fell down, and there was none to help (Psalm 107)
The sorrows of death compassed me (Psalm 18)

Pert stood still on the little beach, looking up. As he watched, two figures appeared in the void above. One was small and pale. It plummeted down, seemed to brush the rock face once and then tumble over and over as it fell, and vanished.

The other was black and square, and he knew without thinking that it was Urethra Grubb. She fell, and then the wind in her voluminous clothing appeared to buoy her up, and she stretched out her arms, and tilted and poised. She seemed to glide out from the cliff, flying in a great circle, scarcely losing height. She raised her head and he could hear, floating down from the air, a harsh croak of triumph. She flashed past the cliff face and out again, soaring on the gale, arms and legs outstretched, clothes billowing, and began another great circle.

Then some wayward gust of wind caught her, or she miscalculated her control or a piece of clothing gave way, because she wobbled, and flapped for a moment, dashed straight into the cliff face, then began to fall.

Headfirst she came, growing larger and larger, her clothes roaring and flapping as she fell, and hit on a flat rock nearer the mouth of the Stonefield with a popping sound like an egg breaking. She stood there on her head, wider than she was tall, silhouetted against the foaming waves with her great boots in the air, and then a wave broke over the rock, there was a flash of pink foam and she was gone.

XXXII

For I am ready to halt and my sorrow
is continually before me (Psalm 38)

Pert stood for a long time. Just as he had known immediately that the second figure was Grubb, he had also known the first faller, the one that had tumbled and gone straight down. He knew that slight, pale figure, recognised the flash of yellow dress. His mouth fell open and he realised that the high keening noise he could hear came from his own throat. Slowly he sat down on the stones. Rosella was dead.

Later when he thought back to that moment and tried to remember what he had felt, the only word he could come up with was "empty". Grief would strike him later, but at that moment he just felt ... empty. He was empty. His life was empty. The world was empty. He had known Rosella since he was six, and she five, when she had first appeared at infant school, a self-contained, confident little tot with almost-blonde hair and dazzling brown eyes. Ever since, she had always been there. True, she had never acknowledged his existence, but there he had been and there she had been, year after year. And he had watched her, and laughed when she laughed, and cried for her on the rare occasions she cried, and been proud when she was clever which was most of the time, and made excuses for her on the rare occasions when she was not.

And now she was not there any more. She was gone, and his life was over. There would be no return for him now. His family would mourn but would manage without him, his sister would certainly weep but would then go on with her life, the town would hardly remember who he was in a week or two. His purpose in being had vanished, and he felt that he would prefer to fade and vanish as well. There was nothing else to do.

He stood and wandered round the little beach vacantly. Overhead the wind still blew but there were stars in the sky now. The

323

rags of cloud were flying away, and the storm would blow itself out. The glow in the sky was dimming too, as the flames died down. There would be smoke for days, but it was blowing inland and he could not see that from where he stood.

He looked at the wreck. It held little interest for him, but he wandered over to it anyway. He climbed up to its deck, which gave under his feet. Some planks still held, though, and he was able to make his way to the little deckhouse. On the side was a piece of wood, nicely carved round the edges with a mermaid at one end and a foul anchor at the other. Incised into the wood were the words *Bight of Benin.*

He smiled wryly at himself. Of course it was. The idea had occurred to him when Walter told him about the wreck. It was obvious, really. This was all that was left of his grandfather's boat, the *Bight of Benin.* Mascaridus Potts, the arch-villain, the ex-pirate who sailed with and was beloved by the infamous Benito de Soto, the upstanding fisherman, the leader of the Free Fishers, hadn't made off with the treasure to sunnier climes at all. He might have stolen the treasure, true enough, but he'd ended here, in the dark and damp at the foot of the Old Man. It seemed rather fitting that his grandson should do the same.

He went back to the *Better Times* and curled up under the sail and looked up at the stars, but could not sleep. He thought of his mother. And Fenestra, what was she doing? Sleeping, probably, and tomorrow she'd give Billy another reading lesson, and tell him a story and be happy. And Rosella?

He thought about Rosella. Where was she, and what was she doing? She was lying broken on the rocks somewhere, all alone. All alone, and cold, and nobody would come and be with her. She would be so lonely and sad. And at last the tears came and he cried. He cried for Rosella, and he cried for himself, and he cried for the afternoon on the moor and for the demoiselles in her hair, and he made a decision. He would lie there till it was light, and then he would go and find Rosella, and be with her.

He woke at dawn, and realised that he had slept after all though he did not feel refreshed, just empty and pointless. But his resolve was the same, so he set off across the rocks.

He looked up and tried to judge just where he had seen her fall. It was not directly above him, but a little way along to the south, in the direction of the town. He looked out to sea, where the lumpen swell was still heaving on the rocks though without yesterday's savagery. He thought he could see the rock where Grubb had fallen, but of course Grubb had flown somewhat first so it wasn't a very good indication.

The clambering was very hard, for the rock was jumbled and young, with sharp edges and many crevices to trap your feet. He lost count of the number of times he came to a dead end, a rock too tall to climb, or a gully too wide to jump, and had to retrace his steps and try another way. The sun came up and presently he was too hot, so he took his jacket off and tied it round his waist. He had nothing to drink, and there was no fresh water here.

By the middle of the day the sun was overhead and burning. He wet his handkerchief in a gully of salt water and draped it over his head, which helped a little. In front of him was a *glacis* of loose rock and spoil, where a piece of the cliff had not fallen but simply slid down. The going was a little easier here and he made good progress. By constantly looking above him he thought he was approaching the place where she had fallen.

At the top of the *glacis* was a raw scar of rock with some earth, where the great mass had slipped down, and above it some hundred or hundred and fifty feet above him was a shelf of green, where grass still grew and a few bushes still clung. The cliff rose above them, but there was a cleft in it, making a ravine that ran back into the body of the cliff and here there were more trees sheltering from the blast. He headed up hill towards them across the *glacis*.

Sometimes his feet slipped, and sometimes the ground gave under him and he slid down the slope with loose stones round his feet, and had to cling to the ground with both hands while the stuff settled again. Then he would have to make good the height he had lost.

Other times he would come to a more vertical section he could not climb for fear that more would break off and carry him with it, so he would have to go left or right until he found a way up. The wind was dying, and the sun had gone over the top of the cliff, so he was cooler though the effort of climbing was a trial to him, and he had still eaten and drunk nothing. He kept climbing though, relying on the numbness of his grief to shut his mind up and keep him from worrying about his own discomfort.

He thought about Rosella, sometimes without meaning to, and the tears would flood his eyes and he would have to stop and weep for a while, crying loudly with his mouth open and not bothering to hide it because there was no one to hear. Other times he thought about her on purpose, reminding himself of her pale body lying somewhere above him all alone, to force himself to keep going. He wasn't sure what he would do when he found her. A grave was an impossibility on these slopes, and he had nothing with which to dig. The idea of dropping her into a hole or over an edge was unthinkable. He only thought about finding her and being with her. Perhaps the best he could do was to lie beside her and hold her poor hands until he died as well, for he was sure he was not going to get off this cliff alive, and wouldn't have wanted to if he could. He knew he might get back to the *Better Times* and sail her home so Walter would still have his good boat, but then he thought of Rosella and knew it was impossible. She needed him more.

As it grew dark he searched for a place to rest, and eventually his strength gave out where a small fall of rock had left a scoop of gravel and a little vertical face above it so that he could lie with his back towards the rock. He laid his head on the gravel and closed his eyes, but the tears came again and forced them open.

Through them he saw the watery void in front. It would be so easy to just roll down and let himself go, and allow the comfortable air to cushion him and let him down and down and it would all be over. He could die so easily and quietly, without effort. It was an alluring prospect, but Rosella kept coming into his mind, lying broken on the hillside somewhere, and he couldn't do it. She was so lonely, and no one else knew where she was. Even the dead need some company, surely? There was nothing else he could do for her, so surely he must do this much, hold her and be with her as she started her journey into oblivion?

He woke at dawn, bitterly cold. His limbs screamed with the cold, and his heart quailed, but even before he made the effort to open his eyes Rosella was there. If he was cold, how bitter must she feel? He was alive at least, but she didn't even have the comfort of a beating heart and flowing blood. He could hear a chattering, clacking sound near at hand, and thought it must be seabirds rattling their beaks on their ledges.

When he finally opened his eyes he saw a small pink flower, shaking in the wind. He saw it hazily, his eyes not yet focused. It had a small spray of leaves around it. As his sight cleared he could see that its roots were half exposed by the wind that whipped the soil from it. Small pebbles lay between it and him, and behind it was a grey sky. Lifting his head a little he could see the brown shale above him, which had fractured and allowed the rock in front to fall away, creating this bed for him.

His limbs ached, and there was an excruciating pain in his hip where he had been lying on a stone. He shifted to avoid it, and the pain got worse. He began to sit up, but had to grab hold of the earth to stop himself from sliding down. He had slept on a ledge that in daylight was barely nine inches wide, and below him was nothing but empty air. That he had not turned in his sleep and fallen to his death was a small and quite pointless miracle.

With infinite care he inched his way along the shelf by wriggling first a shoulder, then his hip, then his feet. Little stones cascaded down at every movement, but soon the shelf grew wider and he was able to haul himself onto a little pocket of grassy slope where several gulls glared at the intruder. One pecked at him, and others hopped to get nearer, thinking perhaps they might mob him. He spoke to them softly, speaking gibberish, and after a while they relaxed and went back to grooming their feathers and making clicking noises to each other.

He lay between the rudimentary nests they had made for themselves, mere scrapes in the earth, and gave rein to the grief that filled him. It was like a blanket at the back of his head, smothering his reason and his throat so that his thoughts ran loose and his throat opened and the tears sprang forth. He wept, and wept, crying and keening, and the gulls cried too, sharing his desolation.

When the spasm had passed he looked around and chose the route of his next attempt at the climb. He would climb for fifteen minutes, and then pause and weep again, then go on. That would be the routine, a routine of loss and hopelessness. He crawled to the top of the slope and took to the hard stone. At first it was not so bad, but then it grew steeper. He had to find a handhold, reach out and grasp it, then look for a foothold not too far below it and transfer one foot to that. Then another handhold, and then the last foothold. Then a small heave, maybe only six inches, and start again.

Some handholds were hard won, scraped out of crevices with his broken fingernails, rooting out small plants that had taken two or three years to win themselves this tiny home, only to be dispossessed rudely by his desperate fingers. Others were easier, a natural ledge or fault that offered enough room for a hand. Footholds were the same, but sometimes just a small protuberance of rock had to make do, a place where the face was not quite vertical and he had to rely on the grip of his leather shoe. When he found a place that offered four reasonable holds and would not let him down, he was able to relax and let the grief well up again, and weep for a few minutes, then gasp and take a deep breath and start again.

Looking down he could see that he had won less than forty feet of height since he had slept, and was clinging like a fly to what from a distance would seem a vertical sheet of rock. From his viewpoint it was a landscape of gaps and faults and crevices, each to be explored or ravaged as he climbed. His mouth hung open, and his breath came in gulps, and his limbs shook with fatigue and, when he looked down at the ridiculous feat he was attempting, sheer terror. Though the gale had passed, the wind had not died completely away, but tugged at him first from one side and then from the other, trying to get underneath and prise his body from the cliff. Once it got under his jacket and wrapped it round his face and he could not see where to put his hands or his feet and had to cling there and wait until the wind turned and blew the jacket back the way it had come. That was a very bad time, and he was very frightened.

As the day warmed the flies found him, and began to buzz round his head, and try to settle on his eyes and mouth. At first he tried to twitch his head and frighten them off, but they were persistent. It seemed so unfair, that with everything else that had happened they should be picking on him now, when he could not spare a hand to brush them away. He even chuckled wryly to himself. It was a bit funny, that however low you fell, there was always something to make you lower. After an hour or two he got used to them and just let them land and crawl on him.

In a sense it was the spasms of grief that saved him, as they prevented him from dwelling on the abyss below his feet. While he hung back his head and bawled in desolation, still his unconscious mind was working away, charting the face of the rock above him and plotting his next moves, so that when he reached a shuddering quietus he could begin to climb again.

He did not know, and could afterwards not remember, just how long he climbed with his muscles shrieking for relief and his bloody fingertips leaving a trail on the rock. He knew that in time the pauses when he wept were welcome, moments when he could turn his mind from physical pain. He summoned them deliberately every few steps, forcing himself to think of the girl, his girl, his poor girl lying on the rocks with no one to hold her or be with her.

He could not remember how long it was, but it must have been the entire day because when the ground he reached up for began to slope away from him and become less vertical, it was evening and the sun had already left him. He did not think to wonder what he would have done if nightfall had caught him out on the bare rock. He certainly could not have clung by his finger-tips through the night, but waking or sleeping must have let go sooner or later and just gently leaned back and fallen. What a relief that would have been.

But here he was, now, on a steep grassy slope again. The light was getting bad, and the air was dropping cool. There were even a few bats flitting along the rock faces, hunting and squeaking. He wondered what they did when the wind blew. There must still be calm places here where they could hunt in shelter. He began looking around for a place to spend his second night. Above him there was the beginning of the cleft he had seen from far below, and there he could make out bushes and even a couple of straggly trees. He thought this was underneath the falling place but as he had moved along, the shape of the cliff above him looked different and he was no longer sure whether he had come too far or not far enough.

In a last scramble he reached the place where there was more grass, and proper undergrowth, and a few last insects buzzed. He lay on the grass facing the sea, the ground falling sharply away before him where he had climbed up. Above him, craning back, still rose six or seven hundred feet of rock, deep in shadow now but he could see the edge because that was where the stars stopped. He turned on his front, and ran his eye down and down towards the place where he now was, and as he did so he caught a glimpse of something light. In the dusk he could not see its colour, but it showed up pale in the twilight, and did not belong.

He got up and forced his weary limbs to climb again, soon having to hand himself from one branch to the next gnarled branch because he had plunged into the bushes and trees that lined the gully. He kept the pale patch in sight as he climbed. Perhaps it was just some paper that had blown there, or a dead animal that had fallen and become desiccated, or a scrap of canvas from some ship in the storm or in the storm before that. Canvas would be useful, because he could sleep under it.

When he got to it, it was caught in the branches of a tree only three or four feet from the ground. In the dim light he had to go very close to it to see, but he wasn't frightened because he had been through all the emotions there were, and couldn't be scared of anything any more.

It was her. Rosella lay on her back on a litter of broken branches, sprawled just as she had fallen and landed. The branches had come down with her when she crashed through them. Her yellow dress was in tatters, and the flesh that showed through was red and lacerated. There was blood on her face, and her eyes were closed. One leg was bent at an unnatural angle. She was almost unrecognisable, but her hair, her lovely hair was still bright.

He touched her. She was cold, but he had expected that. In fact he had expected her to feel colder. He put his face to hers and kissed her, only their third ever kiss and, he supposed, their last. Her lips were cold, bruised and swollen, but not icy and still soft. He tried to stop himself believing, in case it was not true, but he couldn't. She was nearly dead, broken and smashed and hurt, and she was probably dying, but she was not quite dead yet. At least he could make her a little comfortable. At least now he could say goodbye, and she would not die alone.

He held her, cradling her in his arms and putting his face beside hers, and cried wet tears that ran down his face and onto hers, and he felt her stir beside him, and her head turned a little towards him and her eyes opened.

She spoke in a whisper so faint it might have been just the fluttering of a breath, "I knew you'd come. Took your time, though." Her eyes closed again. The merest ghost of a smile played on her lips.

XXXIII

He healeth the broken in heart, and
bindeth up their wounds (Psalm 147)

How good and how pleasant it is to dwell together (Psalm 133)

Rosella lay on a bed of dry branches and bracken, with Pert's coat over her. Beside her a little fire burned fitfully, smoking slightly, and from time to time she would lean and put an extra twig on it, ekeing out their small store with care for it took Pert a long while to gather suitably dry material, searching in the leaf litter up the comb. Over her head the cave arched, with ferns dropping from crevices. Bats lived further in towards the back of the cave, and watching them fly out at dusk and back again at first light was one of her entertainments. She had lain thus for a week or more, slowly gaining strength.

Their first meal in this place had been a grim experience. Pert had found some gull's eggs, and had tried to cook them by cracking them onto a flat stone heated in the fire. The result had been a leathery pancake of gritty substance that tasted of fish and feathers and made her gag, but it had gone down and stayed down and presumably done some good. They had experimented with raw egg beaten in the shell, and that had been even worse.

The fire was a great triumph, and they were careful never to let it go out. It had taken many hours for Pert, hunkered down over a little heap of dry twigs and grass, to coax a spark from a stone when he struck it with his knife, and then to nurture the feeble flame until finally it caught. He had searched for most of a morning to find the right kind of stone, but he was discovering reserves of patience he had not suspected before.

After a couple of days his patience had been rewarded in another way, when he managed to snag a rabbit. Further up the comb it opened out into a broad plateau where rabbits had made a colony. So unused to humans were they that Pert had been able to walk slowly among them and simply pick one up, but then had not known how to kill it. In the end he gritted his teeth, held it by the hind legs and swung it against a rock, and had nearly thrown up when he felt the legs stretching and moving in his hand long after it was dead.

They had cooked it – or rather, Pert had cooked it, for Rosella could not sit up yet, let alone move about – by spearing it with a stick and holding it over the fire. The meat had been alternately burned to a crisp and practically raw, but again it had served its purpose.

Water was a problem. They had plenty, for there was a small spring of perfectly fresh water a little higher up the hill, water that had fallen as rain at the top of the cliff and then spent weeks draining down through the rock to appear as a welcome trickle among the trees that relied on it. But carrying it was another matter. Folded leaves had been a failure, the water draining away before Pert could get it back to the cave. In the end he had taken his trousers off, soaked them in the rivulet and made Rosella suck the water from the cloth. If she felt revolted at the thought of sucking his trousers she didn't show it but had drunk ravenously and sent him back for more. Later he had stumbled on a piece of tin, thrown from the top or blown here by the gale perhaps, and had bent the edges up to make a shallow bowl after first scrubbing it clean with water and gravel.

She lay back and sighed with content. Outside the breeze blew gently, whisking away the smoke from the fire. At the mouth of the cave there was a clump of foxgloves, and a bee was droning its way from one flower to another. She hoped it would go safely home before the bats stirred. She could see a patch of blue sky, and beneath it just a sliver of sea gleaming in the sunlight which would not reach the mouth of the cave until late in the afternoon. When the weather served, she and Pert watched the sunset, she lying back in her bed and he beside her, stroking her hair and not thinking of anything. She felt really happy then.

The first night when he had found her lying head down in the tree was a dreadful time. He thought she was dying, that she had hung on just long enough for him to find her, and would now slip away and leave him so that he would have to go through the agony a second time. He had pulled her down to the ground with great care, but even so her face showed that every movement was insufferable pain. Then he had cradled her in his arms and done his best to keep her warm through the night, not sleeping himself but revelling in her weak warm breath on his throat. Every faint puff of air meant another ten seconds in which she had not died, and they were together. Since he was a little boy he had dreamed of holding her in his arms, but he had never imagined it would be quite like this, the cold wind rushing over them and the hard bright stars slowly wheeling and nowhere warm to go.

He had tried to fix a wood splint to her leg, but she screamed whenever he touched it. In the end they had decided it was not really broken, just wrenched, for she could still move her toes and even her whole leg with a tremendous effort, her eyes screwed up with pain. Over the days there had been a small improvement, and the leg no longer looked so unnatural.

Her yellow dress, almost her only garment, had been torn to shreds in the fall. He had removed it from her, dried it in the sun with stones on it to stop it blowing away, and had even attempted some rudimentary repairs with a rabbit-bone needle and some thin roots pulled from the ground, but the result pleased neither of them. She had not complained when he took the dress. He had tenderly washed her wounds with water and a scrap of cloth, and had spat into some of the deeper cuts, having heard somewhere that there were things in spit that would hinder infection.

But Rosella was young and strong, and she now had food to eat, however revolting it might taste, and clean water and fresh air. And she had Pert, her quiet, patient, determined nurse who loved her and never for a moment wavered in his care. Her face was still a mass of bruises and scratches, her left eye swollen almost shut, her cheek gashed, and her lips puffed and split, but he remembered her only as she had been that day on the hill, with the sun on her hair and the turquoise tails twitching.

Pert returned, carrying more firewood and a dead rabbit. He was getting good with rabbits now, having found how they would die quickly if you just twisted their necks. He felt this was more seemly than bashing them on a rock. He had nothing against rabbits, benign and trusting creatures, and did not wish to subject them to more indignity than he had to. He had tried to catch other things, but without success. Bats he ignored as there would be so little meat on them, but he did wonder if a plump herring gull might make a meal, or perhaps one of the black and white guillemots, their long black feet so awkward on the ledges where they sat tending their solitary chicks. But they were all too wary, taking off long before he got close, and the idea of taking a helpless guillemot chick seemed unfair. What would the poor parents do when they came back to find the empty ledge? He could not bring himself to do it. He knew how he would feel if he came back to the cave one day and found that Rosella had vanished. She was his child now, and he could imagine their pain. Rabbits were different, they had lots of babies. In any case a guillemot chick would probably taste horribly of fish.

One day he came back to the cave with firewood and eggs and found her sobbing in the bed, great tears rolling unchecked down her face. He put down his load and ran to her, holding her head. "Oh Pert," she whispered, "I wet myself!" He kissed her and stroked her hair till the tears stopped, and then set about undressing her. He had thought so many times about her body, but when it came to it the pale limbs so wounded and twisted, and the lacerated skin of her back and chest and stomach, made it impersonal. He took water and a piece of cloth and sponged her, and pulled the bed to pieces and remade it with fresh bracken, and covered her nakedness with what dry material he could.

"You're such a good boy," she said. "I'm sorry to be a nuisance."

"You're not. You'd do the same," he said gruffly. He spoke roughly because he thought he might cry as well. To make it right he kissed her hair again, and stroked her and whispered soothing words until she went to sleep.

Washing Rosella became a daily routine, and Pert tried to be methodical about washing out scraps of cloth and rag he found, and drying them by the fire or in the sun. Each day he uncovered her, and they sat together while he wiped and cleaned, and discussed each wound, saying that this one was healing well, and wondering when this other one would stop weeping or this bruise would fade. Her body became a familiar territory to him, her small breasts, the pale skin of her armpits, the lovely swell of her buttocks. She accepted his attention happily, and he enjoyed the intimacy and tried to put other thoughts out of his head. But he had favourite parts, like the downy hairs in the small of her back or the slim bones of her ankles. He often wanted to kiss them but did not, for this would have been taking advantage. Unless she were strong enough to kick him or push him away if she wanted, it wouldn't be fair, and somehow it wouldn't count. While he worked he was aware of her gaze on him, and hoped she understood his lack of affection.

Day by day Rosella grew stronger. Soon she was able to sit in the mouth of the cave and watch the insects flying among the low growth of thrift and sea plantain. There was a blush of blue across the ground where spring squill was coming into flower, though she did not know the plant's name. Further up the comb where the little stream flowed Pert had found crowfoot and spearwort and other plants he did not recognise. He remembered his mother naming flowers when they walked, forget-me-nots, and ragged robin and willowherb. He wished he had paid more attention. Probably there were plants here they could eat, or put on Rosella's wounds for a poultice, but he did not know which. He nibbled leaves to see if they would poison him. None did, though none tasted nice either. He thought that later there would be berries they could eat.

Rosella was delighted by a little bird which arrived one day and took up residence in a narrow crack above the cave entrance. It was the size of a sparrow, but entirely black except for a patch of white on its rump. She watched it fly in and out, and followed it as it went down the cliff and out over the water, fluttering and brushing the tops of the waves, then turning and coming home again. It was a trusting little body and took no notice of her. There were other birds like it further down, but this was her special one. She wondered when its mate would come and they would start making eggs in their tight nest.

She made Pert cut her a great stick to use for a crutch, and began making little forays from the cave, holding on to the stick and dragging her injured leg. "See," she said, "I can move it this much!" and waved it in the air, supporting the thigh with one hand.

"It's a very nice leg," he said. "Pity you've only got the one boot."

"You could look for the other boot. It must have come off when I fell. Perhaps it's lying somewhere, and you could find it for me."

"I expect a mouse has found it and made a nest in it. We couldn't just turf all the little baby mice out. You'd have to wait until they moved on."

"You're a daft head," she smiled. "What's more important, me or a mouse?"

"You could wait. You're not ready to do much kicking yet. I know what Fenestra would say. She'd be on the side of the mouse."

Rosella sat back and smiled. "I don't remember falling," she said, "well, not landing anyway, but I do remember before. I did half kick Grubb's shins! It felt lovely. I'd been so frightened, and she'd chased me and chased me and I couldn't get away, and then to turn on her and give her a good kicking ... it was the best thing I ever did! How she yelled!"

"I thought you'd get away easy. She couldn't possibly run as fast as you."

"She just kept coming. She couldn't catch me, but she just wouldn't stop. It was awful. And the men, they were all round us. The pirates. And the others behind them."

"Who were the others?"

"People from the town, I think. I don't know whether they were after me, or after Grubb, or after the pirates or what. I couldn't tell who was on which side."

"Why would they be after you?"

"I don't know. I couldn't think. And I could hardly stop and ask them, could I? What would I have said? 'Excuse me, could we just take a minute to discuss who's hunting who, because I'm a bit confused?' I'd just have got thrown off the cliff."

"You were thrown off the cliff."

"No I wasn't. I pushed Grubb off the cliff. That's quite different. I have to go and sit down now. Come and sit with me."

They sat, and she snuggled into his side. "That's nice. What did you see? Tell me again?"

"I saw you fall. I knew it was you, and I thought you were dead. And I saw Grubb. That was unbelievable. She flew, she actually flew. And then she hit the cliff, and then she just fell, and her head went pop on a rock."

"Serves her right. You know ..." she squirmed round and looked at him, "... you know I'm a murderer now? I killed her. I meant to, as well. When we go back they'll lock me up and send for the magistrate."

"So we won't go back, then. We'll stay here and eat rabbits, and raise a family of mice in your boots."

"They could be our children. I'd rather have both my boots, though."

Pert did find her other boot, and there was no mouse in it. It lay half in the water, half out, a little way upstream from where she had fallen. He took it back to the cave and she greeted it like a long-lost friend. It took over two weeks to dry out, but after that she put it on.

"It feels all stiff. I'll have to walk about in it and soften it up again."

"You look just like yourself now, with both boots. Mind you, that dress is a bit of a disaster. You're not decent. Don't you mind?"

She looked down at herself, at her long bare legs, and the holes in the dress. "I don't if you don't," she said shyly.

"Of course I don't. But you'll be cold when the summer's gone."

"It hasn't even started yet. It'll be ages. We don't have to think about it. And I'll have you to keep me warm."

"I'll be cold myself."

"Then I'll keep you warm. We'll warm each other."

Pert felt a hot flush creeping up his cheeks, and a peculiar feeling in his stomach.

"Yes, we will," he said, and bent over the fire to hide his confusion. "I'd better go for some more firewood. Don't want it to go out."

XXXIV

They passed by together (Psalm 48)

*As for man, his days are as grass: as a flower of the field,
so he flourisheth. For the wind passeth over it, and it is gone;
and the place thereof shall know it no more (Psalm 103)*

The days passed, and the weather grew warm. Rosella discarded the stick and began to limp about on her own, and it was not long before she was able to join him when he went rabbiting or egging, though he would not let her climb along the ledges while the neat kittiwakes whirled round his head. He often thought that one small slip, one careless move, would send him crashing down and all this would have been for nothing and she'd have no one to look after her, so he moved slowly and thought about each handhold.

Crows arrived, and a jackdaw or two. They hopped about the meadow slope, and once Pert found that they'd pecked and pecked at a small rabbit until it died, and then fed upon it messily. After that he drove them off whenever he saw them. They were his rabbits, and no one else was going to eat them.

Their exploration took them further and further afield as Rosella grew stronger, and they began to make some interesting discoveries. By climbing to the very top of the comb they found they could get down into another one just like it, that ran down to the south of theirs but faced less towards the sea and more along the coast. There were several sloping meadows here, one below the other in terraces, all with their own populations of tame rabbits, and a much deeper and more forested gully with a substantial stream at the bottom. Here birds twittered and flitted that were not seabirds at all, and swallows swept overhead, and a hawk patrolled high above. There were dragonflies over the stream, and Pert looked for demoiselles but couldn't see any. The dragonflies perched on stalks near the water, and arched their tails into the water, then flew on.

From the very top of this comb they could just catch a glimpse of the top of the town. They could see grey roofs glinting in the sun, and patches of black where the fire had been.

"What do you think they're doing?" Rosella wondered. "What are my sisters up to, and who's looking after them?"

"Your mother, I expect. And Floris is probably helping her."

"I didn't know Floris. Is she nice?"

"Yes. And she's in love with the curate, and he's in love with her. I think he couldn't pluck up the courage, so she just told him they were going to get married. She's a managing sort of person."

"I should think he needs managing."

"He does. My mother did it a bit, but now Floris is in charge."

She thought for a while, watching the roofs in the distance. "You know, when my father's head came off I didn't mind at all. Do you think that's awful of me? But he wasn't very nice, I don't think. I never liked him. He was very taken up with Grubb, and he used to shout at Mother. He always did that, even when I was small, and she never shouted back. They'll be better off without him. I think that's why I kick. I never want to be like her, frightened."

"You won't be."

"And you'll never shout." She smiled at him, and tucked her arm in his. "Let's never go back, shall we?"

"No, let's not. I'd like to see Fenestra one more time, though."

"She's got her Billy, hasn't she? I didn't really know him, just through the grating. He seemed nice."

"He is. He's not scared of anything, and he worships Fenestra."

"Is she up to it? I mean, can she take being worshipped, and not be cruel to him?"

"Oh yes. She ... sort of ... dotes. Is that the right word? She dotes on him. She calls it lusting, but really it's doting."

She laughed. "She's a bit young to know about lusting! How old is she?"

"She'll be fourteen soon."

"Much too young. You have to be at least sixteen to know anything about that."

"Do you, then? You're nearly sixteen."

"Ooh, look at that pretty plant!" she exclaimed, running to the rock face and examining a small, orange-leaved plant growing in a crack. "It's a roseroot, I think."

"You're changing the subject."

"Yes, I am, aren't I? I'm not ready to talk about some things yet."

"There are some things to talk about, then?"

"Yes." They stood very close together, and she looked at the plant, not him. "We will. Just not quite yet."

The days grew longer and warmer, and the sun stayed for most of each afternoon on the patch of level ground in front of the cave. Rosella's limp had gone, and the swelling on her face had subsided though one place on her temple would always be a little red. She moved lightly and well, and could leap from rock to rock as well as he. They went up the comb and down into the next almost every day, and found some plants that could be eaten.

There were green leaves of watercress waving under the surface of the stream, that tasted fiery but pleasant when mixed with other leaves from the banks, almost like lettuce but with a greener taste. There were still some eggs to be had, and always plenty of rabbits. Their stack of firewood in the cave grew larger for when the nights drew in, and they made a much more elaborate bed of branches and bracken and dried grasses. Clothing was still a problem, but they were rarely cold. The west wind was warm, and the sun shone each day, and down on the sparkling sea they could see fishing boats as the town returned to normality.

Rosella's dress was gradually falling into total ruin, and one day she became impatient of the tatters that remained and took it off, and went round in her drawers all day. Pert found it hard to keep his eyes from her breasts, and in the afternoon she declared that she wanted to wash her drawers and took them off too.

"If I'm going to be like this," she said, "so should you. Your clothes could do with a wash as well," so they went bare-skinned to the stream and washed themselves and their clothes on the stones, and laid the clothes out on the rocks to dry. After that there didn't seem much point putting them on again, so they ran around and hunted like a pair of savages among the rocks where the red valerian bloomed in every crevice. Rosella picked a flower head and put it in her hair.

"Just imagine if they could see us!" she giggled. "Imagine Miss Throstle, and all those other frosty old dames! They'd have a heart attack!"

"It would be old Merridew who had the heart attack," Pert said.

"We could just walk into the classroom and sit down as though nothing was happening, and he'd go red in the face and his head would explode!"

That night they lay in their prickly bed, arms entwined, and watched the bright moon rise over the ocean, making a silver track that reached towards them. A soft chill wind blew into the mouth of the cave, but they were warm.

"I'm just thinking about all the things that happened," she said. "The nasty things, and the brave things you did. It all seems a long way off now. How do stories end? This all happened to us, and that's our story. But what happens now?"

He kissed her hair "Stories don't end," he whispered, "I don't suppose. They go on, but they get boring."

"Boring sounds good to me. Put your hand there. That's nice."

There was a moment's silence broken only by the soft crackle of the fire and a fall of ash. "But ours can't end here, not in this cave. It'll be winter soon. We'll freeze, and starve, or get blown away or something."

Pert grunted. "We'd better make a move, then, before it happens. I climbed up here, so we must be able to get down again if we take our time and go careful. The boat will still be there. We can't go back or we'll be arrested, probably. But we can go north, along the coast, and find somewhere no one knows us."

"Yes. All right, let's do that. Ooh! What did you do just then?"

"Sorry, I ..."

"No, it was lovely. Do it again. Do it quite a lot." And she pulled him down on top of her and breathed rather hard in his ear, and he thought he had never felt anything so soft in his life.

It took them three whole days to get down to the beach, resting each night when they found enough ground to perch, and two days before that to put their clothes in some sort of order. Pert's shirt and trousers would serve one more turn, but Rosella's dress was a wreck so they cut it and sewed it together with the rabbit bone needle and thread pulled out of the dress itself, and made a passable skirt from it. Then she put Pert's jacket on over the top, and was decent at least.

The climb down was not pleasant, and they went very slowly. Going down was physically less tiring and they were fresh and rested, but it was no safer than coming up. In fact, there were times when it was decidedly more dangerous, and their hearts were in their mouths as their feet slipped and missed their grip, or the gravel fell away beneath them and they clung to each other as a small landslide rattled away into the void.

But with care, and helping each other, and being on the whole quite brave, they made it to the jumble of great rocks at the bottom, and then it was just a long and tiring clamber over and around and through until the little beach lay before them, and the *Bight of Benin* just as Pert remembered it, and *Better Times* lying faithfully half in and half out of the water as though she knew they would come back and need her again.

Pert handed Rosella in and pushed off, then jumped in and took up the oars. As he turned the boat he looked back at the *Bight of Benin* and thought of what lay within. There was still something he had not told Rosella, something that had happened the last time he was there, something he had done, or thought he had done.

He had climbed down into the deckhouse. A ladder led down into a small cabin. In front would be the fish hold, but in this narrow space with two benches along the sides and a table down the middle the crew would have eaten and sheltered when not working on deck. Pert looked down at his feet. The floor of the cabin was gone, just a few cross members remaining,

346

and below he could see straight down into deep water. The *Bight of Benin* had made it to this safe haven, but the rocks had ripped her bottom out on the way.

He had sat down at the end of one of the benches and put his arms on the table.

"Hello, grandfather," he had said.

The body sat at the far end on the other side, slumped back in the corner, its head on its chest. It wore the lacy remains of a canvas smock and trousers. In its hand was a knife, the ivory handle intact but the steel blade almost rusted away. In its chest, buried between the yellow ribs, was another.

"I'm Pertinacious, your grandson," he said.

"Obadiah's boy?" asked the body.

"Yes. I'm not sure what happened to him, but I think he might still be around."

"Ah. Nice little tyke, he was. I was quite fond of him."

"Why did you go, then? Did you really take the treasure, like they said?"

"Ha!" his grandfather said. "Ha ha! They said that, did they? Well, they would. And they were right. Of course I took it, what do you think? I found out where they'd hid it, under the floor in the church vestry, and I snuck in and lifted it clean as a whistle, and put it in sacks and carried it to me barky and stowed it in the hold. I'd 'a got away with it, too, but for the weather and that stinking little turncoat Teague!"

"He's dead now," said Pert. "He sailed in here and the waves scrobbled him up."

"Good. So they should. He did this to me, you know." His grandfather seemed to point to the knife in his chest without actually moving.

"Why did he do that?"

"He didn't want to share. Greedy, he was, he wanted it all. I got him to help me, you see, I told him where it was and how we was going to lift it, but I needed someone to help carry it and then sail the barky out because the weather was blowing up, and he was a man on his own who'd an eye for money, as I could tell. Ha! So much the worse for me! He had an eye for money all right. He had an eye for his own money, and mine as well, and he jumped down into the cabin and stuck me when I wasn't looking, just as we were coming out the end of the creek."

His voice was quiet and gravelly, and seemed to come from a long way off, rising up through fathoms of green water lit by sunbeams, where seaweed waved and little fish swam in schools that flashed in the light. It was the voice of a bad man, a naughty man, who had been washed clean by years and the currents. Perhaps that was what happened to you after Davy Jones had done his grisly work. Perhaps it wasn't too bad after all.

"So he got the treasure, then?"

"Nah, he never had it. I wasn't killed, see, so we fought, and I was bigger and heavier than he was, and I fought dirtier. He was just a beginner, and I knocked him over the side and left him behind. But I knew he hadn't drowned because when I looked the dinghy was gone, that we were trailing astern, so I reckon he got to the dinghy and got back to land all right. But I had the treasure."

"And then you got washed in here?"

"Yes, she's a heavy old girl, the *Bight of Benin*, too heavy for one man, and the waves was bigger and bigger and before I knew it

I was among the rocks and here I ended. And his little pig-sticker was longer than I thought, because I got weaker and weaker and had to come down here and have a little sit, and that was it fer Mascaridus Potts the Pirate!"

"And you were definitely a pirate? Not a fisherman?"

"No, I was a pirate, all right. Learned my trade with Benido, down the Portugee coast and down the Africa coast and right round to the Bight. That's what this barky's named for, the *Bight of Benin*. A dreadful fever-ridden place that is ... *'Remember, remember the Bight of Benin, There's few that come out, though many go in!'* But we had to go in there because that's where the slaves came from. We started as slavers, see, and then after that it was easier to rob the slavers than it was to be one, so we did that."

"And you weren't a fisherman at all?"

"Oh, I tried. I tried to be respectable. Got married, had a nipper – that's Obadiah, your dad – but it wouldn't stick. I couldn't get on with it. Once the fever's got you, it's got you and you has to obey it, that's how it was with me."

"So what happened to the treasure?"

"Gone, lad, all gone. The rocks ripped the bottom out of her as she came in, me being weak from losing blood, and not being able to control her, and the spiky rocks went through her bottom and all the treasure fell out. Bloody great candlesticks, and crosses, and holy cups and golden plates and stuff. All gone, all lying down on the bottom somewhere out there, so the little crabbies can sit in 'em, and the pretty little seahorses can admire their own reflections. Very sad."

His tone brightened, though his face could not. "There was one thing, though, just the one that I'd slipped in me pocket because it was small. Here, you have a feel in my right hand side ... there ... no, the pocket's gone and it's slipped down on the seat. There, you've got it. You can have that. Little present for you. No use to me, not down here. Still, it's quiet ... shut the door on your way out. It gets a bit nippy down here, and I ain't got the flesh to keep me warm like I used to ..."

Pert knew he'd imagined it, of course. He'd been through the storm, and the *Black Joke* had burst apart, and Urethra Grubb had flown and popped her head open, and he'd watched Rosella fall to her death, so it wasn't surprising that his mind wasn't working properly. You couldn't have conversations with dead people. He'd made it up, for sure. It was probably a conversation he'd wished he could have, but he hadn't really had it.

Except ... he looked at Rosella, kneeling on the thwart in the bows, looking out towards the open sea. He was sculling with one oar over the stern so he could see where he was going, and *Better Times* was just starting to feel the waves coming in. She was stirring like the good little ship she was, eager to be out at sea. Out at the mouth of the gully the sea looked blue and inviting, and the breeze stirred Rosella's hair.

They'd be out soon, and then he would raise the sail and turn north and go up the coast away from the Old Man and the town. He didn't know the coastline, but it was gentle sailing weather. There would be fishing villages, or even a town where they could stop and no one would know them.

No, it must have been his imagination. Except that when he put his hand in his trouser pocket, there was something there. It was a little leather bag with a leather drawstring to keep it closed. The leather was salt stained and worn thin, and there was a dark blotch on one side that looked suspiciously like blood.

And the bag was surprisingly heavy, and when you shook it, it clinked. Rosella heard him clinking it, and turned back to see what he was doing, and smiled.

Glossary

Ships and sailing have a vocabulary all their own, hundreds of words that are perfectly clear to sailors but rather mystifying to land-lubbers. Here are a few of them ...

aft	at or towards the back of a boat. "Abaft" is similar, meaning "behind"
barky	an old slang word for a ship, corruption of "barque"
beam	the width of a ship. If the wind's on the beam it's coming from one side or the other, not from the front or the back
beating	sailing ships can't sail straight into the wind, but by careful management of the sails and steering they can go at about 45 degrees towards it. So a ship will make its way to windward by "beating" - going at 45 degrees one way, then turning ("tacking") and going at 45 degrees the other way, zig-zagging towards its eventual destination
bilges	the bottom of a boat where water tends to collect, also used for the lower part of a boat's side just where it enters the water
binnacle	a wooden or metal column near the ship's wheel, with the ship's compass mounted in the top
bone	as in "bone in her teeth", an expression meaning that a boat is moving quickly and creating a bow wave
boom	the wooden spar that holds the bottom of a sail
bow	the front of a boat
bowsprit	long wooden yard that sticks forward from the bow
brig	a square-rigged ship with two masts. The front mast (foremast) will be a little shorter than the back one ("mainmast"). Although most sails will be square and hung from yards across the ship, there will be some triangular foresails or "jibs" in front of the foremast, possibly one or two triangular "staysails" between the masts, and a large fore-and-aft sail on the back of the mainmast, known as a "spanker" or "mizzen"
bunt	the middle of a sail as opposed to the edges
cast off	untie a rope
copper	old sailing ships often had their hulls sheathed in thin copper against various tropical worms that would eat the timber if they got the chance

course	the direction in which a ship is steered. "Course made good" is the track the ship has followed after taking in to account tides, currents and the sideways force of the wind
courses	the square sails of a ship
dinghy	a very small boat
drawing	when a sail is full of wind and driving the ship, it's said to be "drawing"
ebb	the tide when it's going out. Coming in it's the "flood"
fathom	six feet depth of water
foc'sle	short for "fore-castle", the accommodation in the bows of a ship, where usually the ordinary seamen have their quarters
fore-and-aft	a sailing boat that has its sails arranged along the centre of the boat, as opposed to a square-rigger which has them arranged across the boat, though in both cases the sails can be moved to catch the wind. Fore-and-aft is more modern, and usually more efficient, but as the ship gets larger so do the sails, and very large fore-and-aft sails can be so big the crew can't control them, so that the larger the ship, the more attractive square rig becomes as the sail area is broken into manageable units
forefoot	the bit of a boat's bow where it turns under to meet the keel, in other words the bottom of the front of the boat
forestay	rope that runs from the foremast to the bow of the ship. It holds the mast up, but various foresails or "jibs" may also be set on it
forward	towards the bow of a boat
foul anchor	an anchor with a rope wrapped round it
gaff	the spar that supports the top of a fore-and-aft sail
gunwhale	the outer edge of a boat, the top of the sides. Pronounced "gun'l"
gybe	turn the boat with its stern through the wind, so that the wind suddenly catches the sail and bangs it across to the other side which can be very alarming, though less so on a square-rigger
halliards	or "halyards", ropes used to pull the sails up the mast
headsails	triangular fore-and-aft sails that are hoisted between the bowsprit and the foremast

helm	the steering of a boat, either by tiller or wheel. The helmsman usually sits with his back to the wind so if he puts the helm down (i.e. pushes the tiller away from him) the boat will turn towards the wind, and if he puts it up (pulls it towards him) the boat will go downwind or "fall away"
keel	the very bottom of a ship's hull
leeward	downwind, or away from the wind. Pronounced "loo'erd"
leeway	sailing boats don't just go forwards, they also slip sideways a bit. This is called leeway
mooring rope	rope used to tie a boat to the shore, sometimes called a mooring warp
painter	a thin rope used to tie a very small boat up
pay off	a boat with her head (front) directly into the wind will eventually "pay off" or turn to one side or the other
port	the left side of a ship as you face the front. "Port tack" means the wind is coming over the left side of the ship
ratlines	rope ladders in the rigging so that sailors may climb up
reach	two meanings: a fairly straight bit of river, or sailing with the wind coming from the side of the boat. For most boats this is much the fastest way to go. A "broad" reach has the wind slightly abaft the beam (somewhere between the side and the back of the boat)
reefing lines	small ropes used to tie the bottom of a sail into a bundle so the sail is effectively smaller in bad weather
rig	the number of masts a ship has, and the way the sails are arranged on them
rigging	the ropes that hold the masts up, and those that hoist and control the sails
rudder	a vertical plank of wood which is turned to steer the ship
scuppers	the "gutter" round the edge of a ship's deck, or the holes in her sides to drain away water
sheave	a pulley
sheet	rope attached to the bottom corner of a sail to control it. The mainsheet is the most important rope in a fore-and-aft ship, controlling the angle of the main sail to the wind
splice	join lengths of rope by unravelling them and "plaiting" the strands together. Stronger than tying a knot

square rig	see "fore-and-aft"
starboard	the right side of a ship as you face the front. "Starboard tack" means the wind is coming over the ship's right side
stay	rope that holds up the mast.
staysails	fore-and-aft sails hoisted on the stays
stern	the back of a boat
sternsheets	any space at the back of a boat where you can sit
thwart	a seat, usually just a plank of wood fixed across the boat
tiller	length of wood used to turn the rudder in a ship that doesn't have a wheel for steering
windward	towards the wind – in other words, towards where the wind's coming from, not where it's going to. It's the opposite of "leeward". Sailing ships can't sail directly to windward – see "beating". Sailors often tend to think of "to windward" as "up hill" and "to leeward" as "down"
yard	a wooden spar that holds the top of a sail. On a square-rigged ship the yards go across the ship, and on a fore-and-aft ship they are in line with the ship, but in both cases they move to present the sails at the best angle to the wind

A brig

3143389R00193

Printed in Great Britain
by Amazon.co.uk, Ltd.,
Marston Gate.